B

For Margaret ther
banished and forb
remaining to haunt and disturb, never totally abandoned.

She lay in the quiet darkness and knew that she was destined to remember in greater detail now that the truth must be told. Again, a pang of guilt filled her and she almost sobbed. She grieved for her daughter and for the love she wished she could have given her when she was small. Miriam, the child born in sorrow and despair. There was delight and sorrow together in her feelings for her lovely young granddaughter, and it was for Hannah that she must now tell what she must tell, the facts that perhaps should have been revealed long ago.

Alix Atkinson is very familiar with the setting of *BOUNDARIES* as she was born and raised in Bristol. Although she has written numerous travel articles and over twenty short stories, *BOUNDARIES* is her first novel. Alix is happily married with two children, a son and a daughter, and lives with her husband and two Labrador dogs in Devon. She enjoys travel and walking across the moors.

BOUNDARIES

by

ALIX ATKINSON

WORLDWIDE BOOKS
LONDON · SYDNEY · TORONTO

First published in Hardback in 1990 by
Worldwide Books, Eton House,
18–24 Paradise Road, Richmond, Surrey TW9 1SR

This Paperback edition published in 1991
by Worldwide Books

ISBN 0 373 57927 6
09–9104 95918

Set in 10/11 Times
Printed and bound in Great Britain

Dedicated to Ted,
and also to Teresa and Miriam.

With thanks to the members of the Writing Group who gave me so much constructive criticism, to all the friends who helped with research, and to my husband who was always there to listen and encourage.

The boundary lines have fallen for me in pleasant places
Surely I have a delightful inheritance

(Psalm 16 verse 6)

PART ONE

MARGARET

CHAPTER ONE

1987

IT WAS her granddaughter's letter with its bright Israeli stamp, arriving among all the cards on the morning of her fifty-ninth birthday, that suddenly and unwillingly took Margaret's thoughts winging back to that forbidden and long-buried summer. Perhaps the gulls too helped to shatter her precious façade of peace, the carefully protected tranquillity of her day-to-day ordered environment.

There were seldom any gulls in the skies above her lovely home in the little village outside Bristol. Sometimes a storm at sea would drive them inland. She heard the screaming, haunting cries as she read the letter, and she looked from her kitchen window and saw them, a whole flock riding the wind in the gathering clouds and exulting in the power of their spreading wings.

Then suddenly she was back beneath the hazy Cornish sun, her seventeen-year-old eyes blazing with anger as she looked at the muddied white feathers lying in a pathetic heap on the recently ploughed earth at her feet, and at the young man standing there, his tall blond figure etched against the sky, and forever in her memory. She had watched helpless as he'd smashed his spade down on to the head of the gull, and for a moment, until her sturdy common sense had reasserted itself, his boots had been jackboots and the spade the butt of a gun.

'You had no right,' she had screamed, 'you Nazi thug, no right!'

Her remembered words flashed back to her from across the years, and she looked again at the angry sky, seeing once more those other gulls of a time long past, and the quiet words of the young German as he too, reading her thoughts, had looked upwards at their soaring flight.

'That one would never have flown again,' he had said. 'Someone had taken a shot at him. He would have died miserably or been taken by a fox tonight. I had to do it.'

Margaret, angry with herself for remembering, brushed away the tears, tears that came unbidden, tears for a man she had known and loved forty years away in time, a man she had tried to forget, tried to banish from her thoughts as though he had never been. It was Hannah's letter, read that morning three times over, that had jerked her so unwillingly back, her granddaughter whom she loved so much. Her photograph stood on the sideboard, and Margaret glanced at it as she often did. The girl smiled at her from the bright silver frame, smiled with Karl's smile and Karl's eyes, and her heart lurched suddenly, as it had done so many times before during that lovely Cornish summer so long ago. She put the letter in her bureau, wondering how she should act, how to cope with this new complication. She wondered why she hadn't taken the signs more seriously when Hannah and her mother had last visited.

'She's very young,' she had told her daughter hopefully. 'I shouldn't worry. She'll meet someone more suitable and forget all about him.'

But Hannah had not forgotten. Her love for the young man shone through every line of her letter, as well as her distress over her mother's anger, and Margaret knew that she herself was the only person who could help.

The day passed quietly enough, with Margaret doing ordinary things, walking the dog, preparing for the evening's meal.

'I would rather cook it myself,' she had told Graham when he suggested a celebration for her birthday. 'We'll have something special, but at home. You can take me to the theatre next week—there's that play that I want to see at the Old Vic.'

Graham was always punctual. She heard the car in the drive precisely at half-past six and she took off her apron and glanced in the mirror. Her slightly greying hair was arranged carefully today. She had made a fairly unusual visit to the hairdresser during the afternoon. She was wearing a new dress too. Its elegant lines made her tall body seem slimmer and she was pleased with the effect.

He came into the kitchen and she saw the bunch of orchids held awkwardly in his hand. He kissed her gently.

'They're beautiful,' she said. 'I must find a vase.'

'Marks and Spencer's,' he remarked, trying to sound casual and spoiling the effect somewhat. 'I bought them in Marks. They have nice flowers!'

She laughed at him, seeing the funny side. 'Go and get changed,' she said. 'The meal's nearly ready.'

'It smells jolly nice,' he said when he came back into the kitchen five minutes later, and she laughed again. The words were predictable, ordinary. Then she smiled at him affectionately. He was her anchor, her rock, and would defend her resolutely whatever past secrets her granddaughter's letter might force her to reveal. She kissed him with enthusiasm, and then bent to the oven. Cooking was one of her joys, and she carried the casserole and vegetables to the table. She had set out the best cutlery, made a flower arrangement, and she looked at it with pleasure. Graham lit the birthday candles and poured the wine.

'Just the two of us now,' he said. 'Remember how it used to be?'

She remembered.

'Charles and James both sent me cards and there's a little parcel that I've kept to open after dinner. Miriam telephoned; she said that she has a present for me but it won't post. She's keeping it for our next visit to Israel.'

'Anything from Hannah?'

'A card and a letter too!'

Graham looked at her closely. Her voice had changed.

'We'll talk about it after we've eaten,' she said. 'I don't want you to read it yet.'

'Not bad news!'

He was suddenly concerned. Margaret knew that he loved his daughter and granddaughter very much and Miriam's decision to live in Israel had always been a grief to him.

'No, not bad news. Something that we have to talk about, though. Later, not now.' She wanted to enjoy the meal, to forget for a while.

Graham read the letter quietly when they had finished eating and were sitting at ease, coffee on the small table and liqueurs poured. He put the closely written pages down and got up and kissed her reassuringly. He handed her a cup and a glass and still said nothing. Then he sat down again and sipped his drink.

'Stop worrying. I love you,' he said.

They sat and talked and planned, and because he was the man he was Margaret knew that she would cope however difficult the next days and weeks might be.

She slept fitfully that night. She must go to Israel; Graham would arrange everything for her. From time to time she stretched her arm across the width of the enormous bed she shared with him and touched him gently. She had to assure herself that he was there, a solid reality and a refuge from her dreams. He moved sometimes in his sleep and once he responded to her touch, grasped her hand and squeezed it.

'Love you,' he said, and whether he was awake or still asleep she knew that the words were true, wonderfully true. For nearly forty years she had known and revelled in that love, and returned it too in her own way, but always, always disturbingly in the deepest recesses of her mind, there was that other passion, banished and forbidden, but there still, remaining to haunt and disturb, never totally abandoned.

She lay in the quiet darkness, and she knew that she was destined to remember in greater detail now that the truth must be told. Again a pang of guilt filled her, and she almost sobbed. Her grief was ethereal, usually buried and under strict control, and it was a grief for many things intermixed and tangled in her emotions. She grieved for her daughter and for the love she wished she could have given her when she had been small and needed it so much; Miriam, the child born in sorrow and despair that dismal autumn in a ration-weary Bristol almost forty years ago. There was delight and sorrow together in her feelings for her lovely young granddaughter, and it was for Hannah that she must now tell what she must tell, the facts that perhaps should have been revealed long ago.

She had always had a special place in her life for Hannah. There was a deep bond between them and she had cherished it through all the years since Hannah was born. She remembered when she'd first seen her grandchild, and she recalled the tiny blue eyes and the fuzz of golden hair. The baby had brought tears to her eyes and a fierce love in her heart. She could hear, even now, her daughter's bitter words as she'd looked critically at her newborn child.

'She's not like us at all, Mother, is she? Where does she get that fair skin and those blue eyes? She doesn't look very Jewish, does she?'

Margaret had taken the baby in her arms and loved her immediately, sorrowing that her upbringing in this strange kibbutz home in Israel would preclude frequent visits. But a deep friendship between grandmother and granddaughter had grown nevertheless. Hannah had come to England and stayed with them as often as possible, and there had been letters, frequent newsy letters. They had formed a closeness that both of them cherished.

Sleep refused to banish all the memories that crowded Margaret's mind, and she got up and crept downstairs and sat in her beautiful kitchen with a cup of tea on the sturdy oak table. The soft light and the mellow wood, the trailing plants and gleaming copper comforted her, and she allowed her mind to wander back, to recall those forbidden and golden days. . .and that wonderful summer of her twentieth year.

CHAPTER TWO

1940–1945

EVER since she was a child Margaret had loved the farm. It nestled among the gentle hills of south Cornwall, and every summer her mother and father had taken her there for two glorious weeks of holiday. Weeks that were remembered for sunshine and plenty, freedom and fun, and when in 1940 the threat of invasion struck terror into her mother's Jewish heart, Margaret, aged twelve, was sent away to safety until the war should end.

'Now you'll be a good girl, and help Auntie Annie,' her mother directed when it was time to go. Margaret was embarrassed by the tears she saw in her eyes. Adults should never cry. She herself felt little grief. It was different for the other children, the official evacuees. They hadn't known where they were going, but she was lucky. There was John for a start, four years her senior. She had always longed for a big brother, and during every summer holiday she had followed him about the farm, worshipping from afar. His parents had long been known as Uncle Bill and Auntie Annie to her, and she waved goodbye to her mother on the gloomy Bristol station with excitement in her heart, her gas-mask in its square cardboard box and home-made cover on her shoulder, and all her possessions packed in an ancient battered suitcase.

The pony trap was waiting for her at the station gate when she arrived some hours later, and she climbed aboard happily, if a little disappointed at the absence of John.

'He be working hard,' Bill told her. 'He got his school studies to be thinking about as well as the farm just now.'

The clip-clopping of the pony's hoofs along the road and the movement of the trap was exciting, different, and Margaret felt her heart lifting with joy. This was better than Bristol. The air-raids had offered some change from the dull routine of life, but even the gathering of shrapnel on the way home from school and the bartering of the best pieces the next day couldn't match this—this wonderful place where the gulls cried and the sea crashed on the rocky shore. She remembered the excitement of gathering fresh eggs straight from the nest, taking tiny potatoes from the earth, and best of all there was the beach, the sandy cove with its rugged, sloping cliffs. Perhaps John would take her swimming there. She knew that he was a strong swimmer and would see that she didn't drown. She had always been forbidden even to go and paddle on her own. And there was the old castle on the hill that made her shiver and dream and make up stories. John had frightened her to death one evening when she'd been only ten years old with a tale about a ghost who came from the old gateway and roamed the country road at night.

' 'Tis all in his mind,' his father had said. 'Don't listen to him, maid. He makes it all up!'

John was just carrying in the jug of milk from the evening's milking when they arrived, and he stared at her, his sixteen years making him seem more grown up and unattainable than she ever remembered before.

'Still as skinny as ever, then,' he said as she jumped down from the trap. 'Mum's just waiting to fatten you up like the pigs!'

She blushed and then, without stopping to think, put out her tongue at him. He laughed and went inside.

Auntie Annie laughed too. 'I'm that glad to have you, dearie,' she said. 'You don't know how awful it is here with those two men around and no woman to keep me company.'

Margaret blushed again, but with pleasure this time. She had never been called a woman before. She returned Annie's hearty embrace with enthusiasm and decided that this was the one place in the world where she wanted to be, the one place that she never wished to leave.

'It's lovely to be back,' she said. 'Mummy sends her regards.'

It was a wonderful, untrammelled life, and as the weeks passed into months Margaret grew and matured. Her parents came for visits sometimes, but she was always secretly glad when she kissed them dutifully goodbye and the trap carried them away down the lane and out of sight round the bend in the road. This treachery in her heart caused her a small twinge of guilt each time they left, but one of Annie's glorious apple pies topped with vast amounts of rich yellow cream usually disposed of the unwelcome feelings. A smile and a wink from John could do even better, sending her heart into a flutter and the colour rushing to her face. At fourteen she was beginning to be almost beautiful, and she noticed John's eyes sometimes straying to her young and gently blossoming figure.

'I wish he was your age,' Annie said one day, and there was a desperate anxiety in her voice. 'Farming's a reserved occupation. He need not go, but now he's eighteen he'll be wanting to join up.'

It was then that fear gripped Margaret and for the

first time in her life the war became a reality. Even the few Bristol air-raids she had experienced hadn't any personally disastrous results. No one she knew had been injured. Since she'd come to Cornwall it had all become even more remote, something happening a long way off, a voice on the wireless, a worried frown on Bill's face now and then. There were very few food shortages on the farm. Most of the necessities of life they produced themselves, and it was only bananas and sweets that she occasionally missed.

John was her main concern, and her other was her total ignorance of any of the facts of life. She watched the animals. They mated happily in fields or yard without any embarrassment and in due course a calf or a lamb would be born. Margaret often shuddered when she saw the small, neat Jersey bull. He lived in splendid isolation in a big shed and he had his own yard where the cows were taken now and then. She was strictly forbidden to go anywhere near him.

'He might be small compared with those great black and white things, but he be fierce. Jerseys be known for their fierceness,' Bill warned. 'You keep right away.'

She could still see the animal's performance with the cows, though, and she said little, wondering. Surely it couldn't be that. . .her mind completely failed to make the jump from creature to man. It was too rude!

Annie put her right one evening when Bill and John were out in the fields working late. When all had been told Annie got up to make a cup of tea, and Margaret blushed and turned away from her.

'It's horrible!' she protested. 'I wish I need never have known.'

'You're growing up,' Annie said. 'Your mother should have told you.'

'She couldn't, could she? She isn't here often enough,

and I'd rather you told me anyway. I couldn't have borne to have heard it from Mummy!'

John volunteered for the Army a few months later, in spite of his mother's angry protests.

'You need not go. We need you here on the land,' she said. 'You're of more value keeping the country fed.'

'How can I stay here, Mother, with all my friends gone, and a war to be won? There are others to work on the farm, land-girls.'

'I'll never have one of those in my house,' Annie said angrily. 'They just bring a pack of trouble.'

'Then you'll have to manage. I'm going, whatever you say. It's something I must do.'

Margaret looked at him sadly. At eighteen he was tall and handsome, his rugged, wind-browned face and dark hair making her heart flutter a little every time he spoke to her. She couldn't imagine how it would be here without him. He had been part of her life for the past three years, at first as a brother, but recently becoming, in her dreams, more than that. It had all started with Annie's embarrassing little talk. In spite of her revulsion there was a fascination about what she had been told that she failed to understand, and it seemed to be focused in John.

He came home on embarkation leave some months later, and in uniform he appeared to be far removed from her, remote and inaccessible. When he worked on the farm again during those short days he became more the John she knew, but she was at school most of the time and saw little of him. In the evenings he went into the town, coming back long after she was in bed. It was on his last evening that he asked her if she would like a swim.

'It's a lovely evening,' he said.

Margaret was careful to put on her costume beneath the cape Annie had stitched for her especially for the beach. It was long and loose and made of several old towels sewn together with a cord to pull it tight at the top. You could change quite demurely beneath its voluminous folds.

John laughed when he saw it. 'Whatever is that you're wearing?'

'A bathing-cape!'

'My mother's work, no doubt. Well, you won't be able to race me down in that.'

'I don't want to race. It's still too hot.'

They walked through the lane thick with wild flowers, and the branches of the trees made a delicate arch of green above their heads.

'I shall miss all this,' he said. 'It's so beautiful, and so are you, Margaret. I shall miss you too.'

He suddenly took her hands, both of them in both of his, and pulled her into his arms and kissed her. It was a gentle, chaste kiss, almost that of a brother for a sister, but she pulled away from him, frightened.

'I'll race you now,' she said, and she ran down the whole length of the lane, dropped her wrap on the dry sand at the top of the beach and rushed into the sea. Its cold shock took her breath away, but she struck out for the rock that she could see at the side of the cove. It was safe to swim to it when the tide was right. John followed her; she could hear his powerful crawl in the water behind her. They reached the rock together and he sprang on to it first, pulling her up. But he dropped her hand immediately and there was a space between them. Shivering, she slid back into the sea, and swam to the beach. She took her wrap and threw it round her shoulders.

'I'm going back. It's colder than I thought!' she called to him, and she pushed her wet feet into her sandals and walked quickly back to the farmhouse beneath the darkening sky.

The next day she stood white-faced at the gate as Bill brought the trap round to take John to the station. He kissed his mother, and Margaret saw her take her handkerchief out surreptitiously to wipe away the tears. Then he came and stood in front of Margaret and tilted her face up to his.

'You'll be quite grown up by the time I come back,' he whispered. 'Goodbye, Margaret. Look after Mum for me, and be good.'

They stood watching as the trap swayed and jolted up the lane, and then Margaret ran up the creaking stairs to her room. Was this strange fluttering that she felt in her heart love? she wondered. She was fifteen, and it was the first time she had experienced anything like it. But he had gone now. She might never see him again. She sobbed her young grief into her pillow, and Annie came and put her arms round her.

'He'll be back, dearie,' she said. 'Don't you worry about that. My John'll be back soon enough. Come down and keep me company now and we'll have a nice cup of tea and a piece of my fresh carrot cake.'

That was it, Margaret thought. Tea and carrot cake. They were really what life was all about!

She dried her eyes on her sleeve. 'That'll be lovely, Aunt Annie,' she said. 'I'll have a big, big piece to cheer myself up!'

There was news occasionally and a few letters, but John's war didn't last long, and then there was silence—a long silence. He was in one of the dreaded

Japanese prison camps. He was still alive, they knew that much and that only. Margaret watched Annie grow, if not thin, then certainly haggard and grey with her worry and her desperation. Bill seemed to cope more adequately, but underneath his rugged exterior there was searing grief. He carried on doggedly with his work, ploughing, planting and reaping, and tending his animals, doing more than his strength would allow. But always his thoughts were his own, never shared.

As the war dragged on Margaret grew up. She began to see that her feelings for John were just early teenage dreams. There was probably no substance to them. But there was no one else; she was too busy. She did more and more work on the farm in the evenings and at weekends, finding great pleasure in it and a complete change from the school work that took up most of her days. She knew that her help was valuable too. Another pair of hands was always needed to feed the hens, help with the milking, or bring in the harvest, and she loved to be able to contribute something to the home that she was fast coming to think of as her own.

The coming of summer was always something to celebrate in the countryside, but 1945 brought the greatest celebration of all. When the trees were almost in their full glory, when the fields were full of lambs, and the young corn standing, the news came that the war in Europe was over. Hitler was dead. Margaret watched the village come to life. Union Jacks and red, white and blue streamers fluttered from every lamp-post. The people danced in the village square and a Victory tea-party was arranged for the children. But although the curtains could remain undrawn now, and the lights shine out over the fields for the first time for six long years, there was little rejoicing in the grey stone farmhouse above the beach. The Japanese were still fighting. There would be no release for John, and no one knew if he could survive many more awful weeks and months.

Margaret looked at the tears in Annie's eyes as she heard the faint sounds of revelling coming from the village just over the hill. She could smell the smoke of the bonfires that were triumphantly burning in celebration of victory, and then suddenly she thought of Bristol and her parents. The end of the war must surely mean the end of her time in Cornwall.

'Please say I can stay with you, Auntie,' she whispered, putting her arms round the older woman. 'I'm seventeen now and I've already done almost an extra year at school. I want to leave in July, but I don't want to go back to Bristol just yet. Could I work on the farm full-time instead?'

Annie pushed her gently away, and Margaret could feel the embarrassment in the stolid countrywoman.

'Please write and ask Mum and Dad if I can stay until John comes back,' she pleaded, desperate now. 'I'm as good as any land-girl—John used to say so.'

Annie brushed tears from her eyes. She wouldn't allow the luxury of visible grief to be seen for more than a moment if she could help it.

'You're a good girl, Margaret,' she whispered. 'Like my own daughter. I'll see if your parents can spare you for a bit longer.'

So the letter was sent and it was eventually arranged. Margaret would be allowed to stay and work on the land as she had done in all her spare time since she'd left Bristol five years before. She hoped the arrangement would stand for more than the few months promised.

CHAPTER THREE

1945

IT WAS the coming of Karl into their sheltered world that changed Margaret's life.

Annie had warned her. 'We need more help,' she had said. 'German prisoners are strong, and they work well. Always known for hard work, the Jerries. No fraternisation, though—that's the rule. We don't talk to him except to give instructions.'

Margaret's feelings were mixed. Bill was getting older, his wife's senior by more than a dozen years, and he seemed to do a little less every week. There had been Italian prisoners to help during the earlier years of the war, but they had made no impression on her, and had not stayed for long. Now, with the harvest soon ready to be brought in, and all the potatoes to gather, she knew that help was vital.

She saw Karl for the first time when he arrived for work a few days later, dropped at the gate by the prison van. He stood in the soft Cornish rain, damp and unsure of his reception, and they stared at each other with no smile between them. Margaret stood looking at him in silence, and wondered how it would work. He looked strong enough, but his blond good looks seemed slightly threatening to her inexperienced seventeen years, and she was uneasy. He was German, the enemy, and suddenly from the recesses of her mind came the acknowledgement that she had resolutely put behind her for so long. She was Jewish. Her parents had never been rigid in their beliefs and practices, adhering to their faith only superficially, but she still felt a faint loyalty to her race. Only recently had news of the unbelievable horrors of the concentration camps come trickling through. The obscenities of the photographs she had seen in the newspapers flashed before her eyes in that moment as she stared at the young German.

Annie came out of the farmhouse door and looked the young man over with ill-concealed dislike. Margaret could almost sense the resentment in her. In her aunt's heart he would encapsulate all the misery of John's imprisonment, his obvious good health almost a reproach.

'Don't think you're going to eat with us. You can have your food out in the shed with the dogs.'

Those were her first words to him, and Margaret could feel herself trembling, although she couldn't tell why. Then on a kinder note, Annie continued. 'Good food, mind you—better than the rubbish they feed you up there at the camp, I shouldn't wonder. It's all home-grown and home-made.'

Margaret wondered if he understood a word of it. She hoped he didn't. Annie's accent was strong, and she herself had had a job to follow some of the local conversation when she'd first come to Cornwall.

He bowed ever so slightly, and then he smiled. 'I shall work hard for you in return,' he said. 'What do you want me to do?'

Margaret gasped. His English was almost perfect and the smile was warm. She felt guilty that she was not allowed to reply. His speaking her language made it worse. She must not utter a word—it was forbidden. Girls particularly must be blind and dumb to these handsome blond strangers. They had even been warned in school. With the ending of hostilities, they had been told, more and more freedom would inevitably be given to the Germans. Their help was needed to get the country back on its feet. They would be working mostly in groups, in factories, making roads, and on the farms. The more reliable of them would be allocated to farmers in ones and twos, unsupervised, and there the rules must be more strictly kept. Margaret turned and went into the house. She would leave him to Uncle Bill. Nothing in her previous sheltered existence had prepared her for that smile and that alien voice.

Her last few weeks at the small senior school passed uneventfully. She worked on her books with less interest than previously, and her headmistress told her that she was wasting her life if she didn't continue her education. She should do yet another year and take her Higher School Certificate, which was the passport to university and greater things. But Margaret suddenly had no interest and no enthusiasm. The farm seemed to be waiting for her.

'Perhaps I'll study again in years to come,' she told anyone who remonstrated with her, and she wrote comforting letters to her parents. She was needed on the land, she told them. Food was necessary in ration-hungry Britain. The whole of Europe was full of starving refugees and she couldn't sit at her books any longer. She felt as justified in her decision as any young man who had left his studies for the Army. Her mind was made up, and there was no budging her. So one day in July when school was over for the summer, she packed her neatly filled exercise books into a large cardboard box, put her uniform with it, rolled her long plaits round her head, and with a sigh of relief presented herself to Bill.

'I'm your new land-girl, Uncle,' she announced

triumphantly. 'Full-time now, not just weekends and holidays.'

He laughed. 'And I need you,' he said, puffing at his old pipe. 'I need you until our John comes home, anyway.'

It would be a long time. Japan was fanatical; there would be no surrender.

Then, in August, Hiroshima! Three days later, Nagasaki! The first atomic bombs that brought so much terror and devastation to these previously unknown places on the other side of the world brought only joy to Margaret and to the two people she had come to love so much.

'He's going to be all right,' Annie said as she heard the clipped tones of the announcer's voice from the clumsy brown wireless that sat proudly on the table beside the fire. 'The Nips have given up. He'll be coming home!'

She dabbed at her eyes frantically, and Margaret ran across the room and kissed her. There was rejoicing that night, as Margaret had never seen in her life. The war was truly over. Japan, the last enemy, had surrendered. Life would be normal again. It was the war to end all wars, truly this one was that. It had to be.

But what of her own life? She lay in her little room thinking of John. She had felt herself in love with him once, and she smiled a little in the darkness. It had been a very young teenage love. He had kissed her in the lane on that evening just before he went away, a fond, brotherly kiss, but she had idolised him throughout her adolescence, and even when she was a little girl. She remembered following him puppy-like around the farm when she'd first come on holiday in those happy years before the war. She wondered how he would have changed. Terrible stories were rumoured about the Japanese prison camps. Well, they would soon know. She listened to the roaring of the sea, and her thoughts turned to Karl. He would probably be going home too, back to Germany. She had obeyed the rules. She hadn't exchanged one word with him in the three months he had been working for them, but there was no ban on smiles. They had smiled, frequently!

It was when they were in the milking shed a week or two later that Karl first broke the silence.

'John?' he questioned suddenly. 'He will be home soon. Tell me about him, please.'

Margaret looked up and stared at him, the milk gushing between her trembling fingers. He was concentrating on the job he was doing. He wasn't looking at her. She didn't answer his question.

'We're not supposed to fraternise,' she said.

'That terrible word!' he almost shouted. 'We're talking—that only.'

'Be quiet, then,' she told him anxiously. 'Whisper. Where did you learn your perfect English?'

'My grandmother was English. She taught me—talked to me always in English. She died just before the war. She would have been so unhappy about it. I'm glad she didn't live to see me fight her people. I was doing languages at university when the war started. Had to give it up.'

His sentences were short, disjointed. There seemed to be so much that he wanted to say. In the long silences endless thoughts had been stored in both their minds so that they had to be revealed, words tumbling over themselves. Margaret felt overwhelmed suddenly. What should she begin with now that they seemed to have made their own armistice?

'Your John will have suffered,' he said. 'I've heard a

bit about the Japanese. Have you any news? Is he all right?'

'Why should you care?' she said, her voice suddenly harsh. The wizened, starving old faces of children from the camps all over Europe flashed suddenly into her mind, the pictures that were too awful to be seen. Jews, mainly—her people. 'You haven't been exactly blameless!' Her words were thrown at him angrily.

He looked at her from his seat beside the placid cow, and for a moment his hands were still, and she could see the colour drain from his face.

'I've seen the pictures too,' he said quietly. 'We've been shown them in the camp. Re-education, they call it. They've been telling us how evil the Third Reich was, that Germany is the villain of Europe. I think I almost believe it!'

'Almost, almost!' The words were more angry than the last. 'How can you *almost* believe it?'

'I can see why we shouldn't fraternise,' he said, an edge of sadness in his voice. 'Perhaps it's too difficult to understand each other. But I'm not a Nazi—I want you to know that. I never was.'

Margaret turned back to the gentle cow, and wondered as she had wondered so frequently lately why men couldn't be more like the animals. Why was the human race supposed to be superior? It was vastly inferior. 'A little lower than the angels', the Bible said. She often thought it should have read, 'lower than the animals'. In 1945 it would certainly have been more apt.

It was the following day that she saw Karl kill the injured gull, and she was surprised and horrified at the intensity of her sudden anger and fright. She knew she would never forget the sight of him, and the angry words she screamed out, so swiftly spoken and so swiftly regretted. She saw in one intense second his long, artistic fingers holding the spade that had killed, and the sensitive face with eyes momentarily shut in horror as he looked down and saw the still and muddied feathers. She knew that moment would be with her forever. She turned and ran away across the field, hearing but not registering until later the words he shouted as she fled. The mud sucked at her shoes, and the gulls in the sky above her were screeching their haunting cries—almost, she imagined, in angry lament for one of their number slaughtered.

She knew she had been foolish and, feeling heartily ashamed of her outburst, and determined to make amends, she smiled warmly when she saw him the following day. Annie was watching her from the window, so she said nothing. The milking shed was their private place. There she would offer her apologies, make her peace.

'Sorry I was so stupid about the gull,' she said. 'And I'm very, very sorry about the things I called you.'

'Nazi thug', she had said, and she knew within herself that what he had told her earlier must be true. He couldn't be a Nazi. At least that was what she desperately wanted to believe.

'It was sad about the bird,' he said quietly. 'I hated doing it.'

She looked at him, and felt the sincerity of the words, even the pain of them. Suddenly life was good. The war was over. Her spirits lifted and outside the sun was shining.

The sun shone frequently during the rest of that summer, and the autumn brought the constant hope of John's imminent homecoming. They all tried not to think too much of the reports in the newspapers about the condition of the returning prisoners from the Far East. John had been strong, filled since childhood with the rich, healthy milk, cream and eggs from the farm. Annie was sure that this would have sustained him for the appalling years of near-starvation.

'He'll be all right, my John,' she said frequently, and Bill, sitting in his large old chair by the range, would take an extra pull on his pipe for comfort and look at her steadily.

'He'll be all right,' he would repeat, mainly to reassure himself. 'Soon have him out in the fields again.'

Margaret, listening, wondered. She thought about his return often, and Karl featured in her thoughts in ever-increasing intensity. How would the two young men come to terms with working together? It might happen for a time. The Germans were not being repatriated as soon as they had hoped, and some even were expressing a wish to stay. A shattered and vanquished Fatherland seemed unattractive, especially if their own bit of it was in Russian hands.

Eventually the news arrived that John was soon to be sent home, flying out from the hospital in Rangoon to another in England, and Annie started to plan for the great day.

'He always liked my steak and kidney pies best,' she said, brushing away the tears of happiness that streaked her face as she read the letter, 'and that's what I shall make him for his first meal, with stewed apples and lots of cream for afters!'

Privately Margaret thought that so soon from the hardships of prison camp the young man would hardly be able to face an enormous steak and kidney pie, but it was Annie's only way of coping with her emotions. All her joy, her worries of the past mind-weary years, and her hope for the time to come, would go into that pie, as well as the saved-up meat ration. Margaret laughed to herself gently and wondered how she herself would prepare for this momentous home-coming. A new dress? A new hair-style? Her old dungarees were pretty unsightly, and her recently cut hair upswept at her forehead and neatly rolled round a band at the nape of her neck was hardly flattering. It hadn't seemed to matter much when she had had her long, thick plaits cut off—they had got in the way. Only the daily struggle to work the land and produce as much food as possible had been important. But now there were other things. It was time to forget the past, time to start again, and she had some clothing coupons stored up. Perhaps she could get into Mevagissey and find a length of material to sew into something new.

She looked at herself critically in the small mirror in her bedroom later that day. She had always been larger than she would have liked, but the hard work on the farm had helped to shed a few pounds. She couldn't see very much of herself anyway. The only long mirror in the farmhouse was on the door of the old wardrobe in Annie and Bill's bedroom, and she didn't like asking to go into their room. It was dark and old-fashioned and strange. She hated to think of Annie and Bill in any kind of close physical relationship—she couldn't understand why, but the feeling had been with her since she was little. She felt the same way about her parents. Shut out, perhaps, and the marriage bed was a symbol of that union of which she had no part, a private place that belonged to the couple who slept on it. She didn't want to look at Annie's bed, or at the elaborate and enormous patchwork quilt that covered it. Her own little scratched and discoloured mirror would have to do.

She pulled the band off her head and shook her hair down over her shoulders. She hadn't let the barber cut too much off, and she loved to have it loose sometimes. It hung in thick waves that blew in the wind, and she loved the feeling of it when she stood on the cliff or at the sea's edge.

Her thoughts began to rise at the idea of new clothes and some fun. She had always liked the idea of dressing up, but there hadn't been much opportunity or need to think about anything remotely glamorous for a long time; throughout most of her life, in fact. But her mind was made up now, and she decided to draw Annie into her plans.

She rushed down stairs again and bounced into the kitchen suddenly, with her new-found enthusiasm for life.

'I've got some coupons, Aunt Annie,' she said, 'and some money saved too. Let's get the bus into town one day soon and buy ourselves some clothes!'

Annie took her hands out of the sink and wiped them. She caught some of the girl's brightness and smiled.

'You're right, Maggie,' she said. 'We'll get ourselves decked out for my John. He'll want more than food, I'm thinking.'

Margaret laughed at the prophetic words, and wondered just what he would want. What did a man need when he'd been shut away for all those years? Probably just peace and his own place to enjoy and savour with no complications and no stresses. No Karl? She wondered again about Karl.

'Tomorrow. Let's go tomorrow,' she said to Annie, putting the German firmly out of her thoughts. 'We haven't long now before John will be here, and there's so much to do.'

'We'll get the nine o'clock bus,' the older woman said. 'I'll go and count my clothing coupons right away. Get yours, Margaret. I'm sure we'll have enough between us to get some nice lengths of material. We'll get the old sewing-machine out when we get back.'

The sleepy little fishing town nestled into the south Cornish coast, all its tiny streets leading web-like to the harbour, the centre, the pulsating heart of its life. Boats just in from the night's fishing clustered round the quays, and boxes of shining mackerel stood ready for the journey to the ration-hungry towns, while eager gulls swooped and cried in their thousands waiting for the waste and refuse of the morning.

Annie insisted on buying some fish for their tea, and Margaret stood impatient as she looked over the catch laid out for local buyers. One fish looked much like another to her, their bright, sad and sightless eyes somehow staring reproachfully at the handing over of coins for their lives. She turned away with a shudder. She wished she could overcome her ridiculous horror at the various untimely but necessary ends to the lives of the creatures around her.

'Eight nice ones. Two each,' Annie said with immense satisfaction, putting the newspaper-wrapped parcel at the bottom of her basket. 'We'll eat well tonight. Come on, then, now for the fun bit of the day!'

No shortages of the war years had kept Annie's figure neat and trim. In fact there had virtually been no shortages in the farmhouse, except for bananas and various other fruits from abroad that Margaret sometimes guiltily longed for. There had always been a great bowl of clotted cream on the table at each meal, and Annie loved to spread it liberally over her toast, her apple pie, her thick slices of white bread, and it even sat in a great sensuous lump on top of her breakfast porridge. Margaret laughed as she saw her look down at her ample curves a sight ruefully as they walked away from the sea towards the small draper's shop.

'I'll need twice as much material as you to make anything to cover me,' she said.

The bus dropped them at the village later that afternoon, and they walked down the narrow road to the farm. They carried their parcels triumphantly, and Margaret was looking forward to an evening of cutting out and starting to sew the dress that might make John look at her with more than a casual interest.

Karl was just bringing in a jug from the evening's milking as they reached the gate. He stood back for them to pass, and Annie walked ahead without a glance in his direction. Margaret smiled as he set the milk down on the table just inside the front porch, covering it with a heavy lace cloth bordered with dangling coloured beads, to keep the flies out.

The house milk was always taken from the surface of the churn, and the thick yellow cream from their gentle Jersey cows would reach more than halfway down the jug. When they sometimes filled a quart bottle instead, you could see through the glass that there was only an inch or two of ordinary milk at the bottom. The rest was cream.

Margaret waited a moment until Annie had gone into the house. She bent down, pretending to tighten the laces of her heavy black shoes, then she whispered to Karl.

'Sorry you had extra work to do today,' she said. 'We've had a lovely day in town. I'll try to make up for it tomorrow.'

Karl looked at her as she stood up. 'I hope you got

what you wanted,' he said, and then she remembered that prisoners weren't allowed in the towns. She wondered how long it had been since he had walked free in the streets.

Angry suddenly with the war and angry too that they couldn't stay and talk normally, Margaret felt her pleasure in her planned new dress evaporate a little.

'Yes, yes, we did, and some nice fish for supper.' At least the food was somcthing he could share. Margaret had noted that Annie had bought two fish for him.

She walked quickly into the house and rushed up to her room with her parcel, flinging it on the bed. She looked out of the small window and saw Karl walking away from the cosy brightness of the kitchen. He went into the yard where the cows were waiting to be taken back to their field. She saw the gentleness when he spoke to them, and the way they did his bidding willingly. She watched man and beasts disappear out of her sight, and part of her heart went away down the lane with him, reluctantly, until she deliberately wrenched her thoughts back, back to ordinary mind-restoring things, to the meal being prepared below, and the chickens waiting to be shut up for the night.

Her healthy appetite had easily overcome her pity for the silvery fish in Annie's basket, and the smell wafting up the wooden staircase soon sent her scurrying downstairs, eager to get her evening tasks done.

'Hurry up, maid,' Bill said when he saw her. 'Evening's drawing in now, and the chickens have all put themselves to bed. Fox might be round if you don't get them fastened in soon.'

She went out into the sudden cold of the late October day, and heard the lowing of the cows from over the hedge, as though they sensed that their daily freedom must soon be curtailed. She shuddered as she thought of all the extra work that the coming of winter would mean, with sheds to be cleaned out each day and hay and straw to be carried. She was grateful for Karl's enormous strength, and knew that he would do his full quota of work, and probably some of hers too, without grumbling. He had been sharing their evening meal with them lately. Annie had relented a little in her antagonism towards him, recognising reluctantly that he was a good worker. It had been her idea that he should have a meal before being picked up and taken back each evening, but she would never allow him to sit down in the kitchen with them. He must still eat in the shed!

'Take the meal out, will you, Margaret?' she said later when the day's work was done, and the light almost gone from the sky. 'It's a treat today, the like of which he'll never see up in that camp.'

Margaret carried the succulent fish and a bowl of butter-shiny potatoes across the yard into the building where Karl was waiting, his small table ready, and the sturdy chair that he had mended set beside it. She noticed that his hands and face were scrubbed and clean, and the farmyard smell was mixed with that of carbolic soap which Annie insisted was kept beside the pump and granite trough.

She set the plate and knife and fork down on the table.

'Thank you,' he said. 'It looks delicious.' Then he looked at her and smiled. 'I look forward to seeing the new dress,' he said.

Margaret's usual composure left her and, embarrassed, she brushed down the old tweed skirt that she was still wearing. He had never seen her in anything other than dungarees before.

'You look nice. Like a girl I used to know.'

'Thank you.'

She could think of nothing else to say. Their relationship was usually one of work, seldom overflowing into ordinary things. She turned and walked back to the safety of the farmhouse, her face flushing with the unwelcome red that still overcame her at times.

In bed that night Margaret thought again unwillingly about Karl as she frequently did. She felt the pain he must feel, still to be a prisoner, and to be the vanquished, when all around was the rejoicing of the victorious. The home-coming of John would make his position more difficult to accept. Although they had been able to talk to each other very little during his time on the farm she realised suddenly that there was a depth of feeling between them that she had only half acknowledged. It had been born during their long silences together, and she turned her face to the old stone wall of the bedroom and tears slid from her eyes, tears for the foolishness of the world, and for the sudden, totally forbidden love that was beginning to form in her heart for a man whom she knew she must never love.

The morning brought little relief. They worked together, washing the cows' udders and milking, seated close, close enough to talk.

'Your John?' Karl questioned again. 'Tell me about him now, please. He will be home soon. I must know something about him.'

'He's not my John.' She emphasised the 'my'. 'He's tall—about your height. Same age, roughly, I should think, but he's not like you at all.'

Karl went steadily on with the milking, his hands working automatically now that he was so used to this daily slow and gentle job.

'What do you mean, not like me?'

'Well, he's dark, for a start—Celtic and all that. Cornish. He'd never want to go to university either, and he doesn't read much, only the sky and the land and the sea. The land's in his blood, I suppose. He just wants to farm. Only that really.'

She shrugged. It was true. As she tried to recall conversations with John nothing came into her mind. 'We talked about sheep and cows and the weather, and——' She stopped suddenly guilty. She was being unfair to John. There must be more than that.

Karl broke into her thoughts.

'How shall we manage?' His words were quiet, filled with misgivings, worry almost.

Margaret looked up at him. 'It'll be some time before he's well enough to do anything much, so I shouldn't let it bother you. And it won't be forever. You'll be going home.'

The words were spoken too suddenly and without thought, and when she saw Karl's reaction she desperately regretted them. She was heartily ashamed of her total insensitivity. He turned away from her and she could both see and feel the bitterness in him.

'Do you know where my home was?' he said. 'Dresden.'

Just the one word, Dresden, was enough. He gave no explanation. None was needed. The word stood between them, making a barrier that neither could immediately penetrate. It was one of the obscenities of war, like Auschwitz or Belsen, something completely incomprehensible. Margaret had heard of the terrible bombing of this most beautiful of towns by the Allies. She knew that it had been left a blackened and smouldering ruin, and she remembered Bill saying that it was in the part of Germany now in Russian hands. She had noted the past tense too in the flat hopelessness of Karl's words, and she turned away from him, concentrating on the job she was doing, trying to find some slight comfort from the steady flow of the milk between her fingers and the placid munching of the cow.

At last she forced herself to speak.

'Have you any news? Have you heard from your family?' The words were uncertain and hesitant. She was frightened of his reply, and it was a while before he spoke.

'No one can tell me anything. There's such devastation that it's impossible to get any news. I won't know if they're alive or dead until I can go back.'

His voice was cold, utterly without emotion.

Margaret shivered in spite of the warmth of the animals around her, and she thought momentarily of her own parents safe in Bristol and of John coming home soon. It was only in the reported sufferings of unknown millions that the war had intruded into her safe little world. Her life was almost untouched by its tragedies.

'I'm sorry,' she whispered, and she wondered if there was any way she could reach him, show him her sorrow.

He turned to her and there was a frightening blankness in his eyes. 'I'll have to go back,' he said, and Margaret's heart sank at the iron-cold determination in the words.

She suddenly wanted to leap up from her stool and throw her arms round him, to give comfort in the only way she knew and to keep him here with her for ever, but she sat anchored to the small, uncomfortable seat and was silent. There was nothing more to say, no words that were adequate to express all the jumbled emotions that filled her heart. She set herself resolutely to think only of the ordinary everyday things that were safe and trouble-free. She grieved for the barrier between them, and she was glad when Annie came in for the jug of house milk.

With the milking finished Karl carried the buckets into the dairy and Margaret started the twice-daily task of preparing the milk for the churns. She concentrated on each process with more than usual care. First the warm, frothy liquid must run over the rippled surfaces of the cooler, and these must be immaculately clean, as must everything else in the small room adjoining the cowshed. When the process was finished and the churns stood filled and gleaming they must be loaded into the small handcart and taken to the stone platform at the farm gate to be collected by the milk lorry. One churn was kept each morning for their own use and for neighbours who came every day with their jugs to take the thick, creamy yellow liquid that made such wonderful cups of ever-sustaining tea, and could be turned into either butter or thick clotted cream.

Margaret thought about the cream as she worked. It was one of the small pleasures of life here in Cornwall. She had always found that when there was something miserable or frightening dominating her thoughts, then it was good to fasten her mind on little comforting things, things even as ordinary as cream on her porridge! She had always looked forward to seeing the bowl on the table at every meal when she'd come to the farm as a child, and she still enjoyed it. Deliberately she made herself think about it, deliberately she cast the other disturbing, troubling things away.

'Why can't you make it like that, Mummy?' she remembered asking, and the reply had always been the same.

'We don't get milk like that at home.'

Before she came to the farm she had only seen

churns in the back of the milkman's cart as he had come down the long street where she'd lived. She'd used to run out sometimes with a sugar lump for the old horse, and her mother would follow with the large green jug that always stood on the kitchen table. The milkman would fill it from the aluminium pint measure that he dipped into the white, chalky substance that had no resemblance at all to the rich Jersey milk that now flowed twice each day from beneath her fingers' pressure.

In Cornwall she had soon learned how to make the firm, delicious cream that they all loved. After each evening's milking it was her job to take the great shallow pan and set the richest of the milk to simmer. Hours of gentle heat would produce a thick yellow crust that was carefully taken off and drained into a large glass basin. There was always a vast amount, enough to cover scones and toast, porridge and home-made bread and to eat by the spoonful if you wished. The unwanted skim milk that remained was for the dogs, pigs, and other assorted animals.

She was not alone with Karl any more that day. There was no opportunity to talk, and Margaret was strangely relieved. But she smiled at him warmly whenever there was no one close enough to see, willing him to take some comfort from her sympathy, and gradually she felt that the hurt was receding a little from his eyes.

When she lay in her small bed that night, however, she kept hearing his words hammering through her brain. 'Do you know where my home was?' he had said. 'Dresden.'

CHAPTER FOUR

October 1945

'WE'LL be able to travel as far as Bristol together,' Graham Bantry said, and John looked with gratitude at his friend. The ordeal of the long train journey to Liskeard had worried him, and he despised himself for that. He stared down at the grass at his feet, green and fresh, the newly cut smell of it suddenly overwhelming his senses. This lovely hospital garden enfolded him, and he tried to banish from his mind yet again the past years of non-living. The effort brought the usual shudder to his thin body.

There had been two hospitals since his release from the Japanese prisoner-of-war camp, one in Rangoon, and then this one set in the gentle English countryside. He had slowly learned to eat and think and live normally again, and now there was just one more day left of the ordered routine, the prescribed existence, and of safety. Then every man would be on his own. For the first time after the long nightmare months each would have to direct his own life. The longed-for dream, the day of going home, had become both a great excitement and a feared experience.

John looked up at the autumn sky and at the leaves beginning to turn, the red and golden showing through the green. He had forgotten all about the seasons, and he stared at the glowing colours in the hazy English sunshine almost without comprehension. He registered its beauty vaguely without words, and then he was back unwillingly, beneath another, crueller sun, and he wondered if he would ever forget. He judged himself harshly, and felt a deep shame that he hadn't coped with the terrible privations of the camp as well as his friend. There had been long hours of boredom at first, and then endless hours of mind- and body-destroying toil beneath that same sun that shone so gently now in this peaceful place.

It was a toil that had killed and maimed and made every normal human thought a torment and every movement an agony. Life had become just a succession of misery-filled days, and without Graham he thought he would never have survived. He could hear suddenly in his memory Graham's wonderful occasional laugh. Even there, in that hell, Graham could find something to laugh at now and then and make of that moment a tiny second of heaven. There was kindness too. He was always kind. It was a virtue often despised, but precious beyond belief in the pit of horror into which they had been cast. Graham, with his tall, slim and delicate-looking frame and his white accountant's hands, had coped, but he, John, the supposedly tough young farmer, had not. Perhaps it was those very years of freedom and plenty on the farm before he joined up that had not prepared him for the trauma of a prison camp.

He remembered going proudly to Bodmin to sign into the Duke of Cornwall's Light Infantry. War had seemed splendid then. There was nothing splendid now. Even victory had a hollow ring. There were so many who were not going home the day after tomorrow, or ever. . .He saw them more clearly than he saw the long hydrangea hedge still resplendent in its pink and blue glory beneath the row of identical windows of the ward.

Making a supreme effort, he wrenched his mind back to the present.

What had Graham said? They could travel to Bristol together? John rallied his thoughts and tried to picture his beloved farm. He was going home. He visualised his mother and his father as they had looked when he left, and then he thought of Margaret. He smiled a little as he recalled that last day—the day when they had swum together, when he'd first become aware of her attractiveness. He had pulled her into his arms and then felt guilty because she was so young, only about fifteen. His kiss had been brief and light, more like that of a brother for a sister, but she wasn't a sister, and the remembered feel of her came back to him, her small breasts beneath that ridiculous wrap pressing into his body. She had been frightened, pushing him away. And now it was he who was afraid. He couldn't cope with girls yet, not for a long time. The bleak months of starvation, illness and grinding toil had blanked from his mind and flesh most of the normal reactions that he wished he could feel. And she would be grown up, he thought anxiously, seventeen or eighteen now.

Graham was speaking again.

'Wake up, Johnny boy! Did you hear me? We can travel to Bristol together.'

John forced his mind into a response, made himself look at his friend. 'Great. I'll manage from there,' he said, and wondered if the relief in his voice was obvious.

'You can stay with me for a night before going on, if you like,' Graham said. 'My mum would like that. The folks are getting pretty excited about our arrival and I'd like some support.'

John laughed. Suddenly and surprisingly he wanted to laugh, wanted to be normal, a young man free and going home. He made another great effort.

'Thanks, I think I'd like that too, but I don't know how my family would take it. They're planning something, I think. I'd have two doses of welcome, wouldn't I?'

'We'll have to send telegrams,' said Graham. 'Let them know when we'll be arriving.'

Graham's home was a surprise to John. It was a large sturdy stone-built house that was both his father's surgery and the family home. John looked in amazement at the vast bookshelves that lined the walls of the big living-room, and at the piano that dominated it, and he saw his friend in a new way. His own simple home set beneath its surrounding hills, with the sea always in sight and sound, was suddenly precious. Strangely, he wanted to defend it.

There was no need. After the first joy and emotion of Graham's greeting with his parents they turned to him and welcomed him warmly so that he had no feeling of being an intruder in their immense private happiness. He knew that his own moment was to come. He was to finish his journey tomorrow.

'Go and have a lie-down for a couple of hours,' Graham's mother said to both of them during the afternoon. John glanced at himself in the mirror over the fireplace. Their weakness must be evident to everyone, he thought.

Graham just laughed. 'We've got to look after ourselves,' he said, mimicking the doctor who had signed their hospital discharge.

Thankfully John stretched himself on the soft bed in the carefully prepared vistor's bedroom. He stared at the ceiling with its elaborate mouldings and unsullied whiteness. There was a quietness in the house. He suddenly realised that he had not known any quietness for years, since he'd joined up, in fact, and neither had he slept alone in all those weary months. All around had been the noisy breathing, snores, groans sometimes, of other men. It was a strange, exotic feeling lying on that bed, alone, its very softness and the smell of clean linen adding to the other-worldliness that he found difficult to contain.

There was to be a small celebration that evening. He wondered how he would cope. He must do his best. Graham would manage very well—he knew that.

He stood uncertainly at first, welcoming the guests with his friend as they arrived. Then at the meal he ate slowly, carefully savouring each precious mouthful. Graham's mother had cooked simple food, knowing and understanding their needs. There were girls, two of them, cousins, and John looked at them without interest. Nurses had been the only females in his experience recently. These two tried to talk to him, and he made vague replies to their questions. Eventually they left him alone and turned their attention to Graham. John watched him when the meal was over. He stood, a glass in his hand, and he made them laugh. That was it, John thought. To be able to make people laugh was to survive. For a short time he was almost jealous of his friend, and then Graham sat down at the piano and John listened, incredulous. He hadn't known that he had this gift too.

'I haven't forgotten how to play,' Graham said as his fingers coaxed something classical that John didn't recognise or understand out of the old grand. 'I thought I might have lost it all.'

Suddenly the music changed. Graham swung into a quick ragtime, and John stared unbelieving as the sturdy piano seemed almost to rock under the throb and pulse of the beat. Then gradually a small miracle began in John's mind. The past horrors began to pale and fade, and he responded automatically to the rhythm. The music changed again, became music to dance to, and one of the girls came over to him and held out her hands. Before he knew what was happening he was dancing, laughing, and whirling her round the big room, and there was clapping and everyone else was laughing too.

Graham's father drove him to the station the next day. A car was a necessity because he was a doctor, he told John. Careful control of his mileage left him a small amount of petrol for occasions such as this, he explained, and John felt that there was almost a guilty edge to his explaining.

The early morning streets were almost empty of cars. Trams clattered noisily along their predetermined courses, and sturdy buses, full of earnest workers, mostly women, turban-headed, wound their ponderous ways to the factories and shops and various other establishments of a city coming to life again after six years of war.

The buoyancy of the previous evening was still with him, and even the grey stone bulk of Temple Meads Station couldn't force him back into the mist and fog of his past despondency.

'I'll see you on to the train,' said Graham, and John was grateful but not dependent any more.

They walked to the ticket office and he pulled his pass from his pocket. He held it clutched in his hand, a ticket to Cornwall, a precious symbol of freedom. He was going home, starting a new life. He handed it to the man behind the glass and watched as it was marked with a small punch, marked carelessly. No ticket collector could know its significance. He took it back into his hand and slowly put it back into his wallet and tucked it into his safest pocket. Every event that morning was of moment and importance, invested with a magical quality that he would never again experience. He took out a sixpence. There was a chocolate machine on the platform. He put his coin in the sliding chromium tray and anxiously pushed it in and waited. Then he saw the notice, 'Out of order', and, disappointed beyond reason, he pulled the tray out again and retrieved his money.

'Sweets and chocolate are still rationed,' Graham reminded him. 'We seem to have won the military war, but not the food war.'

They both laughed then, and knew how much they had to learn, how much had changed since they'd gone away.

'It's like being born all over again, isn't it?' Graham commented. 'Almost everything is a whole new adventure.'

The train arrived eventually, and the smell and sound of it reminded John of the occasional outing to Plymouth with his parents. They had gone to visit his grandmother there, and he could still feel the childhood excitement. He had blotted from his mind that other railway on which he had worked in heat and pain for so long. . .it had no part, no connection with this friendly monster coming to a noisy halt in front of him.

The train was crowded and smoky, but his uniform earned respect and both women and older men let him through. He found a seat, heaved his bag on to the rack, folded his thick greatcoat carefully and put it on top and sank into the soft, yielding space. He could see Graham, but dimly now through the dirty window, and there was no way of communicating. It was a sudden parting, expected but never actually accepted until this last minute. They had suffered so much together, and now they would each take up their lives and perhaps never meet again. Graham's environment was so different from his. It had been as nothing in the camp, but here at home it was real, a barrier separating them as surely as the cloudy glass. The train was moving. Graham was running down the platform waving frantically, and John felt tears stinging behind his eyes, then pushing through on to his face. He brushed them away desperately, and when he looked up there was only the grimy wall of the station to stare at, and then houses, rows and rows of identical scruffy houses standing like sentinels ranged up and over the hills against the grey sky.

He closed his eyes and slept.

CHAPTER FIVE

1945

JOHN spent most of the journey either sleeping or gazing out of the window. This was the day of a thousand dreams. He stared at the hedges and the autumn gold of the trees against the grey sky and his heart leapt in repeated joy and wonder, and as the train crossed the old bridge over the Tamar he knew that he was truly home. This was his Cornwall. His own, his native land.

The station was just as he remembered it. There were the flowers carefully tended still, the shabby waiting-room and the ticket office where he had so proudly shown his pass and briskly said goodbye to his father. He shuddered, recalling his bouncy confidence.

There was no car outside to take him the twelve miles to the farm. He had deliberately told them not to meet him. He wanted to manage the two buses alone, to savour the journey through the familiar lanes and past the old landmarks without anyone at his side to see the tears that he felt sure would come. He needed this time to restore him to himself, make ready to face the people he had left so joyfully, and who were now probably preparing to welcome him with noise and merrymaking that he wasn't quite sure he could cope with.

He chose a seat right at the back of the bus, and he hoped that no one he knew would recognise him. He put his bag on the empty place at his side, daring anyone to come too close, and then he allowed his mind to wander ahead to the farm, to his mother and father and again to Margaret. He remembered more about her with each mile that passed. There had been a letter to say that she was working full-time on the farm, although it was not from her. He had always hoped that she would write, but the news had always come from his mother. A sudden chill gripped his heart. Perhaps she was walking out with someone else. Perhaps that was the reason that she had not gone home when the war ended!

He had to change buses at a small fishing town where he shouldered his bag and wandered down to the harbour and smelt the sea and heard the cry of the gulls. He stared at the gently rocking boats and the fish just landed from a small, solitary craft, and was wrapped around in the total glory of this, the most traumatic and the most wonderful afternoon of his life.

The bus finally dropped him at his village, and he stood in the road alone. They thought he was arriving later. That had been another of his plans for the much desired quiet walk up the familiar road to the farm. It was about two miles, and he had to prove to himself that he could manage it. He knew he was weak, and the excitement of the last few days hadn't helped.

He stared at the bent hedgerow oaks, blown almost horizontal by the fierce winds from the sea. There were still leaves on them, brown and golden, and he shivered slightly as he looked up and remembered the winter gales that blew in from the west, gales that would rip every remaining leaf from the branches and tear cruelly at tree and man alike. He wondered how he would manage after years of stifling heat and burning sun.

Suddenly he heard the cows and the excited yapping of a dog, and then they appeared round the bend in the road, swaying along, reluctant to leave the succulent grass of the roadside, their udders heavy with milk. John stood back and watched as they moved towards him, and then he saw the tall blond young man who walked easily behind them, a stick in his hand. He had little need to use it. The animals responded to the gentle tap on their rumps that he administered now and then, and the dog dashed from side to side, nudging the most greedy from their snatched titbits. John watched curiously and wondered who the cows belonged to. He didn't recognise the stranger.

The man looked at him, his eyes travelling over his uniform and there was a moment's pause. Then he spoke, and his voice was friendly with a slight accent that John couldn't place.

'You must be John. They aren't expecting you until the next bus.'

John stared in surprise and felt immediate resentment for his ruddy good health and strong bare arms.

'These are your cows.' The man indicated the beasts and laughed a little. 'We hadn't reckoned on giving you such a smelly welcome.'

John relaxed briefly and looked expertly at those nearest him. 'They look in good condition,' he said. He wanted to ask the man who he was and why he looked as though he had never known a moment's fighting or deprivation in his life.

'My father? Is he all right?' he asked instead. They had never needed help on the farm before, even when he was at school. Sudden fear gripped him. Perhaps there was something he didn't know.

'Fine. Yes, they're all fine, but there's a lot to do and I come every day to help out as much as I can. I'm no farmer, but I'm learning.'

They walked together as far as the bend in the road,

and then, where the hill swept down towards the house and the wood on the hillside brought back countless memories, John stopped and leaned over an old gate that led away into the trees.

'I'll come on later,' he said. 'Please don't say that I'm here. I want it to be a surprise, and I need to be alone for a bit. What's your name, by the way?'

There was a moment's hesitation and then his companion looked him straight in the eyes.

'Karl Schormann,' he said quietly, and it seemed to John as if the world spun around him in a thousand flashing lights.

'I'm sorry that I was the first one you should meet,' the voice went on, and John heard the words through a haze of sudden shock. 'It was intended that I would be gone back to camp when you arrived.'

John gripped the bar of the gate and his knuckles turned white under the force of his grip, but he mustered every vestige of control and turned to face the enemy, the enemy in a country lane near his beloved home, the enemy taking his own cows to the milking, the enemy free and well fed in *his* Cornwall.

'Half an hour,' he said. 'I'll be there in half an hour.'

He tried to regain control of his emotions and his thoughts. He knew that hundreds of German prisoners were helping on the land, and in various rebuilding projects all over the country. He remembered reading something of the programme of re-education to which they had to submit as well, and he had wondered what it must feel like to belong to a beaten and humiliated race. But his thoughts had all been academic. None of it had related to him or to anyone he knew until this moment just past. In the good-natured and healthy face of the man driving a herd of cows peacefully down the lane John suddenly saw the real dilemma of war, and he stared unseeing at the road and the hedgebank, and wondered how he would cope now with this added threat.

Then unexpectedly he laughed. He laughed to himself and to the quiet sky. Of course he would manage. At least the man wasn't a Jap—that would have been another matter.

He held his head high and walked slowly down the lane that took him to his home, coming at last to the low grey farmhouse standing firm and reassuring as it had stood for a century or more, just round the bend in the road. Then his hand was on the gate and his mother was shouting and running towards him and he was enfolded in her ample embrace. Chickens scattered and gulls screamed, and his father ran too—and then John saw the girl. She stood at the door, her long hair falling on her shoulders, her brown eyes staring at him. His mother turned to her.

'Come, Margaret,' she said, and suddenly the girl's young hands were in his and there were tears on her cheeks.

'You've grown up,' John said simply, and he kissed her gently and they all went inside, and there was tea and cake and the sound of the kettle on the hearth, and suddenly he was crying with the rest of them.

The German was nowhere to be seen, and he was glad of that. His family and Margaret were enough for the present. He looked at her frequently, but each time their eyes met she dropped hers and she hardly spoke. She busied herself with the dishes and various tasks in the kitchen from time to time, and although there was so much to say none of them quite knew where to begin. There were silences, but it didn't matter. Just to be there was enough.

'The party is tomorrow,' Annie said suddenly. 'A

village party on the green with all the children and flags and things. They are all so proud of you, John.'

'They'll want you to say something, son,' his father added. 'Not a lot, just a few sentences.'

John's thoughts had strayed momentarily, back to the camp, back to the heat and the flies and the horror, as they frequently did, and he wrenched his mind away, pulled himself again into the present. He took another piece of his mother's fruit-cake and smiled at her.

'I'll manage somehow,' he said. 'I'm glad it's not today.'

Then suddenly his need for quiet and rest overwhelmed him, and his mother, obviously seeing and understanding, picked up his bag.

'Come and have a lie-down before supper,' she said.

Obediently he followed her, and was glad that she stood back at the top of the stairs, allowing him to go into the room before her. It was almost the same as the day he had left it. There were flowers on the small desk beneath the window and the patchwork bedspread was clean and welcoming. The window was open and he could see and smell the cliffs and the sea. The gulls were crying as they had cried ever since his earliest childhood memories, and always in his dreams. It was the sound of home, and he went to the window and leaned out. Suddenly there was another sound and another smell. A large, battered truck was pulling up outside the farm gate. He saw the young German spring on to the back and he heard voices, German voices talking and laughing, and the noises made him blanch. He pulled the window shut angrily and for a moment forgot where he was and that his mother was behind him.

'It's just Karl going back to camp, dear,' she said calmly. 'He comes to help each day, and we've needed help too. Your father isn't so well these days with his rheumatism and all, and although Margaret works hard we needed a man about the place.'

She seemed to be making excuses.

'He never comes into the house,' she went on. 'He has his meals out in the barn. I'll not have him sitting at the same table as the rest of us, although I must say that he's polite and a hard worker. They all are, I believe.'

'I met him on the road,' John said briefly. 'We talked a bit, and he seemed all right. Rather a shock, though, that's all, finding a Jerry herding your own cows.'

'Of course, dear,' she said, and she laid a hand on his arm. 'Tomorrow your dad will show you the farm. We've made a few changes, but not many. I think he wants you to approve!'

She went away down the old, uneven wooden staircase, and he was alone. Again the luxury of a room to himself, he thought. He closed the door quietly, savouring the pleasure of the heavy old latch, and then he emptied his bag, took off his uniform carefully and put it in the big oak wardrobe, and lay on the bed beneath the cover. It was soft, the same old feather bed that he remembered since he was a small boy. It gathered him to itself and drowned his fears and his memories in its soft warmth and cosiness. Soon he was asleep, and he remembered little more until a gentle tap woke him. The sky outside was darkening and Margaret stood there, a cup of tea in one hand and a candle in a wide green tin candlestick in the other. He remembered there was no electricity upstairs in the old house. They had only had it put in downstairs a short time before he'd gone away.

'There will be a meal in half an hour,' she said, and she put the cup down on the bedside table and the candle on the chest of drawers.

She stood and looked at him, and he put out his hand to her.

'It's wonderful to have you back, John,' she said, ignoring his gesture 'We've all longed for this day.'

'Sit down and talk to me,' he said, indicating the bed, but she backed away.

'Not now—I've to help your mother. She's in quite a state trying to have everything just right for your first meal.'

'And I probably won't be able to eat much.' He laughed. 'I'll do my best, though.'

Margaret turned and walked out of the room, and he heard each creaking stair as she went down. Then he sat up, savouring the luxury of a cup of tea in bed. He looked at the square of sky through the tiny window and saw the first stars, and he knew something of peace at last.

Margaret fled down the stairs. She clearly remembered feeling a little in love with John when he'd gone away, but was it just the glamour of the uniform, of the warrior leaving for war? she wondered. Just a young girl's romance that had been mostly in her imagination? This flesh-and-blood man up there in the bed wanting her to sit near him and talk was another matter. Talk? Her experience of men was minimal, and in spite of her seventeen years her life on the farm had been totally sheltered, but she knew that there was more to it than that. One thing led to another! Annie had warned her not to be out alone after dark for fear of various briefly hinted at terrors, and she had read certain of the lurid paperbacks that some of her school friends had used to keep hidden under innocent exercise-book covers in their desks. These were not the permitted romantic sort of stories that she loved, but they had held her fascinated when she'd read them secretly in the school shed, or dangerously by candlelight in her bedroom. She recalled them now, and shivered both with apprehension and with excitement, and then she laughed at herself as she frequently did. It was her way of dealing with most of her problems. She had long ago discovered that worries and fears, and strange disturbing desires too, lost their power to trouble her if she laughed.

She kept her distance from both John and Karl for those first few weeks of John's return. She watched the two men, though, as they tried to come to terms with their predicament, each struggling to cope with the presence of the other. For Karl it seemed easier. He merely carried on with the jobs he was given. He spoke little, except to the dogs. Margaret heard him sometimes calling to them in rapid German, and when the weather was fine he would sit in the yard eating his dinner with the three animals gazing adoringly into his face waiting for the scraps that inevitably came their way. It seemed to annoy John. He would stare out of the window and then turn away to the table amply laden with food and pick at the soup or home-made bread his mother was urging him to eat. His health was improving gradually, but he did little on the farm. Two or three hours' work were enough, and his frustration was obvious.

At the beginning of December he was recalled to his unit, and his demob followed.

'I'm a free man at last,' he announced when he arrived home, and he laughed as he stood in the kitchen wearing the suit they had issued him with. Karl had come to the door at that very moment with a jug of milk from the evening's milking, and as Margaret took it from him she saw the pain in his eyes, and she wished he had not heard. She smiled at him gently and longed to speak, but words between them were still officially forbidden and it was a long time since they had been able to talk. John had taken over some of the milking, and it was really only in the milking shed that they were private. Margaret felt that she was watched sometimes. Perhaps Annie saw the threat that this tall, handsome German might be to her John.

It was a threat that Margaret knew had some substance, and she shivered sometimes when she lay in her small bed and thought of the two men with their obvious longings and passions, and the events of war that had brought them together. Together into a relationship with each other and with her that was bound to be complex and difficult.

They had all rejoiced on the day of John's return after his demobilisation, rejoiced in his freedom at last from all the traumas and restrictions of the past grim years. But for Karl freedom still lay far in the unknown future, and Margaret knew that she alone was aware of his grief. She longed to talk to him, to tell him that she understood, but there was never a chance. The others were always around and she wasn't supposed to care.

She had felt his pain deeply as the other three could not, but she knew vaguely that there was more in her feelings than mere sympathy, and she was confused and unhappy as she went about her normal duties on the farm in the following days.

The next market day held the promise of sunshine to cheer them all. It was one of those golden winter days when the trees and the hedges seem to breathe a hope of spring, even summer perhaps, when the birds broke their silence and sang of the joys to come. Margaret too felt her spirits lifting, and when John took the reins of the pony and Annie heaved herself up into the trap behind him she wondered if perhaps there might be a moment today when she could talk to Karl undisturbed. Bill wasn't as observant as Annie, and he would be out in the fields anyway. She would try to contrive a small, private space where they could be alone, understand each other a little more, perhaps, and her heart sang at the thought, sang with the birds in a flurry of excitement. She was surprised and slightly dismayed too at the happiness that the thought gave her, but she blithely disregarded any slight misgivings as the clip-clopping of the pony's hoofs sounded further and further away on the road to town.

She was busy all the morning inside the house, and at lunchtime she heated the pan of soup that Annie had left for them and poured it into three large earthenware bowls. There was home-made bread too, large white slices with plenty of butter, thick and yellow, from their Jersey cows. She carried the tray with Karl's meal and placed it on the old wooden table that stood in a sheltered spot beneath the house wall. The weather had fulfilled its early promise, the sky was a cloudless blue and the usual cold wind from the sea was still.

Her own food she unwillingly put on the kitchen table with Bill's. He was out in the top field but would be in soon, and she must sit and eat with him while her only wish was to be outside in the sunshine.

'It's ready!' she called to Karl, and he came out from the shippon and washed at the sink in the yard. He looked at her and smiled.

'It's beautiful here today,' he said quietly. 'I wish you could have yours out here with me.'

Margaret blushed and knew that he must have guessed her thoughts. 'I'm sorry. Bill will be down soon. It's good soup, though—Annie made it.'

The words weren't those she wished to speak. She

wanted to offer Karl comfort for his continued captivity, to show him that she understood and cared. If only she could alleviate that lost and desolate look that she saw so frequently on his face lately.

She looked around and there was no one to see, no sound yet of Bill's boots on the gravel. Perhaps actions could speak more deeply than words, and impulsively she put out her hand and gently touched the rough cloth of Karl's jacket, and she smiled, hoping he would see the depth of compassion that she felt.

'Don't be sad,' she said. 'It will end some time, the hostility and the hatred. The world will be a good place again—I'm sure of it.'

Karl looked away from her and stared at a robin who was hopefully pecking between the cobblestones near by.

'I too can be optimistic today,' he said, and he turned and took her hand in both of his and raised it to his lips and kissed it gently.

Bill looked from one to the other as he came into the yard. He had not seen the kiss, and although he was always kind and fair, a keen perception of the feelings of those around him was not one of his gifts.

'Dinner ready, maid?' he questioned. 'I'm hungry as a horse!' He turned to Karl. 'Get on with it, then, lad,' he said, indicating the steaming bowl on the table. 'Won't do to let my Annie's soup get cold.'

The spell was broken, the magic past, and they all laughed and Margaret went inside with Bill and ate, but her heart was fluttering with surprise and with consternation. The kiss had been an ephemeral, fleeting thing and she knew she must put it from her mind, for it surely meant little to Karl. But she could not, and every night before she slept the sweetness of that snatched second of time flashed before her, and she knew that it was an event that was to be cherished, in her memory for ever.

There was no time for them to be alone after that for many days, but Margaret went about her work with a lighter step and was aware of Annie's questioning gaze resting on her from time to time.

'How about inviting Karl to have Christmas dinner with us?' Bill asked one evening a week or so later when they were sitting round the fire. 'The war's over, and he's a decent enough chap. Don't know what we'd have done without him, in fact.'

Margaret looked at Annie and then at John, waiting for the outburst that she knew was bound to come from one or other of them.

Annie was the first to speak. She put her knitting down in her lap and stared at her husband as if he had suddenly gone completely out of his mind. 'Over my dead body,' she said quietly, but there was an iron coldness in her voice. 'He's not allowed in for ordinary meals, and I'm not having him here for our special day, John's first Christmas home. Never! I don't know how you could dare to suggest it, Bill Trevarrick.'

'I don't think I shall be here for Christmas either,' Margaret announced suddenly. She had made the decision abruptly. She knew that she couldn't sit here with these three, in spite of her love for them, knowing Annie's and John's feelings for Karl and their rejection of him, inevitable and understandable though it was. Christmas too was not really a festival that she felt deeply about, although she had fully enjoyed the presents and the fun and even the carols in previous years. Her mother had written asking her to come home for a week or two. Well, she would go. She recognised that this lonely farmhouse was almost fully her home now, these three more her family than her own parents, but she needed to get away.

She was conscious of John staring at her and she looked across at him. 'I know it's your first Christmas and all that, John,' she said. 'But my mother hasn't been too well lately, and it's a long time since I was there.'

'That's OK,' he said, 'I was just thinking that you haven't met Graham yet. He kept me going in the camp. He lives in Bristol, and I'd like you to meet him. I'll write. He'll invite you to his home—they're a great family.'

'That would be nice,' Margaret said without much enthusiasm. She knew that her thoughts would be with Karl and here with John too, and she wasn't looking forward to any more complications.

'Don't stay too long, dear,' said Annie. 'Can't do without my adopted daughter now.'

Her thoughts had obviously moved away from Karl, and anyway Margaret knew as she looked at her affectionately that Annie had no need to worry. Both her menfolk would do as she wished. Annie had always been the boss, and her gentle, round figure bustling about in the kitchen was deceptive. Inside the submissive little wife was a woman with an iron will who was always obeyed. There was no hope for Karl this Christmas.

CHAPTER SIX

December 1945

MARGARET decided to allow herself two weeks—two weeks away from the tensions of living in the same house as John. Fourteen days of freedom. Freedom from the pressures of other people's lives, of the constant demands of the farm, and from the ever increasing consciousness of her forbidden and angrily denied feelings for Karl. Every day lately the strengthening perception of his awareness of her made her awkward and uneasy in his presence, and she wondered frequently if the ever watchful Annie noticed.

It was a cold, wet day in late December when she arrived at the large, grimy station of her home town. There was always a slight thrill, a strange romance about the name Temple Meads. It was a place of so many memories. There had been day trips from here years ago to the seaside at Weston-super-Mare. With the piercing shriek of the trains in her ears, and the smell of smoke, Margaret recalled clearly the excitement of those long-ago pre-war outings. She could almost feel the handle of the enamel bucket clutched in her small, sticky hand, and the new shiny red spade that her father had always bought for her each year. Then with his slightly increasing prosperity had come the holidays in Cornwall, and she remembered her mother's pride when they had stood on this very platform waiting for the steaming monster that would carry them away to the seemingly magical place of real sea and soaring cliffs.

But there was that other time in her memory too. The day when she'd been twelve years old and her mother had brought her here again and had put her on the train, waving her goodbye bravely, sending her to safety and to a new and different life, a life that was to claim her and change her for ever. She had only made occasional short visits home since then.

'Stay where you're safe,' her mother had written. That had been during the worst days of the Bristol blitz, and during the worry-filled time when England had prepared for invasion and the Jewish population had shivered with apprehension. Margaret remembered lying beneath the heavy patchwork quilt in the quiet peace of the Cornish night, praying to the shadowy Jewish God she only half believed in to keep her mummy and daddy safe from the bombs.

Well, He had answered her prayers, she thought, and they had all been kept safe from Hitler too, although why her family, and not those millions of others, she could not surmise.

She knew that for the next two weeks she must put her parents back into their rightful place in her life again, must become a daughter once more, and try to achieve some sort of meaningful relationship. She looked about her at the bustling crowds. The noise shocked her as it had done on previous visits. She had stayed then as short a time as she decently could, and quickly retreated again to the peace of the Cornish countryside, the place that brought a contentment that was never found in any city.

Gripping her small battered case in one hand and her ticket in the other, she pushed through the crowds and out eventually into the street. Black taxis were standing in rows, their drivers scanning the advancing rabble for signs of wealth. Her sturdy shoes, darned socks and ancient tweed coat obviously merited no attention, and she climbed thankfully on to the waiting bus.

'Centre, please,' she said, remembering.

Then she stared through the dirty windows, dismayed as always, as the vehicle made its dreary way through bomb-damaged streets, cleared now, but leaving empty spaces like toothless gaps in a wrinkled and ravaged face. She had forgotten the devastation!

She hadn't told them the exact time of her arrival, and half an hour later she stood looking down at the brightly polished brass step of the terraced house, excited and scared together, almost afraid to knock.

'It's me, Mother!'

It was an older and a weary-faced woman who opened the door and stared at her. There was a pause as the two women looked at each other. Their relationship was a shallow affair, the long years of separation making any closeness or friendship difficult to achieve, but there was some love, surely, Margaret thought, and she smiled uncertainly.

Then suddenly Sarah Seddon came to life. She threw her arms round her daughter and hugged her. Margaret dropped her case and returned the embrace.

'It's lovely to be home,' she said simply. 'I'd love a cup of tea!'

The first day of the holiday was easy and pleasant. Margaret lay in bed late.

'You enjoy yourself,' her mother said. 'Stay there nice and cosy as long as you want. No cows to milk here!'

The remark was meant to cheer her, but it took her thoughts winging back to the dark, musty shippon, to the animals she had become fond of, and of course to Karl.

Her mother turned from the bed and stared out of the window at the large grey buildings that they had always been able to see from the back of the house. Margaret had grown up with those great ugly barracks her only view, apart from the tree that stood at the end of the garden, one bit of glorious nature in a uncompromising mass of solemn grey stone. They were houses built for orphans, though, not soldiers. Built at least fifty years before on one man's faith and prayers, they had been a refuge for hundreds of poor children, but for Margaret those sturdy houses had presented a kind of threat, a place where she might have to go if her parents died. The sight of the long row of sombrely dressed little girls walking up the street with their teacher each day had always made her shudder, made her mother seem more precious, a bulwark between herself and a similar fate.

'They took the children away when the air-raids started,' her mother was saying. 'The War Office took the place over. We've had all sorts billeted there since. The GIs were the last, poor lads. Before D-Day, it was. We didn't know then, but that's what they were there for, getting ready to go to France. Most of them in graves by now, I shouldn't wonder!'

Margaret shuddered a little, remembering Karl and not wanting to remember. The war was over, wasn't it? Finished. She was young and the future was hers. She drank the hot, sweet liquid quickly and pushed the covers back, shivering in the cold bedroom.

'Let's go and look at the shops,' she said, banishing the past. 'I've saved a little for Christmas presents. I want to get you and Dad something.'

The first three days of the holiday passed happily enough, and she began to feel that Bristol had something to offer after all. Perhaps she could one day learn to live in a town again. Maybe there were other things that might take the place of the fields, the crying gulls and the crashing sea. Perhaps somewhere there was something that might free her from Karl, and from John too.

Friday evening, and a sabbath quiet had descended on the little house. Margaret had been surprised to see how her parents had slipped in their keeping of the faith.

'Partly deliberate, I suppose,' her father tried to explain. 'The threat of invasion and the Germans being so down on the Jews. We tried to fade a bit into the background, be more like our neighbours.'

It wasn't very convincing, but he refused to talk any more about it, and Margaret was left wondering. Perhaps the God of the Holocaust was too difficult to come to terms with!

Old habits were hard to cast aside, though, and sunset on Friday spelt the start of a time of rest. The meal had been prepared in the morning and the dishes would remain in the sink for nearly twenty-four hours.

'We'll do no work,' her father said firmly. 'We may have lost our faith, but one day's rest in seven is a sensible rule, and that's how it's to be.'

There were no candles lit, no special meal, just a quietness, and Margaret settled into the small red plush chair by the fire between her parents and wondered how to pass the evening. A knock at the door some time later caused her to jump in nervousness. There were no callers after dark. Her parents had few friends, none that she could recall. Her father rose from his enormous old chair and shuffled into his slippers. He looked at her almost suspiciously.

'Stay there,' he commanded the two women. 'I'll go and see.'

They sat in silent obedience and listened. The door was opened eventually. They heard the shooting back of the large bolt, then there were muffled voices and finally footsteps in the hall. They came along the passage and a young man stood in the doorway, with Samuel Seddon awkward behind him. Margaret sprang to her feet. Of course, John had said something about a friend. She had forgotten his name.

'Someone to see you, Meg,' her father announced. 'Go on in, lad. Mother, find a chair for him and a cup of tea.'

Before the stranger sat down he smiled, and Margaret warmed to him instantly. He held out his hand and took hers, and his grasp was firm and strong as his dark brown eyes searched her face.

'I've heard a lot about you from John,' he said. 'He wrote and asked me to call when you came home.'

She scarcely knew what to reply. His voice was cultured and assured, his clothes well cut and obviously good, and he was holding her work-roughened hand as though she were some precious treasure. She was conscious of her mother fluttering about in the scullery, boiling a kettle, looking for the best cups, all her Sabbath principles cast aside, and she was aware too that she herself was wearing her oldest dress and that her hair had escaped from its neat roll at the nape of her neck into unruly tendrils that dangled over her collar. She could feel herself blushing.

'Graham Bantry,' he continued, introducing himself and obviously understanding her confusion. 'John and I kept one another going when things were tough. He's a great chap.'

For a moment Margaret wondered what on earth

these two men could have found in common. John cared only for the farm; Graham was obviously well educated, from a different social class.

'Have a bite to eat,' her mother said nervously, bringing in a tray with the ever-comforting tea and some home-made carrot cake set out elaborately on one of the best plates, with a lace doily that Margaret had never seen in use before.

Graham got to his feet, taking the tray from her and setting it carefully on the old oak table beneath the bay window. They ate and drank, and conversation was slightly stilted and difficult.

'My parents would like you to come to tea on Sunday,' Graham said, turning directly to Margaret. 'Shall I come for you at about two o'clock? It gets dark early.'

'I could meet you at the Tramway Centre,' she replied, scared now. She glanced up at him shyly. He was looking straight at her again with those kind, wide eyes of his, and she warmed to him, but she wanted no complications in her life. She had enough of those already. Perhaps she should refuse to go, but it was too late. The words of acceptance had been spoken.

'No, I'll come for you in the car. I can borrow my father's—he's not on duty on Sunday.'

Her heart somersaulted. She had never been in a car. There were always buses in Cornwall, and the pony and trap, of course. How old-fashioned it seemed now!

Her mother looked up from her nervously held cup of tea. 'That'll be nice,' she said, answering for her daughter. 'A motor car! Do you like driving, Mr Bantry?'

The car was a small Austin Seven, and Margaret tucked her legs beneath the leather seat with a thrill of excitement. Graham shut the door carefully, swung the starter handle and then climbed into the seat beside her. She gazed entranced as they seemed to glide at incredible speed through familiar streets, across the Gloucester Road and up towards the green expanse of the Downs. She knew that Graham's family lived in Clifton, the leafy and spacious area of the town where the air was clean and the houses large and opulent. She looked with regret as they passed the large grounds and imposing buildings of the old Red Maids School. She remembered the thrill when she'd heard that she had passed the scholarship and so earned herself a place there back at the beginning of the war, but her parents had been too frightened of Hitler's bombs and their Jewish blood, and she had never been able to take advantage of the education offered.

Graham saw her staring at the school. 'My sister went there,' he said, 'and I was at Queen Elizabeth's High. How I hated those yellow stockings and long coats!'

They both laughed. She remembered seeing the boys from the old school in their strange uniform that was still worn, and she looked at Graham and imagined how handsome he would have been in the old medieval clothes.

'I just went to the local senior school in Cornwall, but there were only a few of us and we had a very dedicated teacher,' she said, striving for self-esteem. 'She kept us on a strict diet of poetry and the classics, and although my maths isn't up to much I'm not too ashamed of the rest!'

She had only been with Graham for a short time, but he was so easy to talk to, and she was surprised at her desire to impress him. He mustn't think her an uneducated country bumpkin!

They pulled up outside a large, four-storeyed house.

It was elegant and well kept, and when Graham led her inside, she was as impressed as John had been two months before by the spacious, book-lined rooms, and by the kindness of both of Graham's parents. Tea was served in civilised luxury, and there was even a young maid to bring in the tray. A painting of a severe but very handsome lady in grey silk hung above the fireplace, and Margaret stared up at her as she sipped her tea.

'My great-grandmother,' Graham said, following her glance. 'She was a very strict and dour sort of person, I'm told. She makes me feel guilty every time I sit in this room.'

'I don't think any of her descendants have inherited her character,' Alan Bantry said. 'I'm tempted sometimes to take her down and hang her in one of the attics!'

They all laughed, and when the sandwiches had been eaten and the meal cleared away Graham suggested a walk.

'There's just about an hour of daylight left,' he said. 'Should be a lovely sunset.'

The house was on the edge of the Downs, and they walked along the path that led to the spectacular views of the Avon Gorge and the graceful Suspension Bridge that spanned it. Margaret looked around her and remembered those occasional special days of her childhood when her parents would take her on a bus to have a picnic here on the edge of the town. There were great hollows that children called Dumps. You could run up and down them and pretend that they were castles or fairy dens. There was a small slide in the rocks, polished by countless young bottoms, her own included. She looked at it and laughed a little.

'I slid down there lots of times long ago before the war,' she said.

'Me too,' Graham replied, and he took her hand and squeezed it companionably in their shared remembering.

They stared down to the Portway far below and watched the infrequent car trundling along looking like a little Dinky toy you could buy in Woolworths for threepence.

'As beautiful as Cornwall?' Graham questioned.

'Perhaps it is, in a different way,' she admitted. After all, this town was her birthplace. She felt slightly guilty that all her love and devotion should go elsewhere—a place in which she surely had only temporary dwelling. Thoughts of marrying John had occupied her mind for many of the months that he had been away. The farm would be her permanent home then and Bristol just a memory. She had often wondered lately if it was the sea and the cliffs and the old stone farmhouse that she had fancied herself in love with. Had John just been an unconscious means to an end? She turned to look up at the tall man at her side. If only she could fall in love with someone like Graham. Someone without complications, acceptable and with a secure job, and kind too. She knew instinctively that Graham was kind, a nice sort of man. Funny word, 'nice', but that was just what he was, she thought. Very, very nice.

She met Graham once more during her two weeks at home. He suggested a walk during one of his lunch hours, just an hour, he said, and if the weather was good they could go up to Cabot Tower. She was to meet him outside the Cathedral.

She knew that he was an accountant. At least he would be, one day, and he was working hard every evening for his exams. She stood nervously waiting for him, wondering why she had come and why he had asked her.

The winter sun shone on the stone of the ancient Cathedral, giving it a subtle beauty, but she shivered, partly for the cold wind that blew through the archway behind her, and partly for an apprehension she could not understand. She pulled her thick woollen scarf more tightly round her neck.

Then she saw him come down the steps of the building where he worked, and he waved and hurried towards her. They walked up past the shops and past the gaps left by some of the bombing and turned towards the green hill behind, crowned with its strange tower. It was quiet and peaceful, and they climbed up and up until they could see a great panorama lying below them, the city of Bristol with the devastation of its bomb sites, the docks still busy with a few small ships, and its church spires pointing to the sky. So many spires.

'I'm beginning to feel that it wouldn't be so bad to come back here to live after all,' Margaret said. 'It's a lovely town—I'd forgotten how lovely.'

Graham turned very suddenly to look at her, and she blushed under the gaze of those eyes.

'John wouldn't like that very much, would he?' he said.

It was the first time that he had suggested that she might belong to John. The first time that anything personal had been allowed to intrude into their conversation.

'John?' she questioned, hoping her voice sounded all innocence and amusement. 'What has John got to do with it?'

Then his tone changed, matching hers, and he suggested that they go and get a hot drink, and they both laughed, and turned to retrace their steps down to the shops and the busy, impersonal street.

Christmas was an event with little significance in the small terraced house. Margaret could remember being desperately jealous of her friends years ago, of their presents and decorated trees. Her parents had tried to make it up to her.

'But we have Chanukah,' her mother had always reminded her, 'and Purim, and lots of other special times that your friends don't have at all.'

In spite of the candles that they had used to light for Sabbath each Friday when she was little, and even the presents at the Feast of Lights, nothing had made up for the lack of a Christmas tree and its hazardous little candles that she could see through the windows of the houses as she walked down the long road on her way to school. Now, years later, her parents seemed to have given up all the fun of Judaism and accepted none of the pleasures of Christianity. Margaret sat gloomily through Christmas Day, and her heart was on the farm with Annie and Bill. She thought of the large stuffed cockerel that they would be eating, the paper chains saved from last year that Annie would string across the front room, and the holly with its bright red berries cut from the hedges by John or Karl and decorating every available corner. There might be mistletoe too; she knew that there was some growing on one of the old apple trees in the orchard. Her thoughts went to Karl as they constantly did, and she wondered what he would be doing in the camp. There was still a drastic shortage of food, and not much chance of any of the prisoners going home to Germany yet, so there wouldn't be much cause for celebration.

It was with tremendous relief that she greeted the

morning of her return to Cornwall. Her mother, sadly sensing that her daughter was glad to leave, insisted on going with her to the station.

'Don't argue,' she said firmly. 'I shall come. It'll do me good to have a trip out.' There was a loneliness in the brave words that left Margaret feeling guilty again, a guilt that she was getting used to. Why was there not more room in her heart for her mother?

Sarah Seddon stood in the kitchen that morning spreading margarine thinly on some of her meagre rationed bread, and she managed a little cheese too. Margaret knew that they would have to go short because of these sandwiches. She thought of the home-made butter that Annie put on the table each day, and the cream too, and the guilt increased.

When, some hours later, the train finally rounded the bend in the line and she could no longer see her mother's frail figure waving sadly, she settled down in her corner seat and wondered what the New Year would have in store for her, for them all. 1946 was going to be the first year of peace and of hope for a future.

CHAPTER SEVEN

1946

THE journey to Cornwall was long and tedious, but the train chugged over the Tamar Bridge at last and Margaret knew she would soon be home. Home? Where was home? Where did she truly belong?

'Welcome back,' John said. He met her at the station, and mercifully the weather was dry and not as cold as it could have been for early January. He put her case into the trap and wrapped a thick blanket around her legs.

'Thanks. That's lovely.' She was grateful for his care for her. Gulls were in the sky, the air was fresh and clear and the pony trotted briskly along as he always did on the homeward journey. The reins lay lightly in John's hands.

'Enjoy your stay?' he asked.

'Yes, thank you. Graham came.'

She could feel John looking at her—wanting to know more, anxious that his friend should have pleased her, but probably not too much!

'He's nice, and his family too,' she continued. 'I went for tea.'

'I don't think I should have survived in the camp without him.'

Margaret thought again of the quiet confidence and the warm smile, and she knew what John meant. Graham would always be a bulwark of strength to his family and friends. She sighed, and a sense of sudden gloom overcame her. There was no reason for it and, dismayed, she turned to John and smiled.

'Soon be home,' she said brightly. 'I hope your mum has something nice for supper. I'm starving.'

Her welcome from Annie and Bill was as enthusiastic as she'd known it would be, and four huge, mouth-watering Cornish pasties were waiting in the oven.

'Come on, maid, tuck in,' Bill said when they were sitting round the kitchen table later. 'You must be hungry after those towny meals you've been eating the past couple of weeks.'

Margaret laughed. 'Mum does her best, but it's not easy with all the shortages,' she said, anxious to defend her family.

After a few days of work and fresh air the time in Bristol was almost forgotten. She was needed too. She knew that they really couldn't do without her help. Although John looked well he did very little on the farm. He tired easily, and his frustration seemed to grow with each day that passed. The years of worry had taken their toll of Bill too, and Annie watched over her two men anxiously. It was mainly Karl and Margaret who shared the work. They laboured together in an uneasy companionship, both keeping their feelings firmly under control, but talking when there was no one else to hear. Margaret loved these times of closeness and treasured them in her heart, but she determined that her relationship with Karl must be like sister to brother. She told herself firmly that there could be no hope of anything deeper than that.

He hadn't mentioned his home for some time or said anything about his plans for the future, and she frequently wondered if he had received any more news from Germany. He was sawing and stacking logs in the big barn one day when she went in to fetch another load of dry ones for the fire. He looked at her in the dim half-light and she smiled.

'You've been working hard,' she said. 'Shall I bring you some coffee?'

'Thanks. That would be nice.'

The superficial words hung in the air between them, and Margaret wanted to scream at the barriers they each made for the other. She put the log-basket down on the ground and stood up straight, facing him. She watched fascinated as his powerful arms, bare below the rolled-up sleeves of the old shirt, forced the saw steadily through the hard, resistant wood. She could see the strength of him, but strangely the gentleness too, and suddenly, without warning, all her instincts rebelled against her carefully considered resolutions. She wanted to throw herself into those strong arms and to cry out that the differences between them mattered not at all. She wanted to tell him that she loved him, for the certainty of the knowledge came upon her at that moment. She had felt it that day in the milking shed, but not so intensely as this. She stood still, looking at him, and she could feel the blood rushing to her face. She started to tremble, overcome with the violence of the emotions that filled her.

But the longer she stood there the more impossible it became to take one step in his direction. And he wasn't looking at her any more. He was gathering up the last of the sawn logs, was stacking them neatly in a pile.

She turned and walked steadily out and across the yard towards the farmhouse kitchen, and by the time she had made the coffee and carried it carefully back she had achieved a kind of calm.

Karl took the cup from her and sat down on an old wooden bench beneath the window, and she was aware of the quietness and the sweet smell of fresh sawdust.

'I shall miss all this,' he said. 'I've been happy here in a way.' He looked up at her and smiled. 'It'll be strange to go back to studying again, and I shall miss you most of all, Margaret.'

'Studying?' Her voice was blank, without understanding.

Then she saw the misery descend once more as it frequently did, closing like a shutter over his features.

'One day I suppose I'll study, when Germany has recovered. Languages, music, who knows? It'll be a long time. I sometimes forget and imagine I'm going home to Dresden as it was. It was so beautiful. I should have loved to show it to you!'

She stood for a moment sharing his impossible dream.

Dresden, Dresden. It was a name that meant so many things, and she said it quietly to herself, wondering if she would ever go, ever stand beside Karl looking at the river and the German skies.

'I should like to see it,' she said.

He was silent for a time, drinking the scalding coffee, and she could see that he had retreated from her as he sometimes did. 'No, you wouldn't. Not now you wouldn't.'

The words were measured and quiet, and she shrank from the misery in them. He handed the empty cup to her and she knew that once again the magic of their time together was shattered, the barriers between them too great for crossing. But as she turned to go he smiled at her.

'I'm sorry, Margaret,' he said. 'I'm so sorry.'

As spring gave way to summer John tried hard to do more, but he was still recovering, and Margaret watched as he and Karl tried to work out some sort of rapport together. She watched them often as they ate their sandwiches when they were out in the fields. They sat apart, each one locked in his own world, his private experiences of war and suffering, each one aware of the other yet for the most part silent. Sometimes she wanted to scream at them to forget their backgrounds, forget the war, the horror of the past, but it seemed to her that they were like robots, each programmed by a different maker and never able to come together. Often Karl, seeing John's weakness, would come quietly, take the heavier load, the difficult job, and John would shrug wearily and watch the handsome face and the strong body, and Margaret sensed his bitterness and his anger.

She knew that both men watched her too. They watched as she milked the cows, as she forked the hay on to the elevator, and often one or the other would take the heavy pail of pig food from her hand as she staggered out to the sty. The three of them swam in the little cove below the farmhouse too, but she always went alone just as they did, each one avoiding the other two. Sometimes she laughed at the incongruity of it all. Three young people who should be free of all cares enjoying the summer and the sea and each other. There they were, victims of a war that was over, but which still held each one prisoner.

It was John who broke the mould and asked her to swim with him one golden evening in the autumn. The sun had been shining from a cloudless sky all day, and the sea lay still and welcoming. Margaret knew that Karl was watching as she walked towards the beach. He was waiting at the gate for his transport back to camp, and he looked the other way as they passed. Her heart beat strangely as she glanced at him and she felt a betrayal that hung about her, cold and clammy in the warmth of the evening air.

As soon as they were out of sight of the house, John took her hand, and she remembered at once that other time and felt again something of her early fears. She had been so young and so frightened. Even now she still hadn't the confidence and maturity that she longed for.

'I'm beginning to feel almost normal again now,' he said, laughing. 'A beautiful girl, a beautiful evening and a beautiful place. What more could a man want?'

Margaret smiled. She turned to look at him. He was bronzed and looking better. The gentle Cornish sun and his mother's cooking had worked a miracle during the long summer months. He was almost handsome, shc thought, though no one could compare with Karl's outstanding golden beauty. Immediately she felt guilty. It was her greatest fault, this constant feeling of guilt that engulfed her over so many things. She almost felt that John must be able to know her heart, know of her unacknowledged love for Karl. Yet she hoped desperately that it wasn't so. There had never been any outward sign from her. Her Jewishness alone shouted against her feelings, feelings that were firmly forbidden too by law for all English girls, as well as by every decent thought in her body. Feelings that could have no fruition and must be squashed mercilessly, just as mercilessly as the German jackboot had trodden all over her people throughout Europe.

She shivered and tried to shake off the panic that fell again like a great all-encompassing blanket. Did Karl know she was Jewish? Had John perhaps forgotten? Even her name wasn't Jewish; her parents had given it to her deliberately because they had wanted her to be fully integrated into English society. She knew that she didn't look Jewish, and how much did it matter anyway?

They reached the cove, and the sea lapped gently on the sand, gulls curved and wove their effortless flights lazily above, and the old castle on the cliff gave a sense of peace, peace that Margaret desperately needed just then.

She had put her bathing-costume on beneath the same wrap, the one she had worn all those long years ago, and she dropped it as she always did on the dry sand at the top of the beach. Then without looking at John she ran swiftly into the sea. It almost seemed like a replay of that other time, but she felt sure that John wasn't still feeling like the brother he had almost been then. The water's shock struck her young body with the freshness she always delighted in, and she struck out firmly. She turned on to her back, staring into the darkening sky, and suddenly John's powerful crawl brought him past her, round to her again. He splashed the salt water on to her face, and she laughed and gulped and swam to the rocks at the edge of the bay. She knew where the sand led safely to the flat rock, the same place as before, the rock that she had made her own now that Annie and Bill allowed her to swim alone. She had become a powerful swimmer and she knew the dangers and the safe places. Quickly she climbed out of the water and shivered as the evening breeze, cooler now, rippled the waves at the edge of the rock. She dived back into the sea, a beautiful and effortless dive, and swam strongly for some time, feeling the stress draining slowly from her mind.

Then she turned towards the shore and swam lazily to the tiny breaking waves at the sea's edge. She ran out of the water and up on to the crunching sand and, picking up her wrap, vigorously towelled herself with it. John followed close behind and pulled the towel from her, dropping it with his in a damp heap on to the ground. His arms went round her, and she stiffened slightly in his embrace, the wetness of his body seeming to increase the restraint she felt.

'I love you, Maggie,' he said. 'I've loved you ever since I came home, I think, but I was such a wreck then, and Karl. . .'

'I know,' she whispered. 'I think I have always known.'

Then as John held her to him she knew too that there was a deadness in her that she could not fan into life, no response that she could make, however much she wished it. She looked beyond him to the hill above the beach. She breathed the clean, sea-washed air for strength, and pushed him gently away.

'It's no good,' she whispered. 'I'm so sorry.'

He released her suddenly, almost violently. 'I think I've known too,' he said bitterly. 'I've known, yet chosen not to know.'

He bent down and picked up his towel. She saw its frayed edges as he rubbed himself violently, perhaps to rub off the feel of her as well as the salty wetness of the water. His face was suddenly covered once more with the fixed-mask expression that he had worn for so long after he'd first come home from the prison camp, a mask to cover his insecurity and his fear bred during those terrible years locked away from everything that made life a progression, a unity, a thing of sense and sanity. Years when his life had hung in some awful unknown suspension of time. She could know nothing of his suffering, and now she was increasing it, bringing it back, yet she was powerless to do anything about it, powerless to pretend a love and a passion she could not feel.

She stooped and retrieved her own wrap, now covered with sand, and threw it round her shivering body. A terrible sadness engulfed her. She hurried up the path under the cloud-darkened sky, aware of John somewhere behind her. She could hear his footsteps dragging now in his disappointment, and she wondered how she would manage to get through the next months. Perhaps she should leave and start a new life with her parents in Bristol?

It was only a week later that Bill took to his bed. Margaret was about to announce to Annie that she had decided to go home for good, but the words were not spoken. Bill would never work on the farm again, and she was needed more than ever. There was talk of Karl going back to Germany too, and John seemed unwilling, once more, to tackle anything other than the easiest jobs.

'Don't leave us yet, dear,' Annie said and as Margaret looked at her she sensed the desperation in the plea and made up her mind.

'I'll stay just as long as you need me, Auntie,' she promised rashly. 'I love it here.'

The longer she worked with Karl, the more she knew that the promise she had made to Annie was rash indeed, and the friendship with him that she treasured was becoming more and more difficult to sustain.

'The sea is still warm enough for swimming,' he said to her one day, and she knew that there was more to the statement than a mere comment on the weather. They were eating sandwiches in the shelter of the high hedge that faced the coast and the sun was warm on their bare arms. The sea stretched away to the horizon, blue and sparkling, and the cliffs shimmered in the sunlight clear all the way down to the most distant headland.

'When it's like this with no haze it probably means bad weather soon,' Margaret said dully.

'Then all the more reason to swim now.'

She turned to face him, and blushed as she became aware of his blue eyes searching hers.

'You know that's impossible,' she said. 'Annie would have a fit if we went down there together. Bill would be upset, and John—well, I don't know what John would do!'

'Just because we happened to swim at the same time? Well, yes, I know. It was only a stupid dream. I saw you going to the beach with John last week just as I was leaving for camp. You were both so happy, so free. I suppose I was jealous!'

Margaret ignored the implication. 'At least we're able to talk without restrictions now,' she said. 'Annie doesn't seem to worry about that any more.'

'She has other things to think about,' he said. 'I'm sorry for Bill. He's always been good to me.'

They sat in silence for a moment, and then Karl turned to her again.

'You don't talk much to John. Are you. . ?'

'Not going out with him, if that's what you mean,' she replied quickly. 'When we were on the beach that evening I told him it was no use, so you needn't have felt jealous of his happiness.'

Karl hadn't touched her since that first time, that chaste kiss on her hand, and now he put the sandwich box down on the grass at his side and took both her hands in his. He pulled her towards him and kissed her urgently on the lips, and in spite of her inexperience she could feel a strong emotion and tenseness in him that both thrilled and frightened her.

'Yes, I know it's forbidden,' he whispered at last, 'but there are only the gulls to see!'

She gasped as he let her go and she pushed him aside. 'It's impossible,' she said. 'It can never be, so please, Karl, don't try.'

She remembered the headlines she had seen in the newspaper recently, headlines appearing on the same day. Top Nazis had been executed at Nuremberg for terrible war crimes against the Jews, and British servicemen had been killed by Jewish terrorists in Jerusalem. She sighed and lay back, staring into the sky.

Throughout her childhood and her growing up she had hugged her Jewishness to herself like a precious secret, but now she suddenly wanted him to know, needed to shout out to him that this was why they could be nothing to each other. The barrier was too great. In spite of her feelings for him she felt she could never truly reach him through it.

She didn't move. She looked at the gulls soaring majestically above her in the great blue dome of the sky and then she spoke, and her voice was flat, deliberately without emotion. The words were the hardest she felt she had ever uttered.

'I'm Jewish, Karl. Jewish. Do you understand what that means for us? Jewish!'

She just lay there quietly in the long grass and waited, her heart thudding a sort of tattoo. She continued to stare at the screaming birds and she waited. . .

He was sitting beside her, his back against an old granite gate-post, and the quiet, controlled words hit him like a blow from which he felt he would never recover. Shame washed over him like a great tidal wave, and for the first time in his life he wanted to run away, not from her, but from a situation totally beyond his ability to control. The shame was for Germany, for himself, for everything that he had previously held dear. Suddenly all his carefully preserved pride evaporated and he put his head in his hands.

'Why haven't you told me before?' he whispered at last.

Misunderstanding his words for a moment, imagining rejection, Margaret looked at him in despair and anger. 'I don't know. Fear perhaps. So you regret your kisses now, do you?'

He turned to her, and she saw his ravaged face and the tears in his eyes. 'You don't know what you're saying. It just makes you more precious.'

He pulled her towards him again as he spoke and kissed her once more, but it was a gentle kiss as though she had suddenly become fragile and inaccessible to him. It was the kiss of love and homage and without passion, and she felt tears on her face too.

They sat for a long time and his arms around her were tight and comforting.

'I'm glad you know,' she said at last. 'I'm so glad that you know.'

Then suddenly, like the sun bursting from a sky full of storm clouds, she felt her spirits rise. She brushed the tears quickly away and jumped to her feet, pulling him up beside her.

'The weather's too nice to be solemn any more,' she said. 'Come on. We've work to do, and all on our own if John doesn't come back this afternoon.'

The three of them had been working all the morning mending hedges and stone walls in the big field that overlooked the bay. It was hard work, and at lunchtime John had complained of a headache and had gone back to the house to lie down for an hour instead of eating the picnic meal that Annie had prepared for them.

Margaret wondered if he perversely wanted to throw her and Karl together after that disastrous evening bathe and her rejection of his advances. He had been strange and distant, withdrawing into himself since then, and she worried about him with a tinge of guilt when he complained of his frequent headaches.

Things changed gradually on the little farm as the evenings shortened and the wind blew the red-gold leaves into great heaps against the wall. Annie at last relented a little in her attitude to Karl and he was sometimes allowed to eat with them in the house. It was usually when a storm was blowing furiously from the west, bringing stinging rain and cold winds that whistled round the old farm buildings. Or when there was something to be done inside that only Karl's strength and skill could manage. Then she would invite him to share the warmth of the big kitchen range. And when Bill could no longer move from bed to commode without help it was Karl who stood at one side of him and John at the other. Together they nursed him, doing the things that Annie could not do, and Margaret watched an uneasy friendship at last begin to blossom between the two young men.

So it was natural that Karl should be asked to join them for the next Christmas. Annie often looked at the tall German, with his charm and his smiling face, and felt guilty at the remembered words that she had spoken a year before when Bill had suggested the same thing.

'We could let him have the old cottage to sleep in,' she said to John. 'You and he could do it up a bit. It needs a bit of new glass in the upstairs window and a good clean-up. There's some furniture still there and plenty here that we can do without.'

The cottage stood at the bend of the road a short distance from the farmhouse, and had been used for a farm worker before the war. It had been empty for over five years, but its sturdy stone walls still kept out the worst of the winter gales and, unlike the old barns, the roof was sound.

'You mean have him stay here permanently?' Margaret enquired in alarm. Some specially chosen prisoners of war were being billeted on the farms where they worked. Did they intend this for Karl?

'Don't know about that,' Annie said, her hands covered in flour as she thumped and banged the bread dough on the scrubbed kitchen table in front of her. 'But I'd like to get the cottage cleaned out anyway. They're letting them have a lot more freedom now,' she went on, 'and I'm beginning to wish I hadn't been so against him when he first came. Now the war's over we've got to try and forget. I feel a bit sorry for the poor lads, Germany being in such a state and all.'

She took the bread tins and greased them with some home-made butter, wiping her hands on her ample apron. 'Mind you're careful, my girl,' she said warningly, looking up at Margaret. 'We're allowed to be friendly with them, but no hanky-panky. You know what I mean.'

Margaret laughed at the words, but knew that they were true. Amorous relationships, as the War Office more sedately phrased it, were strictly forbidden.

'I'll keep my distance. Don't worry,' she said, but the promise so lightly made would be almost impossible to keep, she thought.

'I heard today that those two Smith girls were seen with a couple of them down on Bullen's Cove,' Annie continued as if to give more importance to her words. 'Right little tarts, if you ask me.'

'You won't tell on them, will you, Aunt Annie?' Margaret exclaimed in alarm. She knew Jean and Edna Smith. They were twins, evacuees like herself, but from London. There was some mystery about their parents, and the girls couldn't go home after the war. They had both got jobs in Mevagissey. Margaret had always felt sorry for them.

'No, I'll not tell,' Annie assured her. 'It would get the young men into a packet of trouble if the authorities knew. Stupid all round!'

Whether she meant stupid of the girls or the men or the authorities, Margaret didn't dare to speculate. She hoped it was the latter!

Christmas came and went without much festivity that year. Bill's continuing illness cast a shadow on the home, and Annie had no enthusiasm for putting up paper chains again or bothering much with cooking. Margaret filled the gap, and when they all sat down together on Christmas Day and enjoyed the goose she had cooked and the puddings she had made she blushed with pleasure at the praise they all showered on her.

'Wonderful. As good as Mother's,' John said with a grin, and Karl smiled at her across the table, setting her heart into its usual frantic signalling.

'Very nice,' he said. 'Thank you for my first English Christmas.'

They stood together at the sink and washed the pile of greasy dishes and pans, and his nearness disconcerted her again. She had carefully avoided any closeness during the past months. With her love for Karl acknowledged now in her most secret heart she knew that she must be doubly vigilant over her actions. It had been easier when he was kept at a distance by the family, but Annie's new tolerance for the young

German was making it increasingly hard.

John and Karl together did the evening milking. Cows must be attended to even on this special day, and then the four of them sat together round the fire and played cards. The little cottage down the lane had been made ready and Karl was to spend his first night there. Margaret hoped it was not to be a permanent arrangement, but she suspected that it would be. She could see the cottage from her bedroom window, and she knew that fact would make it worse. Could she keep her feelings sternly suppressed when he was so close, when she could see the candle in his window from hers?

She sat staring into the glowing embers of the fire while the other three went upstairs to make Bill comfortable for the night. The old black kettle steamed gently beside her on the hearth. There would be a cup of tea before they all went to bed, and enough water too to fill the stone bottles that were such a comfort to herself and Annie in the cold, unheated bedrooms. John refused one, and she guessed that she shouldn't offer one to Karl. Strange how stupidly proud men sometimes were, denying themselves some of the little comforts of life.

She sensed Karl's eyes on her when he came down. He watched her pour the tea into the slightly chipped china cups, and she smiled as she handed him one.

'I hope you'll sleep well,' she said in confusion, not knowing what to say. The intensity of those blue eyes was devastating in the intimacy of the cosy room. The cowshed, the potato field or the garden were less personal.

'I know I shall,' he said quietly. He turned to Annie. 'It's very kind of you, Mrs Trevarrick, to allow me to stay tonight. I haven't known the quietness of a room to myself since I joined up.'

'I know just what you mean,' John said, coming into the room behind his mother. 'That first night in Graham's house in Bristol was an experience I shall never forget.'

Graham! Margaret remembered his lovely home and her Christmas last year in Bristol. Suddenly her heart began to rise in hope. Another year would soon be over and 1947 beginning. She congratulated herself silently for the way she had managed to keep her feelings in check, the way she had dealt with the strain of living in close proximity to both of these young men. They too now had a tolerance of each other, a respect that might grow into a lasting friendship. Maybe this was the year when she and everyone else could finally forget the war, when people could look at each other without hate and distrust in their eyes.

Annie was smiling at Karl and in the look was the vindication of Margaret's thoughts. Annie, who had loathed the idea of a German in her house, was now drinking tea in the chair next to him, and she was offering him a hot-water bottle! Margaret laughed out loud and handed round the tin of carrot cake. Always carrot cake. Everyone made carrot cake. It was a symbol of the war. She resolved never to make it again.

CHAPTER EIGHT

1947

KARL lay on the narrow bed that he and John had carried into the cottage a few days before. The candle flickered on the table beside him and he stared up at the wooden beams above his head. He could just hear the roaring of the sea. The tide was in, and he was aware of each wave as it sucked and worried at the sand and shingle of the beach. The bed was hard, but he stretched his long legs down to the end of it and felt the heat of the stone hot-water bottle that Annie had insisted he should take. The weather was bitterly cold, and he was grateful.

'There's been no fire over there,' she had said firmly, 'and it might be a bit damp. We've got the stove here to warm us.'

Karl was amazed at the change in her. She had been so antagonistic at first. But even John was beginning to accept him now. The war seemed a long way off in time, and he was becoming fond of these simple people. He was incredibly sad for Bill, hating to see him so helpless.

His thoughts turned to Margaret, and his body went stiff with frustration and rage that she could never be his. He knew he loved her. He had fought the unwelcome knowledge with every ounce of energy and fortitude he possessed. He knew that his love could only bring her misery. Germany was beaten, divided, an economic and social mess. The fact that she was Jewish made no difference to his feelings for her at all, but he could never take a Jewish girl home to Germany. Even if the ghosts of the horror camps could be obliterated, which they could not, it was no place for her. And he wanted to go home. God, how he wanted to go home!

He turned restlessly on the bed and an owl hooted through the trees. He felt the intense heat of the hard, unyielding bottle on his cold feet, and he fell at last into a deep sleep, only to waken in the morning to find himself hunched up away from the now cold and unfriendly lump of stone. The light was already showing round the thick curtains that shielded the tiny window, and he leapt out of bed, knowing that he should have been out with the cows an hour ago. He pulled on his clothes roughly and rushed down the stairs and into the yard. She was already there. He could see her through the open door, sitting on her small stool, her hands busy, and she looked up and smiled at him.

'We let you lie in,' she said. 'I suppose it's the first time in years!'

'Yes. Yes, it is. I can't think why I didn't wake as usual.' He took the stool and bucket and started working on the next cow. It was a long time since they had been here alone together. John usually did the milking instead of her. It wasn't too strenuous, something that he could cope with.

'Where's John?' he asked.

'Helping with his father. He's been ill in the night.'

'Do they want me? Any lifting needed?'

'No, not yet. They may later. He's very poorly.'

They worked easily together but mostly in silence after that, and eventually it was finished and the milk in churns at the roadside waiting to be collected. Margaret took the large jug of milk for the house and carried it in.

'There's some breakfast when you're ready,' she said.

It was a few days later, just as the church bells in the village were chiming their welcome to the New Year, that Bill Trevarrick died, and Margaret knew that for the rest of her life she would remember the dawning of 1947.

Karl was still living in the cottage. With Bill's increasing weakness it had been good to know he was near, and during that awful night he had been with them, sharing the pain, and it had been Karl who had taken the old bicycle and hurried to fetch the doctor, riding through the grey sea mist that enveloped the farm and the hills. The booming of the foghorn throughout that night and the crashing of the sea on the invisible shore added to the strange foreboding that seemed to be wiping away Margaret's previous optimism about the New Year. It was bitterly cold too, one of the coldest winters that any of them had ever known.

It was she and Karl again in the shippon the next morning. After the events of the night there was little restraint between them.

'I can't make any sense of life,' she said quietly as her hands pulled gently at the patient cow. 'Why does Bill have to die like this when he's only fifty-five and with years of life left for living? And what about the war, the camps and all?'

Karl stared at her. He had left Germany with a Christian faith intact, but the experiences of the last years had left doubts and problems he felt powerless to answer. He knew what she meant too about the camps. The nightmare pictures that he had been forced to watch swept over him again in waves, like bouts of returning nausea. He saw the girl beside him through a haze, and he saw those others who could have been like her, of her race, with outstretched arms and skeletal bodies, and he turned away from her so that she couldn't see the tears that shamed him. Or perhaps they did not shame. Perhaps they purged the wrong instead.

'There's no answer to that,' he said when he felt able to speak. 'No answer that I can give you, anyway.' Then he made an effort to throw off the gloom. 'But we're young, Margaret, and the war's over. It's a new year. Let's try to find some happiness.'

He carried his stool round to the next cow and put it down, but he came back to where she was standing preparing the cooling machine. Suddenly he threw all his carefully guarded caution away and caught her hands in his and pulled her towards him.

'A happy New Year, my dear love,' he whispered, and his arms went round her and he felt her body melt into his as he kissed her again and again, and only the chewing cows were there to witness their love and their desire for each other.

It was not like that other time out in the harvest field above the sea. Margaret was sure of his love for her now, and she felt herself responding to him with a passion that she did not know she possessed, a strength of feeling that frightened her in its intensity.

Yet she shivered with the joy of it, with the new sensations flooding through her body. Her arms tightened round him as if she never wanted to let him go, and she felt in that moment of perfect happiness that the love of this man was the most precious thing she had ever known, and probably would ever know.

Then gently he put her from him and stared into her eyes. 'I love you, Margaret,' he whispered. 'You know that, don't you?'

'Yes, oh, yes! And I love you, Karl,' she whispered. 'I love you so much.'

Only when she was alone in her room later that night did she allow herself the luxury of dwelling on the feel of Karl's embrace, of his body against hers, and the desire for more of him. But it was impossible. A bleakness swept over her. If she gave in to her love for Karl, declared it openly, she would have to leave the farm. Her parents would reject her, and for Karl? She shuddered. Only a few weeks ago the papers had reported a similar case. There had been outrage, and the young man doubly imprisoned. They would have to either meet in secret or reject each other. Either solution appeared to be impossible, and Margaret curled up in bed and sobbed her desolation to the pillow, but she must be quiet. Annie had enough sadness of her own. The usual guilt encompassed her. To think that on the very day of Bill's death—the death of the man who had been to her almost as a father for the last six years—to think that on this day she should be sobbing for someone else! She thumped the unoffending pillow angrily again and again, and then she heard the muffled sobbing of Annie's tears coming through the wall, and she got out of her warm bed, hurried down and made a cup of tea and carried it in to the older woman and tried to comfort her.

Those early weeks of the year were bitterly cold. They read that even the sea froze in places. There were food shortages in the towns, sometimes worse than during the war, and while they guiltily enjoyed the milk, butter and eggs that were plentiful on the farm, the snow-bound roads meant that they could do little about sharing them. It was a strange winter, each of them struggling to cope with the work that had to be done, and which the freezing weather made doubly difficult, and at the same time trying to come to terms with the different problems of their lives.

John looked at Margaret frequently with a sad hardness in his eyes. There was not enough fight in him to try to win her for his own. He knew that her heart was given to Karl anyway. It was obvious from the way they smiled sometimes at each other and from the faraway look in her face when she stared out of the window towards his little cottage. What would happen to the two of them John couldn't imagine. He was still taken up with his own personal battle to achieve full and perfect health again, and he had little sympathy to spare for others with abundant energy, whose war had appeared to be no great disaster.

Then of course there was Sybil, the daughter of the neighbouring farmer. John's spirits lifted a little. She was uncomplicated and easy-going. Why shouldn't she fill the gap in his life? She certainly appeared keen to do so, always fluttering those great blue eyes at him when he saw her with her father on market days. He decided to give the matter some thought.

There was no privacy for Margaret and Karl, and they were both secretly glad of that. John and his mother were always around, and it was only a quick squeeze of the hand in the cowshed, or a surreptitious smile, a smile that held all of their love. They wouldn't allow anything more.

Gradually the terrible weather passed, and the lengthening days brought a lifting of their spirits.

May was especially beautiful that year, and on the morning of her nineteenth birthday Margaret sprang from her bed and leaned out of the small window. The air was full of birdsong and the sound and smell of the sea. No one could remain gloomy for long in such a place and in such weather, she thought. She went about her chores that day with a new spring in her step, and even Annie was beginning to respond to the beginning of summer. Perhaps there was hope for the year after all.

There was a birthday cake that Annie had baked for her, and they all sat on the lawn in front of the house and ate it after lunch and sang 'Happy Birthday'. She felt that she had not been so happy for a long time.

'Sorry that we have to go out for the rest of the day,' Annie said. 'It seems a pity to leave you on your special day.'

'Never mind. When the work's finished I shall swim. The water's beginning to warm up a bit. I put my toes in yesterday and I've promised myself the first dip of the year this evening.'

'Be careful, then,' Annie warned. 'Don't go out too far, and don't get cold.'

Margaret laughed. 'I'll be very, very careful, Aunt Annie,' she said. 'And we'll have a nice nightcap together when you come back and you can tell me all about the new baby.'

Annie had a sister in Liskeard, and she had been invited to the christening of her new granddaughter, and to the family party afterwards. John was to drive his mother there in the pony-cart. They still kept the old pony and the little wooden trap. It was a bit of the old way of life that Annie loved, and the pony was a friend anyway, never to be sent to the knacker's yard.

Margaret waved them off later, and as she heard the clip-clopping of the pony's hoofs on the road become fainter, her heart thumped a warning and a desire, both. For the first time she and Karl were alone, would be alone for five or six hours. She hoped she could contain her love for him, keep her emotions under strict control.

He kept away from her at first, but the milking had to be done together, and there was the meal, the pasties that Annie had left for them. They would eat in the kitchen, and Margaret wondered what they would say to each other.

They were silent in the milking shed. Margaret was consumed with excitement and foreboding, and she hoped desperately for resolution and strength. Their fingers coaxed the milk from the placidly chewing cows, and at last the churns were once more ready beside the road, the dairy cleaned and the jug of house milk, carefully covered, on the kitchen table. Margaret put the pasties to heat and fried up the potatoes from yesterday. She made gravy and called Karl to come in. They sat opposite each other and ate, and still said very little, only what was necessary to say.

They washed up together, and Karl's closeness was more than she could bear.

'I'm going to swim,' she said, and she left him with the tea-towel in his hand and ran up the stairs for her costume and her wrap. She thought of John for one brief moment. It was when they had swum together that he had wanted to make love to her. Perhaps a swim was not a sensible thing for tonight. She hesitated, and then she heard steps on the stairs, and Karl was looking at her, and she knew that nothing could stand between them any more. Neither the war, her race, John. All meant nothing in the power of her love and desire for this tall blond man looking at her as if she held the riches of the whole world in her hands.

He covered the space between them in two strides and took her in his arms. His mouth covered hers, and his hands were exploring the softness of her. She sank on to the bed and he gently removed her clothes and his own. Then he stood up and looked at her as she lay before him.

'You're so beautiful,' he said.

She had never seen an unclothed male before. She knew about the animals. That, plus Annie's brief and embarrassing words, and the few forbidden books she had read in her schooldays, was all, but instinct took over where knowledge failed, and she reached up and pulled him down to her. She felt and knew his passion, but she was aware of his gentleness too, and his hands set her body on fire as he stroked her and wooed her with all the love and skill he possessed. They moved closer together, and she cried out for the pain and the joy, and then they lay still for a long, precious time, their arms about each other, and there was the sound of the sea from the open window, and the cry of the gulls, always the crying of the gulls. After that he loved her again, and more gently this time, making it last longer. She savoured the full depths of his love and he gave her all the pleasure that her body could take, and without the pain.

'Karl,' she murmured later, still in the circle of his arms, 'we've made the war truly end in our love-making,' and she saw his smile and felt that, whatever life held for her in the future, this was the moment of her fulfilment, of her growing up.

'How about that swim?' he said, bringing her back to normality, and he rose from the bed and pulled her towards him. They stood together, swaying with the closeness of their bodies, and then she pushed him gently away and pulled her bathing-costume on to her damp body, and took another towel, not the wrap that reminded her of John, and they ran together to the cove and plunged into the cold water, exulting in their youth and their strength. They swam and kissed in the splashing waves, then Karl pulled her costume from her and she felt the thrill of the kiss of the cold water on her bare skin as well as the hands and lips of the man she knew now that she loved above all else.

John and Annie were late back that night, and Margaret was glad. She felt that the glow of her skin and the radiance in her eyes must be visible for anyone to see.

She knew that Karl mustn't come into the house again, though.

'It's too risky,' she said. 'They'll be back any time. You'd better go straight back to the cottage.'

She sat in the kitchen for a while on her own and the memory of what had happened to her enveloped her in a kind of golden haze. She refused to think of the future. It was only the present that mattered.

CHAPTER NINE

1947

IT WAS quite dark when Margaret heard the cart wheels on the road and she rushed to stoke up the old black range. Even though it was May, Annie might be feeling chilly after her long journey, and she would be ready for a nice cup of tea for sure.

'Had a nice time?' Margaret enquired, hoping that they would be so full of their outing that they wouldn't notice the glow all about her.

'Lovely, dear,' Annie said. 'Quite took me out of myself, it did.' She eased her feet out of her best shoes and sank into the soft, accommodating chair near the stove. 'I've never been one to envy others—the Good Book forbids it—but I must admit I was jealous today.'

Margaret busied herself setting some cake and cups and saucers on the kitchen table. 'Why's that, then, Aunt Annie?'

'Well, the baby, of course. I've always hoped that I'd have grandchildren—especially lately. Give me something new to think about.'

Margaret could feel the colour flood her face, and sudden shame for what she had done that afternoon swept over her like the mists that came so silently from the sea, hiding everything that was familiar and safe. There was fear too. She had been so caught up in her love for Karl that all the taboos of her upbringing had been cast aside, forgotten in that wonderful hour. Surely something so beautiful couldn't be wrong? But she knew in a flash of horrifying insight that it could, it could be terribly, horribly wrong.

With a supreme effort of self-control she poured the tea, handed the cake, listened to glowing accounts of the new baby, the house and the prettiness of the young mother.

'Well, I think I'll be having an early night,' Annie said at last, and to Margaret's intense relief she heaved herself wearily out of the chair and went to fill her hot-water bottle.

It was a long time before Margaret slept that night. It was on this bed in this little room that Karl had loved her. She could almost smell the clean male scent of him still, and she lay and clutched her arms around herself, remembering the ecstasy and the pain. But as the night wore on and the church clock chimed out its early morning hours the guilt that always came to her so easily took over. And there was regret too. It would have been possible to stop what had happened. Karl was good and honourable, she was sure. She had given herself to him easily like any street-girl.

Yet there had been glory in it. Such glory. She chose the word carefully in her mind because that was how it was. She relived the wonder and the absolute beauty of those moments in his arms, and then she turned her burning face into the pillow and wept, wept with a terrible desolation and emptiness, for she knew with a cold, clear logic that it must never happen again.

She slept at last, a disturbed, dream-filled sleep, and when the first cockerel crowed his welcome to the day Margaret woke sluggishly and she knew what she must do. Perhaps there might be a future for herself and for Karl one day, but not yet, not for a long, long time. It would be difficult even to face him again. The memory of their lovemaking would hang between them now like an impenetrable wall, making friendship impossible. Her upbringing had seen to that.

'You're very quiet today!' Annie's voice was bright and cheerful as she stirred the breakfast porridge.

'I did a lot of thinking yesterday,' Margaret lied. She hoped she sounded convincing. 'It really is time that I made another life for myself now, Auntie. My mother needs me, I think, and I should like to study a bit, get some qualifications. I could do a year's shorthand and typing at college if I went home.'

'You, indoors all day!' Annie laughed and tipped the steaming porridge into large bowls. She set them on the table, then went to the door and called to the men. 'Still, I suppose you've always been one for books and learning. Not like me. Gave up reading when I left school!'

John and Karl came quickly, expecting the call and hungry for breakfast. They stopped to take off their muddy boots, and Margaret's face flamed as Karl looked at her and smiled. It was a special smile just for her, private, excluding the others, reinforcing his love. Then why had she to go? There was no logical reason, just a deep inner conviction, more a compulsion, and she smiled back briefly and busied herself pouring tea from the large brown earthenware pot. There was always tea, always the great comforter. She sat down and drank, then ate a little of the porridge, stirring the rich yellow Jersey milk into it, and she wondered why she frequently had this need inside herself to do the very thing that was most distasteful to her, why she couldn't be uncomplicated and easy-going like the paper heroines of some of the romantic novels she read in secret by candlelight. But Karl's smile had perversely strengthened her resolve. It would be impossible to keep their love for each other a secret thing between them, and it was too precious to be reviled and destroyed.

That her one afternoon of loving might have other more frightening consequences she refused at first to acknowledge. 'Please, please, God, let it not be so,' she whispered, on her knees on the third day of her lateness. She was always so regular, twenty-seven days always, and now it was the thirtieth, and two weeks since the day of her shaming, for that was how she had come to think of it lately.

There were ways of ending something so terrible, weren't there? But there was no finding out, no one to ask. Annie would be too horrified, and of course there was Karl to think of too. If the authorities knew, there would be double shame, his added to hers, and for him, severe punishment and a possible end to his hopes for the repatriation he was longing for.

As the anxious days passed and June came with its long golden evenings and there was still no sign that her fervent prayers were being answered Margaret knew that she must go very soon, before it became obvious. When did it become obvious? She shuddered at her own ignorance. Perhaps in the anonymity of a big city she could find an answer to all her questions. She would have to get to Bristol soon.

For Karl there was only a deepening knowledge that this was the girl he loved and wished to marry, yet she was totally forbidden to him. Forbidden by race and by circumstances and by the laws of both their countries. He worked steadily and bleakly throughout the long, busy days of May, making his body as weary as his youth and strength would allow. He gave himself no respite, hoping that intense weariness would ensure the bliss of dreamless sleep. But in the lonely little cottage every night he could not prevent his mind from dwelling on those lovely precious hours he had spent with her, hours that gradually achieved a quality of almost ethereal and unreal beauty that had little to do with the hard realities of the everyday. If he looked from his window when the sky was dark at last he could sometimes see a candle flickering from the farmhouse, from her bedroom, and he wondered if she put it there for him, a symbol of their love.

Every day when he sat across from her at the table in the farmhouse kitchen he searched her face anxiously. Sometimes he wondered and worried. He knew he should have been more careful, made sure that his love made no problems, no difficulties for her. He looked at her lovely slim body and her clear, untroubled eyes, and the terrible thought of a pregnancy sent his heart racing with fear. He drew constant comfort from the serenity of those eyes and from her frequent smiles and jokes. She couldn't be so carefree if there had been any results from their loving. With those thoughts he reassured himself, not knowing that the very lightness of her conversation was an act deliberately played out for his benefit. They were never alone now, so there was no way he could talk to her, no other way of telling.

Karl wasn't the only one in that troubled house who was worrying. Annie looked at Margaret frequently too and wondered why the girl suddenly wanted to go home so much. She had hoped for years that she would marry John. There was no one else who could ever take her place, and now he had chosen Sybil. Perhaps that was the reason behind Margaret's wish to leave. Annie frequently tried to make her change her mind, but she was adamant, strangely detached, and seemed to have already left the farm in spirit. Annie frequently watched her going about her tasks, and sighed for the things that might have been.

But in spite of all of her regrets, the arrangements were eventually made, train times decided upon, drawers and cupboards emptied and case and bag packed.

'I want to be alone for a little while after supper, Auntie,' Margaret said on that last evening.

Annie could hear the desperation in her voice.

'Yes, of course you do,' she replied with an enforced brightness that she was far from feeling. 'I think Sybil's coming over later. Now that John's walking out with her I mightn't be as lonely as I thought after you've gone tomorrow.'

Sybil was a quiet little thing, and lately John had taken to bringing her in for supper now and then, and only the week before had surprised them all by announcing their engagement. Her father farmed the adjoining land, so it was convenient. Annie was happy for them, hoped it was a love match, and she was determined to make the best of it anyway.

'Off you go, then, and say goodbye to that sea of yours that you love so much, though what you can find good about it I'm sure I don't know.'

Brought up within sound and sight of the sea, and with a brother lost to it manning the lifeboat years before, Annie could never understand others to whom it was a constant delight, almost a religion.

Margaret hurried down the cliff path and hoped that Karl hadn't seen her go, but as she rounded the bend and saw the cove spread out before her and the waves making a gently moving silver line on the edge of the sea, she saw him. He was sitting on the large rock from which they often swam, but the tide was out and he was staring out to the horizon. Suddenly, before she had time to rush away, he turned and saw her. She stood paralysed, desperately hoping for resolution and strength. She must not tell. For his sake she must not tell. She would bear the burden of their child herself and she would love it. In that moment as she looked at him and her heart nearly melted within her for love, she knew that Karl's son was the most precious gift she would ever have, a secret treasure that for his sake he must not know about yet. Circumstances would decide when. To bring up his child with all the care of which she was capable would be her pledge to him of their love. If there was ever a new Germany free and undivided and where a Jewish child could grow up without any stigma or fear then she would go to him, perhaps. It wasn't a consideration for now. And in spite of all her longing she still wouldn't trap him into staying here. She knew his heart was in Dresden.

He sprang from the rock and ran over the wet sand towards her and wrapped her in his arms. It was the first time they had been alone since their loving and she couldn't stop responding with equal enthusiasm.

'When shall we see each other again?' he said, and his breath was warm and sweet on her face. 'Why do you have to go, Margaret? Are you sure that you're all right? There was no. . ?'

She pushed him gently away. She knew what he was asking and she felt his love and his concern. 'I'm fine, really fine,' she said, lying again. 'I'll write.'

'They're sending me home, probably—in the autumn, I think. You know Dresden is in Russian hands?' His voice was sad, uncertain. 'Perhaps I should ask to stay here?'

For a moment a ray of hope lit her thoughts, but it was a sudden, fleeting thing.

'No, Karl. You've told me about your family. Go and find them. But come back perhaps one day?'

She was amazed at her own resolution and her strength. All she wanted was to sink into his arms, tell him about the baby, leave him to settle the problems, but she knew it was impossible.

They both sensed the finality of their love, knew great sadness, and they walked hand in hand along the lonely sea-washed beach and spoke little.

Then suddenly, like the great waves breaking on the jagged rocks at the edge of the cove, all the misery of their parting seemed to erupt. Karl pulled her angrily and forcefully against him.

'It's no good!' he shouted. 'We can't part like this, Margaret. I love you—I love you more than anything in the world. You mustn't go to Bristol!'

Then it was her turn to shout, to feel anger instead of the grim acceptance that she had held before her like a shield for so many miserable days.

'Not go? What do you mean, not go? You're going away yourself soon, you've just said so, and for all your fine words you don't love me more than you love Germany. You know you don't!'

There were tears in her eyes, but in spite of her anger she didn't push him away this time. She just stood there in the circle of his arms and cried hopelessly, for there was no hope. She could see no possible way, and Karl was silent. It seemed that he was not going to deny her bitter words.

He held her gently, and every shudder of her body was his too. He had never felt so desolate in his life. Even on that day when they had taken him prisoner his misery hadn't equalled this.

'You know I love you,' he whispered. 'You mean more to me than my life, Margaret, more than

Germany, than Dresden, than anything.'

For a moment hope flared in her heart and then died down as suddenly as it had come. For them there could be no hope. For Jew and German there could be no future. She had made her decision. There must be no last-minute weakening.

'I'll come for you,' he said. 'You know I must go back. I couldn't live here for the rest of my life not knowing what has happened to my family, my home, everything, but I'll come back, Margaret. I'll come back.'

She heard the words through a dim haze of misery, for she knew in her deepest heart that he would not come, that however much he wished to return to her he wouldn't be able to leave. Dresden was in the Russian sector, and everyone knew what that meant. The words held a dread finality. She kissed him and her tears streaked his face. Then she loosed herself from his grasp and ran from him.

Her feet stumbled in the dry sand at the top of the beach, but she didn't look back until she had gained the path where it led through the bushes to the farm.

Karl was standing where she had left him, and she knew that she would always remember him so, with the sea behind and the gulls sweeping and soaring in the evening sky, their haunting cries matching the sadness and desolation in her heart.

John and Annie went with her to the station. There wasn't much luggage to show for all those teenage years of living, and John, much stronger now, managed to carry it and would take no offers of help. He found her a seat and heaved the case on to the rack above. There were a few more difficult minutes to fill before the little train steamed its way out of the station and a section of her life closed for ever. Annie's tears were hard to bear.

'I'll come back and see you all,' Margaret said, wondering how and when and if ever the words would have any fulfilment.

'You'll come for the wedding.' It was a statement, not a question, and Margaret's heart thumped a warning. How could she come? October was the date set. She would be five months pregnant.

'If I can,' she said. She turned to John, who stood uncertainly on the platform now, not knowing what to say. 'I'm so glad for you and Sybil. She's just right for you.'

'Thanks, Margaret,' he said. 'Perhaps you and Graham can come down together. He'll be coming, of course.'

Graham! She had forgotten Graham, or almost forgotten him.

'Yes.'

There seemed nothing else to say.

At last the guard, whistle in mouth, waved his welcome green flag, and the chugging engine pulled her away from those kind people, from the family that had meant such a lot to her, from the place she had grown to think of as her own, and from Karl. She sank down in the corner seat of the little shabby carriage and cried silently behind the newspaper that John had thrust into her hand.

Bristol was a shock again, as it always was. Its rows of dilapidated houses and bomb sites depressed her, and thoughts of settling permanently into her parents' respectable terraced house became more and more frightening.

Margaret looked around at the familiar Tramway Centre where she must change buses and remembered her last visit when she'd been still young and carefree. She had laughed then at the gloomy man with the sandwich boards who felt it his duty to berate the sad-faced passengers with his dire message.

'Prepare to meet your God,' the placard said, and to emphasise the words he shouted them out in deep, resonant tones to the assembled queue waiting for the bus. Then he turned the board round so that the other side threatened them all as menacingly as his frowning face. 'The wages of sin is Death!' Margaret read, and she wondered for a fleeting, horrified moment if he could read her soul, and if he saw there the sense of betrayal and shame that so frequently filled her thoughts. Now that she was going home her Jewishness was the part that she felt she had betrayed, and it added to the conflict. 'Jew and German. Jew and German. The wages of sin is Death.' The words made a mad litany that revolved in her brain and would not be erased.

'Cheerful bloke!'

She turned to the man who stood next to her. His face puckered into a grin.

'Always enlivens the waiting. Don't know what we'd do without him!'

Margaret laughed, and felt immediately better, and incredibly grateful. Suddenly there was warmth and humour again, and hope too. In those few words and in that friendly smile she found strength to overcome the gloom. Perhaps her baby would defy the misery of the war, the camps, the deaths, everything that turned life into a horrifying nightmare. He would be a new beginning, a hope for a future. She climbed on to the bus, and the man beside her took her case and lifted it into the luggage rack.

They rattled through the dismal streets of St Pauls,

climbed the steep Ashley Hill, and then it was her stop. She must leave the safe anonymity of the bus and face her parents.

Her case felt heavier and heavier as she passed house after house, all alike, most with high privet hedges so that you couldn't look into the front rooms. At last she was there, and she stopped and put the case down, her heart beating madly, trying to call up some reserves of strength that would carry her through the space where the front gate had been. She stared at the gap. They had told her last time that it had been taken away with all the other metal gates in the road years ago to make tanks or Spitfires or something. Now the dogs could roam unheeded into each tiny front garden. Margaret laughed suddenly to herself. She remembered swinging on that gate when she was small, and wondered vaguely where it was now, in what secret bit of the world it had ended. Perhaps it was rusting away on some desolate German hillside. Germany! Karl! She closed her eyes momentarily to hide the pain, and then she stepped through the gap, looked at the shining brass step, and rang the bell.

CHAPTER TEN

1947

THERE was little time to worry after that, no time for Margaret to consider her own problems. Her mother flung open the door in response to her ringing, and her face was white. She was wearing a patterned and rather grubby apron tied round her thin waist, and her hair had escaped from its usual tight roll at the nape of her neck. She took the bag from Margaret and kissed her briefly.

'Your gran's had a stroke,' she said. 'We've to go down as soon as we can. Last night it was. They found her in the kitchen, collapsed. Dad's with her.'

There was just a snatched cup of tea, a bit of cake, and then they were retracing the bus journey back to the city centre, to the grey, impersonal hospital that stood, huge and forbidding, on one of the busiest streets in the centre of the town. Margaret walked down the long, bleak ward and her heart failed within her for fear. There had been no experience in her life of old age and disability. The only illness she had watched closely had been that of Bill, and she had no wish to remember the sadness of those awful weeks.

She was aware of many pairs of eyes watching her as she followed her mother, envying her youth and health, perhaps. Then she suddenly saw her father sitting beside his mother's bed, and perversely she was glad she had come, happy to be part of the family and to be able to support and take part. She sat down in the chair that her father fetched silently for her and hesitantly took the old woman's hand in hers, but there was no sign of recognition in the faded eyes, and tears streamed down Margaret's face as she looked at the old Jewish woman, the grandmother whom she hardly knew.

They were only allowed to stay for the prescribed hour, and she was secretly glad to get out into the heat and noise of the street afterwards. It was necessary to find some normality again, to exchange the hospital smell and quietness for the traffic fumes and cheerful noise and bustle outside.

It was two days later that the old woman died, and Margaret was there, sitting silently at the bedside, watching, scared and apprehensive. In her grandmother's dying she felt she had lost a relationship that could have been precious to her. Yet it was a kind of detached grief and a guilt that there was nothing deeper. She resolved to make more efforts now to try to build a relationship with her parents that would see them all through the next difficult years. She hoped they would allow her to do so.

When everything was done, the funeral over, and friends and relations gone home, she sat in the cold, formal front room, the room that was only used on special occasions and which she had seldom been allowed to enter as a child, wondering how her resolution was to be achieved. Her father looked worn and old, and she dreaded adding to his burdens.

'There's the house,' he said suddenly, looking at his wife. 'What are we going to do with the house?'

Samuel Seddon had been an only child, an unusual occurrence, and his father had bought the tiny terraced house in St Pauls as a security for his wife and son.

'Leave it for a bit,' Sarah said sensibly. She had never been over-fond of her mother-in-law, and she didn't feel up to coping with any clearing out just yet. She was glad Margaret was here to help. It would be an unpleasant job.

'Will you sell it?' Margaret asked.

'Possibly,' Samuel said, 'but it'll not fetch much, although I've kept it neat and clean—a lot of folk are trying to move out from St Pauls now. Up around here is more popular.'

'I heard that a few black families are moving in, snapping up some of the houses that have been going cheap,' Sarah commented. 'If that happens too much, the prices will go down even more.'

Margaret had noticed a few, a very few coloured faces here and there. There had been none in her childhood, only in picture books.

'They're coming looking for work, and there's plenty of that around at the moment, though for how long I don't know.' Samuel's voice was gloomy. 'There'll be trouble one day, if you ask me.'

It was two weeks later that Sarah suggested that perhaps they ought to do something about the house.

'You'll be starting your job in a few days, Meg, and I thought you could help me sort things and that.'

'Of course I will, Mum,' Margaret said, glad that there would be something to occupy her thoughts. The job she had found was in a large bookshop in the town, and she was thrilled to have it. She loved books, not just the romantic ones she read secretly, but serious ones too, classics and the like. She couldn't start until the beginning of August, though, when the girl who she was replacing was leaving to get married. She hoped they hadn't any policy of sacking their staff automatically on either marriage or motherhood, but she knew that she could get a couple of months' wages earned anyway before she need tell. They didn't know her, might just think she was a bit fat! It was near the library too, so she could spend an hour or so there before she came home each evening. She often bitterly regretted the scholarship to the grammar school that had had to be given up to go to the safety and peace of Cornwall. What a lot of things might have been, and not have been! There was no use in regrets, though. There were plenty of ways of improving one's education, and if she was to earn enough to keep herself and her baby she would have to get some qualifications.

'We'll go on Monday and start clearing out,' her mother said. 'Your father hasn't time, and it'd upset him anyway. He was very fond of her. Never got on with her myself.'

The house was in one of the poorest streets of St Pauls, but it was painted bright and clean on the outside, the net curtains were spotless, and when they opened the door and let themselves in Margaret gasped at the order and cleanliness. Her grandmother's stroke had been sudden. There was still a cup and saucer on the table and stale milk in a jug, but the aspidistras had survived their waterless days, and their leaves still gleamed with the love and care that had been lavished on them. The mantelpiece with its brown frill and numerous ornaments all lovingly set in their correct places, the silver-framed photographs, one of herself as a baby, and the old treadle organ with music open upon it, all combined to bring the tears again to Margaret's eyes.

'It's lovely, Mum,' she said. 'It's a lovely little house. I just wish it was mine.'

'Perhaps it could be one day if you get married and find a good man to pay your dad a bit of rent.'

'He said he was going to sell it.' Margaret's voice was

sad; she couldn't bear to think of it going to other uncaring hands.

'He's doing fairly well in the shop. He doesn't need the money. If we could find a tenant perhaps we'll let it out.'

Suddenly Margaret knew that here was the answer to all her problems. Perhaps she could have it, have her baby here where no one knew her. It was far enough away from her parents' home to give anonymity. She sank down into the armchair, a green plush one with great comforting arms, and looked at her mother.

'Sit down for a minute, Mum,' she said, frightened now. 'I've got something to tell you—there hasn't been time before.'

Sarah sat down a little unwillingly. There was a lot to be done, clothes to sort, the larder to empty.

'I'm expecting a baby.'

The words hung on the quiet air like a threat of doom, something that only happened to others, an event of such horrifying magnitude that at first Sarah couldn't grasp the full import.

She was silent, uncomprehending, then as the whole terrifying meaning swept over her she felt sick. Her daughter was one of those, one of the loose girls that other mothers had, never herself.

Sarah heard herself speak at last, but the silly, inane words seemed to come from someone else.

'How could you? However could you? I thought you were a good girl!'

She started to cry, and Margaret sprang up and went to her, kneeling before her. She took her hands in hers and cried too.

'It'll not be so bad, Mum. I promise you I'll go right away, if that's what you want.'

Sarah looked at her with pain-ravaged eyes. 'You'll have it adopted!'

It wasn't a question, and Margaret's heart thumped unsteadily. 'No. I'm going to bring him up myself.'

'Him, him!' The words conveyed a sense of reality, and suddenly Sarah realised that it was her grandchild they were talking about. She tried to calm herself, to think. 'Who was it, Meg?' she asked. 'Who is the father?'

'I can never tell you that, and I can't marry him, so please don't talk about it.'

There was a finality in her daughter's expression that warned Sarah not to probe any more. Not for now, anyway. She would try to find out later.

'Perhaps this house might be the answer,' she said in a sudden flash of inspiration, or perhaps catching Margaret's unspoken thoughts. 'No one here knows you, and we could say that we'd let it to a widow. You'd have to get a ring.'

'I don't want to do that, Mum, call myself Mrs somebody or other and deceive everyone. I should like to bring up my baby on my own without everyone pointing a finger.'

'Perhaps you would, but it's not possible, not around here anyway, and you've got to think of us and the child as well as yourself.' Sarah was well aware how hard it was to do what Margaret was suggesting. She knew of one or two who had tried it and ended up with the world against them. 'You'll tell everyone your husband was killed or something or I'll have nothing to do with it. If you don't, then you can't live here and you'll have to go right away out of Bristol.'

'What about Dad? How do you think he'll take it?' There was anxiety in Margaret's voice, and Sarah too was scared.

'He'll be very miserable, angry, and goodness knows what else. You'll just have to see. You must tell him tonight, and if he takes it well I'll probably be able to get him to agree about the house.'

Sarah's eyes swept the room with new interest now. Perhaps it might just be the one thing that would save them all from the disgrace her daughter had brought upon them, if only she could persuade Samuel.

Although neither felt like starting the work they had come to do they eventually went into the bedroom and packed clothes into boxes for the second-hand shop, stripped the bed and parcelled up a bundle for the laundry. They sorted and cleaned the kitchen, and when all was done they locked the door behind them and walked slowly to the bus-stop. Net curtains moved from the occasional window, and Margaret wondered how she would get on with her neighbours if her father allowed her to live here. It was a far cry from the lonely farmhouse, but it could be a wonderful refuge and home for herself and her son—Karl's son. She knew she would be very lucky and privileged indeed to have a house to herself, even one so small and in a terrace of others all alike. It seemed too good to come true, and she sat in the bus in an agony of suspense. Samuel Seddon held the happiness and security of her future in his hands. She didn't know her father very well at all, and she feared his reaction desperately.

It was not what she expected. He looked at her sadly and there was no anger, just a searing grief that was far worse.

'I'll not throw you out,' he said. 'You're my only child as I was my parents' only one, and they were good to me.'

He sucked at his pipe and stared into the grate where

a small coal fire smoked languidly. Even in summer the fire was lit to keep the damp away from the old house, and for hot water. The large black kettle simmered constantly on its equally black stand over the weakly flickering glow.

'It's my grandchild, so you'll not have it adopted either, and I don't go along with your mother about taking some other name and calling yourself Mrs. That would be living a lie.'

Margaret stared at this man she hardly knew. She deeply regretted giving him so much sorrow. She would make it up to him somehow.

'You can have the house, and I'll give you a bit each month to help out with food,' he told her.

Margaret had been sitting awkwardly on the edge of her chair as she made her confession, and now she sprang up and went to him and kissed him shyly on the cheek.

'Oh, Dad, you're wonderful,' she whispered. 'I'm so grateful. I thought you'd be angry!'

'What use is anger?' he said, embarrassed. 'What's done is done, and I won't see any of my flesh and blood on the streets with nowhere to go, while I can afford to help. No call to be extravagant, mind, but none of us will want for food, and a roof over our heads. If you refuse to go to the scoundrel who did this to you, then it'll have to be me you turn to!'

At the beginning of September Margaret moved into the little house.

'You can let the big front bedroom to someone,' her mother had suggested. 'You'll need more money than your dad can give you, and I'd like you to have company anyway—some nice woman to keep an eye on you. It's not good for you to be alone with the baby coming and all that.'

An advertisement in the corner shop brought a lot of hopeful enquirers, and the choice was difficult. Each one was anxious to pay their half a crown for the sanctuary of the clean little room with its bay window and net curtains, and share of the bathroom and kitchen.

'No men,' Sarah ordered, and Margaret hoped that the first applicant, a smiling West Indian, would know that it was his sex rather than his colour that brought the hasty refusal. A pleading young man and his very pregnant wife were also turned away, and several ladies of dismal appearance and uncertain age all received polite refusals.

But when the flamboyant figure of Dottie stood at the front door, suitcase in hand and fair hair blowing loose beneath a bright red beret, Margaret was immediately intrigued. Here was someone whom she sensed immediately her mother would not approve of.

'Come in, and we'll talk about it,' she said, trying to be careful.

They sat drinking tea, and Margaret stared at her prospective tenant, trying to place her. She fitted into no convenient category.

'I'll try not to be noisy or anything,' the girl said, 'but I desperately need somewhere soon. I'm starting at the school in three days' time. I'm the new infant teacher and I'm scared stiff.'

Margaret gulped on her tea. She didn't look like the proverbial teacher, all tweed and sturdy shoes.

'I was in the Wrens for the last three years of the war, and then did this one-year emergency training when I was demobbed. It was jolly hard work, and now they've thrown us all to the lions and expect us to cope. I hope I'll make the grade.'

'When do you start?'

'Next Monday. I need to find somewhere to live today. All my worldly possessions are in that bag and I don't feel like humping it round much longer.'

Margaret looked at the heavy case standing in the corner of the room and at the slender girl who was staring at her hopefully. She made up her mind immediately. There was something lost about Dottie, a sense of need that penetrated the hard shell and the ostentatious clothes. Perhaps they would become friends. It looked as though they both could do with some mutual support.

'I'll show you the room,' she said.

CHAPTER ELEVEN

1947

DOTTIE settled in quickly.

'Dorothea,' she explained. 'What a perfectly awful name it is! Everyone calls me Dottie because I suppose that's what I am—at least, that's the impression I give.'

'I could do with someone a bit dotty to cheer things up,' said Margaret. 'I think we'll get on fine.'

'Why to cheer things up? You don't look particularly woebegone. I mean, with this nice house you can't possibly be too desperate.'

Margaret looked around at the small front parlour where they were sitting, seeing with a stranger's eyes. Yes, it was nice, but it still had signs of her grandmother's fifty years of occupancy. There had been no time yet to impart to it anything of herself.

'My father's only letting me borrow it for a bit,' she explained. 'I wish it were mine—I think I could become quite fond of it.'

She wondered if her new friend, for that was what Dottie was rapidly becoming, had realised that she was pregnant. At four months she could hardly do up her skirts and fastened them with elastic hidden beneath two shapeless jumpers she had bought at the second-hand clothes shop on the corner. They hadn't noticed yet in the bookshop where she was working. She dreaded the day when it would become obvious.

'Will you stay on here after?'

Dottie looked at her frankly, and suddenly Margaret knew that her secret wasn't hers any longer.

'So you know?'

'Well, I've heard you being sick a few times, and it happened to a friend of mine, so I'm not too ignorant. Want to talk about it?'

The temptation was great. It would be good to share the burden, and the grief too. It was mainly at night that she lay and wept silently for Karl and for the life together that they would never know. In her worst moments she wondered if he really cared for her as she did for him. Wouldn't he have stayed on in England as so many prisoners of war were hoping to do, if he had truly loved her? Perhaps if she had told him about the baby? She always banished the tempting thought almost as quickly as it came. She wouldn't imprison him all over again with that.

Would Dottie understand all her complicated reasons for everything she had done? Could she dare risk telling her? She had never had a close friend of her own age, and she had longed desperately for one through all the years of her growing up. Although, in her own mind, Cornwall was more her home than Bristol, there had always been a barrier between herself and the local girls. All her efforts to break it down had failed and the kindred spirit that she so much sought had never materialised. Perhaps here was one at last.

'I can never marry him.' She brushed away sudden unexpected tears as she spoke the incredibly difficult words. 'And I'm not going to have it adopted, in spite of all the pressures.'

'You'll have a pretty tough time. My friend went to an adoption agency. She only saw her once—a little girl, it was. They took her away a couple of hours after the birth. I don't know how she could have done it. She's married now, though, so I suppose it was the right decision for her. Are you sure you can face it?'

'Not really, but I'm going to anyway! Having this house will help. I'll live on the rent you pay me and maybe I'll try to fit a lodger in too if I have to. It depends on how long they let me keep my job. Mum said no men, but if I got someone who wanted his meals doing and generally looking after I could charge a bit more.'

'Good for you. How'll you manage the accommodation, though?'

'I'll sleep in the back kitchen on the settee. You can keep the front bedroom and he could have the back.'

'So we might have an unknown man in the house! The neighbours won't like that!'

'Well, it's none of their business, but I don't think I shall like it much either. I hope it won't be necessary.'

'I'll pay you a bit more—I can just afford it,' said Dottie. 'And now do you mind if I do some school work in here? It's cosier than in my bedroom.' She took a pile of cards out of her bag and spread them on the small table in the bay window. 'That headmistress of mine is a bit of a tartar. She expects every child to have a new work card almost each day.'

'Carry on,' Margaret said. 'I'm glad my job doesn't extend into my spare time. I get tired enough as it is.'

She got up and went into the little scullery to make coffee. It would be nice to confide everything to Dottie, she thought, tell her about Karl and have her advice, but a strange reluctance held her back. One day, perhaps.

She carried two cups back into the living-room and put one down on the table among the colourful work cards. She looked at them idly. Maybe she would have trained as a teacher if she had taken up that scholarship. It was strange how the circumstances of life altered the course of your existence so completely.

'Could you bring me a couple of books from the shop tomorrow, please, if you've got them?' Dottie asked, breaking into her train of thought.

'Of course,' Margaret said, taking the paper that was held out to her. She enjoyed working in the bookshop. It was on the hill that ran from the great Cathedral near the city centre up to the University Tower. It was often full of students, and she used to look at them, envying their seemingly carefree lives, and wishing that she too had nothing to think of but herself. She constantly regretted her own lack of education, feeling inferior when asked for a book that she had never heard of. As she unpacked boxes of new books and stacked them on the shelves she would handle them reverently, remembering each title and frequently going across the Green in her lunch hour, to the library, to find and borrow a tattered copy of the same book.

To reach the library she had to pass the old Cathedral Chambers, and although the small building was interesting and beautiful it would not normally have caught her close attention. But there was a brass plaque on the door, and it was during the fifth week that she was working at the shop that she noticed it. The sun was shining on the brass illuminating it so that it seemed to demand her attention. She glanced at it, and immediately the name registered. 'Bantry and Son, Chartered Accountants.'

In the turmoil and worry of her home-coming she had almost forgotten that John had suggested that she should contact Graham Bantry again. She remembered suddenly the kind young man who had called to see her when she was home on holiday, the walk on the Downs with him and tea in his parents' lovely home. She looked down at her expanding waistline and shuddered at the thought of meeting any of that family now. They were so respectable, so conventional, and she would hate to see their previous friendliness towards her change into a polite disgust, as she guessed it would. She hurried past, hoping that their paths would never cross. Not until after the baby, anyway. It might be different then.

'Weather's changing. It's chilly this morning,' Dottie remarked a few days later, and with relief Margaret rummaged in her wardrobe for the square-shouldered and back-pleated short coat that would hide her condition admirably. She produced it triumphantly and swirled in front of the mirror.

'Perfect to keep a secret,' she said. 'How do I look?'

'Nice, but the rumour I heard about a new tight-waisted fashion coming in won't do much for you!'

Margaret laughed. 'Just you wait! Only five more months to go and I'll look as skinny as you!'

'Don't you believe it. Mums are always fat!' her friend teased as she stuffed her books into a battered old tapestry bag that she used for school.

'Mine isn't. Never has been.'

Margaret thought about her mother as she spoke. She was due to go and visit her parents during the coming weekend, and she shuddered. Only with them did her condition really embarrass her.

Saturday morning was always busy in the shop. She wished that she hadn't to work on Saturdays. It would be nice to have two whole days free. The shops in Park Street closed at lunchtime, though, unlike those in other parts of the town which were shut on Wednesday afternoons.

'Have you a copy of the *Oxford Dictionary of English Literature*?'

Margaret looked up from the bottom shelf where she was straightening some books. The voice was vaguely familiar. She stood up, and colour suffused her face and neck. She smoothed down her voluminous smock and put a hand to her hair.

'Yes, yes, I'm sure we have. I'll go——'

'We've met, haven't we? You're Margaret. What on earth are you doing here?'

She forced a smile, a smile to match his, and to cover her confusion. 'I live here now. Didn't John write? He said he would.'

'He was never one for letters.'

Margaret was suddenly aware of the eyes of her boss looking in her direction. 'I'll get your book,' she said, glad of an excuse to go to the other end of the large shop. 'I won't be a moment. Will you wait here, please?' She was once more the efficient assistant, taking refuge in the job to be done.

She brought the book back and wrapped it carefully, concentrating all her efforts on the simple task, taking time to think of something to say, and wondering desperately whether Graham had noticed. She was standing behind the counter now and the barrier between them gave her confidence.

'That's ten and six,' she said. It seemed a lot of money to spend on a book.

'Could we have lunch somewhere?' I should like to catch up on all the news from Cornwall, and yours too.'

For a moment Margaret searched for an excuse, but the brilliance of those brown eyes and the smile he turned upon her weakened her defences, and there was the coat. She would keep her coat on and he wouldn't be able to tell.

'Just a snack,' she said. 'I'm going to my mother's tonight, and she always cooks mountains of food! Saves up all her rations for my visits, I think.'

It was the end of Sabbath at sundown and there was always an appetising smell from the little terraced house an hour or two later. Margaret forbore to say anything of this to Graham.

'Right—I'll be outside when the shop closes. One o'clock. See you then, Margaret,'

The rest of the morning passed quickly, but while her hands were constantly busy her mind was in a turmoil. She liked Graham. She had been attracted to him in a sisterly sort of way when they last met, but she must make this one meeting their only one. If he knew that she was expecting a baby he would assume that it was John's, and she would of course have to deny that. Suppose he mentioned it in a letter to Cornwall! Annie would guess that it was Karl.

Her heart thumped a warning and her face paled at the thought. Karl hadn't had his repatriation yet; Annie had mentioned it in her last letter. She'd said that he was hoping it might be soon, and the thought had brought a feeling of desolation and despair to Margaret. While he was still in England she felt a sense of support, although she knew that it had no substance and was totally illusory. Karl never mentioned repatriation in his letters to her, and she questioned herself constantly about the tone of the short, bright replies she sent to him, words full of confidence and happiness. 'I'm doing it to free him,' she told herself firmly and with an element of anger. 'He must be free. He must go to Dresden and come back for me a free man if he ever wants to!'

That was for the distant future, probably an impossible dream, and meanwhile no one in Cornwall must find out about the baby, at least not until Karl was safely back in his beloved Germany, and even then she wouldn't tell if she could help it. It was a secret that she wanted to keep safe and secure for a long time yet.

'Just tea and a sandwich, please,' she said.

'Surely you can manage something more than that?' queried Graham.

'No. Truly, I couldn't face anything else.' Her stomach heaved with the tension of their meeting, and she wondered whether she could cope with anything at all. It was a good thing that tea hadn't become odious to her as it was supposed to do in pregnancy. It was a constant source of comfort!

The young waitress wrote their meagre order quickly and disappeared, leaving a silence between them. Graham stared at her and she could feel his eyes searching her face, wanting news, needing reasons for her presence here. He must have had some idea about John's feelings for her. The two men had been very close and they had met a couple of times since their demobilisation. How much had John said? Had he mentioned Karl?

'You're looking lovely, Margaret,' he said, and she blushed. This was the time in pregnancy when you were supposed to blossom, and she knew that she did indeed look good. There was a bloom on her skin and a glow in her eyes that all the sadness of her despairing love for Karl could not dim.

'I'm fine, but what about you, Graham? Tell me about yourself.' There would be safety in switching the conversation to him, and men liked to talk about themselves, she reflected.

'Nothing very startling,' he said. 'I'm working in my grandfather's firm. He's taken me on as an articled clerk, so I suppose I shall be a fully fledged accountant eventually and after lots of exams. He's due to retire very shortly, and I'm the hope of his declining years, making up for the disappointment of my father's going into medicine instead of the family firm.'

Margaret nibbled at the sandwich before her. The lettuce was wilting sadly and the tiny bit of cheese that was hidden in its soft white interior was scarcely edible. She gulped the hot tea to wash it down.

'It's a good job, I should think. Is it what you wanted to do?'

'I suppose so. I've always been good at figures. I missed university, though—because of the war, of course. A lot of accountants start off with a degree, so I'm at quite a disadvantage.'

'I'm sure you'll overcome that.' There was certainty in her words as she looked at the confident young man across the table. In spite of his prison years, years that had destroyed so many, she was sure that Graham would cope. He was a survivor.

'Enough of me,' he said firmly. 'Tell me about yourself and why you've left the farm and poor old John?'

This was what she was dreading. How could she answer? Lies wouldn't do. Evasion was the best course. Her mind searched for words.

'John's always been a sort of brother to me,' she explained. 'I couldn't think of him in any other way. It was terrible leaving them all, but there was nothing else I could have done!'

'So you're living with your parents again?'

Another difficult question. Another difficult answer!

'No, I'm not, actually. My grandmother died and my father's letting me have her house for a bit. It's in St Pauls.'

'You mean you wanted to live on your own?' There was incredulity in his voice, and a questioning too.

The colour flooded her face. 'A teacher lives with me. I rent her a room. She's nice, and we've become good friends.' Again it was a statement wholly true but giving away nothing. Margaret was beginning to feel desperate, hunted. She must somehow turn the conversation to general things. 'That book you bought this morning. It isn't anything to do with accountancy?' She was questioning him now. Perhaps they could talk about books. It was a subject in which she was just beginning to feel confident. Her interest in the classics was sustaining her in so many ways.

He laughed. 'No. I need to get away from facts and figures and accounts into the realm of literature and fantasy. I wanted something to allay my ignorance, help make up for all I missed in my education.'

'Me too,' Margaret added. 'At least you went to a grammar school. I only managed a village secondary. I'm reading like mad now. It's great having the library so close.'

The time passed quickly after that, and for a while their shared tastes in books brought a false sense of peace to Margaret. It was almost as if the past months hadn't been and they were taking up their friendship where they had left it on that previous winter visit.

'Can I see you again?' Graham asked when the meal was finished and they rose to leave.

'I would rather not,' Margaret said, suddenly aware again of her figure and her worry.

A hurt and surprised expression passed briefly over his face. 'Just friendship,' he said. 'No strings or anything.'

'I'll be in the shop,' she said, stalling for time. 'I'll be there for a few more weeks, anyway.'

The words had slipped out. She looked at him, embarrassed, not knowing how to explain.

No explanation was needed. He took her arm and they walked on to the Cathedral Green. They walked for a long time in an uneasy silence. The winter sun made pale shadows behind them on the path and pigeons walked unafraid round their feet. Suddenly Graham pulled her down beside him on to a seat and put his hand over hers. It was the first time he had touched her since they had met all those months ago. There was a gentleness and a concern both in his touch and his eyes, and she shuddered a little, not from antipathy, but from fear.

'Well, if there's any way I can help you I'm just a telephone call away,' he said.

It was a simple statement, but she felt a sudden terrible dismay. Did he know after all, then, or was he guessing? Was it so obvious? She tried to appear casual and serene. She must make him think he had made a mistake. No word of suspicion must get to Cornwall.

'Thanks, Graham. I'm fine, though, and very independent. I've a good job and a house. What more could I want?' She forced a laugh. 'I'll be in touch one day!'

She slid her hand gently from beneath his and stood up. Without looking back at him she strode off to the safety and anonymity of the library, and then, trembling violently, she hurried up the wide steps and into the silent world of the reference section. The partitions dividing each working space would hide her tears and her terror, but nothing could salvage her peace of mind. She needed to think and plan. The most important thing in the world at that moment was to protect Karl. Karl! She rested her head on her arms and sobbed silently, her tears falling relentlessly on the old oak desk. The gulls called outside where they flew high over the city docks, but she could hear only those others whose calling mingled with the crashing of the sea, and her heart wept for the baby she carried and for the man she loved and would never see again.

Graham watched her go. As she walked away from him he saw the vulnerability in every proud step she took, and he wondered why this girl whom he hardly knew tugged at his heart-strings so. He remembered their first meeting. He had sensed something special about her then, something to which he responded, and he was suddenly angry, angry beyond reason with the man who had done this terrible thing to her. He thought of John and the letter he had received a few weeks before telling of an engagement to someone called Sybil. Furiously he kicked the stone base of the seat on which he was still sitting. John, his friend, the man who had been with him through those horrific years in the camp! It could only be John.

He got up eventually and walked slowly towards his office. His heart was heavy with his new discovery, and heavy too with the knowledge that he could really do nothing to help either of them. He sat at his desk all that afternoon trying to concentrate on his work, but the more he stared at the big leather-covered ledgers before him with their lines of copperplate writing and figures, the more he saw Margaret's face staring at him, white and afraid, and yet so brave with its mask of confidence that he knew had been put on just for his benefit.

CHAPTER TWELVE

1947

DOTTIE was sitting deep in the big green plush chair with her feet on the mantelpiece when Margaret arrived home late that Saturday evening. She was reading the newspaper, one of her favourite pursuits.

'How are the parents?' she asked. She put the paper down on the floor and jumped up to make a cup of tea as she spoke. Margaret always came home looking weary and somewhat dejected after the weekly visit, and this Saturday she seemed more depressed than usual. A cup of tea was vital.

'Sit here,' she said, indicating the chair. 'I've warmed it for you!'

Margaret laughed, flung off her coat and did as she was told. The two girls had become firm friends and shared the cooking and food. Neither kept to her own domain.

'They're fine, I suppose. Mum told me I looked terrible, and Dad gave me five pounds to go and buy a new winter coat!'

'Then mind you get a nice bright one to cheer us all up a bit. None of those dreary greys and browns you're so fond of wearing.'

'You shall come with me next weekend and help me choose.'

'Done! I love buying clothes. Anything else interesting happen today?'

'I met someone.'

Dottie put the cup down on the floor on top of the

newspaper and stared at her friend. 'Come on, then—tell all!'

'He's nice. Good-looking, good job, good prospects, and I was rude to him.'

Dottie collapsed on the rug beside the newspaper and the tea and sighed elaborately. 'Why don't these kind of things happen to me? I'd have been charming and encouraging and wonderful, and he'd have been here having supper with us and in love with me by now!'

Margaret laughed and bent to poke up the fire. 'He's a friend of John's. I was frightened that he'd see I was pregnant and write to him.'

Dottie was silent for a while, staring into the flames that were beginning to curl reluctantly round the few bits of coal they could afford. She wondered constantly about all the secrecy. If this baby was John's then surely he ought to help a bit, financially anyway. Privately she thought it might be a good thing if he did get to know.

'Why don't you tell him, Maggie?' she said. 'Keeping it to yourself is half killing you. It's his baby too, remember.'

There was a silence between them and Dottie put a hand out to Margaret and grasped hers in a gesture of friendship and support.

'It's not his!'

The words were forced out, and Dottie saw the tears and gasped, regretting her own insensitivity. She had always been so sure that this John who was mentioned casually now and then was the father. Margaret hadn't talked about anyone else that she could remember.

'I'm sorry—I'm so sorry,' she said quietly.

'I do need to tell someone. Can you keep a secret?'

The words were childish in their simplicity but

genuine and sincere nevertheless. Speechless, Dottie nodded her reply.

'He's called Karl Schormann—a German. I can't marry him, and no, he doesn't know about the baby. It was only once, the first time ever for me, and the last!'

Dottie listened to the incredible words and at first they made no sense. She stared at her friend and tried to comprehend fully what she had just heard. She said nothing. There seemed to be no sentiment at all that she could express. There was a strange silence between them.

Margaret looked up in fear. She couldn't bear to lose the friendship of the one person she felt she could trust. Then suddenly she felt a strange fluttering within her. The baby moved gently, and she clasped her hands passionately over the folds of her smock.

'His child is precious to me, Dottie. It's part of him and me, a symbol of our love for each other. I can't explain really. It's like a sort of healing of the wounds of war, a new beginning. Can you understand?'

Dottie quickly regained her composure. 'Of course I can. It was just a bit of a shock, that's all. I was so sure it was this John you sometimes talk about. Nationality makes no difference to me. It all sounds a bit too romantic and up in the clouds, though,' she added. 'He goes free, you get all the trouble, and no one will care about healing wounds and all that when the child is born. They'll just criticise you for fraternising if they find out. Sorry, love, but I do think you ought to get him to take some responsibility, German or no!'

Not stopping to think about the incongruity of her words, she suddenly jumped up and started turning the pages of the now tattered newspaper on the floor.

'I saw something in the paper,' she said, scattering pages everywhere as she searched. 'Somewhere

. . .here it is. A girl is getting married to a POW in Yorkshire. So it can be done.' Her finger stabbed the article and the fuzzy picture of a smiling bride and her slightly shabby-looking groom. She pushed it into Margaret's lap, then sat back and wondered what she had done. Why did she always speak her mind so bluntly? She hoped that she hadn't hurt her friend too much.

'But I thought it was forbidden?' Margaret said, and her face paled as she read.

'Apparently the marriage ban was lifted by the Government last July. It says so further down the page.'

'Why didn't I know?'

'I don't suppose it was much talked about. It wouldn't have been a very popular move, would it, and you told me that you never read newspapers.'

Karl sat in the hazy autumn sunshine and ate the pasty he had brought with him to the field. He wanted to work every hour of daylight to get the harvest in. He wouldn't be on the farm much longer and he didn't want to leave any of the heavy work for John. He took the newspaper that Annie had wrapped round the food and idly glanced at it as he ate. Suddenly his attention was riveted by what he read. 'First British Bride For German POW' was the headline, and he stared at the fading photograph. He read through the article, then angrily screwed the paper up and pushed it deep into a hole in the hedgerow behind him. He had known about the lifting of the marriage ban, but Margaret had gone by then, and he hadn't mentioned it in his letters mainly because of the tone of her replies. Her letters had always been brief and cheerful, and lately there had been mention of John's friend, Graham Bantry. In spite of the intense jealousy and sadness that her loss brought to him he was glad that she was obviously contented with her new life in Bristol, and he wanted to put her happiness before his own, however great the struggle. It would be better in the end if she could forget him. He couldn't ask her to face the deprivation and horrors of living in Germany; it was too much to ask of any girl. And he couldn't settle in England as a few POWs were doing. He needed to get home. It was vital to him in a way he didn't really understand but couldn't change.

He thought of Dresden as it had been when he'd left to join up—beautiful, serene, a place where one could live and breathe freely, and make a good life. Perhaps one day in the new land he wanted to help build there would be hope. . .Perhaps he could come back for Margaret! He sighed, knowing that it was probably only a dream.

He looked up at the gulls screaming above him and threw a small portion of food for them. He remembered the time Margaret had seen him on the beach, and her fury when he had killed the injured bird. He smiled sadly to himself. 'Nazi thug', she had called him—angry words soon regretted. He would never forget her, even if she had so quickly forgotten him. He got up decisively. This part of his life was almost over and there would be a new beginning. In spite of the great sadness in his heart there was excitement too as he thought of the longed-for repatriation papers which had recently arrived. He had to go to Sheffield and then they would arrange transport from there. Cornwall was beautiful, but Germany had his heart, or most of it, now, although a portion would always remain here under an English sky with the girl he had loved so much and lost.

It was when he looked at the map and saw that

Bristol was in a direct line between the farm and Sheffield that temptation overcame all his strong resolutions. Perhaps he could meet Margaret again for an hour or two? He had no idea how it could be managed, but he determined to try. He had always been amazed at her sudden departure for Bristol, and he felt that he would like to see her once more, find out the truth perhaps even if it was hurtful. If he heard from her own lips that she was happy, that she was in love with someone else even, then he would be content for her. It would be their last chance.

Margaret always kept Karl's letters until she was alone, until she could savour them and feel the touch of him from the thin white paper. She was in bed when she opened the latest, and she gasped as she read the words. He wanted to come to see her on his way to Sheffield. It would be the last opportunity, he said. He was to go back to Germany soon.

She put the letter down and sobbed, and the baby in her womb moved restlessly. She put her hands over the swelling of her stomach, and her tears would not be stopped, and the throbbing of her heart echoed her baby's moving. For a long time she struggled with her emotions and almost gave way to her desperate desire to have Karl here, his arms round her again, his protection shielding her from all the insults and stares that her condition provoked, and his love enfolding her and their baby. It was the most natural thing to crave, and for a time she gave herself up to the dream of his presence, here in this house, in Bristol.

Then common sense reasserted itself and she groped for the letter and read it again. Never, she told herself, never would he see her like this, because it would demand his help and prevent him from doing what he obviously so desperately wanted to do. There was happiness in the letter—his years of captivity were almost over. He would soon be free again and going home at last, he said. He just wanted to see her again for an hour or two before he left. Never would she shatter his chances of going back to Germany, she told herself firmly, and she certainly wouldn't bind him with cords of duty. Once more she thought of the future. Karl would come back for her freely and without coercion. That was the way she wanted it to be.

So the next day the reply was sent. She was sorry, but it couldn't be done, she wrote. She couldn't meet him. She knew it was for the best, she said, and she gave no reasons, just sent him her love and best wishes for his future, and hopes that they might meet one day in a new and free world. Her eyes were full of tears as she posted that final letter, and after she heard it fall with a soft thud on to the others in the box she turned and walked away down the grey, rain-filled street with the deepest sense of loss and hopelessness that she had ever felt in all her life.

John was smarting a little over a loss too, but he had to admit to himself that it was more a loss of pride than of love!

'What do you mean, it's all over?' Annie demanded angrily that evening when he sat down heavily at the table in the farm kitchen and looked blankly at the ample meal she put before him.

'Just what I say, Mother. Sybil has changed her mind. She doesn't want to marry me any more.'

Karl looked up, shocked and surprised. The marriage with Sybil had seemed to be so safe and so good for John.

'And why, may I ask? What have you done to make her back out so suddenly?'

The wedding had been arranged for early December, not October as originally planned, and Annie was looking forward to having a daughter-in-law moving in to share some of the work, and she would be company too. Sybil was a nice girl, homely and used to farming.

'I suppose she sensed that I'm not in love with her, that's all,' John said.

'What do you mean, not in love?' Annie's tone was disgusted as well as totally amazed. 'You like her well enough, don't you?'

'But that's not sufficient, is it?'

John poked the food on his plate and wasn't sure whether to be relieved or downcast. When he really examined his deepest thoughts he supposed he was secretly glad. He had been catapulted into the relationship with Sybil on the rebound from Margaret's rebuff. Once the ring was on her finger and their respective families rejoicing about the highly suitable match, it had been too late to withdraw. Now the breaking of the relationship had come from her, and he was free. Free.

Suddenly he attacked the meal in front of him and ate with gusto. Margaret! He thought of her again. Karl was going soon, and their friendship had obviously come to nothing. Once he was safely back in Germany John would go to Bristol, stay with Graham and visit her. The idea took root in his mind, but he determined to say nothing yet. And he would have to get someone in to look after the farm. That wouldn't be easy. He wouldn't tell them he was coming. Make it a surprise—perhaps. January or February would be about right. There was no desperate rush.

1948

In spite of all her fears the birth was easy, and on a cold February day Margaret was delivered of a daughter, a dark-haired, crying scrap who bore no resemblance at all to the blonde Aryan super-race that Hitler had hoped to create, no resemblance to Karl. Margaret looked at her and turned her face to the wall and cried. All the agony of mind, sacrifice of love, and the pain, for this—this daughter, this little Jewish child, for Jewish she certainly was. It was stamped on the baby face indelibly, and Margaret knew no throb of emotion or love in her heart.

'Well, you seem to have given up your race and religion,' Sarah Seddon observed as she looked down at her new granddaughter, 'and she's been sent to remind you of it. Remind us all, no doubt.'

She had no idea how prophetic her words were. The baby in the white hospital cot waved a tiny fist and her eyes stared up at a hostile world.

'You know that it's the mother who determines the race of the child, not the father, in Jewish law,' Sarah went on. 'So whoever he is makes no difference. She's Jewish.'

Margaret wanted to fight the words and she couldn't understand why. 'I'll give her a Jewish name,' she heard herself saying, 'and that's all. Miriam. She shall be Miriam.'

'It's a lovely name, but why?' Dottie asked as she bent over the cradle on their first evening at home.

'I don't know. Something perverse in me, I suppose. It just came to me on impulse and I decided to stick to it. A sort of expiation of my guilt.'

'What on earth are you talking about?'

'I'm Jewish, he was German. She's a sort of battlefield, or an armistice!'

Dottie sat down abruptly. Was there no end to all the shock waves Margaret imparted?

'Jewish? You didn't tell me. You went to chapel on Christmas Day. We had a tree. You don't look it!'

'I forget it myself sometimes. I was brought up mainly by Annie and Bill on the farm, good Methodists, and I just conformed. It seemed a good idea at the beginning of the war when we thought Hitler might invade. My parents aren't religious now. I don't suppose they ever were really. They just kept up some of the traditions because of my grandmother, I think. They still vaguely keep Sabbath. That's about all really, and that's because Dad likes a day of rest.'

'I thought he had a shop.'

'He has someone in to look after it on that day!' Margaret laughed. 'Mother thinks that the baby has been sent to remind us of our failings. She looks so Jewish—just like Grandmother, I'm told.'

Dottie took another look at the sleeping child and then at the photograph in its old silver frame on the mantelpiece. It gleamed in the light. Margaret always kept the silver shining brightly and the old woman looked out at them both with a fierce stare. 'Yes, I suppose she does, now you come to mention it. Miriam, look Jewish, I mean. Oh, well, she isn't, is she, not really?'

'Yes, she is. If the mother is Jewish, then so is the child. The father's race doesn't matter! My mother reminded me.'

'I can't believe it,' Dottie said. 'I thought women were rather despised.'

'Not despised—important in the home, I suppose that's the reason. Anyway, she won't get any Jewish teaching from me. In fact, I plan not to make anything of it at all.'

'Apart from the name?' Dottie questioned. 'What will she make of her name? Perhaps she should have been Margaret Rose after the Princess. Something really English.'

'Miriam it is and Miriam it remains,' Margaret said. 'She can make of it what she likes. It'll be a long time before she questions it at all, and meanwhile I've other things to worry about. Will she let me get a good night's sleep, for instance! Today's problems are more important than tomorrow's at the moment.'

But in spite of her tiredness and the baby's quiet breathing, sleep eluded Margaret on that first night at home. She tossed restlessly on her narrow bed and worried about her lack of love for the tiny scrap who was sleeping so soundly in the cot next to her. The baby was good. She had been good in the hospital. She slept and fed and slept, but every time Margaret nursed her she would look down at the tiny dark head and wonder if she could ever have any relationship at all with this daughter. All her love for Karl had been enshrined in the little blond son she had visualised throughout her pregnancy. The sacrifices she had made and would have to go on making would have been worthwhile for the child she had been so sure of, a little boy stamped with Karl's features. She admitted to herself too that in the most secret of her dreams she had dramatised a day when she would take him to Germany, present him to Karl. It had all been a romantic fantasy, but it had kept her going in the blackest moments, and now all that was finished.

She sat up in bed and stared at the baby in the glow of the little night-light that flickered gently in its saucer of water. She wondered how she was going to cope, and for a few frightened moments wished that she had had the baby adopted. Life could have begun all over again, free. Free of the hostility and the stares. And the baby would have been loved. An adopted baby was usually a very much wanted baby.

Then with a sudden rush of terrible guilt for her thoughts she jumped from her bed and snatched the sleeping child to her and took her into bed. Miriam woke and cried a little, and then fastened on to the full breast and sucked gently, and Margaret, enjoying the sensation, felt a slight relief, but there was no sudden love to expiate the guilt. Her tears flowed and she resolved that this baby should have the best that she could offer, everything that her meagre resources could give, and if there could be no love, then there should be care and security instead. She would work and fight for this child with everything in her power. It would have to suffice.

She changed Miriam's nappy and laid her gently back in the cot when she had finished feeding, and then she crept downstairs to make a cup of tea. It wouldn't do to disturb Dottie; she had a class to teach in the morning.

Back in the comfort of her bed and with the hot mug of tea in her hands she began to feel better, and she reflected on the past difficult weeks, and on the future too. There had been animosity from neighbours as soon as her pregnancy had become obvious, and now that she had a baby to take everywhere with her she knew that the prejudice would be much worse. For one moment she wished that, for Miriam's sake, she had taken her mother's advice and bought a wedding-ring. She remembered staring at them in a jeweller's window for a long time back in the autumn, and eventually walking resolutely past, determined not to be tempted. It had been easier then.

'I think you're brave,' Graham had said when she told him. 'It won't be easy, though.'

Margaret smiled to herself when she thought of Graham. He was so predictable, so conventional, and yet he had been a good friend to her during the hardest times.

They had met often, and it hadn't been necessary to have any pretences or secrets from him. None, apart from her love for Karl. She'd hugged that to herself, and only Dottie would know. There had been no need even to appear courageous with Graham. He was like a brother, but without the complications. His own experiences of suffering had given him a maturity beyond his years, and she had felt safe with him, totally accepted with no questions asked, no recriminations. His father was a doctor, and that made it easier somehow. He had grown up with a surgery in the house and pregnancy wasn't anything unusual.

'You need someone, Margaret,' he had said when they had first talked about it openly. 'Let me help you in any way I can.'

'People will talk, think it's yours!'

He had laughed aloud at that. 'Let them. I'm about as tough as an old boot. You don't come through a Japanese prison camp and survive only to worry about what people think.'

They used to meet often in the lunch hour during the autumn and early winter. Brandon Hill was one of their favourite places when the weather was good, and when it rained they often went into the Cathedral. Graham loved the Cathedral and told her stories of its history that intrigued and fascinated her.

'Do you know about the Jew who had his teeth knocked out?' he asked one day as they sat on the stone seats round the edge of the ancient Chapter House.

Margaret turned to him, shocked, but there was no glimmer of amusement on his face. It was the kind of remark that sometimes preceded a joke against her people, but it couldn't be that from Graham.

'No, tell me.'

'It was about the time when this was first built.' He ran his hand over the mellow old walls, 'King John was in power and his terrible cruelty was always causing uproar, but apparently all Bristol was disgusted when they heard that he had tortured a wealthy Jew of the town, finally causing eight of his teeth to be struck out, one a day, until the poor wretch agreed to pay him some thousands of pounds.'

'I wonder why we've always been so persecuted?'

The sentence was spoken before she could stop it. There had been strange headlines and even stranger pictures in the newspapers lately, and although she seldom bought a paper she couldn't help seeing the frightened faces that stared at her from newsagents' stands every day. There was a ship trying to get to Palestine, full of Jewish refugees, pathetic survivors of the Nazi concentration camps. It had been turned back by the British, its occupants put in camps all over again.

She remembered Graham turning to her as he heard her words, and she was aware of a slightly dazed expression on his face.

'You didn't tell me you were Jewish?'

'No. It wasn't really relevant. I seldom consider myself Jewish, but lately I've begun to identify more.'

They had talked about it frequently after that. Graham had been more interested in politics than she was.

'The Jews want a homeland in Palestine,' he had said one day. 'The United Nations gave them a favourable vote. I hope they get their dream—they deserve it after all they've suffered.'

It sounded wonderful, Margaret had thought. A country where Jews could totally belong, a place of their own. But it was a dream without substance, surely, though. It could never happen, and if it did, there would be no place in it for her.

Her baby had not been born when these ideas had first come to her, and she had still been thinking of the little blond German that she was sure she carried. There would be no place for Karl's baby in a Jewish state. Bristol would have to do! Her friendship with Graham had grown and she had often wondered why he chose to spend time with her. She had been terribly conscious of her rapidly expanding figure, and he was so good-looking and attractive that there must have been plenty of girls who were anxious to go out with him. When she had given up her job she had been sure that their meetings would cease.

'Of course not,' he had assured her. 'I'm hoping you'll invite me home sometimes.'

After that he had frequently come to the little house in St Pauls and they had sat and talked in the cosy kitchen, often eaten together, including Dottie in their friendship. At weekends they would walk up Ashley Hill where they could stop when Margaret was tired and lean on the wall and look over the city, spread below them, and at the countryside beyond. When there was petrol to spare he would take her further, occasionally even to the seaside at Clevedon or as far as Weston-super-Mare. She had pined for fields and woods, but most of all for the sea.

He had even visited her during her time in hospital. She remembered the huge bunch of flowers that must have been bought at vast expense at that time of year, and heads had turned to stare from every corner of the ward at Graham's tall, immaculate figure. He had come three times altogether and cheered her immensely. He had even looked at the baby through the glass window of the nursery.

'She's lovely,' he'd said when he came back to her. 'Like you.'

He had bent over her bed and kissed her, his lips brushing hers very lightly, and she had blushed furiously and wondered what the other mothers must be thinking.

She smiled to herself in the quietness of her little bedroom as she remembered, and as she fell asleep at last it was with a sense of gratitude. Gratitude to her father for the safety of this house, and to Graham for his friendship. Her mother too had been kind, and in Dottie she had another wonderful friend.

And her dreams as she slept were of Graham. They were at sea on a small boat, and then the scene changed and it was a hot, sandy stretch of beach, not at all like the one she had loved in Cornwall. Graham was carrying Miriam and someone was telling them that it was Palestine and that they weren't allowed to stay. She tossed restlessly in her sleep, and woke when the skies were still dark outside and her baby was crying for another feed.

CHAPTER THIRTEEN

1948

JOHN was not used to telephones. He thought about the call he would have to make with mounting apprehension as the train chugged its smoky way nearer to Bristol, and he wished more fervently with each passing mile that he had written to tell Graham of his coming. The idea of a surprise had seemed good when he'd first decided on the trip, but now he wasn't so sure. There had been the matter of the relief worker to look after the farm, of course. He hadn't known that the man was free to take over until two days ago. That would be his excuse. He comforted himself with that.

He flexed his muscles as he sat, and tried to banish the rising panic, tried to fix his mind on the good, positive things in his life. He was certainly in better physical shape than he had been for a long time. He smiled a little to himself as he thought of the skinny, pale individual he had been when he last saw Graham. Well, he was fine now, or as fine as he would ever be. He had felt slightly injured when Sybil had turned him down, but the sense of freedom had more than compensated.

His thoughts turned hopefully to Margaret. Karl was gone, safely out of sight and out of mind. His home town was Dresden, in the Eastern Sector, and from the little John had heard there wasn't much chance that he would ever be able to come on visits to England. John knew that Margaret had been attracted to him, with his winning smile and his golden good looks, but he wasn't sure how much. God, how jealous he had been! He had come to like Karl eventually, but those early feelings had been almost of hatred. She must surely have forgotten him now. There had been few letters arriving at the farm for the German as far as he knew. Of course, she hadn't written to him either, but the occasional short note had come with a Bristol postmark, always addressed to his mother. She didn't say much about herself, just that she was working in a bookshop. A bookshop! John had been incredulous when he heard. Margaret, who loved the open air, the sea and the hard, physical work of the farm! Surely he could persuade her to come back. His pulse quickened and he glanced impatiently at his watch. Only another ten minutes.

It was easy to find the telephone box; its cheerful red paint contrasted with the grey of everything else. John fumbled with the coins in the confining and grubby space. For a moment, before he took control of himself, he panicked. Ever since the camp he had been terrified of small places.

'Hello.'

He heard the cool, cultivated voice of Graham's mother and for a moment was lost for the right thing to say.

'Hello. Dr Bantry's home,' she said again. 'Can I help you?'

'Yes,' he said awkwardly, and then he realised that he hadn't pressed the appropriate button. He looked at the instructions again and nervously pushed the one marked 'A' and his money fell with a resounding clang. She was still there, at the other end of the line, waiting.

'It's John Trevarrick,' he said. 'From Cornwall. Do you remember?'

There was a second's silence and he felt a sudden alarm. Then a reassuring friendliness filled the distance between them.

'Of course, of course. Where are you?'

'At the station—Temple Meads. I've a few days' holiday and I wondered if——' He broke off awkwardly. The absurd position he had put himself in suddenly dawned. You couldn't just turn up on someone's doorstep and expect to be given board and lodging. Well, he had some money. He would find a cheap hotel. Perhaps Margaret's family might offer him accommodation later. 'I'm staying in Bristol and wondered if Graham and I could meet?'

'Of course,' the calm, reassuring voice continued. 'You know his office, don't you? It's next to the Cathedral—Bantry and Son, in Cathedral Chambers. He'll be free at lunchtime. Why don't you go round there and call on him? He'll be so pleased to see you. Then you can come over here for the evening if you're free. Can you come for dinner?'

She must have suddenly realised that he was not so confident as he was trying to appear, sensed his insecurity. 'If you could stay with us for a night or two while you're here we should like that, and I'm sure Graham would be very pleased. The spare room is always ready!'

John breathed a sigh of relief. 'Thank you, Mrs Bantry,' he said. 'I'll call on Graham and let you know later.' It would be better to see his friend before making any arrangements, he thought.

He found the office, and knocked at the door marked 'Enquiries'. Following the command to come in, he entered and stood awkwardly before the typist who confronted him. She seemed to be only about sixteen, and her frank, interested stare was embarrassing.

'Mr Bantry?' he asked. 'Could you tell him that I'm here? I won't keep him if he's busy.'

'Name, please.' Her tone was brisk and efficient. 'Would you mind waiting a moment? I'll see if he's free.' She indicated a chair, and he sat obediently, wishing himself miles away, back under his own familiar skies.

His doubts and worries vanished when Graham strode into the small room, his tall frame seeming to fill it. He held out both his hands to his friend.

'John! How wonderful to see you after all this time. Where are you staying? How long? What a terrific surprise!' Then there was a sudden silence and his face clouded a little, but only momentarily. 'I'm afraid I've a client in at the moment, but I'll be free at twelve-thirty. Can we meet for lunch?'

An hour or so later the two men sat opposite each other in a little restaurant in a quiet street off the city centre. Each was weighing up the other, wondering about the effects of peacetime, not knowing quite what to talk about at first, and when most of their news was exchanged there was a difficult silence. John broke it at last with the question he was longing to ask.

'Do you ever see anything of Margaret? I want to look her up while I'm here, of course.'

Fear clutched at him suddenly. There was a guarded and strange look on Graham's face. John remembered that she had mentioned something about him once in one of her early letters to his mother. He had come into the shop where she worked, apparently. Perhaps they. . .He couldn't bear it. It would be the final irony, the greatest humiliation, and his flagging self-confidence wouldn't be able to cope with that. He remembered suggesting that they should meet, but that was when he and Sybil. . .

Graham was obviously fumbling for words. 'She's not living with her parents now. But I expect you knew?'

'No. No, I didn't. Where, then?'

'In her grandmother's house in St Pauls. She lives with another girl, a lodger called Dottie. She's a good sort and keeps Margaret company.'

'You see a lot of her, then?'

'A bit. Nothing between us, though, if that's what you're thinking.'

John flushed. Were his thoughts so obvious? 'We were fairly close on the farm and I've known her since she was quite little,' he said, making unnecessary excuses. 'I should like to look her up.'

Another silence. It seemed to go on and on and hang in the air, heavy with some ominous feeling that John couldn't fathom.

'What's wrong?'

He had to know. There was obviously something that Graham didn't want to tell him, and he was alarmed, frightened. If Margaret was in any sort of trouble then he could help her, carry her off to Cornwall and to peace and security.

He dragged his worried thoughts back to his companion. 'There's something you're not telling me!'

Graham stared at him and still didn't speak.

'What's the address? I'm going now, straight away.'

'Calm yourself down, there's a good chap. She's been a bit poorly, but she's fine now. You can't go rushing off there straight away, just out of the blue. Might give her a heart attack!'

His tone was light and bantering again, and John relaxed a little.

'I'll drive you over there tonight,' Graham went on. 'I might be able to get a message to her via Dottie. She's a teacher and I can find out her school telephone number. Then we could take both girls out for a meal. They'd like that.'

So it was all right. Graham's tone implied that there was nothing wrong. Margaret had been ill, that was all, and now they were going to make a foursome for the evening. It suddenly seemed so pleasant and normal that John laughed in relief.

'Your mother asked me to dinner,' he said. 'I'll have to telephone and tell her we won't be there.'

'Don't worry—I'll ring from the office. Are you staying with us, or have you made any other arrangements? I hope you haven't.'

'I'd love to stay.'

Graham looked around. 'No bags?'

'At the left luggage place on the station.'

'Can you meet me at the office at five-thirty? We'll pick them up then.' Graham looked anxiously at his watch. 'I shall have to rush now—I'm still only a very junior junior in spite of the name. Got to make a good impression and all that!'

Graham left him sitting there with another cup of coffee and hurried back across the Cathedral Green, his thoughts in a turmoil of indecision. He had to see Margaret and work out some sort of strategy before he took John to her house. He ran up the stairs as fast as the steep winding steps would allow and pleaded some urgent business. Could he have an hour off?

Dennis Bantry was the senior partner in the firm. The years that Graham had been a prisoner of war had been one of the greatest ordeals of his life. This grandson was his hope and his deepest joy. He looked at the young man standing before him and smiled.

'Of course, Graham—take as much time as you want. I won't ask any questions, but I hope it's nothing serious.'

'No, Grandfather,' Graham lied. 'I'll be back as soon as I can.'

He reversed the gleaming old Austin out of the parking space behind the office. He was grateful to his father for the gift of the car and he lavished much loving care on it every weekend. He drove carefully in spite of his anxiety, or perhaps because of it, and was soon in the drab little street where Margaret lived. Unaware this time of the stares of the children playing in the road, he parked at the kerbside, and looking neither to right nor left strode up to the front door and rang the bell. She had to be in. She must be there!

'Graham! This is a funny time to visit. Come in.'

He saw the welcoming smile die as she searched his face and obviously saw the concern that he couldn't hide, but he followed her through the narrow passage into the back kitchen before breaking his news.

'It's John,' he said. 'He's here in Bristol. He wants to come to see you.'

She sat down abruptly at the table and stared at him. He could see the dawning of panic on her face and he wondered for the thousandth time whether John was the father of her child. He must be. Surely there couldn't be anyone else. Yet why then was she so terrified of his knowing?

In spite of her dismay she was surprisingly calm. 'Have you seen him?'

'We've just lunched together. He could only get a stand-in for the farm at the last minute, apparently, and decided to come and surprise us. He came to the office.'

'What are we going to do?'

The fact that she included him so completely in the plans that had to be made brought a strange glow, and an overwhelming sense of her need for his protection.

He didn't understand the reasons, but he had to shield her from whatever in her past caused her such anxiety. He wanted to put his arms around her and hold her tightly where the taunts and the gibes and the sneers couldn't reach, but he knew he could not. Not now anyway, not yet.

'He'll have to know!' he said.

Margaret looked out of the window to the tiny back garden where Miriam was sleeping peacefully in her shabby old pram. She was wrapped up against the February cold, and when Graham followed her glance he couldn't see anything of her at all beneath the shawls.

'Isn't it a bit cold for her out there today?' he asked, prevaricating, putting off for a second the need to think, to decide.

Margaret laughed a little. 'Of course not. The sun's shining, and fresh air is good for babies. She'll get nice rosy cheeks.'

Suddenly he had to be sure. If John was the father he must know. His heart sank and his eyes almost misted over as he looked at the girl before him. She wouldn't need his protection, in that case, or his love. Love. It was the first time he had admitted the word to himself.

He reached across the table and put his hands over hers. She didn't pull them away as she usually did. There had never been anything very physical between them.

'Is it him, Margaret?' he said quietly, and felt that his whole future was poised waiting for her answer.

She stared at him for a moment in silence, and then she shook her head.

'No, Graham. Miriam isn't his baby.'

He wanted to ask her more, probe and find out, but he looked deep into her clear brown eyes and was silent. He squeezed her hands, then got up from the table.

'Thank you,' he said simply. 'I told him we would take you both out for a meal—you and Dottie. We can take the baby too, can't we?'

He was making it sound so simple, and that was how he wanted it to be. It was how he had stopped John from making a headlong rush down here without him.

'Shall I tell him first?' he asked. 'Do you want to release me from that promise I made to you?'

She was quiet for a moment, considering, and when she spoke at last her words were matter-of-fact as if they were talking about a new job or a simple everyday occurrence. He knew that beneath the calm exterior was a seething torrent of worry.

'If you could I should be grateful. See if it's possible.'

He too kept a serene shell to hide the suffocating anxiety. Again the question that tormented him: if the baby wasn't John's then whose was it? She wasn't the kind of girl to. . .He desperately marshalled his thoughts. He had to take control of himself, of the whole situation.

'We'll be here about six-thirty, then. I'll take him for a drink or something first.'

He bent and lightly kissed Margaret on the cheek, a brotherly kiss meant for comfort.

'Trust me,' he said as he got into the car, and she smiled at him, trusting. It was all there was to do.

It was already dark and cold when John returned to the office. He was glad to get into the warmth of the small waiting-room, and within minutes Graham joined him.

'Come on, then,' he said brightly. 'To the station to get your things, and then we'll find somewhere to get some coffee or something before we call on the girls. Better not arrive too early.'

John sat in the passenger seat of the car and for a moment envied his friend. His easy self-confidence, his ability to drive, even his possession of this vehicle, were all desirable attributes that he felt he would never attain. He thought of the cart at home and Daisy, the small pony who had been faithfully pulling it for so many years. Well, he loved Daisy in a way, and he smiled to himself at the incongruity of his thoughts.

They retrieved the battered suitcase and stowed it in the car.

'What do you want to drink?' Graham asked. 'Coffee or something stronger?'

'Coffee,' John said. He wasn't used to alcohol. Good Methodists knew it was the ultimate evil, and although he didn't totally agree with his mother's ardent belief in this direction he felt that this wasn't the time to start a rebellion. He must keep a clear head for the important evening with Margaret!

'Then I know a nice little ice-cream parlour where they do passable coffee. We'll go there.'

The two men pushed through the door into the bright, welcoming glitter of the small café. It was crowded with young people, and John immediately felt old. These others had missed the war; you could see that by their faces. Two girls were just getting up to leave and Graham grabbed the seats they had vacated.

'Sit there and keep the table,' he directed, and he pushed through to the counter, returning eventually with two large mugs of steaming coffee. He stirred two spoonfuls of sugar into his, and John again felt a slight unease. He had lived in the camp with Graham for countless months. He knew him pretty well, and there seemed to be something wrong.

'There's something you don't know,' Graham said

suddenly, and he didn't look at John, but kept on stirring the swirling coffee and staring into its brown froth. 'Margaret has a baby, a little girl, Miriam.'

For a moment the words didn't mean anything to John. There was no sense he could make of them. Then they sank into his consciousness and he could feel the colour drain from his face.

'What do you mean, baby? She can't. . .'

'Awful shock, I know, but it's true.'

John stood up, fists clenched. All the words that he had learned in the Army and at camp and that his upbringing had locked into him, words never spoken, flooded into his mind, and he looked at the man opposite him with more hatred than he had ever felt for anyone in his life, even the Nips. He wanted to scream the filth at him in the loudest voice he could muster and run from the place into the cold and the blessed anonymity of dark, unknown streets. Instead he stood silent and white, swaying in a lost limbo of time until he saw, eventually, Graham's instant concern and sudden understanding.

'She's not my baby. Not mine, John—I swear to you. She won't say whose. Sit down and we'll talk. We're going there, remember.'

The calm, quiet words penetrated the angry recesses of John's mind and he flopped back on to the chair. He was dimly aware of staring faces around them, and he concentrated desperately on curbing his rage. He was left with a numbing emptiness.

'I can't go and see her now, not after this!'

'You must. I've told her, and she's expecting you. She's suffered terribly and she's been very brave. She's changed. Please come.'

John stared at the dimly lighted shabby streets as they

drove from the city centre towards St Pauls. His thoughts were such a tangled web of conflicting emotions that he couldn't bring himself to talk very much to Graham. The idea of Margaret pregnant, bringing forth, and now caring for some strange unwanted infant was totally repugnant to him. All his hopeful dreams of the past weeks lay ruthlessly shattered in the abyss of some other man's passion. Then a sudden unthinkable suspicion flashed across his mind. Karl!

'When did you say it was born?' He couldn't even bear to give the child gender or humanity.

'February—early. The seventh, I think.'

There was silence while John calculated. Nine months back, nine months! 'The bitch, the stinking bitch! Let me out, Graham. I won't see her!'

The car swerved slightly and Graham pulled it over to the kerbside. He switched off the engine. 'Steady on,' he said, angry now. 'What on earth's the matter?'

'Some German swine, that's what's the matter! Karl Schormann. Worked on our farm and was billeted with us, in fact. I knew she fancied him.' He felt sick. He was going to be violently sick. 'Open this bloody door, for God's sake!' The inhibitions were gone. He would swear as much as he liked.

Graham leaned across and released the catch, and John lurched out and vomited into the gutter. Then he sank back into the seat and closed his eyes.

'And I thought I was in love with her. I just hate her guts. To think of her with that damned bloody Hun!'

They sat in silence for a time and John could feel the anger slowly draining out of him. He had no strength left for the luxury of intense rage. The weakness that he had been fighting for the past three years swept over him, and he put his hands over his face and wept.

CHAPTER FOURTEEN

1948

AN HOUR and a couple of whiskies later John stood at the front door of Margaret's house, pale, shaken, slightly drunk, and still angry. Graham was beside him, firm and silent.

It was Dottie who answered their knocking. She stood and looked at them, peering at John in the dim glow of the street lamp. The light was behind them and she couldn't see very clearly, but he seemed fairly ordinary and not very fearsome.

She had been regaled with all Margaret's fears and worries as soon as she'd got home, tired from a day's teaching.

'I can't see why you're so scared of this John,' she had said after listening to her friend's outpourings. 'He's not a relation or anything. He has no hold on you. You're a free person, and this isn't the last century!'

But she had not been able to comfort Margaret very much, and she felt an outsider anyway. Perhaps she didn't fully understand. She would just stay around in the background and try to give some sort of support if it was needed.

'Hello, Graham,' she said. 'Come in.'

They followed her through the dark passage into the cheerfulness of the back kitchen. Margaret was nervously poking the fire, needing its warmth.

Dottie stood back and watched.

'Hello, John,' Margaret said simply, and then she

held out both her hands to him. It was a friendly but pleading gesture.

He stood stiff and unbending, and on his face was a strange mixture of anger and sadness together. 'Graham told me,' he said. 'He made me come.'

Margaret dropped her hands helplessly to her side and looked at him and then at Graham. There was a silence in the small room broken only by the crackle of the fire, and then suddenly by a wail from upstairs. Miriam was crying.

'Go and deal with your German bastard,' he said suddenly and unexpectedly. 'I never want to see you again!' and he turned on his heel and strode out. The angry words were a surprise, even to himself. It was the child's crying that had brought everything into focus from a nightmare to a horrible reality. He wrenched the front door open and ran from them into the dark and the cold, caring not at all where he went, or what happened to himself or to any of them. He knew that all the dreams he had so carefully cherished were shattered into a thousand fragments, shattered by a small child he had never seen and whom he hated with every ounce of feeling he could muster. He hated her for just being. Her very existence made his own insufferable.

He pulled his coat round his body against the chilling wind and walked the length of the street and into another and still another. They were all alike. Then he came to a wider road with shops, one or two still open. The misery and the shock, combined with the whisky that Graham had insisted he drink, and the terrible sickness before it, began to affect him and he swayed uncertainly. He suddenly realised that he was ill and lost. He had no idea how far he had come or how to get back to Graham's car. He stumbled into the doorway of a newsagent's and fell.

'Get out of my shop, you damned drunken lout!'

He heard the words through a haze of pain and then there was a gentler voice.

'He bain't drunk, Sid. Can't you see the lad's ill?'

'Ill, my foot—drunk as a lord! I can smell the whisky.'

John struggled to his feet and a woman took his arm and led him to a rickety chair in front of the counter. One or two others had gathered and were looking at him curiously. A mug of water was pushed at him and he drank gratefully, and slowly the room ceased its spinning.

'Thank you,' he said. 'I'm sorry for all the trouble.'

He wasn't sure how long as he sat there. It could have been five minutes or an hour, but suddenly he saw the girl and his fuddled brain recognised her. It was the one who had opened the door to them—the one with a funny name. He had registered the hair, the flying blonde hair, that was all. A bright red beret sat on top of it now and she was smiling at the woman in the shop.

'Yes, I know who he is. I'll take him.'

It sounded as though he was a stray dog, he thought, and he looked up helplessly. He would have to go with her. There was nothing else he could do.

'I'm glad I've found you at last,' she said. 'You look as though you need a good meal. Come on, I know just the place.'

John felt that food was the last thing in the world he wanted just then, but the girl was taking his arm, helping him to his feet, and he rose unsteadily and leaned on her young, sturdy body, glad of her strength and her direction.

They found a small café just along the road, and Dottie took his hand and led him to a secluded table in a corner.

'I'm starving,' she said. 'What shall we order?'

He still hadn't spoken, and the smell of food caused his stomach to heave again.

'A pot of tea for two,' he heard her saying, 'and some soup and bread.' Then she smiled at him. 'You've got to eat—you'll feel better. The soup in this place is home-made and good. I come here quite often when I can't bother to do anything myself.'

She was wearing a thick tweed coat, and he watched her take it off and drape it over the chair on which she was sitting. He could see the shape of her small, firm breasts beneath the red jumper. She seemed to be fond of red, not a bit like the brown, mousy Sybil, or even Margaret. His thoughts nosedived again as the events of the evening flashed into his brain. Margaret!

'I can't eat!'

'Please try—just a little. Just for me.'

Her smile was dazzling, and the vitality and brightness that seemed to spring from her gradually penetrated his cloud of bleak depression. He stared down into the thick soup that was placed in front of him, and at the fresh, crisp white roll, and slowly he took his spoon and sipped. The food warmed him and eventually he felt his head clearing a little.

'Thank you,' he said quietly, and he looked up and saw that she was staring at him. She smiled again.

'We'd better go and find Graham. He was very worried when you disappeared. He's probably still looking for you.'

'How did you know where I was?'

'I didn't. I just guessed you might be here by the shops.'

The waitress put the bill on the table in front of him and Dottie picked it up.

'No,' he said. 'That's mine, please.'

She handed it over, and he searched in his pocket for the money. He counted it out, remembered to add something for a tip, and then unsteadily rose to his feet. Dottie was putting on her coat. He moved round to her side of the table and awkwardly helped her. He was aware of her perfume. It was spicy and heavy, and it suited her.

'Let's go, then,' she said, and he followed her out into the dark and cold of the street.

Once out of the light of the café Dottie took his hand and squeezed it. 'Will you come back?' she said quietly. 'Please.'

He knew she meant to the house. He had eaten because she'd asked it of him, and now he felt drawn by some unknown force, perhaps just the strength of her personality. He knew that he would do again what she wished.

'I don't want to.'

'I know that. It's been tough. Tough for Margaret too, though.'

They walked together along the dark pavements and stood at last before the front door. The car was standing at the kerb, and John looked at it with a sense of relief. It was an escape.

'I'll wait outside,' he said. 'Just tell Graham I'm here.'

He saw Dottie's disappointed look and then she disappeared through the front door, leaving it open, inviting him to go in. Instead he went to the car, longing for its comfort and safe enclosure. It was locked.

'Graham's not here,' said Dottie. 'He must be still looking for you. I'll go and try to find him.'

She had come out again, and he noticed that she was still wearing the beret and that it made a bright flash of colour in the greyness of the night. She moved over to him.

'Do go in, John,' she said. 'You're not well, and it's cold.' She looked up at him and smiled her encouragement, and then she laughed a little. 'She won't eat you, you silly!'

She took his hand again and half pulled him towards the open door, and he followed reluctantly, drawn by the warmth and the light. Once more he felt a victim of circumstances he couldn't control. She guided him gently down the passage, pushed the door of the kitchen open and went before him into the room. Margaret was sitting at the fireside, and she half rose as he entered, but the baby was at her breast, and he noticed her nervousness as she pulled the shawl over, hiding the child.

Dottie took his coat from him and pushed him into the large, comfortable armchair.

'I'll have to go,' she said. 'Do you know where Graham might have gone, Maggie?'

'He was going towards the park,' she replied. 'Look there first.'

Dottie went out quickly into the night and he was alone with Margaret. They didn't speak for a long time. He could hear the baby noises, noises of contented suckling, and he felt he had never been so embarrassed and so desperate to be elsewhere in his life.

At last it was finished, and Margaret got to her feet. He watched her take the child and walk out of the room. Strangely he wanted to look, to push the shawl aside and torture himself with the sight of this baby who would have the blue eyes and the blonde hair of the man he now hated more than he had ever hated anyone in his life, even the guards in the camp. She came back alone, and then she took the heavy black kettle from the fire and carried it into the scullery. He could hear the rattle of cups.

'Tea?'

'Yes, please.'

She carried a teapot in and set it before the fire, and he watched her pour milk and tea into two china cups. She handed him one and he stirred two large spoonfuls of sugar into it.

'I'm sorry, John,' she said. 'Sorry about the shock. I didn't want you to know, or Aunt Annie. Not for a long time, anyway.'

Another long silence. Another fumbling for words. His desire to swear and shout had gone. His anger was still there, but quiet and controlled now, mingled with an emptiness and an unutterable despondency. 'I was going to ask you to marry me.'

He saw her grip the cup and watched the colour drain from her face.

'I couldn't have done—you must know that.'

'No, I didn't know. Oh, yes, I remember that time on the beach, but things change. Well, it's all over now. Karl has seen to that.' He could feel the anger beginning to rise again. 'How could you? A Jerry, a bloody Jerry?'

'I loved him, John,' she said simply, and he stared at her and saw for the first time the grief on her face, and he dimly perceived something of her suffering, the suffering that Dottie had mentioned. Well, he wanted her to suffer. He was almost scared of the strength of his hatred in that fleeting moment.

'I don't want him to know, ever,' she went on, and her voice was urgent, frightened.

'Well, I'll not tell—you can count on that. I never want to have anything more to do with him. He's back in his damned precious Fatherland now anyway, and from what I hear about the Russians he won't be able to leave, so you're safe.'

She looked at him with pain in her eyes, but the pain was not for him, and he knew that for his own sanity he must get away from here and forget this girl. He heard Dottie's voice at that moment, and Graham's deeper one.

'I've found him!' she said as she burst exuberantly into the room. 'Now what about some food?'

'I think we'll get home now,' Graham said. 'My mother will be wondering where we are.'

John looked at his friend with gratitude. All he wanted was a bed and a quiet room where he could be alone, where he could sleep. He had had enough of today! Graham understood that need.

Dottie was obviously aware of his feelings too. She took his coat from the chair where he had dumped it and held it out to him. She smiled as she did so.

'We'll have that meal another time,' she said. 'I shan't let you forget.'

She took his hand and squeezed it as she had done before. and the gesture was warm and friendly. It seemed to say that she understood, and could share his grief.

'Thank you for rescuing me,' he said, and he smiled at her and was comforted. He turned to Margaret. 'I'm sorry for my outburst, and I won't tell my mother about your secret. Or anyone else.'

Then he turned abruptly and walked up the passage and stood with his hand on the car door waiting for Graham.

The two girls sat either side of the dying fire, and for a while there was nothing to say. Each was lost in a maze of her own thoughts, disturbed and upset by the events of the evening. At last it was Dottie who broke the silence.

'I think they're both in love with you. Only that could account for the strength of John's feelings about the baby.'

'He told me how he felt once,' Margaret said. 'It was one lovely autumn evening after we'd been swimming.' For a moment she was back in time and place and she could almost hear the sea and feel the warm sand beneath her feet. 'He suffered so much in the prison camp and he wasn't fully recovered. I hated telling him that there could be nothing between us.'

'He's a long way from well even now,' Dottie said. 'I've met others who've been prisoners of the Japs, and it takes years. Perhaps the scars will be there always. That was probably why he behaved as he did tonight. He couldn't cope with the stress.'

'Graham seems to be all right. He went through the same trauma.'

'Graham's different, tougher somehow. More resilient.' Dottie got up and went to the scullery door. 'Anyway,' she said, making an effort to change the subject, 'I'm going to prepare something for us to eat. I've only had a bowl of soup and it looks as if you've had nothing.'

Margaret laughed and looked at her friend with affection. She wasn't sure whether she believed in a friendly God any more, but it was certainly a benevolent deity who had sent Dottie to her. Or perhaps it was just good luck. Either way she was very, very grateful.

'There are two eggs in the larder and I got our cheese ration today,' she said. 'Let's be extravagant and make omelettes.'

'You know,' said Dottie as she carefully broke the

precious eggs into a basin, 'I like John. I think I like him very much!'

It was Dottie who retrieved John's holiday from total disaster.

'It's half-term,' she told Graham when he called alone the following day. 'I've got three days off this week. I'll take him around if you like, show him a bit of Bristol. I don't suppose he's very keen on being by himself while you're at work.'

'I'd be very grateful,' he said. 'He's having a rest this morning, but he'll be fine tomorrow, I should think. He was talking about going back to Cornwall, but apparently he's hired this man to look after the farm for a week, so he might as well make the most of it.'

The weather was kind, and the winter sun cheered John. He felt at ease with Dottie. They went to the zoo, walked on the Clifton Downs, stared in shop windows, enjoyed the museum, and spent hours sitting in small cafés eating little but talking, talking until almost every subject that they could imagine was covered. By the end of the three days they both felt that they knew each other very well, and liked what they had discovered.

'I'd love to show you the farm,' John said on the last day. He was going back on Saturday and suddenly realised that he would miss this girl. She gave him confidence and strength, attributes that he always lacked in Margaret's presence, and she was fun to be with, made him laugh constantly, and he needed to laugh. He felt his vigour returning with every hour that he spent with her. Even Sybil with her quiet, unassuming ways hadn't made him feel like this. It wasn't all one-sided either. Beneath Dottie's bright exterior there was a vulnerability that she had confessed to him that afternoon as they sat staring down at the impressive Avon Gorge in the winter sunshine. The river wound its way far below them, sensuously curving between steep wooded banks, the trees bare now, and the graceful span of the Suspension Bridge seeming at that distance to be ethereal and insubstantial, a thing of fantasy.

'I haven't got anyone,' she said, staring at the stupendous view but not really seeing it. 'I was brought up in a children's home. I managed to get a scholarship to grammar school and determined to do well. Then the war came and the Wrens, and the emergency training schemes for teachers, and here I am.' She shrugged her shoulders. 'There was never anyone to tell me I was doing well, no one to give any praise when exam results arrived. It wasn't easy.'

'Life seldom is. Easier for some than others, perhaps.' It was John's turn now to administer the comfort. He leaned towards her and kissed her lightly, and they walked along the path to the bus-stop hand in hand. Suddenly the world held hope again and life was good.

As the train carried him back to Cornwall the next day and to everything he loved, he marvelled at the quick and easy friendship he had found with Dottie. Perhaps it would develop into something more. Perhaps not. He wasn't going to rush anything now. It wouldn't do to get hurt again.

CHAPTER FIFTEEN

1948

'I DON'T love her, Graham,' Margaret said, and there were tears in her eyes as she looked down at the baby lying fast asleep in the old pram in the back yard. 'I haven't any love for her at all. I've tried, but I can't make it come. I've always suffered from an excess of guilt about everything, but this is the worst.'

Graham didn't offer any solutions or any cheap comforts. He couldn't understand Margaret's feelings. Miriam was beautiful, meriting love. He couldn't understand himself either. Men weren't supposed to feel much for tiny babies, especially men like himself who had always lived in a man's world and gone through a tough and terrible war. The war! Because of it this child had come to be. He looked at the gently breathing baby and wondered if it was just because he loved the mother that he felt the stirrings of love for the child.

Margaret was staring at him. He became aware of the intensity of her eyes upon him.

'Do you mind about Karl?' she said.

The question surprised him. She stood with her hands on the handle of the pram, wanting an answer, desperate to know. He could see that. Since John's revelations he had frequently questioned himself about his own feelings. He hadn't had much to do with Germans during the war, but his parents had had friends in Germany a long time ago. He vaguely remembered their visit to his home once, or was it twice? It was a memory dredged from the forgotten past, dim and uncertain, obscured by the years. There had been a little boy about his own age. They had played together in the large garden of the house in Clifton, and he recalled his amazement that this five-year-old could only speak alien words he couldn't understand. War was a strange phenomenon. You fought and killed, and the man you were killing could have been your friend. He stared down again at the baby in the pram, the child that Margaret couldn't love, and a deep wave of sadness engulfed him.

'No, I don't mind,' he said. 'Margaret, will you marry me?'

The words were spoken quickly and without premeditation. He knew suddenly that it was the one thing in the world he wanted at this moment. He could, in some small measure, put right some of the wrongs of the previous decade of war and destruction. He loved Margaret, and he loved her baby—loved Miriam more than her mother did! The new understanding surprised him, and he looked at the two of them and knew that this was right, the thing he had to do. It had been there at the back of his conscious thoughts for months, not given form or substance until now.

He was aware of Margaret's amazement, shock almost. She was staring at him as though he had taken leave of his senses.

'Graham, you don't know what you're saying! You can't take on another man's baby, and a woman who. . .'

'Who what? If you're going to say that you don't love me I'm ready for that, expected it.'

'Then why?'

'I love you very much. I think I always have, but I suspected that John must be Miriam's father. He's always been there between us somehow. Now all that's changed.'

'But it's not changed. Don't you see? It's Karl who comes between us instead, and that must be even worse.'

'Worse?'

'Yes, the enemy and all that!'

Graham sighed and took Margaret's hands and held them in his. Miriam was still fast asleep. 'Come inside,' he said.

Obediently she allowed herself to be led into the warmth of the house and she sat down at the table beneath the window. The pram, standing near the old stone wall of the yard, was visible from there and Graham saw her staring at it with unseeing eyes.

'You're being dramatic,' he said. 'The war's over—it's been over for nearly three years. The Germans aren't our enemies any more. That isn't the problem.'

'There are plenty more, though.'

'I love you, Margaret.'

He kissed her gently, and suddenly all the passion that had been so strictly denied for so many months came rushing to the fore and he had to fight harder than he had ever done to resist it. He knew he mustn't hurry her.

She turned her head away from him for a moment, but then responded and returned the kiss, surprising him with her warmth. Then they both heard the key in the front door and Dottie bouncing through it in her noisy, exuberant manner.

'Hello, folks,' she said, throwing her battered old tapestry bag on the chair. 'Phew, what a day! I've got forty-five little horrors now. Just had three more landed on me.'

Suddenly she looked at Graham and Margaret.

'Gosh, have I disturbed something? Can I just make a cup of tea and then I'll disappear?'

'Don't disappear!' Her coming at that moment was just right for Margaret, crystallised her thoughts in a way she didn't understand. 'We'll all have one.'

Graham, misunderstanding her obvious relief as she pulled away from him, was saddened, but there was time. He would wait. 'I won't stop for the tea,' he said. 'I'll be in touch.'

Margaret walked with him to the door. She put her hand on his to prevent him opening it. 'Thank you, Graham,' she whispered. 'Yes, I'll marry you!'

For a moment he couldn't believe the words he was hearing. 'You mean it? You're saying yes?'

'Yes, yes. Oh, yes! What a silly word, but yes.'

He pulled her into his arms, then held her back a little and looked into her eyes. 'My precious girl. My precious, precious girl,' he said, and crushed her tightly and kissed her desperately with all the longing and hope and dreams of the years of war and prison and peace. 'But I thought——'

She put her hands over his mouth to prevent further words. 'Never mind what you thought,' she said, taking control. 'Go now. Please go now, but come back soon.'

'This evening. About eight?'

'Yes—about eight!'

Margaret shut the door behind him and leaned on it and closed her eyes. What had she done? Why had she done it? Why make so sudden a decision? The words had seemed to come from her of their own volition, without conscious reflection or resolve. She gathered herself together and walked slowly through to where Dottie was pouring the newly brewed tea.

'I'm going to marry Graham,' she announced, and she sank down into the depths of the old armchair and waited for the response. She had no idea what it would be. There was a moment's silence, and then Dottie put the teapot down, nearly crashing it into the milk jug in her surprise. She clapped her hands, and Margaret looked at her friend and saw the delight in her clear blue eyes.

'That's wonderful! Just wonderful. About the most wonderful news I've heard for a long time. Tell me all about it.'

She turned and retrieved the teapot and continued her pouring and stirring, eventually handing over a brimming cup.

The wedding was in May.

'No, not on my birthday,' Margaret said, remembering that golden day a year before. The thought was firmly banished. 'How about the fifteenth?'

So it was fixed, and the two sets of parents eyed each other with a little suspicion at their first meeting.

'In our parish church, of course,' said Graham's mother. 'The vicar's a friend. I'll be able to persuade him,' and Sarah Seddon sighed.

'I'd hoped for the synagogue,' she confided to her husband later.

'Just be grateful for such a reliable man for our Margaret. It's not many would take on a baby too,' said Samuel Seddon drily.

'There are so many nice, respectable girls he could have chosen,' Iris Bantry complained.

'It's his choice. He's a grown man. I like Margaret anyway. She'll be good for him.' Alan Bantry, for over thirty years a GP in the same practice, had had long experience of dealing with people, and there was a strength and resilience that he recognised in Margaret.

'Graham's still got a few mental wounds from that damned camp. He needs a good, steady woman.'

'So you really think that's what she is, steady?'

'Sure of it. Stop worrying.'

It was the last word on the matter, and, although spoken only to his wife, seemed to penetrate the minds of all the others involved, and when Samuel Seddon walked down the aisle of the ancient parish church with his daughter on his arm he tried to forget the aversion he had always felt for the bastion of Gentile domination. He was proud of his lovely daughter and happy for her. That was all that mattered.

Sarah Seddon sat awkwardly in the front pew. The altar cross was an offence. At the cross Jews had been forced to convert or die in countless pogroms all over Europe. She had never thought to find herself sitting peacefully in front of the gleaming gold symbol. She looked across at Graham standing stiffly, nervously, then saw him turn as her daughter came down the aisle, and the smile on his face was enough to set all her fears at rest, and to smother all her misgivings.

Dottie felt foolish in the long dress that Margaret had bought for her. It had taken so many of their precious clothing coupons too. She hoped it would be of some use afterwards, and that she didn't look too silly in it—especially as John was standing there at the front with Graham. John! She blushed and laughed at herself a little for her feelings.

John stood beside his friend, hoping that none of the turmoil of emotions he was feeling were showing in his face. He had been amazed at Graham's decision to marry Margaret and at her ready acceptance, and he had been angry too, although he couldn't easily understand his anger. Was it because he was afraid that Margaret wouldn't make Graham happy? Or was he still jealous? He didn't know, and he was trying desperately not to care.

When he had been asked to be best man he had experienced many hours of anguish and heart-searching. The last thing in the world that he'd wanted to do was stand there at the altar waiting for Margaret to come down the aisle! It was only when he'd realised that Dottie would be close behind her that he began to feel he could go through with it. Since his visit to Bristol her letters had been arriving regularly at the farm, fat, bulging letters full of cheerfulness and fun. They had brought him great happiness, given him self-worth again and a precious hope for the future. So he stood there beside Graham, and when the strains of the Bridal March brought everyone to their feet he turned and looked not at Margaret but at Dottie, Dottie in that crazy dress! He saw the welcome in her eyes and the ready grin, and he smiled and was content.

He had promised not to say anything to his mother about Karl when he told her of Miriam's birth. Annie Trevarrick must never know. She wouldn't count up the months—at least, they all hoped not.

She didn't. She sat beside Margaret's mother, wearing a new outfit and a hat of enormous proportions. Keeping this in place had taken most of her thoughts as she'd walked through the churchyard. It was a windy day. And now inside she found that she couldn't tilt her head back to get a better look at the bride in case her difficult headgear fell off into the pew behind. Fancy Margaret and that nice Graham having to get married like that, though! It must have happened soon after she left the farm too. Ought to have had more sense, both of them. Well, it just showed what living in a town could do for you!

Margaret walked up the aisle and her usual guilt

surfaced for a moment as she thought of her little daughter. She was at home being looked after by a friend. Graham had wanted her to be here with them all, 'where she belongs', he had said, but Margaret had insisted that Miriam must not be present, and had got her own way eventually. This day was just for them. She looked at him as he stood waiting for her and she felt the beginnings of love in her heart. Karl must become a memory, was almost that already. Precious, but only a dream of the past. Graham was here, a flesh-and-blood man, here in the present, waiting for her. She saw him turn and smile, and her heart leapt with happiness and peace. They were two commodities that were often in short supply in even the best of marriages, and she knew that they would always be hers as long as she kept faith with Graham. And she would. There would never be anyone else for her now.

Graham turned to look at his bride, and as he saw her walking towards him he knew he had reached his safe haven. After his prison years he needed a haven. Everyone thought he had fully recovered, and mostly he had, but he was aware of a need deep within himself of another source of strength and stability to turn to sometimes. They both needed those things and would give, each to the other.

'Wilt thou, Graham, have this woman. . .?'

And his reply rang out firm and clear.

'I will.'

PART TWO

MIRIAM

CHAPTER SIXTEEN

1958

'HAPPY birthday, darling,' Graham said. 'Ten today,' and he put a large white envelope beside Miriam's dish of cereal. She looked up at him and smiled, and then opened it carefully. Inside was a card and a key. She knew that key. It fitted the garden shed. Excited now, she jumped up, breakfast left uneaten. Margaret started to protest, but Graham, sharing his daughter's enthusiasm, took her hand and together they rushed out of the kitchen and into the garden. Miriam fitted the key into the lock, opened the door, and there before her was the gleaming new bicycle she had so desperately wanted. She stood silent for a moment, staring at it, and then threw her arms round Graham.

'Daddy, thank you! Thank you so much. It's just super! The right colours, everything!'

She hugged her father and planted a milky kiss on his cheek, then she pulled away from him and went over to the new blue and silver Raleigh and stroked its shining handlebars.

'Can I try it out now, right now?'

'Just down the drive and back,' Graham said, 'and then go and finish your breakfast. We don't want to make Mummy cross on your birthday, do we?'

He watched her cycling unsteadily down the long drive, and at the end she wobbled around and waved to him before coming back. His heart went out to her, and he marvelled at the amount of love he had for this child, just as much as, perhaps even more than, for his two sons, twins, born a year after his marriage to Margaret. He had legally adopted Miriam and she had never questioned her birth. He knew that one day she would start wondering about dates, and he dreaded that time. Margaret had made him promise never to tell her about Karl.

'Hurry up or you'll all be late!' Margaret called from the kitchen door.

'Lucky you,' Charles said as he pushed past his mother and watched his sister's unsteady progress up the drive. 'Can I have a bike like that for my birthday too?'

'Not this year. Nine is too young. When you're ten like your sister, perhaps,' Graham said, and he ruffled his son's dark hair. 'Now go and get your things ready for school.'

Back in the kitchen Miriam opened the rest of her birthday cards.

'This one is from Dottie and Uncle John,' she said, 'and there's one from Auntie Annie as well. They've sent me a whole pound note each. And there's a letter for you inside too, Mummy.'

Margaret had looked at the Cornish postmark when she'd collected the cards from the mat, and wondered when she would be able to go back to the farm without a feeling of guilt. Probably never. It was almost eleven years now since the day she had left. She could see the cliffs and the lovely curve of the bay clearly in her mind, and sometimes Karl's face seemed to come to her when she allowed her memory to cast back to that other time, that other life. The misery of her leaving, and the bleakness of her heart that day as she had contemplated the lonely years ahead, were part of the memory too, though, and it was Graham who had rescued her from all that. Graham, who had brought her the deepest contentment and happiness that any woman could ever want.

He had driven her down to Cornwall to visit them all for short trips now and then, just a day or a weekend. She had never wanted to stay longer at the farm, although she loved the sea so much. She had never gone to that special beach with the children, always making excuses.

She watched him and Miriam. They adored each other, and she smiled to herself. That was one of the greatest bonuses that her marriage to Graham had brought. His love for the child compensated a little perhaps for her own lack of it. She knew she could never really love Miriam as a mother should. It was the deepest grief of her life and a constant further source of guilt, but she could do nothing about it. She had tried hard over the years and had achieved affection but not love. She had given her daughter everything that was in her power to give. It was not really enough, but it had to do. There were her sons now, anyway—Graham's boys, and very, very dear to her. Charles and James were like their father, dark-haired and sturdy, sensible and clever, and she loved them very much.

Graham came into the spacious kitchen and shivered a little. He shut the door on the chilly winter morning outside, and sat down to the bowl of porridge that Margaret placed in front of him.

'Five minutes and we've got to be out of the house,' he said to all three children. 'Mustn't be late for school on your birthday, Miriam. Your teacher won't excuse you for that.'

There was a rushing for satchels and books, a scurrying to find coats and to tie up shoes, and eventually they were all packed into the back of the new Hillman and Graham reversed carefully down the drive. With their cheerful goodbyes ringing in her ears Margaret closed the large wooden gates and went back into the house. She turned on the wireless as she put the dishes into the sink, and the honeyed tones of Anne Ziegler and Webster Booth sang out one of their love-songs. She laughed as she listened and sang along with them.

She was happy, so very happy. She was almost frightened to admit to this contentment in case anything should happen to destroy it. She washed up, replenished the Aga from the hod that Graham had left filled for her, and then sat down with another cup of coffee to read Dottie's letter. They corresponded regularly, and the sheets of scrawly writing that came every couple of weeks were one of her delights. John and Dottie had married a year after her own wedding, just after the birth of the twins. Margaret remembered the occasion with pleasure. It had brought happiness to everyone concerned. They were so right for each other, and Dottie had given up her classroom with the greatest of joy, exchanging it for the farm where she declared she felt totally at home from the start. She had settled into the old grey farmhouse above the sea, filling it with light and laughter and babies, and was constantly asking Margaret to stay for long holidays. But even after so many years of happy marriage there was a fear in the depths of Margaret's heart that to go back would be to stir up the past, to remember again those golden days of her twentieth year when the gulls had called and the sun had shone and she'd been so hopelessly and so sadly in love.

Well, she was in love again now, she told herself firmly as she started to read. She loved Graham deeply. At first, in the early days of marriage, it had been more a very close friendship, and his lovemaking had not stirred her greatly. But love had grown in the way many people believed it could. It never had a sudden brilliant flowering, but was all the better for that, she thought. Something that was swift and intense could be fleeting and transient. Her love for Graham had grown steadily and was as firm now as the great oak tree that stood at the back of the lovely house he had bought for her. Not like the roses which bloomed in summer and were gone.

Dottie wrote that they were all well on the farm. The children were fine and John had just bought a new chicken house. 'Deep-litter,' she said. 'Keep them warmer in the winter, and I shan't have to go messing around in wellies in the mud to collect the eggs.'

Margaret laughed, hearing her friend's voice in the written words, and remembering her own egg-collecting days. Annie too was in her element doing all the cooking for the seven of them, the three adults and four children. There were two boys and two girls now. Dottie had always said she wanted a big family. She came to Bristol to visit each year, usually bringing the latest baby, and the days they spent together were precious both to her and to Margaret.

With the letter read and the cleaning done, it was time to take the dog for his morning walk. Margaret loved the boisterous yellow Labrador. He was her shadow and constant companion, a present from Graham for her last birthday.

The ordinary, pleasant life she was leading filled Margaret with happiness as she climbed the hill at the back of the house. From where she stood she could look out across fields and woods to the distant line of the River Severn at Portishead. She pulled her sheep-skin coat round her against the February cold and suddenly heard gulls calling in the sky above. They always took her thoughts, sometimes unwillingly, back, made her think of Karl. She wondered momentarily, as she often did, what he was doing now. After her marriage to Graham there had only been one letter sending his good wishes for the future. She had wept a little when she read it, but she had deliberately torn it into small shreds, trying to put thoughts of him aside for ever, she had hoped. She knew that it was a vain hope, of course. There would always be a corner of her heart kept secret and secure for Karl, and no one would ever know. Dottie might guess, but nothing was ever said, although she gave her news from Dresden now and again. There were a few infrequent letters sent to the farm. Karl was married now and had a son, apparently, Miriam's half-brother! The thought had caused Margaret much heart-searching at first. Would there ever be a time when she would feel that Miriam ought to know? She ruthlessly put the misgivings behind her. The relationship between Graham and Miriam was too precious to risk. An unknown father was surely better than a real, known man?

And the present and the future belonged to Graham and the three children. She loved him in a quiet, determined way, loved him very much. She smiled to herself as her thoughts passed from one man to the other and she strode on up to the woods above the hill. Life was good, and the troubled times were all past, gone and usually forgotten, just as her Jewish blood too was now totally unacknowledged and denied. Both her parents had died in the years following her marriage, and she had been sad, cried a lot at the funerals, but she had never been really close to either of them, and with their passing she had finally rejected that part of her background which she had secretly renounced years before. Henceforward she had decided she would be completely Anglican, Gentile by adoption, taking Graham's faith and way of life totally to herself. She was baptised and confirmed, and if there was any secret regret occasionally she would never admit to it.

Miriam was quiet when Margaret picked her up from school later that day. They drove from the expensive little private school, which Graham had insisted that she attend, to fetch the boys from theirs. In the two miles that separated the two schools she failed to say a word apart from a muttered reply to Margaret's questions.

'Whatever is the matter, Miriam?' her mother asked irritably. The child had been given a new bike as well as a heap of other presents, and here she was sullen and subdued.

'What's a bastard?'

The question shocked Margaret so much that she had to take a grip on herself and concentrate on her driving.

'Why do you want to know that?' she asked curtly.

'My friend said I'm one, and she said it's a terrible thing to be.'

'You shouldn't listen to silly little girls who don't know what they're talking about.'

'She's not silly, and she's not very little either. She's a prefect.'

For an awful moment Margaret wanted perversely to laugh. From the dramatic heights of a school prefect had come the knowledge from which she had been at such pains to protect her daughter! 'Why did she say that?'

'Her mummy worked in Daddy's office a long time ago, and she says you married him after I was born!'

'We'll talk about it tonight, later. We've got to pick up the boys now, and you don't want to discuss things like that in front of them.'

'Why not? Are they bastards too?'

'Be quiet, Miriam! I forbid another word on the matter.'

Charles and James came running out exuberantly from the school gates, dirt on their faces, and shirts and ties awry.

'Hey, Mirry, can I have first go on your bike?' Charles wanted to know. He was always first in everything, leaving James trailing behind.

'No, you can't. Neither of you can have goes. It's all mine tonight.'

The arrival of the boys seemed to take Miriam's mind off her problem, and Margaret was comforted a little. There was the birthday party to think about, anyway. Perhaps Miriam would forget.

With ten small guests to entertain and feed there was little time for worrying, but when the last parents had driven away and peace had descended on the house again the anxiety returned. There had been no time to warn Graham, not one spare minute when they had been alone.

'She said I'm a dirty Jew too. I don't know what that means either.'

Miriam was in bed with three of her new books lying neglected on the eiderdown. She looked up at her mother and there were tears in her eyes.

'Please, Mummy, tell me! She was my favourite person before she said those awful things, my best friend!'

Graham, standing in the doorway, heard the remark. Margaret looked at him and saw his face go pale and his eyes become angry. He was so seldom angry.

'Who said that to you, poppet?'

'Jenny Trand, and she says I'm a bastard. What's a bastard, Daddy? Mummy won't tell me.'

Graham strode over to the bed and sat on it, pushing the books aside. He put his arms round the little girl and kissed her gently.

'It means someone whose parents weren't married when he or she was born,' he said quietly. 'And that's right. Your mummy and I had our wedding-day when you were just a few months old. But it makes no difference at all to you. We love you very, very much.'

'But you are my real mummy and daddy, aren't you?'

Graham heard the desperation in her voice and he paused for a moment, wondering how to reply. She must have the truth, or he would lose all credibility in her eyes now and for ever.

'I'm your real daddy because I loved you so much that I adopted you when you were very, very tiny,' he said, 'And yes, your mummy is your real mummy.'

The answer seemed to satisfy Miriam for a while, but then the worried questioning returned.

'What's a Jew, then, and why did she say I was one, and dirty too? I'm not dirty, am I?'

She smoothed the spotless white cover of her bed, and her hand went up to her shining hair. Margaret, watching, wanted to scream out in her anger and grief. Surely a war had been fought to prevent this sort of thing? Suddenly she felt a stab of protective love for the little girl, and she bent and kissed her, an unaccustomed gesture.

'To be Jewish is something to be very proud of,' she said, believing it momentarily. 'I'm Jewish, and that makes you Jewish too. When someone says the word "dirty" like that, it just shows their ignorance and silliness.'

'But what does it mean?' Miriam wailed.

Both Margaret and Graham were at a loss for words.

Both suddenly realised that in their denying of their children's heritage they were depriving them, all three of them, of something that might become precious in time, something priceless and not to be disregarded.

'It means you're special, and Charles and James too. Now go to sleep, and we'll explain all about it in the morning.' The comforting words were from Graham, and he tucked her up and kissed her again.

Satisfied, and totally secure in her father's love and in her mother's caring, Miriam slept.

Very little explaining was necessary after that.

'Do you know we're Jewish?' she announced to her brothers the next day when they were having breakfast. 'And it's something nice, and makes us special.'

'Gosh, are we really?' Charles seemed impressed, and he turned to his mother for confirmation. 'Is she just being silly, Mummy?'

'No, dear. She's telling you the truth.'

'I know about Jews,' the studious James said. 'My teacher told us that Jesus was a Jew, so it must be good!'

'All his friends were too,' Charles added, not to be outdone. 'We've been having the stories in Scripture.'

'They didn't like him doing good and put him up on a cross with nails in his hands and feet!'

Miriam listened, crunching on her cornflakes as she took in this information. 'Oh, well, I don't mind being Jewish if Jesus was one. I'll tell my friend. That'll shut her up!'

Margaret looked across at Graham and he winked at her and grinned, and after she had waved them all off once more she went inside and laughed at the incongruity of her children's solution of their problem. She hoped it would always remain as simple!

CHAPTER SEVENTEEN

1966

'THEN you'll agree, both of you?' Miriam looked at her parents with unrestrained excitement in her eyes. She threw her arms round her father. 'I really thought you would be the one to refuse, Daddy.'

Graham laughed. 'As long as you come back safe and sound and ready to take up that precious place at Oxford in September, I agree, with reluctance.'

Miriam at eighteen was beautiful and clever, the joy of his life, and her delight at gaining a place at university, and the one she had always dreamed of too, had been a triumph for the whole family. He was very proud of his lovely daughter. When she had announced that she wanted to spend the whole of her long summer holiday working on a kibbutz in Israel his heart had plummeted.

'It's dangerous,' he had told her. 'There's a lot of trouble over there. Can't you go somewhere a bit safer and nearer to home? How about Scotland?'

'Stop worrying about me,' she had told him. 'I'm eighteen now, an adult, and I want to find out something about my roots!'

For a moment he had blanched at that. Roots! The German! She still didn't know the truth about her natural father.

There had been questions now and then as she grew into her teens, but Margaret had always stalled, and Miriam had learned to be content, although she often wondered what lay beneath her mother's reluctance to tell. But she knew that to probe more deeply would cause strife and unhappiness and that the one it would hurt most of all would be her adored adoptive father. She and Graham had a deep and loving relationship that transcended all her curiosity, and she had pushed her questioning to the depths of her mind and seldom thought about it.

'Roots, Daddy,' she had explained. 'My Jewish ones. I've been a good Anglican like you wanted me to be, but I want to find out a bit about Mum's part of me. After all, I *am* Jewish really, more than Gentile!'

Margaret, listening to the conversation, remembered her mother's remarks when she'd first seen Miriam in the little hospital crib just after her birth. 'She's Jewish,' she had said. 'It's the mother who determines the race of the child, not the father, in Jewish law.' Miriam certainly looked Jewish. There was something stamped on her lovely features that proclaimed the fact boldly, and, to Margaret, seemed slightly incongruous as she knelt each Sunday beside her daughter, receiving communion at the altar of their beautiful old parish church. The boys hadn't inherited those distinguishing features, taking after their father almost totally. They never bothered about it as Miriam did. Perhaps it was her name that caused her to do so. Margaret sometimes regretted the choice she had made so quickly out of a sense of guilt, so long ago. She sometimes felt guilty too about her reluctance to tell Miriam about Karl. Her reasons were complex, only half understood even to herself. She supposed that a loyalty to Graham was one of the main grounds for her continued silence. The right time would come eventually, but she was sure that it wasn't yet.

Full of excitement and not a little apprehension, Miriam kissed her father goodbye and clung to him tearfully as they stood waiting at the airport for her flight to be called. She sensed that there was something special about this parting. It wasn't like the school trip to Austria last year, or even the months she had spent in France studying for her A Level exam. This was different. Israel! The very word sent shivers of expectation through her slim body, almost as if it had some mystical force that drew her with cords that she couldn't understand or control.

'See you in September, Daddy,' she said desperately. 'And I'll write as soon as I arrive.'

She wasn't prepared for the heat. It met her as she left the plane and engulfed her, sapping all energy and even taking the edge from the intense excitement that she had felt throughout the flight. The security arrangements at Heathrow had been long and tedious, but they gave a sense of safety and she had submitted fairly cheerfully. Here there were more checks, and when they were over she emerged thankfully, clutching her heavy bag, and sweating profusely. She had seldom felt so frightened or so alone. She stood not knowing quite what to do. There would be someone to meet her, she had been told, and she stared at the busy crowds, all intent on their own concerns, not one of them bothering about her. There were young soldiers too, in green uniforms and mostly chewing gum. Each one carried a terrifying-looking machine-gun as though it were a toy just purchased from Woolworths. Miriam was prepared for this, but the reality unnerved her, made her think suddenly of home, the quiet, tree-lined road in the little village near Bristol where she lived, and of her parents' cool and beautiful house with its spacious rooms, and well-kept and shady garden, and most of all its total safety.

'Miriam Bantry?'

She turned with relief, and looked at the tall young man who was smiling and holding out his hand to her. He took her bag and led the way outside into the even greater heat.

'The others arrived on earlier flights,' he explained. 'There are a dozen students coming today, so they sent me with the mini-bus.'

They were all waiting in the small crowded vehicle, hot and impatient, and they looked at her without smiling.

'From the States and Germany,' her escort explained. He stowed her bag at the back with a heap of scruffy rucksacks and kitbags and two girls shuffled along the wooden seat to make room for her. The incredible heat, the noise and the closeness of so many hot bodies did nothing to comfort Miriam. Embarrassed, she slid into the small space allotted to her.

'Trust us to be allocated to a kibbutz miles away,' the girl next to her said. 'Rosh Hazim, apparently, and it's somewhere up north, where we're likely to get shelled too.'

'Not very often. I shouldn't worry about that.' The young man in charge laughed and turned to Miriam. 'We've had a long wait for you in the heat, so we're all a bit snappy. By the way, I'm Chaim Macleod.'

'Macleod!' Miriam couldn't help remarking at the surprising name. Why Macleod?

'Scottish father. I'll explain more later. We must be off if we're to get home at any reasonable hour.'

The old vehicle rattled its way out of the airport complex, and on to the open road. Miriam turned from her fellow passengers to stare out of the window at the countryside. So this was Israel, the land that meant so much to so many. There were tears in her eyes, and she couldn't be sure whether it was emotion or tiredness or just that she was incredibily homesick. She brushed them away hastily and hoped that no one had noticed. The route took them north along the busy main road that bordered the sea for many miles, and she tried to picture the famous map at the back of her Bible with its well-remembered old names and its sacred associations. This modern road had no likeness at all to the land of her imagination. There were ugly modern concrete buildings scattered here and there, and sometimes signs of tourism.

'Netanya,' Chaim called back to them as he drove, 'there on your left. Beginning to be a holiday resort. We'll make it a great attraction one day.'

Miriam looked at the long stretch of beach, and at the sea, the incredibly blue sea, and for the first time since she landed felt a small tremor of excitement. This was a new land, full of promise, needing young people like herself to take up all the challenges it offered, prevent it being ruined, perhaps.

They rattled north and then turned inland through a green fertile region with farming settlements and small villages, some of them old and dilapidated, looking as though they had been there beneath the blazing sun unchanged for a thousand years, and others modern and brash, surrounded by well-cultivated fields.

'Not far now,' their driver told them eventually. 'The kibbutz is a few miles north of Nazareth.'

The road climbed steadily, and Miriam stared with mounting excitement through the dusty window. This had more resemblance to the land she had dreamed about. There were terraces of fig and olive trees, and countless dark, spear-like cypresses pointing to the sky. It reminded her slightly of Spain, and happy, carefree holidays she had spent there with her parents and brothers years ago.

Nazareth! They drove slowly through the maze of tiny streets with their small dirty-white houses, crowds of tourists, overladen, pathetic donkeys, shouting, rushing inhabitants, and stalls selling every conceivable commodity, their owners desperate to capture the unwary visitor. Combined with the suffocating and mind-blowing heat the effect produced a totally unspiritual hullabaloo, and Miriam was glad that she wasn't here on any pilgrimage where she had to visit holy shrines and pretend a reverence that she couldn't in any way feel. She reminded herself too that this special little town mustn't be special to her. She was determined to be strictly Jewish while she was here!

'You can come back and do some sightseeing on your day off,' Chaim said, 'in a group. We'll arrange a trip. The Arabs here are mostly friendly. A large number of them are Christian, not Muslim, and it makes a difference. They're Israeli Arabs too. That means that they have citizenship of Israel.'

Miriam, listening and looking, realised what a lot she had to learn.

The kibbutz buildings were spread across the crest of a small hill, and when the old mini-bus screeched to a halt all its passengers breathed a communal sigh of relief, tumbled out and stood and stared.

'Grab your bags,' Chaim directed, 'and I'll show you to your quarters, then you can shower and come and eat. The others will have had their meal by now. The cooks said they would leave something for you in the dining-hall.'

Obediently they followed him along gravelled paths between strange beds of cacti and brightly coloured flowers that Miriam didn't recognise. She could smell the scent of them, heavy in the cooling evening air, and their exotic fragrance increased her sense of homesickness and her excitement, in equal measure.

The accommodation was basic—a long room with bunks and one small cupboard each to stow their belongings; no wardrobe. The showers were communal, one for women and the other alongside it for the men. The girls stood gratefully under the comforting sprinkling water, letting its coolness caress their hot, sweating bodies, and listening to the bawdy remarks of the men through the thinness of the separating screen.

The first day was hard. It was the hardest day's work that Miriam had ever done.

'You'll be in the chicken house,' Chaim told her when jobs were allocated. 'That's my responsibility at the moment. We change around every now and then. I'll be able to show you how things are done and all that.'

Was she imagining it, or was there a special smile aimed in her direction, a little more time spent with her than with any of the others? She wasn't sure, but this tall young man with the curly brown hair and smiling dark eyes looked as though he would be more at home striding around the Highlands of Scotland in a kilt than farming beneath the blazing sun in this strange land. There was an attractive ruggedness about him that she liked. He seemed to be at her side frequently, and she was glad. She had never met anyone with such enthusiasm and energy.

'Tell me about yourself,' he said one evening when the day's work was done and they were all sitting in the welcome coolness on the grass beside the dining-hall.

'Not a lot to tell,' she said. 'My mother is Jewish, my father as English as he could possibly be.' She hesitated a little as she sometimes did lately when she talked of Graham. She loved him so dearly, and she sometimes felt a sudden sense of deprivation when she remembered that he wasn't really her father.

'Then you're Jewish,' Chaim said.

'Yes, I know, but I wasn't brought up Jewish.'

'That doesn't matter. This isn't a religious kibbutz—you'll have found that out already. Most of us are agnostic. Zionists yes, religious no!'

'It's strange,' Miriam said. 'I hadn't thought about that when I was in England. I thought it would be all Jewish festivals and things.'

'We keep some, and the kitchens are kosher, of course. How about your mother? Doesn't she observe any of the rules?'

'None at all. She's gone over completely to my father's way of life. Baptised and confirmed, a fairly enthusiastic Anglican.'

Chaim laughed. 'I hope you're not,' he said. 'Agnostic or even atheist views are acceptable, but Christianity is definitely out.'

'But I thought Israel boasted tolerance, freedom of religion?'

'Only for non-Jews, I'm afraid. If you admit your Jewish blood then your Christianity wouldn't be acceptable.'

'That's crazy,' Miriam objected. 'I'm still Jewish, whatever I believe. Anyway, tell me about the Zionist bit of yourself,' she added, anxious to change the subject, to talk about him instead.

'Scottish father, Jewish mother, hence the name,' he told her. 'My father was killed in the war—the German war, I mean. I was born on Skye. We lived there for a few years, then my mother decided to give up everything for the kibbutz way of life. She was a teacher and came out here in 1950 when I was just four, so I don't remember much about my Scottish roots.

This is home to me and I almost consider myself a Sabra.'

'What's a Sabra?'

'Israeli-born, born here in Eretz Israel, the land of promise and all that. I know I'm not, but I feel like one.'

'What about Scotland? We had a holiday there a few years ago. It's beautiful and romantic. Skye particularly is wonderful. Don't you feel anything for it?'

' "From the lone shieling of the misty island",' he quoted. 'It's about as remote, I suppose, from the heat and dust of this place as it could possibly be, and I admit that I'd like to go one day, but here is home. My mother died here when I was only ten and they brought me up on this kibbutz. It's the only life I know. This is my Israel, my place, and it's got me in some sort of tight grip that I can't explain. I love it.'

'Lucky you, to have two such terrific places in the two halves of you,' Miriam said.

He turned to her seriously. 'What about you? Haven't you a special place?'

She searched her mind for an answer. 'Bristol. I was born in Bristol, and yes, I suppose I feel a kind of affection for it, but it hardly possesses a romantic atmosphere like your misty islands, or the challenge and magic of a new country like this, nothing to get steamed up about.'

She suddenly thought of Margaret. 'My mother, now. She's got a special feeling about Cornwall, seagulls and lonely cliffs and so on. In fact my father is considering buying a cottage somewhere down there for her, for holidays.'

'It sounds wonderful.' Chaim caught her hand and pulled her to her feet. 'Let's go for a walk,' he said.

CHAPTER EIGHTEEN

1966

'WILL it do?' Graham asked, and he caught Margaret's hand and held it in his as they stood together staring at the cottage. They had driven down from Bristol that day and the roads had been busy, the weather too hot for travelling, but Margaret could smell the fresh, tangy fragrance of the sea as soon as she opened the car door, and her heart lifted.

The little house nestled safely into a gently rising hillside and there was a glimpse of cliffs and calm blue water through a gap in the hedge. The sea, so often wild and restless on this beautiful and remote north Cornish shore, was today placid, almost still, welcoming them.

She looked at the neat grey roof of tough Cornish slate, at the sturdy stone walls of the little house, and then turned to him with tears in her eyes.

'It's the most perfect thing I've ever seen in my life,' she replied. 'Can we really afford it?'

'If you want it, yes. You've always yearned to be near the sea, and I know you can't bear to go to the farm very often. I thought this might suit. We can come down for weekends and holidays. Here's the key, let's go and have a look.'

He handed her a bunch of keys and followed her up the cobbled path. Silently she fitted one of them into the lock and slowly pushed the heavy old door. Almost reverently they went inside, into its cool quietness, glad to have some respite from the unusually hot August sunshine.

The ticking of a large grandfather clock gave an immediate sense of peace and timelessness, and she stroked its mellow wood gently, almost paying homage. There were other pieces of lovely antique furniture set about the room, and the sunlight filtering softly through the tiny panes of the small window illuminated them here and there, giving a quality of strange, ethereal beauty. A large bowl of dried flower petals had been placed on the table, lending a slightly exotic and strange fragrance.

Margaret ran her finger along the polished oak table. There was no dust. 'Who cares for it? It looks as though the old lady left only a few minutes ago.'

'A woman from the village comes in every day, apparently.' Graham went to the window. 'Come over here and look,' he said.

The window was set in the thickness of the old wall and Margaret had to bend to see clearly through it. Then she gasped in delight.

'I can see the sea,' she said. 'I've always wanted a house with a view of the sea!' She stared almost unbelieving at the small waves breaking lazily on the great rock that lay just beyond the bay. Then a gull cried, and she knew that here she would find peace. Here within sight and sound of the sea she would come face to face with herself and find peace. It was a strange irony that she needed the wildness of the sea to purge the restlessness which she often felt at its sound, but she knew that it was so. However, peace was more than mere happiness. It was deeper and more enduring. The ghosts of the past would be laid to rest here.

'You like it, then?'

The question was unnecessary. Margaret turned and threw her arms around Graham.

'What have I ever done in all my life to deserve such a perfect husband and such a wonderful gift?' she said.

He laughed. 'Just being yourself, and bringing me constant happiness!' He kissed her lightly. 'We can have the furniture too if you want it. It's for sale just as it stands.'

'Yes, oh, yes. All of it,' she said.

'Then it's yours. A belated thirty-eighth birthday present!'

'We can spend all our holidays here,' Margaret said as she went, like a delighted child, through the tiny rooms and up the uneven stairs. 'I shall never want to go anywhere else! No more uncomfortable camping or noisy hotels!'

'And when we're old and in our dotage, we'll leave Bristol and spend our declining years staring out at the sea and listening to the gulls!' Graham added.

They were calling at that moment, riding on the gentle summer breeze, and suddenly their plaintive crying seemed to be in the room, close and compelling. Margaret gasped at the nearness of the sound, and Graham went to the large stone chimney that dominated one side of the room.

'Why do you think it's called Gull Cottage?' he said. 'Apparently they like to sit on the roof and the sound comes straight down the chimney. You probably won't be so thrilled with them after you've been here a while.'

'I'll always love gulls,' Margaret said. 'They've fascinated me since I was a little girl. The sound of them always meant summer holidays when I was small. There's a magic about them that I can't describe—magic that works for me, anyway.'

Suddenly her thoughts strayed. Perhaps it was the

gulls' cry that reminded her of her daughter.

'The children will love it here, won't they? I'm longing to show it to them. If we've got possession of it before Miriam goes to Oxford perhaps we could have a weekend here, all of us together?'

They travelled back to Bristol the following day, and the letter was lying innocently on the mat. Graham picked it up, glanced at the Israeli stamp and carried it through to the kitchen. He put their suitcases down and slit it open impatiently. Letters from Miriam came regularly every week, long, happy letters full of the life she seemed to be enjoying so much. He started to read this latest one with his usual pleasure.

'Anything new?' Margaret asked as she put the kettle to boil. It had been a hot journey and she was ready for a cup of tea. For a few moments he didn't speak, and she looked at him and saw his expression change suddenly. He sat down heavily at the kitchen table.

'She's not coming home,' he said. 'She's met some Israeli fellow. She wants to stay. Someone called Chaim—damn silly name!'

The short, disjointed sentences spoke worlds to Margaret, and she moved over to him and took the letter from his trembling hands. She read it with mounting anger. She could bear to lose her daughter as long as the girl was happy; they had never been close, and she still had her sons. But Graham! How could Miriam think of bringing such grief to the father who loved her, who had cherished her so deeply all her life? She read thc letter again. It was brief and sounded almost uncaring. Even Oxford seemed to count for nothing.

'She can't throw her life away!' she said furiously. 'I'll go out there straight away and try to persuade her to come back; get some sense into her silly head. Israel! How do I go about it?'

'It's I who should go,' said Graham. 'I'll go.'

He turned and went to the small room that he called his den and lifted the telephone from its hook. His mind blanked out suddenly. He knew he must call the airport or the travel agent or someone, but he was suddenly powerless to do anything. He stared unseeing at the wall and thought about Miriam whom he loved so much. He stayed like that for minutes, or hours, he couldn't tell. It was in fact only minutes, and Margaret came in and found him speechless and staring and silent. She folded her arms round him and he wept, and she knew that the prisoner-of-war years, so long ago now, still had their moments of power over him, a weakness that he couldn't control in times of stress. Beneath the calm, successful businessman was someone very, very vulnerable. Her anger against her daughter threatened to stifle her, and for a time she had no sympathy or understanding. Miriam was just being selfish and stupid, bewitched. How could one give up Oxford anyway? It was the chance of a lifetime. She would regret her decision desperately and must be persuaded to change her mind. There was no doubt about that.

It was Margaret eventually who went. She flew out of Heathrow on a dull September day a week later. She had delayed, knowing that Graham was her first priority. She had to wait until he had recovered from the first shock. They had spent hours talking, and at last he seemed to have come to terms with the situation a little.

'I'll do everything in my power to get her to return,' she assured him as they stood together at the airport. 'Trust me!'

When her flight was called she kissed him again and left quickly, scared at the prospect of what lay before her, wondering how she would relate to this obviously new and determined daughter and the unknown young man, Chaim, the one with the damned silly name! She laughed grimly to herself as she remembered Graham's first remark. And what was a kibbutz like? They had booked her into the guest-house, Miriam had told her over the telephone, but she had said little and her young voice, distant and remote over the crackling line, had been full of defiance and pride.

'Get a taxi,' Graham had commanded her. 'All the way from the airport to the kibbutz—and no, it isn't extravagant. It's a dangerous place to be.'

She had promised reluctantly, and when the heat met her as she walked from the plane she was glad of his instructions.

In fact it wasn't so much of a luxury as she had supposed. She found herself directed to a *sherut*, a large Mercedes car with six other passengers, all apparently going north.

'Good way of travelling about,' she was told. 'It's a communal taxi.'

They all stared at her as she stood uncertainly, wondering if it would take her where she wanted to go. Her smart sandals and fashionable cotton suit suddenly seemed ostentatious and unsuitable. But she was reassured by the driver, and timidly she tucked herself and her luggage into the one remaining seat.

'Your first visit to Israel?'

The questioner was a large, friendly man in his fifties or sixties, she guessed, wearing ancient well-patched trousers and open-necked casual shirt. She was aware that her appearance made her stand out vividly from all the others.

'Yes. I'm going to visit my daughter at Kibbutz Rosh Hazim.'

He was immediately interested. 'That's a great place. Is she one of the summer volunteers, or permanent?'

'Just for the summer,' Margaret said hurriedly. 'She's going to Oxford in three weeks' time.' She hoped the confident tone of her voice would make the prediction a certainty.

'Jewish?'

The question startled her. Was he talking about herself or Miriam? She hesitated. She hadn't really thought of herself as Jewish for a long time, not since her marriage, certainly. More a Gentile convert, if one could be such a thing.

'Yes. Yes, we are, sort of!'

It certainly wasn't the right response. Not here. Not in Israel. She could feel every face turned towards her and was acutely aware of a unanimous disapproval. Worse than disapproval, perhaps, and she had to spend the next two hours at least cramped up in this vehicle with them. When they spoke to each other it was in some strange language that she had never heard before, and she guessed it was Hebrew. It was the language of modern Israel. She was glad her questioner had fluent English.

She smiled and tried to make it her most charming smile. 'I'm just out from England,' she said, pleading slightly. 'This is my first visit to Israel and everything is very strange. I had to come very suddenly, you see, without any plans or preparation.'

Her first questioner relaxed a little and smiled. 'It's a wonderful place. You won't want to go back.'

It was a confident, assured statement. Margaret stared through the car windows at the sea, the Mediterranean with its waves only little ripples breaking lazily on the hot sandy beach. She thought suddenly of the little cottage set on its Cornish hillside with the wild Atlantic visible from its small windows, and of the harsh and beautiful granite cliffs and she knew that she belonged there, not in this strange unknown place with its alien climate, difficult language and frighteningly earnest inhabitants. She longed to get this visit over and to go back to Graham, to everything that held her heart. And Miriam would be with her. Miriam would definitely be with her.

They talked a little throughout the journey. All of them appeared to speak English, indeed probably were English, European certainly, but the heat and the motion of the car induced a stupor eventually and before long most were asleep. Nothing would allow Margaret to close her eyes, though. This was the Holy Land, after all, her first glimpse of it, and if it was to be her last she must try to understand what made it such an object of passion and devotion. She stared at the coastal sprawl of houses and at the traffic without enthusiasm, and tried to come to terms with modern Israel.

The taxi dropped her at the gate of the kibbutz and she saw Miriam standing there, small and alone and frightened. Suddenly Margaret was ashamed of her angry thoughts, her fierce refusal to have anything to do with Graham's moderating comments, the quiet words that had come later after the first shock.

'Her happiness must come first,' he had said. 'Make sure that this Chaim character is good to her, and that it's what she really wants. Don't think about us. She's an adult now and has her own life.'

She looked extremely young and very vulnerable, Margaret thought, and her antagonism was transferred to the unknown young man who had brought about this state of affairs.

They stood and looked at each other for a moment, and then Miriam ran to her and kissed her quickly on the cheek. It was an unusual display of affection, and Margaret took her hands and held them for a moment in hers and stared at her daughter.

'You're thinner,' she said. 'What are they doing to you?'

'It's wonderful here, Mummy,' Miriam said. 'The kind of life I've always dreamed about, free and fulfilled and. . .But I'm sorry. How's Daddy?'

'Upset, sad and missing you very much.'

The words held some condemnation, and she saw Miriam's face cloud, losing its glow and brightness.

'I thought about him a lot, about you both, before I wrote, but I had no choice. I belong here.'

Both women suddenly realised that this was not how they had planned it, this meeting. Both had carefully rehearsed what they would say, worrying, choosing their words with great deliberation.

Miriam picked up her mother's case. 'Come on in anyway. You're not going into the guest-house after all. Because you're Jewish, and my mum, and because Chaim pulled a few strings, we've managed to get you a little *binyan* of your own for two weeks. It's empty because the couple it's been allocated to aren't coming yet.'

'Whatever is a *binyan*?' Margaret felt she might have been better in the comforts of the kibbutz hotel.

'A sort of apartment. They're only small, but it's all the kibbutz can afford just now. Every married couple has one, but it doesn't need to be big because all the cooking and washing and things are done in the communal house.'

Miriam led the way along the path, and Margaret stared around with an increasing degree of concern.

She felt completely alien, as though everything that was happening to her was happening to someone else and she was merely observing from a distance.

'*Shalom!*' Her hand was suddenly gripped fiercely by a large, elderly man. He had smiling brown eyes and he was dressed in a crumpled blue shirt and jeans. 'You must be Miriam's mother. Welcome to Rosh Hazim!'

She smiled back at him in a detached way. 'Yes.' It was all she could manage at that moment. He said something that she couldn't later recall, but she was aware of his appreciative glance as he looked her up and down.

Miriam giggled. 'He was obviously quite smitten with you, Mum,' she said. 'He doesn't often see glamorous women! He's the secretary of the kibbutz.'

Margaret wondered in an obtuse way if there was any connection between the two seemingly unrelated comments, and then she suddenly realised that almost everyone she had seen so far, both male and female, seemed to be wearing similar ancient blue shirts and jeans. She glanced at Miriam, and of course she was in the uniform too.

'Why is everyone dressed alike?' she asked.

'It's not intentional. I suppose we get a large number of things cheaper because of bulk buying or something, and it's easier for the laundry.'

'How do you know which belongs to you?'

'We don't. We just have whatever fits! At least, that isn't totally true for us summer volunteers, because a lot of us have our own clothes. And some of the others have one or two special things for the evenings.'

Margaret thought of the shopping expedition to choose clothes for this trip, the expensive shirts and the new jeans, and she sighed a little, uncomprehending.

Suddenly Miriam stopped and put the case down.

She brought a key from her pocket and indicated the little flat-roofed concrete building in front of them. It looked like a garage with a window and a porch stuck on at the front! It stood in a row of others all alike.

'This is it, Mummy. All yours while you're here.'

She retrieved the case, opened the door and stood back for Margaret to go inside. The heat was appalling and the sun streaming through the uncurtained window showed the dust that seemed to cover everything.

'The bed is in there,' Miriam said. 'I made it up all ready for you, and there's a shower and toilet just beyond. Some of the older apartments haven't got their own. The place where I'm billeted hasn't. We have to use the communal showers and things. Everyone used to have to do that, apparently, years ago.'

Margaret shuddered at the thought and she stared at the tiny cubicle with its bead curtaining that partly hid the large bed. She concealed her dismay.

'Thank you, darling,' she murmured. 'I'm sure I'll love it here, and I'm relying on you to show me some of the sights.'

She wondered why she was saying these things. They both knew why she had come. How would she broach the subject that neither of them wanted to talk about?

'I'll leave you for half an hour to get unpacked and then we can go over to supper together,' said Miriam. 'It's in the dining-hall.'

Alone in the tiny, austere room Margaret thought again of home and of the little cottage in Cornwall too with its antique furniture, cool, mellow beauty, and thick stone walls. She ran her hand along the bare, rough wood of the table and the two kitchen chairs that stood beside it. Thick yellow dust stained her fingers.

'It gets everywhere. It's a fact of life, the terrible dust

that blows in from the desert!' She remembered Miriam's words in one of the first letters. They had laughed, not really understanding.

There was a sink and a cupboard in a small adjoining room and a two-ring burner. She went through to it and turned on the one tap. The water was warm, neither hot nor cold, and she held her hands under it and washed them and then her face, trying to cool both her skin and her thoughts. So this was the kind of life that Miriam wanted, a place like this, and always this heat, this stifling, unbearable heat. She opened the case that had been deposited on the bed and stared at the unsuitable clothes packed carefully in layers of tissue paper. There was no wardrobe to hang anything, just some hooks behind the door and two twisted wire hangers.

'Shalom!'

The word that she heard repeatedly was called from the open front door.

'*Shalom*—welcome!'

Her visitor was a woman about her own age and she was smiling warmly. Margaret shook her outstretched hand and smiled too.

'Thank you. I'm just trying to settle in. It's so hot.'

The woman laughed. 'You get used to it. I'm from next door and I heard that we are to be temporary neighbours.'

'Yes. I've come to visit my daughter. She was going to put me in the guest-house, but changed her mind and decided that I should like it better here.'

'Well, you'd have been more comfortable over there perhaps, but you might have been lonely. There's no chance of that here! Would you like a cup of tea? It's usually Nes that we drink, but I keep some tea in as well, for my English friends.'

'Oh, please. That would be wonderful.'

'Do you want to shower or anything first, or shall I make it straight away?'

'Oh, right now, please. I shall have more strength to cope when I've had a drink.'

Margaret followed her new acquaintance to the next-door apartment and stared around with interest. The little room was obviously loved and well cared for. One whole wall was covered with home-made bookshelves and a couple of trailing plants made it seem more lived-in. There were bright curtains at the window and colourful rugs on the tiled floor.

'It's nice,' she said as they waited for the kettle to boil. 'Do you live here alone?'

'No, with my husband, Moshe. He's working on the banana plantation down by the lake at the moment.'

She set two cups on the table and stretched out her arm to the fridge which was fixed to the wall near the small sink. It was then that Margaret saw it, the dark blue numbers tattooed on her sunburned skin. For a moment the significance didn't register, but her eyes were riveted on the ugly, disfiguring marks. The woman suddenly turned and saw her expression, and she smiled.

'Yes, it's always a bit of a shock for strangers. Auschwitz. I was one of the lucky ones.'

Margaret had no words. Her mind flew back to those awful pictures they had seen when the news of the Nazi camps were thrust before a horrified world, and for one blinding moment she remembered Karl's face, and recalled his tortured words. He had been so ashamed, almost destroyed by what his country had done.

'I'm Dinah, by the way. Can I call you Margaret?'

'Yes—yes, of course.'

'My mother was English—English-Jewish, I mean—

and we always spoke English at home. I've never forgotten it and I teach it to the children here. She met my father when he was studying in England, and they went back to Czechoslovakia to live when he had his degree. That was in the thirties, and neither of them read the signs well enough. They both died in Auschwitz.'

The conversation was difficult after that. Margaret talked about Miriam and England and longed to escape. She drank the tea and ate the biscuits that were offered, and then made her excuses. So much suffering, there was so much suffering behind the cheerful face of this lean and hardy *kibbutznik* that her own early problems seemed as nothing, and her worries now about her daughter paled into insignificance.

'See you in the dining-hall later, then,' Dinah said. 'I hope the meal's good for your first introduction to kibbutz life!'

Margaret unpacked a few of her things, carefully leaving the smarter items hidden in her case. Only the trousers and shirts were suitable. The shower was basic, but she stood beneath it gratefully, letting the cool water wash away her weariness and hoping that all her worries could likewise go swishing away as simply. Then she dressed, and waited for Miriam. The worries had not gone. She sat in the little wicker chair on the small veranda outside the front door and watched the path nervously.

She saw her daughter come swinging towards her, hand in hand with a young man. Margaret tried hard not to dislike him, not to feel any antipathy before they had even met. She watched them hastily drop their linked hands when they saw her and then Miriam waved cheerfully.

'Everything all right, Mum?' she asked, and Margaret noticed the name. 'Mummy' was gone now. Her daughter was growing up. She must come to terms with it.

'Fine, darling. I've had a nice cup of tea with my neighbour, and I'm all ready to face the hordes!'

'Well, this is the first one. Chaim, meet my mother!'

He took a step towards her and held out a large farmer's hand. It was broad and capable, stained with the earth of this land to which they all seemed so devoted. Margaret recognised the signs. Karl's had looked just like that, and John's too. Graham's never. His were the well-kept hands of the city businessman, strong and artistic, but not calloused by hard manual work.

Chaim's grip was very firm and his smile infectious and friendly. '*Shalom*,' he said. 'Miriam has told me all about you. Welcome to Rosh Hazim.'

Margaret wondered what he had been told, but there was no animosity in the young man's smile, no suspicion of her intentions in coming here, so perhaps Miriam had been kind to her, reporting only the good.

The dining-room was spartan. It reminded Margaret of some of the restaurants of wartime Bristol. There were Formica-topped tables with ugly tubular metal legs and chairs to match. They sat eight or ten to a table and were served from a stainless steel trolley which was pushed round with much noise and laughter. It was the laughter that impressed her. It jarred slightly too, and she was ashamed at her irritation and her longing for quietness, peace, subdued lighting and coolness. But the food was good, and she was surprised at the enormity of her appetite. Miriam, watching her, laughed.

'I've never seen you eat so much, Mum,' she said.

'You'd better not keep that up, or you'll get fat!'

'The life here doesn't seem to have had that effect on you, though!' she replied, looking at the girl's thin body beneath the rather ugly clothes.

'But I'm fit, really fit, and I eat loads. It's the hard work! I've got the next four days off, though. I saved up all my free days and I'm taking them all together so I can show you around.'

It wasn't until much later that evening that there was any privacy. At last the searing heat of the day was past and they sat together on the little porch of Margaret's apartment. Miriam had brought some milk and the ever-necessary Nes, as everyone seemed to call the rather unpleasant instant coffee. She made two cups and carried them out, setting them carefully on the home-made coffee-table. There were sounds of laughter in the distance, the splash of bodies in the newly excavated swimming-pool of which they were all so proud, and the occasional crying of a restless child from the children's house across the central area of watered grass. Margaret could smell the pines too that stood around the perimeter fence and she was reminded of family holidays in the Landes, that part of France where they had used to camp when the children were small. She looked at Miriam sipping her hot coffee. She was staring in front of her with a dreamy expression on her face, and suddenly she appeared young and vulnerable, and Margaret longed to gather her up in her arms as she had done when Miriam was little. Although there had never been love between them she had always felt a great need to protect this child, almost as though her guilt over her conception made the need to guard her from life's difficulties more urgent.

She didn't know how to begin or what to say. It was Miriam who broke the uncomfortable silence.

'You've come to persuade me to come home, haven't you?'

'It's Oxford! You can't mean to pass over the most wonderful chance of your life?' It wasn't what she had intended, but the words came without premeditation. 'We don't want to lose you either, of course. Your father is very upset.'

There was another silence, and Margaret could feel her daughter's intense anxiety and stress.

'Mum,' she said quietly, 'I love Daddy very, very much, but who really is my father? I need to know.'

Margaret hadn't expected this, certainly not at this time anyway, and her heart seemed to turn over in sudden shock. It took her some moments before she could reply.

'I can't tell you that, Miriam. I've told you frequently that it would do no good. You know that he was a good man and that I loved him. He doesn't know about your birth and he must never find out. Certainly not by accident. Perhaps "never" is too final a word, but please believe me and trust me. One day perhaps when I'm very old and it doesn't matter any more then I shall tell you. But for now, no. I can't!'

'But why not, for goodness' sake?'

Margaret saw the tears in the girl's eyes and she felt again the searing guilt that had torn her apart all those years ago. She suddenly remembered the awful marks on the arm of the woman in the next room. No, Miriam must not know, not yet, not for many, many years, if ever.

'Because it could damage several lives. I can't say any more, not without a lot of hurt. Please don't force me.' She could feel tears threatening her own eyes too and she groped for a handkerchief. 'Please, Miriam!' She was pleading now, and suddenly her daughter rose from her chair and knelt on the floor beside her.

'I'm sorry,' she said. 'I will trust you, Mummy. It's bothered me, though, ever since I could understand. I'll try to trust you and not to think about it any more. You've often told me that you loved him, but always there has been a doubt in my mind. I wondered if you were only saying that to comfort me and the truth was that he was bad and raped you. I couldn't live with that.'

Margaret placed her coffee on the small table and put her arms round the now sobbing girl. 'My precious child,' she said, surprising herself with the words, 'I loved him more than I can ever tell you. I shall never forget him, but I love Graham now. He's the father who brought you up and who loves both of us very much. Try to think only of him.' She stroked the shining hair. 'For me that long-ago summer is just a dream, a lovely, magical dream that I must keep in the past for all our sakes.'

'But I've always felt that you didn't really love me as much as you loved the boys. That's why I thought it must have been a bad experience for you!'

Margaret gasped in surprise and sadness. They had never talked like this before, never discussed anything but the practical matters of every day.

'It was a terrible thing to have a baby in those days without a husband,' she said, trying to explain the inexplicable. How could she say that she had wanted a little blond German son? That Miriam had been a daughter, a very Jewish-looking daughter, a terrible disappointment, and never likely to remind her of Karl whom she had so passionately wanted to remember? Even after her marriage to Graham the love for this daughter which she'd then so wished to feel had never come, and the lack of it had increased her guilt complex over the years. Love was so unpredictable, she thought. You could not pretend it or decide to whom you would give it. Was it beginning to rise in her heart now, just at the time when she was about to lose this child? The irony did not escape her.

'Of course I love you,' she said, believing once more that what she asserted with her lips would become accomplished fact.

Miriam kissed her then and they clung to each other for a second or two.

'Come and let me show you around,' Miriam said, suddenly embarrassed. 'It's cool now. Perhaps you'd like a swim? The new pool is super!'

CHAPTER NINETEEN

1966

'WHAT do you most want to see?' Miriam asked as they sat in the noisy dining-room the following morning. 'Chaim has the use of one of the cars for a couple of days, so we could visit some of the tourist sites if you like.'

Margaret would have preferred a day alone with her daughter, but she was too scared to hire a car and drive in this strange, alien land, and she felt fairly helpless. She longed for Graham's capable presence.

'I'll leave it to you,' she said. 'You both know the best places to go.'

The car was battered and covered in dust and the inside smelt strongly of cigarette smoke. Margaret settled herself in the front seat with some misgivings. She hoped that Chaim wouldn't tear along in the abandoned way she had seen drivers speeding past on the journey here the day before.

'I'll drive slowly,' he said, apparently reading her thoughts, 'so that you can see the scenery! We'll start with the lake and my bananas.'

He grinned at her, and she had to admit to herself that he was extremely attractive.

'Our orange groves,' he pointed out as the road wound through vast plantations. 'Jaffas! We export them all over the world, but the bananas are my special joy.'

'I thought you looked after the chickens?'

'That's only temporary. I'm coming back on to

bananas soon. I'm not too keen on chickens!'

'A bit smelly, being kept inside in all this heat, I should think.' Margaret remembered the tough brown-feathered characters that pecked and scratched round the farm in the uncertain Cornish climate.

'They take a lot of keeping cool and clean, certainly. Miriam seems to like them.'

'I feel sorry for the poor things,' said Miriam. 'I've got to learn not to be so silly about animals. That's one of the hardest things for me!'

She suddenly pointed to the view as they negotiated a sharp bend in the road.

'Look, Mum—Galilee!'

'Kinneret,' Chaim corrected as the expanse of calm blue water came into view.

Margaret looked, and for the first time since her plane had landed the magic of the place communicated itself to her. Galilee! It was Galilee, not Kinneret. Galilee. She remembered the hymns she had sung about it in the little chapel in Cornwall and the number of times it had figured in the childish drawings brought back from Sunday school by Charles and James, and Miriam too, years ago when they were little. And now she was here, seeing it in reality. It lay spread out before her between its encircling hills, little changed by the passing of many years.

'Please stop in the layby,' she said. 'I just want to stand and stare for a moment.'

'Yes, it's a nice view,' Chaim remarked casually.

'Nice view? It's Galilee!'

To him it was probably little more than a source of water for irrigation, fish for market and a pleasant place to swim, she reflected sadly.

She climbed out of the car and stood silently for a time shielding her eyes from the glare of the brilliant sunshine. Miriam came and stood beside her.

'It doesn't mean the same things to us Jews, you know, Mum. It's precious because it's our land, our country, part of our history, and it's a fertile region too, but that's all. No great religious significance!'

Margaret turned to look at her daughter. She suddenly realised the full import of her words. 'You mean. . .' She couldn't finish the sentence.

'Yes, I mean that I've adopted the Jewish faith. I'm Jewish and I want to belong fully. Well, I'm not going to be one of those fanatical types. Chaim is agnostic. But I'm certainly not Christian any more.'

Suddenly Margaret knew that she had lost. Miriam wouldn't be coming home with her. This land had claimed her child. She remembered her mother's face and her mother's voice. 'She's Jewish,' she had said all those years ago as she bent over the little hospital cot and looked at her new granddaughter.

Tears blurred the lovely hills and the blue of the sky and lake. The sun beat down on Margaret's uncovered head and she turned and got back into the car.

'Where now?' she asked, brushing the tears away, and groping in her handbag for her sunglasses and a handkerchief. 'I should like to see Capernaum and Nazareth, and I'd just love to go right down to the lakeside and paddle in the water!'

'A quick look at Chaim's beloved bananas first,' Miriam said. 'He's so proud of them that we have to go there before he'll allow us to see anything else. Then Tiberias for some shopping, a picnic on the beach and a swim, the Mount of Beatitudes and then Nazareth and Capernaum. All tourists want to see those places. Does that suit?'

'It sounds wonderful,' said Margaret.

* * *

The bananas were impressive.

'The climate isn't quite right for them,' Chaim explained. 'We have to wrap each bunch of fruit in brown paper in winter and then they have to be protected from the very hot sun in August. It's a lot of work, but I enjoy the challenge. Almost everything here is a challenge. That's partly why I like it!'

Margaret wanted to reply that Oxford was a challenge. 'You're keeping Miriam from the greatest opportunity of her life!' she wanted to scream at him, but she refrained. Instead she smiled politely. 'Isn't there something about the desert blossoming like the rose?' she said.

'Yes. Well, this part of Israel has never been desert, but it wasn't always as productive as it is now. It needed modern technology, and that's what we're able to make use of.'

Margaret looked at him thoughtfully. He knew nothing of the turmoil in her mind. He was so taken up with his life, the life he apparently wanted her daughter to share, and which he believed was the most wonderful on earth. She smiled a little to herself. He was so enthusiastic that he probably carried everyone he met along in his earnest zeal. Perhaps twenty years ago his eagerness might have infected her just as it was captivating her daughter.

They had to leave the car and walk beneath the giant leaves of the trees. They flapped now and then like great fans in the hot and infrequent breeze and the temporary shade was welcome. The ground beneath their feet was damp. Chaim saw her looking down at it, careful where she was treading.

'Irrigation,' he explained. 'We have to flood the fields regularly to keep them damp. We can't afford sprinklers yet.'

'It's all very impressive,' Margaret said, trying to be enthusiastic. 'I can see you're all working very hard and making all the old prophecies come true.'

They both turned to look at her.

'You know about the prophecies?'

'Of course.' She laughed suddenly at the earnest faces of the two young people. 'There are lots of them in my guidebook. I was amazed to find bits of the Bible in a modern guide when I started reading it. I was amusing myself trying to find out a bit about Israel on the plane. How about "He that tills the land shall be satisfied with bread"? I remember that one.'

'Good for you!' Chaim said, and they all laughed.

'And now,' said Margaret, 'talking about bread makes me think of that picnic you promised, and I want to walk on the shores of Galilee. I want to see what I've been singing about for so many Sundays of my life.'

He stared at her. 'Sundays? I thought you were Jewish?'

'Didn't Miriam explain? I've taken the faith of my husband,' she said, determined not to be scared of his vibrant personality.

'But that's terrible. You can't. You can believe in nothing at all, but not Christianity!'

Here it was again, that fierce, adamant statement.

'I'm sorry, Chaim,' she said. 'You'll have to accept that Miriam's family are all good Anglicans.'

To her relief he burst out laughing. 'To Galilee, as you call it, then,' he said. 'But first we've to get some things for the kibbutz in Tiberias.'

They left her in the courtyard of a small café while they shopped. Chaim ordered her a large orange juice, and she was grateful for its icy coolness and for the bamboo trellis with its thick vine leaves that shaded the tables. It reminded her of the South of France.

'We'll be as quick as we can,' Chaim said. 'I hope you don't mind.'

'I'll be glad of the rest. I'm not used to this heat,' she said, settling herself in the comfortable cane chair. 'Take as long as you like.'

She watched them walk together hand in hand down the road to the market and the shops, and for a moment she was content and vaguely happy for them. If only this could have happened in England. If only he were a fellow student at Oxford. She allowed herself the luxury of daydreaming for a time, and then she brought her thoughts back to reality. One couldn't order one's children's lives. It was a painful lesson that had been forced on her lately.

The swinging sixties! She thought of the term reluctantly. All three of her children were grown up, at least they considered themselves to be so. They were straining to be away, impatient of anything or anyone who stood between them and their supposed freedom.

She sipped her welcome drink, cupping the cold glass with her hands.

Miriam will do just whatever she wants with her life, she told herself firmly, and there is nothing that either Graham or I can do about it. Except persuade, of course. There is always persuasion left. Miriam might change her mind, after all. One never knows with the young!

The shopping was done more quickly than she imagined. She saw them returning, each carrying a large cardboard box, and their rucksacks straining at their shoulders.

The car was parked on the roadside; she could see it from where she was sitting. They called across to her and waved, and dumped their heavy loads on the pavement while Chaim groped in his pocket for the car key. When everything was stowed carefully inside the capacious old boot they came across to her and sank down thankfully on the bench opposite.

'Another job completed,' said Chaim. 'More orange juice all round and then we'll start the sightseeing. Tabgha first?'

They suffered the suffocating heat of the car again for a few miles along the road that lined the shore, and then, finding the welcome shade of some trees, parked.

'The beach is just down there,' he said, indicating a path that wound through an olive grove. Margaret looked, and saw glimpses of the sea between silvery branches. They walked over the dusty brown earth, carrying bathing things and towels, the picnic basket that Miriam had retrieved from among the boxes of shopping, and a carrier-bag of large oranges. Always here in the land of the Jaffa there were oranges. They seemed to take the place of tea as the panacea to cure all ills!

'I'm going to paddle!' Margaret said impulsively when they reached the shore. 'I must get my feet in that water before I do anything else!' She removed her sandals and walked into the small, lapping waves. It was cool, welcoming, and she looked back at them and laughed. 'It's just the same as any sea anywhere,' she called. 'It doesn't feel special—just warmer than Cornwall!'

Chaim and Miriam were in swimming things now, and they joined her.

'Why don't you get changed and come right in?' Miriam said, and for a moment Margaret was tempted, but then she felt that her feet were enough. Enough for today, anyway. There would be other days. She had two whole weeks. She stood and watched them go out into the deeper water. They swam together, laughing and calling to each other, and Margaret longed once more for Graham. Then dramatically and without warning her thoughts were back suddenly much further in time. Back to that lonely, sea-washed cove, where the gulls were screaming and the cold shock of the waves was on her skin. She remembered Karl again, and more clearly than at home, remembered the day they had swum and made love, and her heart turned over and would not be calmed. She felt passion and desire rise in her body as she had not truly felt it since that time, that golden English summer day which lay carefully buried in the deepest part of her.

She looked at the girl swimming and laughing in the warm water of such a different sea, the girl who was the result of that loving. Life was turning its full circle, and she suddenly felt very much alone. These two were a unit already. She saw the way Chaim looked at Miriam and she knew suddenly in a flash of insight that this was the man who could make her daughter happy. It was their obvious love for each other that had sent her memories scudding once more back through the years. She recognised it, and she turned away, not wanting to see, not wanting to come to terms with its meaning.

She picked her way carefully over the stony beach and spread out her towel where the stones gave way to smaller pebbles, and she sat down, hoping that the peace and beauty of the place would fill her mind, easing the unwelcome thoughts and removing the sense of loss that the sight of those two together gave her. The heat of the sun and the beauty of the hills and lake gradually induced a kind of stupor, and she lay back and stared up into the unbroken blue of the sky. There were no gulls, only some birds she did not recognise.

The two young people came out of the water eventually, and she heard their laughter as they walked gingerly over the painful stones. She sat up and looked at them again, and wondered unwillingly if perhaps this life was better for Miriam than long years in Oxford. She tried to believe that it could be so.

They found some shade for their picnic, but the burning midday heat drove them back at last to the even hotter car. There was no breath of air now, and even beneath the trees Margaret fanned herself desperately.

'Up into the hills,' Chaim said, opening every window. 'It's lovely up there, and there's usually a breeze!'

The road climbed upwards, twisting its way round tortuous hairpin bends, and Margaret held on to her seat with clenched, frightened hands. At last Chaim pulled the car into a car park, and she breathed a sigh of relief.

'The Mount of Beatitudes!' Miriam said. 'There's the church, and although I don't go much for any of them I really do think this one is quite lovely.'

Its grey dome was encircled by a porticoed balcony, and they walked into its welcome shade. Margaret gasped at the sweeping view of lake and hills, and at the great palms and cypresses that were growing together in the carefully tended gardens.

'Palms from the desert and pines from the Med,' said Chaim the agriculturalist. 'Beautiful, aren't they?'

So he had some aesthetic appreciation of this lovely land, Margaret thought. He wasn't entirely the practical farmer! The thought gave her pleasure.

Miriam was standing beside her staring out at the hills and the vast expanse of cultivated and fruitful acres far below shimmering in the heat. She came suddenly and took her mother's hand, and there were tears in her eyes.

'Bring Daddy to see it,' she said quietly. 'He'll

understand, I know he will. Isn't it beautiful, Mum? It's my land, my Israel. I can't explain. I love it so much and it demands my whole devotion. Can you ever forgive me?'

'I'll bring him,' Margaret said. 'And there's no need to forgive. Perhaps it's I who need forgiveness!'

They visited the lovely ruins of Capernaum later that afternoon when the sun was beginning to cast long shadows on the ancient stones, and Margaret was awed and quiet as she looked. After that the raucous, noisy streets of Nazareth were a shock and she was glad to get back in the early evening to the kibbutz, to her little room and a shower and supper again in the ugly, friendly dining-hall.

'Have you enjoyed today?' Miriam asked anxiously as they sat together outside in the warm night air.

'It's been wonderful, and now I'm quite exhausted,' she said. 'And it was nice getting to know Chaim too. I like him, Miriam.'

She paused, wondering how to continue the conversation that they were both dreading. It was no use going on with only half an understanding between them. Everything must be disçussed. Margaret braced herself, took another sip of coffee and looked at her daughter. Yes, she was pretty, she thought. Her hair looked longer, curling on her shoulders, and there was a serenity and a depth of purpose in the dark eyes that had never been there before. She remembered the photograph of her grandmother as a young girl that she had found in the old house in St Pauls. It stood now in its silver frame on her desk at home, and in the girl before her she could see the features of that other girl from another age, a girl who surely would have leapt at the chance of life here in the promised and unobtainable land.

'So you really want to stay here?' she asked. 'Give up Oxford?'

'I know it sounds crazy.' Miriam was staring at the porch lights just beginning to come on at the front of the other little dwellings as she spoke, and Margaret knew she wasn't really seeing any of it. There was a distant, dreamy expression in the girl's eyes.

'You won't believe me, Mum,' she continued, 'but it's more than just Chaim. Oh, yes, I love him, but I'm totally committed to this place too. I was trying to explain this afternoon when we were up in the hills. Seeing the land spread out in front of me like that makes me quite sure that I'm making the right choice. It doesn't sound very rational or sensible, I know. It's an emotional response, but no worse for that.'

'Wouldn't you be more use here if you got your education first? A good degree from Oxford would make your contribution more valuable, surely?'

'If they accept me as a full member of the kibbutz they might send me to the university in Jerusalem instead. I'll have to wait, of course, and I'll have to learn Hebrew, but I'm prepared for that.' She swiped at the mosquitoes that were trying to eat both of them as she spoke.

'I came here determined to persuade you to change your mind, you know,' Margaret said. A sudden weariness overcame her. She hoped it was only the heat and those horrible little biting insects, but she suspected that it was more than that. Until this afternoon there had still been some hope in her heart. Now there was none.

Suddenly another thought sprang into her mind, terrifying her. She remembered seeing girl soldiers at the airport. 'You won't have to go into the army, will you?' she asked.

'I don't know. I might. Don't worry about that. It'll be fun, and I don't expect there'll be another war for a bit. If I get married I'd be exempt anyway!'

It was all too incredible. Margaret shook her head in wonder and amazement. Perhaps she was getting old. At thirty-eight she hadn't the desire for adventure. Maybe that was it. She remembered her resolutions of the afternoon. She had to let go!

'Then we'll not talk about it any more,' she said. 'I'll just enjoy the rest of my stay.'

'But I want to talk about it, Mummy,' Miriam said. 'I'm so happy that you're not very angry. I want you to try to understand and begin to feel a little bit of my enthusiasm.'

'You mean that you want me to be an Israeli as well?' Having at last accepted the unacceptable, Margaret felt a sudden lifting of her depression. 'Well, that'll never happen,' she said, and she laughed slightly. 'Whatever would your father say?'

'My father? You mean Daddy?'

The smile died on Margaret's face. She could hear Dinah's voice from next door, and she remembered the marks of Auschwitz on her arm. Miriam must never know of the German blood that ran in her veins! She stood up purposefully. 'Let's go for a last walk around the fence,' she said. 'It's lovely now it's cooler. I like to hear the cicadas. They remind me of all those times we camped in Spain and the South of France when you were all little. Remember?'

They walked arm in arm along the gravelled paths, and Margaret thought how pleasant and simple life had been then. War had been forgotten, its aftermath and its effects things of the distant past for her happy little family. Here it wasn't so.

Suddenly there was an explosion, distant, but frightening nevertheless.

'Whatever was that?' she exclaimed.

'Just an incident at the border, probably,' Miriam told her complacently. 'We're fairly near the Golan Heights up here in Galilee, and Syria doesn't like us much!'

Margaret shuddered. It seemed to be of even less importance than the mosquitoes!

'Come home, Miriam,' she said. It was one last final, desperate plea. 'Come home where it's safe!'

'What do I want with safety, Mummy?' she said. 'I'm eighteen and life is for living. That's what I can do here—live!'

Margaret lay in her narrow bed that night scratching at her numerous bites, and then she heard the guns again, and for a moment understood. After all, she was Jewish too and this was the land promised to her fathers. Next year in Jerusalem! She remembered the Passover words and fell asleep full of expectation. Tomorrow they were going to Jerusalem!

CHAPTER TWENTY

1966

THE evening was the best time, the best time in all the twenty-four hours. Miriam could smell the scents of flowers and herbs and orange blossom at night, and it was cool, just cool enough to enjoy being out of doors. She walked hand in hand with Chaim and she was completely happy. This was the first time she had really been in love. There had been boyfriends at school, spotty teenagers who held no attraction for her at all. She had repulsed all their fumbling, groping attempts at lovemaking, usually laughing at them. 'Chilly Mirry', they had nicknamed her, but she had merely smiled, knowing that some day someone would change all that. She had built images of him in her mind and kept herself for him. She looked up at the man at her side and knew that her search had ended.

'Are you sure you don't mind giving up two more days for Mum?' she asked him, and for reply he put his arm round her, pulling her close.

'To show Jerusalem to anyone is a pleasure, and to show it to you and your mother will be the ultimate joy!'

Miriam chuckled at his words. 'Those are rather flowery sentiments for a farmer, aren't they?'

'I'm a poet as well, or had you forgotten?'

'No, I haven't forgotten.' She thought of the letters she had received from him during the few days he was away in Tel Aviv the previous week. They were locked up in her small case, precious both for the sentiments he had expressed and for the words he had used. It was important to know that beneath the practical, tough and commonplace image that he presented to the world lay a sensitive and slightly vulnerable man.

'It's a long way, isn't it?' she queried.

'It would be shorter if we could go through Samaria, but of course we have to go right round, so yes, it's a long way. I presume your mother knows that she can't go into the Old City?'

'I'd never really thought about it. You mean the Arab part?'

'Of course. All our precious sites, the Western Wall, everything. The only part we've had since '48 is the modern town outside the walls.'

Miriam recognised the bitterness in his voice. She was so new to Israel that the division of the land and the exclusion of all Jews from all the holy places that lay within the borders of Jordan wasn't too much of a problem to her yet. There had been no time to travel, little opportunity to find out about the depths of feeling such limitations brought.

'Most of our borders I can accept,' Chaim went on, 'but Jerusalem is different. Having it divided as it is seems just crazy. It's the source of everything, a kind of cornerstone, if you like. It symbolises our whole history.'

'But you say you're not religious, so why are you so steamed up about it—about all those holy places, I mean?'

'That's hard to answer. I've never seen the Wall, but it still means an awful lot to me. It's something in my heart, in the way I feel.'

He looked at her, embarrassed, then went on, and his voice lost its dreamy tone.

'I get so angry and frustrated sometimes that I want

to go right out there and start a war or something to get it back. Do you realise that no Jew of my age has ever been allowed into the Old City?'

Miriam looked up at him, trying to understand. 'Some friends of ours went last year from England,' she said. 'They showed us their photographs, the Church of the Holy Sepulchre, the Via Dolorosa and all that. The Western Wall too.'

Her innocent remark caused him to clench his fists angrily. She could feel his tenseness in the arm that still lay about her shoulder.

'Yes—oh, yes! You can visit Jordan and do a tour of all the ancient shrines of old Jerusalem if you come straight from Europe or America and if you're Gentile and Christian or Muslim, but just beware if they can trace any Jewish blood in your pedigree! You'd be shot for an Israeli spy straight away, probably!'

'There's no hope of Mum going through the Mandelbaum Gate, then, into the Arab part?'

He stared at her and his eyes were cold. 'Are you crazy or something?'

She was shocked and humiliated by his reply, ashamed that she was so ignorant.

'Well, she's a baptised and confirmed Anglican—she converted properly after she married. I don't think there's anything on her passport about being Jewish. I thought she might get away with it.'

'You can't cross from Israel to Jordan unless you're the Angel Gabriel, and they'd probably arrest even him! Diplomats can go over occasionally, I believe, and a few characters with very special passes, but no Jew. They don't even recognise that we exist, and if forced to, then they shoot us!'

Miriam sighed. Politics had never interested her very much. She had been born the same year as the State of

Israel had been declared, that much she knew, but as she grew up it had all seemed so very far away, and her happy, secure home in Bristol was another world. Israel and its frequent wars had mattered very little until a few months ago, until the realisation of her Jewishness had truly dawned on her, overturning her life.

She was suddenly depressed in spite of the beauty of the night. The smell of the pines near the perimeter fence filled the air and the scent of rosemary too. They were walking beside a low hedge of rosemary, and she put her hand out, touching it reverently. It was a herb she loved. She plucked a small piece.

'Rosemary, that's for remembrance,' she said softly, and she held it up to Chaim. 'Do you ever read Shakespeare?' Suddenly it was necessary to think of something else, to dwell on the pleasant, ordinary things, the delights of her past. 'We go to the Bristol Old Vic regularly. We've got season tickets.'

'What on earth are you talking about?'

'Just home. The rosemary reminded me—scents always remind me of places. Mum grows it and she puts it in with the sheets. She makes little pillows with it. It's supposed to make you sleep. The climate's better for it here, though. You don't often see a whole hedge of it in England.'

Chaim laughed and pulled her over suddenly into the sanctuary of some larger bushes.

'Come here, you strange, lovely girl,' he said. 'Life was so earnest and hard, perhaps even dreary, until you came. I didn't realise it, of course, but now it bubbles like champagne!'

His arms were round her and he kissed her full on the mouth as he had never done before, and she responded tremulously, her whole body alive with wanting him.

Rough branches were brushing her bare arms, not the soft, accommodating rosemary now, and he pulled her down on to the dry sandy earth. His weight was hard on her body. Everything seemed to shrink into the small space they occupied. Nothing else mattered. Jerusalem, the kibbutz, Bristol, the whole world, it was all a dream. This present moment, this terrible, wonderful desire was the only reality. Her feet dug into the earth and she could feel his large, strong hands exploring her body, gentle and urgent together. Both sensations were present in the fervour of their passion. She moaned and saw the moon between the leaves above her head, and she wanted to give herself to him willingly and without thought. But it was Chaim who stopped without warning. She felt him shiver slightly and he drew apart from her and sat up abruptly.

'What's the matter?' she asked, suddenly frightened and confused. 'What have I done?'

'Nothing. You've just become too precious to me,' he whispered, and there was a kind of anger in his voice, intense and strange.

He pulled her to her feet and she stumbled against him, her mind in a turmoil. He was holding her hand tightly in his and he led her back to the lighted part of the grounds where they could hear voices, and here and there music very softly played. Work started early and most people were going to bed already. The cicadas filled the quiet night with their gentle strumming, and she hoped that Chaim wasn't aware of the fervent thumping of her disappointed heart. He was silent for a while and then she realised that he was leading her in the direction of the hostel that she shared with the other summer volunteers. Just before they reached it, he stopped and pulled her into his arms again, not looking for seclusion this time. His kiss was brief and without the passion of a few minutes before.

'I'll never let that happen again,' he said. 'I'm sorry, Miriam. Goodnight. Be ready for seven o'clock tomorrow. We want to get away early.'

His tone was dismissive, and she pulled away from him with no understanding. She half ran the few yards to the doorway and pushed it open. Quickly she washed and climbed into her bunk, and the tears came then, but her sobbing was quiet. The others were asleep, and she mustn't wake them. She didn't want any questions asked. The only certainty in her mind was that she loved Chaim and there was nothing in the world that she wouldn't do for him. There were no sacrifices too great for her to make. Oxford, England, home, money, parents, all must take second place. It was the sudden way he had cut short their lovemaking that devastated her. Surely if his love for her was as great as her own he couldn't have left her so abruptly? She tossed and turned in the confining space of the hard bunk and could find no answers. 'Too precious', he had said. In the turmoil of her complete inexperience and suddenly discovered passion the words were incomprehensible.

Sleep came at last, and then the morning, and breakfast, and the prospect of two wonderful days in his company. True, her mother would be with them, but in a strange way she was glad of that. She had never been able to achieve any degree of closeness with Margaret, but yesterday they had begun to understand each other a little. Perhaps her love for Chaim was making her a more mature person, she thought, more able to handle the complicated emotions that life seemed to be throwing around. Well, she hoped she could understand Chaim and his sudden coldness. She needed all her wisdom for that.

* * *

There was an uneasy silence at first as they drove south once more along the dusty road towards Nazareth. But it didn't last long. In spite of the devastating experience of the night before Miriam was excited about the day out, and she stared through the car window at the countryside with its tidy Israeli settlements dotted here and there, the houses bright and brash, sparkling in the early morning sun. There were Arab villages too, older and picturesque, nestling beneath their native hills, with children and chickens and goats mingling at the roadside in attractive disorder.

'Isn't it fantastic, Mum?' she said. 'All that's been done since '48.'

It was important that her mother should get the feel of the place, experience some of the pull and the magic, and then maybe she would convey it to Graham when she got home to England. Miriam couldn't really understand why she felt this deep, obsessive love for this country and why she identified so completely with it rather than with Bristol and everything she had known since birth. Her only sadness was that it separated her from her parents, especially from Graham. And he wasn't even Jewish. It would be so much more difficult for him to understand, but she wanted his blessing very much indeed. She thought of him now as they rattled along the road, and she couldn't imagine him on a kibbutz. He would hate almost everything about it.

'I wasn't very keen on Nazareth,' her mother said, answering her question from the front seat. 'It was a bit of a shock after all the pictures of it I had in my mind.'

'Most people say that,' Chaim told her. 'We won't stop there today. No stops, in fact, except to eat. Straight to Jerusalem.'

Another shiver of excitement rippled through

Miriam. What was it Jews had said every Passover for hundreds of years? Like Margaret the night before, she remembered the words, 'Next year in Jerusalem!' Well, it wasn't next year for her. It was now, today, in a few hours' time.

'Megiddo!' Her mother noticed the signpost first. 'Look,' she indicated, 'it said Megiddo. Isn't that where the last battle will be?'

Miriam's excitement gave way momentarily to a shiver of fear as they stared out of the car window.

'Don't talk about wars, Mum,' she said. 'Chaim will have to fight if there's any trouble, and there always seem to be incidents happening lately.'

'Armageddon I'm talking about,' said Margaret, laughing. 'The end of the world and all that. Nothing imminent!'

'Great battlefield, this,' Chaim commented light-heartedly. 'The plain of Megiddo! Lots of battles have been fought here!'

Miriam looked at the back of his head as he drove, and the thought of him in army uniform frightened her but thrilled her too. She wondered if she would get used to the ever-present threat of war, the thick barbed wire fence around the kibbutz, the guard at the entrance and on the hill outside. And the machine-guns!

No wars had affected her life so far. She had no direct experience of aggression, only a tranquil growing up, with nothing more exciting than netball matches, new clothes, a party now and then, and holidays each year, always until now in quiet and beautiful places chosen by her parents for their serene and untroubled peace. All that was gone. She had come alive suddenly and she was in love with a man, a soldier—more than a soldier, a pioneer. A place too.

She belonged. It was all hers. Life was beginning.

She stared at his back again and at the powerful muscles of his arms as he held the steering-wheel. She remembered telling her mother that it wasn't only Chaim that was holding her here. Well, was it? A small shudder ran through her as she thought of last night and his abrupt ending of their lovemaking. Could she bear to stay on here if he left her? Was all this love for the land, for Israel, just a delusion? She hoped not. She desperately hoped not, but you could never tell.

Jerusalem was almost a disappointment. To be so near to the ancient sites and not to touch them, not to pray at the Western Wall, not to be able to walk on the Mount of Olives, was the ultimate deprivation. Influenced by Chaim, Miriam was now beginning to feel the sorrow too. She felt it more than her mother.

But to Margaret, just to know that she was standing here in these streets, in the Holy City at last, was a mind-boggling experience.

'It's still exciting to be here,' she said, feeling the exasperation of the two younger ones. 'Look over there. How do they manage to wear such clothes in this heat?'

She passed her hand across her damp forehead and they all stared at the two men in long black coats and wide-brimmed velvet hats. Their hair immaculately fashioned into ringlets hanging down over their ears and reaching almost to their collars completed the unreal picture. Margaret remembered her mother putting her hair into rags when she was very small and wanted to look like Shirley Temple. The rags had produced ringlets all over her head, and she stared at the men, irreverently wondering if they suffered similar agonies each night sleeping in some sort of curlers to produce that effect!

'They're from Mea Shearim, the very orthodox Jewish quarter,' Chaim explained. 'Very strict, and they don't approve of modern Israel at all. They are mostly from Eastern Europe, hence the thick clothes!'

'Don't worry, Mum,' Miriam said. 'I'll never be like that. Jewish perhaps, but never fanatical.'

They all laughed and drove round the modern streets, sharing Chaim's pride as he pointed out various achievements of the new state.

'The Hadassah Hospital,' he said. 'One of the best in the world.'

It was at the new museum that they found some shade at last, and after admiring the various exhibits and remarking over the Dead Sea Scrolls they sank exhausted on to the grass beneath the shade of some small trees and ate their picnic. Then suddenly into the midst of the tranquillity came Chaim's suggestion.

'Do you want to see Yad Vashem?' he asked.

Margaret knew that this was the memorial to the victims of the Holocaust, and she knew too that it would torture her mind, bringing Karl back to her yet again. He had seemed to come to her so often since she came to Israel. She recalled his words. They echoed down the years and she could still hear the sorrow in his voice. 'I've seen the pictures too,' he had told her. 'Re-education, they call it. They've been telling us how evil the Third Reich was.'

To walk round that place with her daughter at her side would be a sort of hell.

'Not really.' She answered Chaim's question with true British understatement. 'It's very depressing, I should think.'

Miriam turned and stared at her and she was aware of her look of intense surprise.

'But, Mum, we must go there! It's important. You

were alive when it all happened. Surely you want to see?'

'Well, no, I don't want to see, as a matter of fact.'

The surprise on Miriam's face was replaced by swift antagonism, and Chaim must have sensed the conflict, for he looked from one to the other and burst into the conversation.

'I've only been once, years ago. We had a sort of pilgrimage there from school,' he said. 'I should like to go very much, but it's up to you.'

'We'll go, then,' Margaret decided. 'Yes, you're right. It's something I should do.'

They walked through the Avenue of the Righteous with its carob trees marking the names of Gentiles who had risked or lost their lives helping Jews during the war. Then there were the pictures, the photographs with commentaries in Hebrew and English, photographs so terrible that the human mind mostly failed to comprehend the total horror. Margaret stared at them, and at paintings and drawings done by many of the victims.

'They were hidden and smuggled out, or found afterwards in the ruins,' Chaim told her.

They walked through the Hall of Names. It was all that was left of so many—just a name on a wall. Margaret felt sick.

'Six million slaughtered!' Miriam said dramatically. 'It takes some believing. Yet Germans come here. We've got some working on the kibbutz.'

'They aren't our enemies any more,' Chaim said. 'We have others now!' There was a sinister ring to his voice which Margaret noticed but Miriam did not.

'That's beside the point,' she said. 'They did it, didn't they? Ordinary Germans? They put them in the gas chambers, burnt them in the ovens, experimented on babies and children. Six million Jews! I'll never speak to a German in my life!'

Margaret's heart thumped in fear as she heard her daughter's words. She and Karl had created this child who was voicing these awful, unspeakable things about her father's race. Could she live with the knowledge for the rest of her life and not tell?

'You can't have thoughts like that, Miriam.' Chaim's voice was stern now and he turned his searching dark eyes towards her. 'No one can go through life hating. And anyway, there's no such thing as a bad race, only individuals, a few. The young ones who come here are mostly ashamed. Those we've got now are a nice bunch.'

Margaret looked at him in surprise. His words comforted her. He couldn't know anything of her worried thoughts, but it was almost as though he did. Perhaps he had some second sight. Wasn't his name Macleod? He hardly seemed to acknowledge his Highland blood, but it was there nevertheless.

They walked out into the burning sunlight and were all silent. Margaret thought of Karl again. Here in this bright, vivid land she was always reluctantly remembering. She could see his blue eyes and his smile, and she rebelled against Miriam's words. Had it been such a terrible thing to love him? Was love ever so wrong that it could lead to a lifetime of deceit and fear? She had to admit that sometimes it could be, but for her? In no way could she take that one magical day of her life and push it into a box marked 'evil'. She had loved him so much, and perhaps she did still, but that mustn't be so. It just added to the conflict. She must go home soon. This disturbing place must be left behind to those who could cope with it. In Bristol, beneath a gentler sky and with Graham at her side, life seemed infinitely more simple!

They stayed that night in another kibbutz near Jerusalem, and Margaret accepted the hospitality that was showered upon her. She smiled and talked and no one knew of the sadness in her heart. There was more sightseeing the next day and then the long, hot drive back to Galilee. She wished that she were going to Tel Aviv and the plane that would take her back to nice, safe England and Graham. She longed to see his immaculately suited figure waiting for her at the station. She would manage the whole journey on her own, she had told him. He could meet her at Temple Meads.

Before starting on the road north again back to Rosh Hazim, Chaim drove them to various vantage-points where they could look over into the other Jerusalem across the border, the forbidden places.

'That's the Mount of Olives over there,' he told them, 'and you can see the rooftops of the Old City.'

Margaret looked at the ancient walls just visible from where they were standing, and then she looked at Chaim and she could feel the bitterness in his voice, and the sorrow too. She turned away quickly. Were there tears in his eyes hastily brushed away? Jerusalem had caused so many tears and so much bloodshed that she could hardly bear to look over at its golden stones. She wondered if she would ever be able to go to those hallowed, precious places. She was aware of Miriam at her side taking Chaim's hand for comfort.

At one quiet and peaceful place beneath some shady trees they stopped again, and Margaret got out of the car and crossed the road to get a better look.

'Don't go any further,' Chaim called. 'In fact, better get into the car. This is very close to the border, and you might get shot!'

She looked at him in disbelief.

'There have been incidents, and if there's a shooting then we retaliate, and it escalates,' he told her.

'Miriam, oh, Miriam!' she wanted to shout. 'What are you doing in this troubled place?' But she said nothing. She just obeyed.

'I'll sit in the back for the journey home,' she said. 'Let's get on our way. I think I've had enough for a bit, and it's so hot. All I can think of at this moment is a nice swim in that new pool of yours!'

They all laughed, the tension broken.

'You called it "home", Mum,' Miriam said. 'So you're beginning to think it's not so bad after all!'

CHAPTER TWENTY-ONE

1966

THE remaining days of Margaret's traumatic visit to Israel passed quickly in a panorama of sights and sounds and heat. There was so much to see and to experience, and always people around wanting to talk. Time with Miriam, however, just the two of them together, was almost non-existent. Margaret began to wonder if it was deliberate.

Eventually, on the last evening, they were on their own. Chaim was starting a week of guard duty at the vantage-point on the hill outside the kibbutz.

'I'm a bit frightened for him,' Miriam confessed. 'We're so near the border here.'

Margaret looked at her daughter and grieved for her lost youth. She should be getting ready to go to Oxford now, not worrying about a tense political situation and a boyfriend guarding a hillside with a Sten gun at his hip! They were sitting on the porch of the little *binyan* which had been home for the past two eventful weeks.

'He'll be all right,' she said. 'He's a very capable young man.'

Miriam sniffed doubtfully. 'Capable, yes, but that won't protect him from stray bullets or worse, will it?'

'If you're going to worry every time he has to go out on watch then you'd better not stay here,' Margaret said a trifle cruelly. 'I can see that you need to be made of tough material to live on a kibbutz, especially one here in Galilee.'

'I know that, Mum—I know. I'm going to stay,

though, and I'll learn to be strong. I've just got to!'

'You don't have to. There's home waiting for you, and college.' Suddenly, in spite of all her good resolutions, the words came tumbling out. 'How about giving Oxford a try, just for one term? You can decide at Christmas what to do.'

There was a long silence, and to her dismay Margaret started to cry and she was glad of the quickly falling dusk to hide her tears.

'Don't cry, Mummy. I love you. I do really love you.'

'And I love you too.'

She heard herself speak the words almost as if they were coming from someone else. But it was the second time in these two weeks that she had felt this new deep bonding. Her heart was responding to Miriam's love, the love that had been there hidden between them all through the years since her daughter's birth, denied until now, until this precious time in the land that seemed to cause all pretences to fall, all truth to be revealed.

'But I can't come back!'

Miriam spoke quietly, and Margaret could feel the iron resolve and the desperate sadness too, and she knew that any more pleading on her part could destroy the delicate balance of their relationship with each other. Words were hard to find after that. What could she say? Perhaps there was no need to say much more.

'Then be happy,' she whispered. 'And remember that Daddy and I will always be waiting for you if you change your mind. Don't be proud, Miriam. Promise me that.'

'I promise.'

'Come home for Christmas? Bring Chaim, perhaps? You'll make us all very happy if you do, especially Daddy.'

'I don't know. They might not give us leave. I'll see. How about a swim? I love swimming after dark.'

The abrupt change of tone and mood took Margaret by surprise, but she jumped up, determined to adapt. Nothing must spoil this last evening.

Graham was standing on the platform. Margaret saw him before the train stopped, and her heart beat more quickly in anticipation of the warm, safe encircling of his arms around her. She was unutterably sad for him too. The bond he and Miriam had between them was special, a father-and-daughter relationship that had been almost perfect through the years, and had made up for her own inadequacies as a mother.

Impatiently and with some difficulty she hauled her suitcase from the rack and pushed through the grey crowds on to the grey platform, and for a moment wished for the sunshine and colour of Israel. It was cold for September.

He took the case from her and put it down at his feet, and then she was in his arms and she knew that she was going to cry again. 'I'm sorry.'

He brushed the tears from her eyes and kissed her gently. 'Don't worry. You're back safely, and I love you.'

Holding hands for mutual comfort, they walked through the underpass to the station entrance and to the car.

'You must tell me all about it,' he said, 'but later. Charles is making a special meal for you!'

She smiled. She was looking forward to being with the boys again. They had always been fairly easy, uncomplicated, and Charles's recently discovered love of cooking had surprised and amused her. He always succeeded in everything he attempted, and this latest interest was no exception. It had its obvious uses too! she thought.

'He's done very well in the kitchen while you were away,' Graham said with a laugh. 'In fact, I told him that I would employ him as a cook if he's ever out of a job!'

'He'll never be that,' Margaret said. She was glad to turn her thoughts to her sons and away from Miriam for a time. For the past two weeks every emotion had been supercharged, and she felt exhausted. She just wanted a pleasant, easy time now with no decisions to be made, no complications of any kind.

They drove through the wet city streets and out into the countryside to the large, comfortable house with its well-kept lawns and trees. Margaret loved it, and she looked around with quiet pleasure as Graham parked the car in front of the garage and took her case from the boot. For a moment she thought of the tiny *binyan* and the dust and the heat, the barbed wire fence and Chaim with his Sten gun. Then she remembered Dinah and the marks on her arm.

I'm a very lucky woman, she thought. Very lucky indeed.

The meal was perfect, and Charles beamed with pleasure at her praise.

'Come on then, Mum,' he said when they were comfortably settled in the living-room with coffee percolating and Mozart quietly playing in the background. 'Let's hear about the Land of Promise and all that, and Mirry's boyfriend. What's he like? Must be pretty special to keep her from Oxford! No one would do that to me!'

'Your mother's tired,' Graham said. 'Leave it till tomorrow.'

Margaret touched his hand affectionately. 'No—I'm

refreshed now after that wonderful meal.' She turned to her son. 'Yes, Charles, I suppose Chaim is special—well, different from the boys Miriam knew here. He cares desperately about Israel. It's more important to him than almost everything.'

She tried to visualise his tall, vibrant personality in this room, and he didn't fit, didn't fit at all.

'More important than Miriam?'

It was James who asked the question. He had always been close to his sister, his quiet, thoughtful nature responding to her more buoyant one. Margaret hadn't thought about James being saddened by Miriam's absence. She had only considered Graham.

'I can't answer that,' she replied thoughtfully. 'Perhaps they couldn't answer it either. Israel is a very special place, like no other land, I suppose. It has a sort of magic pull that enslaves its people. You seem to either hate or love it passionately. I can't describe it or even begin to understand the reasons. It's something you have to feel inside.'

'Gosh, Mum, I do believe it's got you too!'

Charles's tone was bantering, not serious, but James stared at her.

'I've read a lot about it,' he said. 'I think I should like to go and experience it for myself. Perhaps I'll visit Miriam some time.'

The words fell on the peaceful room and into Margaret's heart like a knell of doom. She had almost forgotten that her sons were Jewish too, could be Israeli if they wished.

'Not you too, James!' she wailed. 'Not you as well!'

'Oh, don't worry about me going there to live or anything,' he said. 'It's too military and aggressive for me. I can't see myself in the Israeli army, and that's what it would mean, wouldn't it?'

'You'd look good waving a machine-gun around,' Charles said. 'I can just see you now, aiming it at every suspicious Arab you encountered!'

'Shut up!' Margaret shouted. 'Shut up, both of you! You don't know what you're talking about. Don't joke about it. Yes, go there if you want to and see for yourselves, but just don't joke.'

She was dismayed to feel tears coming again, and she knew that she must go to bed. The past two weeks had been even more exhausting and traumatic than she had realised. Perhaps she too was being pulled against her will towards Israel, the Land of Promise, as Charles had surprisingly called it. Well, it had very little promise for her. It had taken her daughter and looked likely to deprive her of one of her sons as well, possibly both. In no way did she underestimate the power of the land, Eretz Israel.

'Sorry, Mum.' It was James who broke the uncomfortable silence after her outburst. 'I couldn't give up my Christian faith anyway, could I, and that's what I should have to do if I took Israeli citizenship. They won't have Christian Jews.'

The statement was another surprise, and Margaret stared at her son in amazement. 'You've obviously been giving it a lot of thought.'

'Yes, I have. It's Mirry, of course. I can't believe it—she wanted to go to Oxford so much. There must be something more than just a boyfriend.'

'Want to bet!' Charles grinned, and got up from the settee. He went to the bookcase and pulled out two books and some records. '*Shalom*, everybody,' he said. 'Old James here is a bit of a dark horse. He's been secretly learning Hebrew.'

James's sensitive face flooded with colour and he grabbed the books from his brother.

'There was no need to tell her about that at this particular moment!'

His voice was angry. They seldom quarrelled, but Charles, frequently thoughtless and fun-loving, often teased the quieter James.

'Let me see.' Margaret held out her hand for the books. 'I should like to borrow them. Everyone seems to speak Hebrew in Israel, and if it's to be Miriam's home perhaps we all ought to try to learn it too.'

There had been little time during the past eventful weeks to think about the cottage in Cornwall, but a few days later a large brown envelope arrived in the post, and Margaret watched Graham open it carefully. Then he smiled and put it into her hands.

'Everything has been completed,' he said. 'It's ours. When do you want to go?'

Israel seemed an eternity away in that moment.

'Now. Now, today.' She laughed. 'It's just what I need. Space to breathe and think and hear the gulls again!'

'You and your gulls! You'll be sick of them after the first night there, I assure you.'

'Never! When can we go?'

'I think I could take a few days off next week. We could go and see Dottie and John. They'll not be too far away.'

'Wonderful and more wonderful,' Margaret said. 'I'd love to pour out all my woes to Dottie.'

Privately she knew that this cottage would solve another of her problems. Dottie was still her closest friend, but visiting her was difficult. The farm held too many memories and there was still a restraint between herself and John. Being so near meant that she could go over just for a couple of hours whenever they were in

Cornwall. That way she could with luck miss seeing too much of him.

'Woes?' Graham questioned. 'I thought you were getting used to the idea of Miriam living in Israel?'

'Who was it said that what you can't change you must learn to live with? Well, I'm trying to learn to live with the idea, but occasionally I still feel a bit weepy.' She smiled at him. 'How about you, though? I always felt you would be the one to be most hurt.'

'I want her to be happy. I want to see her again soon, though, just to be sure in my mind that it's really what she wants. I thought we might go out there for Christmas if she can't get home.'

'We couldn't go to Bethlehem!'

'I know that. It's a pity, but I wouldn't be going to see the sights. Just Miriam and this Chaim of hers.' He folded his newspaper and got up from the table, and Margaret looked at him affectionately. It would be nice to go to Israel with him. She wouldn't feel so alone and so vulnerable.

'We'll mention it when we write. I'm still hoping that they can come here. If not Christmas perhaps we could go in the spring. Apparently the flowers are beautiful then around Galilee.'

Margaret gathered up the breakfast things and carried them into the kitchen. Then she deliberately wrenched her thoughts away from her daughter and back to the brown envelope lying on the table.

'Can we go to Cornwall on Saturday?' she asked hopefully. 'If the boys don't want to come they can look after themselves here.'

'Good idea. We'll go without them. Just us. I must hurry.' He picked up his briefcase and rushed out and Margaret was alone. Charles and James always left early. Only a few more months and they would be finished with school and probably at college. She heard Graham's car reversing down the long drive and then the click of the gates at the end as he carefully closed them. She made herself another cup of coffee and wondered what it would be like with all three of her children away. Just herself and Graham left in the big house. She would only be around forty with almost half of her life remaining to be filled. She thought of Israel, the land of sun and promise and challenge, and for a few moments of dreaming wondered if it could offer her anything after all. Perhaps she herself owed some debt to this land of her fathers?

But surely not! She mentally shook herself and called to the dog for his walk. This was her life, the place where she belonged, and Graham was the man whom she loved, and she was going back to Cornwall in a few days' time. Cornwall was her place too. It held the magic of her childhood fantasies and her teenage dreams.

She pulled on her coat and wellingtons, and shut the door on the washing up and the chores.

'Come on, Ricky,' she said to the dog. 'I've missed you horribly, and I hope you've missed me too. You won't have liked it at all in that stuffy office with the boss every day while I was away!'

For reply he barked excitedly and bounced round her feet like a puppy in spite of his nine years. She fetched his lead, which sent him into further transports of joy, and she remembered to put some of his favourite biscuits into her pocket. She walked quickly across the grass to the back gate that opened on to the field. There was a chill bite to the autumn air and the leaves were turning to a lovely red-gold on the trees. Suddenly it was good to be alive, and this was surely one of the loveliest places to be.

'Yes, I am lucky,' she said aloud to the dog as she threw his ball. 'And so are you.'

Together they walked through the wet grass and into the woods behind the house. The clean, fresh smell of the countryside after rain filled the air, and gave Margaret a sense of well-being that lasted all that day. It was the last day she was to feel at peace for a long time.

The letter from Cornwall lay on the mat behind the front door among a pile of others when she went down to make a cup of tea the next morning. Letters from Dottie were always a treat, and she carried them all upstairs with the tray and the newspaper and got back into bed beside Graham. This was their morning ritual. They took it in turns to get up first before the boys were awake. The leisurely half-hour with each other was a pleasure that made the breakfast rush later on less harrowing. They often read their post together too. They had no secrets.

'From Cornwall,' Margaret said. She poured the tea and settled herself comfortably, plumping up the pillows behind her. 'Shall I read it first?'

'Yes, carry on. I'll see it later.' Graham carefully opened the *Financial Times* and glanced at it. 'Awful rate of inflation in Israel,' he commented. 'It's a good thing Miriam is on a kibbutz where she doesn't have to bother too much about money.'

Margaret hardly heard the words. She was hearing Dottie's voice instead speaking from the scrawled page in front of her.

'We had a letter from Karl. He asked about you and wants your address. What am I to do? Let me know.'

Her heart thumped and she could feel her face going pale. Suddenly the dream of the past was becoming reality. The memory was achieving substance, flesh and blood, resurrection!

Graham turned from his paper and looked at her. 'What on earth's the matter? You look as if you'd seen a ghost!'

'I have!'

He took the letter from her hands. 'It's addressed to you. Can I read it?'

Dottie's letter always began with the usual 'Dear Graham and Margaret'. This was one just 'My dear Maggie'.

'Yes, read it.'

Margaret reached for her cup and drank the scalding liquid, watching him as he read. She would need Graham now. She would need to stay close to him, need his calm, safe presence and the assurance of their love for each other.

'What are you going to do?'

'I don't know. It's quite a shock after all this time. What can he want? He mustn't know about Miriam—that's the most important thing. And she mustn't know about him either. You haven't been out there, to Israel, I mean, heard her speak about the Germans. There's that woman with awful marks on her arm, from Auschwitz. And you haven't been to Yad Vashem. You just can't know how awful it is until you've been there!'

She started to cry, and he put the letter on the bedside cupboard and took her hand, then gently brushed her tears away.

'That was all a long time ago, and people are forgetting. You must try to put all that out of your mind. Israel has different enemies now. It's Egypt and Syria they have to fear, not Germany!'

She remembered hearing Chaim saying something

similar. Perhaps she was over-dramatising. She lay in Graham's arms, drawing comfort from him, and then she gave herself up to his quiet and considerate lovemaking, but at the end it was Karl of whom she thought, and the passion and the splendour of that one day, the day of Miriam's begetting. She knew that she wanted to see Karl again. She wanted that more than she wanted anything else on earth. The thought frightened and terrified her and made her turn to Graham with intense guilt and complete surrender.

'Make love to me again,' she whispered. 'Again—right now.'

CHAPTER TWENTY-TWO

1966–1967

THE promised autumn holiday hadn't materialised, in spite of Margaret's longing for Cornwall. The cottage had been a wonderful birthday present, but she and Graham had only been able to manage one short weekend there to sort out some of the formalities and decide on a few changes that had to be made. He was too busy at the office to get away for longer. He was always busy, and Margaret didn't really like the idea of going to Gull Cottage alone yet. Perhaps later, when she knew the area a little better, she would be brave enough to stay, she thought.

'We'll spend a whole week there at New Year if you like,' Graham suggested eventually. 'I'm closing the office right down for ten days.'

Delighted, Margaret hugged him enthusiastically.

'It'll help to cheer us up,' he went on. 'We're going to be a bit sad without Miriam.'

There had been a letter from Miriam that morning. She was not coming home for Christmas. She was sorry, but she couldn't get permission. She had applied for membership of the kibbutz, so it was important to do all the right things.

Margaret, watching Graham's expression, bleak and hopeless as he read the words, had felt a tinge of anger again at her daughter.

'She'll come when she's ready,' he had said firmly, half to himself. 'She has her own life to lead now.'

The boys too, apparently, had lives of their own.

They were not too happy about the proposed arrangements.

'I can't bury myself down there on New Year's Eve,' Charles moaned. 'There's a party.'

Margaret smiled a little sadly at her son. There was a new girlfriend too, she suspected. 'You can stay here, then. Your father and I will just have the week on our own. What about you, James?'

'I'll stay too. Keep an eye on Charles!'

Although she was sorry that they preferred to remain at home Margaret recognised that the remote cottage in winter would probably be extremely boring to them both. They needed their own friends now that they were growing up, almost adults.

After Christmas she gathered up the cards that were scattered all over the house. It gave her a sense of relief to put them away. She wondered why any family sadness always seemed more traumatic at this time of year. Miriam's absence was a permanent grief to Graham, but on Christmas Day she knew that he felt it more keenly. They had eaten their meal in an atmosphere of forced brightness and the conversation had frequently been stilted. Her thoughts had travelled often to Israel, and she wondered how Christmas was kept on the kibbutz, if it was kept at all.

She was thinking about it again as she packed the lovely carved wooden crib away in its box, and she wondered if she would be getting it out again next year. They had bought the set a long time ago in Austria and it had been part of family Christmases ever since. She handled the handmade figures reverently, stroking the hard wood of Mary's robe and Joseph's cloak gently as she wrapped each one in tissue paper. She remembered that long-ago holiday, and it made her think of Karl. How different everything might have been if his part of

Germany had been in the West. He would have been free to travel, to seek her out. Would he have done so, and how would she have responded? There was no answer to that sort of questioning or any point in it, and she mentally shook herself and brought her mind back to the present.

Dottie had given him her address as he had requested, but there had been no letter yet. She wondered why he wanted suddenly to write to her again after all these years.

She still worried from time to time about Miriam's reaction should she find out. Now that her daughter was becoming so keen to accept her Jewish roots fully it seemed to be more and more difficult. Margaret remembered Yad Vashem and the horrors of the Holocaust portrayed there. A German father would probably be a disaster for an ardent Israeli, which was what Miriam appeared to want to become. There was the chance too that it would form an even greater barrier between mother and daughter. She could imagine Miriam's anger and scorn tarnishing, as it inevitably would, all her precious memories. Then, even more important, there was Graham, of course, and his love for both of them. He wouldn't escape the hurt either.

She had talked about it again recently with Graham, and his advice had been compassionate and unselfish as always.

'Leave things as they are at present,' he had said. 'Especially while Miriam is sorting out her thoughts about Israel. But if Karl should ever be free to come to England then of course I think they would both have to know.'

'But he won't be able to come here, will he, not ever,' Margaret remembered saying anxiously. 'East

Germany is like Russia, isn't it? You can't leave at all, not for holidays or anything?'

'It's called the German Democratic Republic,' Graham had corrected her. 'And no, I don't think he could leave.'

He had kissed her and told her not to worry any more, and the comfort of his strong arms had been reassuring, but she knew that however much she tried not to worry, the concern would still be there until the matter was settled and Miriam knew. She dreaded that day.

With only herself and Graham to consider, the packing for the week away was simple.

'Don't forget Ricky,' James called to her as he saw the suitcases on the bed. 'We don't want him left here. We'll be out a lot.'

The dog, hearing his name, pranced around Margaret's feet, and then fetched his rubber ring and presented it to her.

'As if I'd forget him!' she laughed. She took the ring and threw it down the stairs, and he ran after it joyfully. Margaret looked at him and thought that it might be nice to be a dog, with your whole world encompassed in the fetching and carrying of a rubber ring, a good meal and a warm bed. If you had those things and the love of one or two humans then life was good. She laughed to herself and thought that perhaps that was all she needed too. Well, she had them, hadn't she? Suddenly her mood lightened and she packed the cases quickly and put some food into a cardboard box. It was going to be a wonderful holiday.

The winter gales were battering the thick stone walls of the cottage when they arrived and the sea was angry, increasing the cosiness of the little house. They could feel the welcoming warmth of the central heating as soon as they opened the heavy door, and Margaret saw too that logs were set ready to light in the large open fireplace of the living-room.

'She cares for it as if it were her own,' said Graham, referring to the ageing lady who came in frequently to keep the cottage warm and looked after. He dumped the suitcases on the floor and turned to kiss Margaret.

'A happy 1967, and may it bring you all you've ever wanted,' he said. 'Just seven hours to go to the New Year.'

Margaret returned his kiss, and then shivered slightly at his words. I only hope I want all the right things, she thought ominously. Aloud she said, 'And a very happy New Year to you, my darling.'

Graham went through to put a match to the fire before he took off his coat, and Ricky bounded after him, sniffing excitedly in every corner. Margaret looked at the two of them affectionately, man and dog together. She watched Graham pat Ricky and then hug him gently as the dog pushed his nose into his legs. In simple homely things like this surely lay happiness.

Gradually the gentle smell of woodsmoke pervaded the house, giving her a sense of peace. It reminded her of the farmhouse, and although there had been traumas there, she had also known a great security. She went to the cardboard box of provisions they had brought and pulled out a bottle.

'Drink, darling?' she asked, waving it at him. 'When I've found some glasses, that is. We'll have some more at midnight. Let's just enjoy this before unpacking.'

The letters arrived together three days later, forwarded from Bristol by James. The post came late here and it was almost lunchtime when Margaret took them from the postman. She held them in her hands for a long time, staring at the Dresden postmark on one and the Israeli stamp on the other. Graham was out taking Ricky for a walk. Slowly she pushed the front door shut and walked almost in a trance back to the living-room. She sat down heavily and put the letters side by side on the coffee-table, and then she stared at them, Karl's handwriting beside his daughter's, so close and so alike, and neither of them knew of the existence of the other, and it was her fault.

She couldn't think which to open first. All her powers of decision seemed suddenly to have become suspended. She left them lying there and walked into the tiny kitchen and made a cup of coffee. She brought it back and set the cup beside them on the table, with a small fruit knife to open the envelopes. It would be a pity to destroy those attractive stamps! Then slowly she picked up Miriam's thinner envelope and slit it open. There was only one page and she read it quickly, and then over again. The words seemed at first to make no sense. Eventually they unjumbled themselves and she read once more. Miriam was going to marry Chaim. The wedding would be in the summer, June probably, on the kibbutz, and please would they all try to come! The full import of the letter still really evaded Margaret. Visions of a white wedding in their lovely parish church began to float before her mind. It was how she had always imagined it. For a fleeting moment she even began to plan! Then she took the second envelope.

She was still holding it when Graham came back, his face glowing from the cold winds that were blowing fiercely in from the sea. He bent to take off his boots and to wipe the dog's muddy feet.

'It's cold out there,' he said. 'Invigorating, but jolly cold. What's in the post?'

'Two letters. One from Israel and one from Dresden.'

'Then let's have some coffee and read them.'

The words were calm, surely shielding his true feelings. She stared at him, and then she rose and poured more coffee. There was some ready in the percolator. She had still not read Karl's letter. It lay there on the table where she had put it down again, like a document from another life, from another world, a world of war and bombs and strife and trauma. Here in this quiet cottage there should be peace and tranquillity, the elements outside having the only anger, the only torment, the wildness of the turbulent sea bringing the only restlessness.

Graham took his cup and went to the small window, obliterating much of the light. He was quiet, staring at the sea outside, his back to her. 'Read it. It was a long time ago—it's the past. I don't mind!'

She marvelled at his composure. Perhaps it was because of his self-confidence. He was sure of her love. She had never given him a moment's cause to doubt it since their marriage.

She took the opened envelope and slowly pulled out the thin pages. There were two of them, four sides closely written. Her heart was beating more quickly.

'My dear Margaret, I scarcely know how to begin this letter, or with what words to beg your forgiveness for my long silence.'

'Would you mind if I read it to you,' she said to Graham. 'I should like to read it aloud.'

Secretly it was the last thing she wanted to do. She would have liked to take it in her pocket to some remote corner of the beach below the cottage, to read it in complete privacy, to remember Karl's voice, his face and that golden smile, and enjoy the remembering, but she knew she would never do that. Even if Graham hadn't known of the letter's arrival she could not have kept it to herself. She owed Graham almost all the happiness she had known during the past eighteen years, and she loved him. She reminded herself fiercely that she loved him still very much.

He turned and smiled at her. 'If that's what you want.'

She read slowly in a quiet, controlled voice, and all the time Graham stared out of the window at the sea. When she had finished he came over to her and kissed her gently.

'It wasn't so awful, then, was it?' he said. 'He's happy—as happy as anyone can be in a Communist state. Do you feel better about it now? Can you try to forget?'

'Feel better because he's happy, do you mean? Because he has a good wife and a clever son of whom he's very proud? Is that what you mean? Yes, I suppose I do.'

She found it difficult to say the words. It was strange to think of Karl, prosperous, with a wife and child, a job and a home. She had heard some of the details from Dottie, but to see it there in pen and ink jumping out from the paper in front of her was different. In her mind time stood still for him. He remained the blond young prisoner of war, ever young, ever penniless, and always in love with her.

'Gisela sounds nice. I'm glad he can write to us like that,' said Graham. 'He obviously never had any suspicion about. . .' He stopped, not knowing how to finish the sentence.

'That I was pregnant with his child. No, of course he didn't know.'

It was all so long ago, and Margaret sighed. If it were not for Miriam then she might have been able to put her memories aside as Karl obviously had, buried them where they wouldn't arise to cause conflict and doubts.

'And it seems that his reason for writing to you was simply because English tourists are beginning to go to Dresden and it's made him think with nostalgia of his time in England,' Graham went on.

'Do you suppose he secretly hopes that one day we might go?' Margaret shivered a little at the thought. It disturbed her and frightened her too. She knew that it was something she could never easily do, however much she wanted to see Karl again.

'Perhaps, but he doesn't say so. You don't want to go, do you?' There was a moment of doubt between them and Margaret caught the fear in Graham's words. She could never do that to him, could she?

'Of course not, darling,' she said reassuringly. 'Maybe he just wanted me to know a little about the terrible bombing of Dresden to help redress the balance a bit, and that his wife was trapped beneath the ruins before she was rescued. That was awful. You know, I was very harsh to him about the Holocaust when the news of the concentration camps first came out. I didn't know about the awful raid on Dresden then—well, not much anyway.'

'It was almost completely flattened by the Allies, by the British mostly, I believe, in the last winter of the war. I don't think they did any serious rebuilding until the fifties.' Graham picked up the letter which Margaret had placed on the small coffee-table and looked at it. 'It must have been a pretty grim place to live when he went back.'

Margaret suddenly remembered Jerusalem and Yad Vashem again and Dinah with her tattooed concentration camp number. It wasn't only the victims of the Holocaust who had suffered in that terrible war, she reflected. If only she could make Miriam understand the total horror and not just the part, then perhaps she would eventually come to accept the German blood that flowed in her veins.

They went to visit John and Dottie the following day.

'Hi,' Dottie said, and she kissed Margaret warmly, then stood back and looked at her. 'Well, you look just great. Slim too. How do you do it?'

'No cream and never a pudding.' She laughed. 'I remember Annie's cooking, though, but even that didn't make me fat. I suppose I'm just one of the thin kind.'

'Lucky you!'

They went inside, and Dottie bustled about in her well-remembered, bright, busy fashion, making coffee and setting out a large plate of home-made scones and cream as well. Margaret, looking around her at all the changes she had made in the old farmhouse, was glad that her friend was here. Without Dottie's cheerful presence she felt that she could never have returned. She rather dreaded seeing John, though. She still felt ill at ease with him. The passing years made little difference. The bitter encounter in Bristol, so long ago now, seemed to be always remembered between them, and they seldom mentioned Miriam.

'Lunch will be ready in about an hour,' Dottie said, turning to Graham when they had finished their coffee. 'John's out in the bottom field. I don't expect he knows you've arrived yet. Like to go and find him? He'll want to show you round. I hope you've brought your wellies?'

Graham laughed. 'I can take a hint,' he said. 'I know

you two are just longing for a good old gossip. Where are the children, by the way? The place seems exceptionally quiet.'

'David and Ian are out on the farm somewhere, and the girls have gone to Mevagissey with their gran. She passed her driving test a few weeks ago, by the way.'

'Annie driving a car?' The idea seemed totally incredible to Margaret. She remembered her sitting in the old pony trap. She wasn't keen even to take the reins of that on her own. 'And how old is she now, for goodness' sake?'

Dottie laughed. 'She won't tell anyone her age, and she has sworn John to secrecy. I think she must be around sixty-five, but she seems as young as ever. The children have given her a new lease of life.'

'The girls must be fourteen and fifteen now,' Margaret said, swiftly counting the years.

'Absolutely right, and David is seventeen and Ian sixteen.' Dottie turned to Graham, who was struggling into his wellingtons. 'Here,' she said, 'take John's old trilby as well. I think it's going to rain.'

She plopped it on his head, and they all laughed as he looked at himself in the mirror.

'I look like a proper farmer,' he remarked, and he pushed open the door and went out, leaving the two women sitting at the kitchen table.

'Well, now, we've just about an hour, or maybe less, on our own. Let's have all the news, and I'll make two more cups of coffee just like in the old days!'

Margaret looked at her friend as she got up to boil the kettle again. The fair, wavy hair was just as thick and luxurious and her clothes as outrageous as they always had been, but there was a peace about her that hadn't been there when they had first met.

'You're obviously contented and happy,' she said. 'Country life still suiting you?'

'Oh, wonderfully. I suppose that's why I've put on weight. John likes it, though, and I'm not worried. Tells me I look buxom! How about you?'

Margaret sighed. She could feel Dottie's concerned expression as she sat down opposite her. 'I've lots to tell you about Miriam. You know I've just been to see her in Israel?'

'Yes. I had your card.'

'And we had a letter from Karl yesterday!'

There was a moment's pause while the two women stared at each other and said nothing, the air pregnant with their thoughts.

'What did he say?'

'That it's possible to go for holidays to Dresden. He's seen English tourists! That his son is a musician, almost grown up, and he mentioned Gisela. Oh, and he told us that when the town was bombed she was buried in the ruins for a long time before being rescued. Strange thing, that, to write about it so long afterwards.'

'Terrible, though, wasn't it? I've read a bit about the air-raids lately and I've seen pictures of the ruins. Apparently it was one of the most beautiful cities of Europe. Will you ever go?'

'Don't ask me that, Dottie. Just don't ask me that!'

'John said he'd like to see it! He said it might help him to purge his bitterness about his own treatment by the Japs.'

'Go there? Meet Karl?' There was instant panic in Margaret's voice.

Dottie laughed at her. 'Oh, it's only a dream. He never will, of course. I can't even get him to take me to Truro very often—he's a real old stick-in-the-mud. Have you replied to Karl, by the way?'

'Not yet. I don't want to start a correspondence. What should I do?'

'Just send a card from both of you. He'll take the hint. Now let's change the subject. Tell me about Miriam.'

Dottie busied herself with preparing vegetables and making a pudding for lunch while Margaret talked. She poured out all her thoughts about Israel, Chaim, and her feelings for Miriam. Her friend was the only person to whom she could be so honest. It was a relief, and she felt infinitely better afterwards. Nothing seemed so grim any more. She began to wonder what she had been worrying about and why she had been feeling apprehensive and depressed. Even her son's interest in Israel didn't seem so threatening.

'James seems infected with this Zionist thing too,' she finished. 'He's been secretly learning Hebrew, would you believe!'

Dottie turned to her, the wooden spoon waving in the air and dripping gravy over the floor. 'I seem to remember you had the boys circumcised, didn't you? Now why on earth did you do that? Was it some sort of concession to your Jewish blood?'

There was a hint of amusement in her voice, and Margaret laughed.

'Oh, not a religious ceremony—just a very clinical little operation when they were eight days old. I told Graham it was more healthy.'

'Well, that's one hurdle they won't have to overcome if they convert,' Dottie said lightly. 'It must have been meant!'

'Fiddlesticks,' said Margaret. 'I'd forgotten all about it. Trust you to bring up something like that out of the misty past!'

* * *

There were nine of them sitting at the vast wooden table for Dottie's splendid lunch a short time later.

Margaret looked around at John and Dottie's family with intense pleasure, and then she caught Annie's eye.

'Remember how you used to moan about having no grandchildren, Aunt Annie?'

The old womam smiled. 'I've certainly got a quiver-full now,' she said. 'And very good to me they are. Bring your three down to see us soon, won't you, Margaret?'

'One day, perhaps. They're grown up now and don't like trailing around with us any more. Miriam's not likely to be here for a long time, of course.'

There was a silence for a moment, and then Annie spoke slowly and thoughtfully.

'So Karl has written to you, then. Funny how we all came to like him in spite of his being a Jerry. Do you remember how I wouldn't let him eat with us when he first came?'

'Yes. Yes, I do remember very well, Aunt Annie,' Margaret said, and she could feel John's eyes upon her and she knew the colour was suddenly draining from her face.

'Will you help me clear away, Maggie?' said Dottie hastily. 'Come on, everyone, pass your plates. There's apple pie and cream for afters!'

CHAPTER TWENTY-THREE

1967

'WHY are you so obsessed with the Holocaust?'

The question took Miriam by surprise and she turned to look at Chaim as they strolled back together from the dining-hall in the warm April evening.

'But I thought all Jews were "obsessed", as you call it.'

'Not as much as you are. I told you before, we have other enemies. We're surrounded by them—just look at the map. Russia too, even. The Soviet friendship with the Arabs goes on growing. They supply arms and money.'

The quiet peacefulness of the night and the rich scent of oranges that always seemed to be borne on every gentle breeze belied his words, and Miriam shivered slightly. There had been raids near the border and various acts of terrorism committed during her time in Israel, but she had been lucky enough to have no close encounter with any trouble.

'Aren't there people searching for some of the Nazi war criminals, then?' she asked.

'Of course. Eichmann was found and executed here a few years ago—1962, I believe. He was the head of the Gestapo's Jewish Extermination Department. It sounds horrific, but that doesn't mean that we have to go on bearing a grudge against Germany. It's only individuals who are guilty, not a whole nation.'

'I suppose you're right, but after that visit to Yad Vashem and constantly seeing people around here with those awful concentration camp numbers tattooed on their arms I can't seem to get it out of my mind.'

'We mustn't forget, of course. It must never happen again. That's why this land is so precious and we have to defend it against the world if necessary!' He laughed a little at his own words. 'I know I sound rather pompous, but to think of all those Jews just lining up and letting themselves be killed without any resistance at all makes me so mad that I want to——'

'Yes, I know,' Miriam interrupted him. 'Makes you want to go out waving a machine-gun around!'

'Not quite. What I'm trying to say is that it took the Nazis to wake us up, make us realise that we can't rely on any other country to defend us. We've got to fight if we want to survive.'

'It sounds as though you're the one who's getting all steamed up now!'

'Yes, but. . .' Chaim stopped suddenly and grinned at her. She loved that mischievous, childish grin. It was one of his endearing qualities, reminding her constantly that there was fun to be had here as well as hard work and talk of war.

'Let's change the subject,' he said. 'What about this wedding of ours? Have your parents decided when they're coming yet?'

'I'm not sure of the actual day, but they're all hoping to come, Charles and James too. Of course Mum is very sad about it really. She doesn't say, but I know.'

'Sad? Doesn't she like me?'

'Oh, yes, she thinks you're fine. It's just the place and the religion she doesn't like.'

'But she's Jewish! That must make some difference, surely?'

'Not really. She'd imagined a lovely white wedding at home in our little village church. It's very old and very beautiful. She'd like to see me floating down the aisle on Dad's arm with bridesmaids in tow and flowers everywhere.'

'Well, we can manage the flowers!'

'Not a lot else, though, that she would approve of.'

'Plenty of dancing and wine and masses of friends around to wish us good luck.'

Miriam sighed. Secretly she too had dreamed of getting married in the ancient parish church, with a long white dress and the lovely peal of bells echoing around the green English countryside. It had been a dream since she was a little girl.

'It wouldn't be any good going home to get married,' she said half to herself. 'A synagogue wedding in Bristol wouldn't be at all what Mum would wish.' She paused, and then laughed a little. 'I think she would rather come here. There won't be any of her friends to be faintly supercilious about it. Now if my grandmother were alive she would have been really thrilled. I hardly remember her, but Mum told me that she and my grandfather were rather upset about her marrying my father in church. They wanted it to be in the synagogue in Bristol! Slightly ironic, isn't it!'

'Then stop worrying. Your mother survived her parents' disapproval and so will you, and I love you!'

Chaim kissed her gently and pushed open the door of his small apartment. He had been allocated a bigger one now that his marriage was imminent. It was the same one that her mother had occupied during her short stay.

'Sorry I had to take possession before our wedding,' he said. 'I'll be able to paint it, though, and make it ready for us. You've got to decide on the colour and choose the curtains and all that. There's a central store with things we can have.'

Miriam looked around. This was to be her home for years to come. This was the place where they would make love, make babies, relax and enjoy each other after each day's work. The living-room was almost empty—just a table and two chairs at present and some books in cardboard boxes along the wall. She could see a large double bed and a dressing-table and wardrobe in the smaller room.

'No more communal showers,' Chaim said proudly. 'As a married couple we have our own, and a loo. There's a bit of a kitchen as well.' He pulled back a bead curtain and looked at the tiny sink and two-ring burner. 'Not very grand, but enough for all we'll need.'

Miriam thought of her mother's large kitchen at home, and the ever-warm and comfortable Aga. But she wouldn't have to cook. It had never been one of her favourite things.

'It's super,' she told him happily. 'And I'm thrilled about not having to think what to eat every day. It's like constantly going out to a restaurant. That was a luxury at home. I'll never have to look at a cookery book!'

She went into the bedroom and sat on the bed. She could see Chaim watching her from the doorway. He had been careful since that evening a few weeks before, not allowing himself to be alone with her often.

'We'll not sleep together until our wedding night,' he had told her. 'That's how I want it. I want you to come to me fresh and new, my lovely bride. I don't want anything to spoil it.'

She knew that he was slightly unusual in this, and she often wondered why. She sat there on the bed persuading him with her eyes, saying nothing. She just sat there looking at him. Her whole body began to throb as she looked, and new and previously unknown sensations coursed through her. They would soon be married and this very bed the place of their loving, but she wanted him now, wanted to experience the fullness of their love at this very moment. Her very virginity seemed almost a reproach to her and she wanted him to take it, wanted to give it to him without any more waiting. She suddenly held out her arms to him and she saw him hesitate, watched him turn and quietly close the door, latching it securely. Then he came over to her and she was aware of the coarse, brightly woven blanket beneath them. The bed yielded its softness and for a fleeting moment she thought of that other time outside under the dark canopy of the sky and of the earth that had scratched her bare legs.

His mouth covered hers hungrily and then his hands were exploring her body beneath the thin dress. She was wearing a dress, not the usual trousers, and she was glad, so glad. She wanted him to go further, the deepest part of her longing for his touch, and then he was there, his fingers gently stroking, making her call out for the deeper, fuller experience. Then suddenly, as before, she felt a great shudder go right through him and he pulled himself away. He turned from her and went into the shower-room.

She just lay there in a welter of ecstasy and misery both. It was the misery that outlasted the other, though, and she sobbed and clutched at herself to still the throbbing of her body. She could hear the splashing of the shower and knew that he was in there washing away the feel of her, angry perhaps because of her beguiling him, tempting him. But surely her feelings couldn't be wrong? Why was he like this? She wept and pulled her dress around her nakedness, but she still lay there, unable to summon the courage to rise from the bed.

Then he was standing beside her again, a towel tied around his waist. He picked up his pants and his trousers and turned from her to put them on. Then he came over and stood looking down at her, and she feared to see anger in his eyes, but there was only tenderness, and he bent and stroked her face gently. She turned away from him and knew that he saw her tears.

'I'll tell you why later, after we're married,' he said. 'Come on, get up and we'll sit on the porch and drink coffee. I'll make it.'

She wanted to pull him down again beside her, but she dared not. Instead she did as he wished and walked slowly outside, out to the velvet darkness and the sound of the cicadas. He came soon and set a mug of brown steaming liquid down beside her on the floor. There was no small table.

'I'll see if there's a coffee-table in the store tomorrow,' he said.

She ignored his remark and ignored the coffee. 'Why, Chaim? Why? You must tell me. Tell me now, not when we're married. I must know—I must know now!'

He was silent. She could hear him sipping from his cup and she almost hated him in that moment of her disappointment and her shame, for she felt shamed as well as rejected. Then at last he began to speak.

'There was someone else. We were very young and knew nothing, or almost nothing, and she became pregnant. There was an abortion. She was very ill, almost died. I'll never do that to any other woman again as long as I live, and especially not to you. I love you. You're too precious.'

She had to strain to hear the words. They were whispered, and he wouldn't turn to look at her. He stared ahead at the row of buildings opposite, not seeing them.

'I'm so sorry, Miriam. Can you forgive me?'

She was suddenly aware of movements in the next apartment; the walls were thin and the porches joined.

'Forgive? Forgive what? Your making love to me, do you mean? It's your leaving me so suddenly and so cruelly again that I have to forgive.' Her words were whispered like his, but she saw the desolation in his face and she leaned over to him and took his hand impetuously in hers.

'But, Chaim, this is 1967, and babies aren't the necessary end of loving nowadays, you know.'

She tried to keep the incredulity out of her voice, but she could tell that he was hurt.

'I know that—of course I know that,' he said. 'But the other time made it all sordid somehow, the abortion and everything. I want it to be perfect for us. If I make love to you before we're married I shall spoil it. I know I'm unusual and odd, but there it is. Please try and understand.'

'The girl? Where is she? What happened to her?'

Miriam knew there was jealousy in her voice. It was an emotion she had never encountered before in herself, and she felt uncomfortable with it, wished it gone.

He turned to her in surprise. 'Tel Aviv. She left the kibbutz with her parents. She's married now. Don't worry, it was all over long ago.'

He smiled at her and kissed her again, gently taking away the doubts, and she realised with a flash of certainty that here was a man she could trust totally. Whatever his reasons for the things he did or did not do they would be sound reasons and not excuses.

She climbed into her narrow bunk in the hostel later

that night with a deepening sense of having found in Chaim her safe harbour, her destiny.

But the news that dominated the following day threatened to banish that carefully won and precious security. Israel shot down six Syrian planes from the April sky!

'We had to teach them a lesson,' Chaim said with excitement in his voice. 'They've been helping terrorists for too long. If there's more trouble my unit will probably be called up.'

Miriam shuddered. She knew that he was assigned to a reserve unit.

Suddenly he turned to her and spoke quietly. 'It might be a good idea if we tried to put our marriage forward a bit, just in case. Do you think your parents could manage it?'

It was a shock, and she shivered slightly. 'Yes, I suppose so. Can we talk about it after our meal? I can't think straight with all this noise. Do you really think there's going to be a war?'

'Probably not, but you never know, and if I did have to fight I'd be a better soldier knowing that you were here waiting for me, and that it was you I was fighting for!'

It was evening before they had any time together.

'When were you thinking of—for our wedding, I mean?' she asked as they walked over from the dining-hall after supper.

'Early May, before Independence Day—that's the fifteenth. If we had it around then and if your parents were here they could stay for the celebrations. There's going to be a military parade in Jerusalem, I think.'

'Celebrations of 1948, you mean?'

'Yes, the day Israel came into being—May the

fifteenth, 1948. Just nineteen years ago.'

'Could we get married on that day?'

'Not really. Too much going on! I want you to myself for a bit on our wedding night!'

He smiled and kissed her, and she thrilled at his touch and his words.

'How about May the fourth, then? That's Mum's birthday.'

'If you like. Are your brothers coming?'

'Probably. For part of the time, anyway—they might have exams and things. I'd better telephone tonight, the post seems to take such ages.'

'Where are we going for our honeymoon?'

'Where would you like to go?'

'I've an idea swimming around in my head, but it's not very practical and I don't think we could afford it. I'm not telling you at the moment—have to make some more enquiries.'

Chaim's voice was conspiratorial, and Miriam laughed. 'I don't mind where it is really. I just want it to happen soon.'

Margaret was in the house alone watching television when the telephone rang. She knew as soon as she answered that it was from Israel. There was a crackling and the operator sounded faint and far away. Then she heard Miriam's voice and she caught the excitement in the words.

'We want to put the wedding forward a bit,' Miriam told her. 'How about May the fourth, Mum? On your birthday? Can you and Dad manage to get here for then?'

The significance of the date escaped at her first. That it was her birthday she knew, but then suddenly she gasped. Twenty years to the day! Miriam was conceived on May the fourth, 1947, and the wedding was to be on May the fourth. She would be standing beside Graham to witness her daughter's marriage to a Jew in the land of the Jews. It wasn't what she had planned at all! It was certainly not what she had wished for Miriam.

'Is May the fourth all right?' she asked anxiously when Graham came in later that evening. 'They're putting the date forward.'

'Any reason? Did she say why?'

Margaret laughed a little grimly at the anxiety in his voice, guessing his thoughts. If only that could have been the reason. How much better to change the date because of a baby than for a war!

'Didn't you hear the news yesterday? Six planes shot down by the Israelis, Syrian ones, and Chaim seems to think they should marry soon just in case.'

'My God,' Graham said. 'Why on earth did we let her go over there in the first place? I thought I'd finished with having to worry about wars when ours was over. Vietnam doesn't concern anyone I know and I've put it out of my mind, and now it seems that we've to start all over again with some remote quarrel in the Middle East.'

'Hardly a remote quarrel, not if the media coverage Israel gets is anything to go by. It's always in the news.'

'All the more reason for Miriam not to be living there! Do you think we could persuade this Chaim of hers to come over here? I'd find some money somehow, set him up in a little farm if that was what he wanted. It should be possible.'

Margaret looked at his anxious face and she loved him desperately for his concern for this child who wasn't his.

'You don't understand,' she said sadly. 'For Chaim, Israel is his whole reason for being. I think I remember saying to you before that nothing else matters for him except that little bit of scorched earth, and Miriam. He could never be happy anywhere else.'

Graham came over to her and kissed her lightly. 'I must go there,' he said. 'I really must go and try to understand this passion it seems to generate. Even James is a little affected, I think.'

He took out his diary and sat down in the chair on the opposite side of the fireplace. 'I could go soon, towards the end of this month, and stay until the day after the wedding.'

'She wants us to be there for the Independence celebrations on May the fifteenth.'

'Sorry, can't be done. What about you and the boys? Are you free?'

Margaret's life was not so organised. She could go any time, she said, and she would ask Charles and James. She hoped secretly that they wouldn't go. She was afraid—afraid of that fatal attraction that Israel exerted so strongly. The land was like a siren, she thought, waiting for its sons—her sons. It would pounce and swallow them up if she wasn't careful.

The boys both said that they wanted to go. Mirry's wedding was not to be missed. The exams weren't until June and they would do as much extra work as they could cram in before they went.

So it was with some misgivings that Margaret washed and ironed and prepared for the journey. As mother of the bride she wondered if she should buy a new outfit. She wandered disconsolately round the fairly elegant shops in Bristol's Park Street and looked at a great number of outfits. She tried on numerous large and lacy hats and shoes with impossible heels. Nothing seemed suitable for the kibbutz.

'It's a kibbutz wedding,' she explained to one assistant, and for her pains received an uncomprehending stare. What did the word sound like if you had never heard it before? she wondered. Then she suddenly giggled and wished Dottie were here to share the joke!

She telephoned Cornwall that evening. 'I can't think what on earth to wear!' she wailed, and crackling along the wires she heard her friend's infectious laugh.

'Can I come and help you?' Dottie asked. 'I need a little holiday, and Annie will hold the fort.'

They had a wonderful time together for the next three days. They walked the dog in the fields behind the house and poured out all their joys and problems to each other, and they shopped. How they shopped!

There were presents to be bought for Miriam and Chaim, and of course the wedding outfit. Now that she wasn't alone it became fun. Margaret determined that she wouldn't allow any worries or misgivings to spoil this time with Dottie.

'You're so slim,' her friend said enviously as she watched her trying on the tenth dress that day. 'It's important to be thin now, of course, with that wretched Twiggy setting the fashion!'

'I can't wear these awful short skirts, though,' Margaret sighed. 'My legs are too skinny, and I'm not having this new Crimplene either. It'll be too hot for Israel.'

She chose a simple silk dress eventually with a short jacket to match and a hat that set off her hair, which was still glossy and showed no signs of grey.

'You look quite stunning, Mum,' Charles said later when she paraded in her new finery. 'Too smart for a kibbutz, I should think.'

'Well, you're wrong. Miriam told me that they dress up for weddings,' said Margaret. 'And mind you get your hair cut before we go—James as well. None of your hippy decadence in Israel, if you please.' Her voice was light and carefree, and when she waved Dottie goodbye at the station the following day she knew that once more her friend had cheered her and brought her through a difficult time. The prospect of the wedding wasn't so fearful as she had at first thought. She really felt quite optimistic, and even James's excitement at the coming holiday couldn't dampen her spirits.

'Give Miriam my love, and send me lots of photographs,' Dottie called as the train carried her away. 'And enjoy yourself. That's an order!'

Margaret laughed and determined that she would obey!

CHAPTER TWENTY-FOUR

May 1967

MARGARET knew that the first glimpse of Israel was always thrilling. Even on that last journey when she had been in a turmoil of anger over Miriam's decision to stay, even then the lofty snow cap of Mount Hermon seen from the plane had lifted her heart a little. This time she made sure that Graham was sitting near the window and the boys were in seats behind them with a good view too.

It was James who spoke first. 'Look down there, Mum,' he said. 'Look, isn't that Galilee, that little blue shape among the hills?'

She leaned over Graham and peered through the dirty little window. The weather was excellent, clear and bright with no clouds in the sky. 'Yes, I'm sure it is.'

There was silence for a time as they all stared down at the living map spread out beneath them and she wondered what each was feeling.

'The town you can see now,' said a voice over the aircraft's loudspeaker, 'is Acre, an ancient port, sometimes called Acco. It was taken by the Crusaders in 1104 and has had an exciting history, but it's a modern city too and well worth a visit.'

'Gosh, Mum, it is quite something, isn't it? I can hardly believe I'm here at last!' The excitement had even spread to Charles.

'You can see Haifa and the road connecting it to Tel Aviv,' the disembodied voice continued. 'And now would you fasten your safety-belts, please, for landing.'

After the long and involved security checks they emerged into the blinding light and the dust, and eventually settled themselves into a large black *sherut* taxi. The journey to Rosh Hazim passed in a dazzle of sunshine and excitement and heat, and at last when the taxi set them down at the gate of the kibbutz Margaret breathed a great sigh of relief. They had telephoned their safe arrival at the airport, and Miriam was standing beneath a silvery spreading olive tree waiting for them.

She stood for a moment, and then ran straight into Graham's arms.

'Daddy!' she gasped. 'It's just wonderful to have you here. I thought you'd never come.'

'Hey, don't I get a kiss too? All this way and you can only think of the old man!'

Miriam laughed at Charles's words and turned to her brothers, embracing each in turn, and then she looked at her mother and kissed her gently on the cheek.

'Thanks, Mum. Thanks a thousand times for bringing them. It's going to be a wonderful wedding with you all here. I was so worried that you wouldn't be able to manage it. It's such a long way for you to come.'

There was just a week before the celebrations, and Miriam was determined that they should see everything.

'Everything,' she told them. 'I've booked you on a coach tour for three days. Chaim and I can't come with you, unfortunately. They're giving us ten days for our honeymoon, so we can't really ask for any more. The tour will take you to Jerusalem and you won't miss any of the important places—any that we have control of, that is. You can't go into the Old City, of course.'

'I know all about that,' James said. 'I've been reading

everything that I could get hold of about Israel, both ancient and modern.'

'You mean we're going to have to leave you here and go off on our own?' Graham complained.

'Well, it's not long, and you must see Israel. It's more important than seeing me!'

'I'm not so sure about that,' he said. 'But perhaps you're right. Just at this moment, though, all I can think of is a shower and something to eat. Lead on, Macduff!'

Miriam laughed, and Margaret felt a glow of temporary happiness at the old familiar words. Her whole family was together again for a while. She must make the most of it!

'You're in the guest-house this time,' Miriam told Margaret. 'It's like a proper hotel and more luxurious than our accommodation. This way.'

She indicated a path that led away from the residents' area towards the attractive buildings that had been set aside for visitors. There were palm trees and bright flower borders along the route, and Margaret was reminded again of some of the Spanish resorts she knew.

It was fairly luxurious, and they all unpacked, bathed and ate, relaxing after the long, hot journey.

Miriam came to find them after the evening meal. 'Chaim is anxious to meet you,' she said. 'Well, a bit nervous, actually. He got on fine with Mum, but three strapping males are quite another matter!'

'We'll eat him alive if we don't think he's good enough for you,' said Charles. 'Won't we, James?'

'Sure thing. Let's get the shock over with, then. Quick about it!'

The now familiar scents of oranges, rosemary and pine filled the air as they walked towards the main kibbutz buildings, and Margaret sniffed appreciatively. The clicking of the cicadas too took her mind back to her previous visit. It was strange how perfumes and small background sounds could transport one through time, she thought, just as the call of gulls always took her away to those wartime years on the farm, and that one special day and that one special person! She shook herself mentally and concentrated on the present. It was important that her three men should like Chaim. He was already starting with a great disadvantage where Graham was concerned.

She saw him as soon as they turned the corner. He was sitting on the porch of his apartment, engrossed in a book. Then he looked up and rose quickly to meet them.

'My father and brothers,' Miriam said, and Margaret could hear the nervousness in her voice.

Chaim shook hands with each, and then he turned and kissed Margaret on the cheek in the French way.

'It's just great that you've all come so far,' he said. 'I feel very honoured.'

Chaim passed their scrutiny with honours.

'Capital chap,' James said later that evening. 'It must be wonderful to have a constant sort of inspiration and challenge in life as he has.'

Charles roared with laughter at his brother's words, and some of the other guests stared in their direction, much to Margaret's embarrassment.

'Miriam, do you mean?' he teased.

'Of course not, you oaf. Israel. He just lives for the State of Israel. It's obvious when you've been with him for even a short time!'

'That's the only thing I'm worried about,' Graham

commented. 'I wonder if someone so single-minded will make a good husband?'

'Well, Miriam seems to think so, and she's beginning to catch it too, this passion for the land—Eretz Israel, as they call it. I don't think you should worry.'

Margaret's words were quiet and reassuring, and she grasped Graham's hand and smiled at him. Everything would be all right. She suddenly felt a surge of confidence and happiness. Yes, everything was going to be fine.

The three-day tour proved to be excellent, and throughout its almost never-ending panorama of sights and sounds and experiences Margaret's satisfaction with events grew. There was only one small worry: she watched James become more and more entranced. Charles was more matter-of-fact, interested, enthusiastic even, but obviously detached. With James it was different. He seemed deeply absorbed in everything he saw, and there was frequently an expression on his sensitive face that she couldn't fathom. It was most intense when they stared over towards the forbidden golden walls of the Old City of Jerusalem, and again as they walked on the shores of Galilee and through the beautiful ruins of Capernaum.

He said little, but it was obvious that some deep emotions were being stirred, and Margaret longed to wrap him in her arms as she used to do frequently when he was little. She wanted to keep him safe with her for ever. This passionate, possessive land couldn't take her son as well as her daughter! Or could it? She would never underestimate its power. She wanted to fight against it like the proverbial mother tigress, yet in a strange way it bewitched her too. It was almost a seduction!

In spite of her thoughts she knew that there was little she could actually do, especially now. Perhaps when they got home to England the vision would fade and she could influence James a little, but in her deepest heart she knew that it was not so. What he wanted to do he would do. This quiet, studious son had a resolve of steel beneath the sensitive exterior.

The wedding was noisy, colourful and strange. The fact that it was Margaret's birthday too caused some extra celebrations. Only in her secret heart did she acknowledge the fact that it was the anniversary of Miriam's conception. As she watched her daughter, radiant and lovely in her short white dress, standing beside her young Israeli bridegroom, she felt that here perhaps was the expiation of her guilt at last. She was giving this child, half German, half Jew, to the land of Israel. She remembered Karl again as she watched his daughter making her promises and she knew that he would be touched and pleased. But he would never know. There was a great sadness in that.

She enjoyed the ceremony. You couldn't remain sad very long here, she decided. Everything was so different from the wedding she had always dreamed of for Miriam, but no worse for that. There was no solemn music, no cool and ancient aisle to walk down, no bells and no bridesmaids, no altar and no familiar and loved hymns, but there was much more that was exciting and strange. The placing of the glass on to the floor and the ritual stamping on it alarmed her until she saw that it was safely contained in a cloth bag. Miriam smiled at her from time to time, and she knew with a deep sense of satisfaction that her daughter was completely happy, and she was loved too. There was a look of adoration in Chaim's eyes, and Margaret, seeing it, was content.

'Can we know where you're going for your honeymoon?' Graham had asked the night before.

'Sorry, Dad—Chaim hasn't even told me. But it's somewhere exciting, because he said I must have my passport ready! I can't believe it really. The kibbutz doesn't usually have enough funds to let people travel abroad very often.'

Margaret had been aware of Graham's sighing at that. She knew that he longed to give Miriam a handsome gift on her marriage.

'I'll have to hand it over to the central fund,' she had told him. 'It's the way we live here. Everything we have is given to the kibbutz and we don't need money at all for day-to-day living. All we need is provided. If we want to travel or anything we get an allowance.'

'Then I shall only give her a small amount,' Graham had confided later to Margaret. 'Just so that she has something to donate, and the rest I shall put in a trust fund for her at home. Then if she ever wants to live in England one day in the future she'll have the money to do it. Don't tell her—it'll be a secret. If she never wants it she may have children who do!'

Margaret had thrilled slightly at the thought of grandchildren. She hoped there would be some. She was only thirty-nine and she would be young enough to enjoy them. But here in Israel they would be so far away. That was another small grief. And they would be brought up in the communal children's house, not in the little apartment that Chaim had showed them so proudly. It seemed a strange existence.

'It's their own choice, though,' Graham had reminded her. 'There's nothing forced about it—quite democratic and all that. They could move out tomorrow if they wanted. Only a small percentage of Israelis live like this.'

* * *

Miriam and Chaim left in a hail of good wishes and jokes and raucous laughter. Charles and James made sure that their cases were filled with confetti brought from England.

'Don't suppose you can buy it over there,' Charles had said as he packed loads of the stuff, much to Margaret's amusement.

There was no car to decorate, but the apartment was doctored in various ways so that when they returned 'Just Married' notices would fall out of every available cupboard. All the innocent merry-go-round of fun helped to disguise the sadness of parting. They all knew that it would be a long time before they could come to see Miriam again. Years, perhaps.

Margaret kissed her warmly when the goodbyes were being said and Graham had tears in his eyes as their taxi whisked them away. There was just another night to be spent here and then they too would be leaving, back to the English summer and rain. There was sure to be rain.

'I wish we could stay for another couple of weeks,' said James sadly. 'There's still loads that I want to see. I think I'd like to come here and work on the kibbutz after I've finished with the exams, like Miriam did.'

Alarm bells began to ring in Margaret's heart as she heard his words, but Charles's remarks comforted her a little.

'Too much like hard work for me,' he said reassuringly. 'I'd like to take Jinny down to your cottage in Cornwall. Much more fun, surfing and walking and lying in the sun!'

'Jinny? Who's Jinny?'

'The latest girlfriend,' James said. 'He's been keeping her a secret!'

* * *

It was indeed raining as they motored from Heathrow, and Margaret delighted in it. She opened the car door and got out quickly when Graham pulled into the drive of their house, and she stood bare-headed letting the cool raindrops fall on her face and sniffing the warm, rich scent of grass and flowers that always filled damp summer evenings. It was so different from the heavy, dry, aromatic smells of last night!

Later that evening they had the surprise telephone call. It was Miriam's voice, but without the long-distance crackle.

'You'll never guess where we are, Mum,' she said. 'Skye—Skye! Yes, really, Scotland, and it's wonderful. Chaim's aunt wrote and asked the kibbutz if she could pay for the visit. He was born here, you see. It's his father's home! He kept it for a surprise for me.'

Margaret gasped with pleasure. 'Can you come here on your way back?' she asked, desperately hopeful.

'I don't know. I'd love to show Chaim our house and everything, but we haven't got very long—we have to be back by the fourteenth. We'll see.'

There was little time for more. The operator cut in, telling them that their time was up, and then there was silence.

'Perhaps they'll decide they like Scotland best,' Graham said with a laugh. 'Skye! Well, I would never have believed it.'

The weather was wonderful, the hills green and golden with gorse bushes in their full glory when the honeymooners arrived on the ferry from Kyle of Lochalsh. Chaim's aunt had arranged everything for them and she was standing on the jetty waiting when the small boat arrived.

'Good to see you, Ian,' she said. 'My, you've grown!'

She looked him up and down critically, and she smiled. 'Yes, you do look like your father!'

Miriam glanced at him with surprise when she heard the name.

'I didn't tell you, did I?' he said. 'My name is actually Ian Chaim Macleod. I've dropped the first bit completely in Israel. Perhaps I shouldn't have done. My mother only used the Jewish name after we left here. I started life as Ian and was very confused about the change-over when I was small!'

He returned his aunt's kiss with a little embarrassment. 'Sorry, Aunt Fiona,' he said. 'I'll be Ian while I'm here if you wish. Thanks for everything. You've been great.'

The tall Scottish woman smiled at them both, and then turned directly to Miriam.

'Welcome to Skye, my dear,' she said. 'We were so thrilled to hear that Ian was getting married and that he would be able to get away from that kibbutz of his for a visit to us. Do you realise that we haven't seen him since he was four years old? Not that we shall see much of either of you during the next few days, I suppose.' She winked at her nephew. 'You're coming to me for a good meal anyway, and then you can drive out to your hideaway.'

Miriam knew that Chaim had almost no remembrance of his Scottish family or the place where he had been born and lived for the first four years of his life, but there had been letters and photographs that he had shown her.

'Thank you, Aunt,' he said again, a trifle awkwardly. 'It's wonderful of you to go to all this trouble for me.'

They put their cases into the car boot and Chaim sat in the front seat, leaving Miriam on her own in the back. She stared around with interest. Scotland was not so strange to her. She had been to the Highlands with the family on two visits during her teens, but Skye was special in a way, a wonderful, romantic place for a honeymoon. She hoped that this aunt, nice though she seemed, wouldn't be too possessive of Chaim while they were here.

It was not far to the sturdy stone house overlooking the sea where Fiona and her husband lived.

'Here we are, then,' she said, showing them into the living-room. 'I expect you're dying for a cup of tea. I'll make that first and then we can talk a bit while the dinner's finishing.'

Miriam looked round at the old-fashioned room with its well-polished antique furniture and view of loch and hills.

'Mum would love this,' she said. 'She has a great thing about the sea.'

'That little island is Scalpay,' Fiona said as she returned a few minutes later carrying a tray, 'and beyond you can see the mainland.'

'It's so beautiful. Don't you think so, Chaim?' Miriam said. She was suddenly anxious that he should see that there were other places meriting interest and enthusiasm apart from Israel.

He was standing at the window staring out at the sea and the hills beyond. 'So this is my birthplace, and I can only dimly remember it. Yes, it's lovely. I've thought about it from time to time, especially when your letters arrived, Aunt Fiona. Thanks so much for keeping them coming and not minding about my short scrawls.'

'Drop the "Aunt" bit, please. Makes me feel really ancient! Just Fiona.' She set the tray down and poured tea from delicate china cups. 'I was determined that you shouldn't forget about this part of your life. We all hoped that you'd come here one day to live, perhaps. I don't suppose that'll ever come about now, but the croft is out there for you when you want it. It's well looked after—we see to that.'

'It can't be sold,' Chaim explained to Miriam. 'It belonged to my grandfather and then my father, although he didn't live in it for long. He made a will, though, tying it up for me and any children I might have.'

'When he married your mother,' Fiona interrupted, 'I think he knew that she might decide to leave the Island one day. She had Zionist tendencies even then, I seem to remember, and he may have guessed that if he was killed in the war she would try to go to Israel, or Palestine as it was known then. He didn't want the old place to go out of the family.'

'How on earth did he manage to marry a Jewish girl?' Miriam asked.

Chaim laughed. 'Easy. They fell in love!'

'Not very easy, in fact,' Fiona said. 'There was lots of opposition from our parents and from the folks here when he wrote from university to say that he was bringing her home and that they'd been married in Cambridge. I liked her a lot, but she had a pretty hard time. It was no wonder that she left eventually. Must have been jolly lonely out there when your dad was called up.'

'She taught in the village school, didn't she?' asked Chaim.

'Only when they couldn't get anyone else. She wasn't Christian, and that didn't go down at all well!'

Miriam shuffled a little on her chair. She was feeling a mixture of many emotions, and although she was grateful to Fiona for this wonderful holiday she wished only to be alone with Chaim. They had booked one night in a small hotel in Tel Aviv before their flight to

London, and their lovemaking had been restrained, almost a disappointment, the memory of those other times when he had withdrawn from her suddenly a barrier between them. She had lain tense and unyielding and he had hurt her physically. She remembered the moment with fear and with apprehension for tonight, yet there was passionate hope too in her heart. It couldn't be like that each time, surely? She longed to know.

Her thoughts must have shown in her face, and she blushed as she saw Fiona suddenly look at her with understanding.

'Goodness, trust me to go prattling on, and you both look so tired,' the older woman said kindly. 'The meal's ready now and then you can get out to the croft and have a whole week or more to yourselves. No one'll bother you. I've stocked it up with food, and I'm lending you my little car while you're here. I won't need it for a bit, so you can get round the island and enjoy yourselves!'

'You're absolutely wonderful, Aunt—sorry, Fiona,' Chaim said as she handed him a map and a bunch of keys an hour or so later.

'Fiddlesticks,' she replied. 'You're my only flesh and blood now. Off you go, anyway, and perhaps you'll come and see me just once or twice while you're here?' She pointed to the map. 'Now you know where it is, don't you? You can't miss the place really and you can always telephone if you want anything. There's no phone in the house, but there's one in Elgol.'

They settled themselves in the little car and waved goodbye, and Miriam's heart gave a small flutter of excitement. Their precious honeymoon was really starting at last. They were alone—and how alone! The road became empty and narrow, with great hills on one side and the sea on the other. It seemed, when they had left the houses behind, that there was not another sign of human habitation anywhere.

It was about ten miles across the Island, and eventually they saw the croft. It stood, low and sturdy, tucked into its protecting hillside as though it had been there for ever. There was a door in the centre and two small windows on either side of it, and the chimneys, standing bravely on each end wall, gave it a look of surprise as if it were amazed at the presence at last, after so many years, of its rightful owner, a true Macleod.

They got out of the car and stood staring at it for a moment. Miriam was completely entranced with its simple and austere beauty, and she wondered what Chaim was thinking as he looked.

She saw him take the keys in his hand and walk up the path.

'I think I can just remember it,' he said quietly. 'There's a faint memory beginning to stir. I can see my mother coming back from Elgol on her bicycle. She used to go shopping on an old black thing with a big curved bar. She took me with her sometimes on a small seat on the back!' Then he laughed. 'But this isn't the time for memories. It's now that matters, and it's our honeymoon!'

He opened the door, and then turned back and suddenly swept her off her feet and carried her through, setting her down carefully over the threshold. He kissed her and held her close.

'Welcome to Scotland, my darling,' he said.

Miriam shivered a little in his arms with tiredness and emotion. In the kibbutz there were always people; even in the apartment they could hear their neighbours through the thin walls. There was noise and heat and constant activity. Here the absence of human sound was intense, almost frightening. There was only the crashing of the sea on the beach just below the road and the wind whistling round the house. It was cold too. After the heat of Israel it was so cold.

They lit the log fire that was ready laid in the hearth. They sat before it and drank the coffee that Fiona had left, and then Miriam trembled as Chaim took her hand and gently led her through to the spotless little bedroom with its large patchwork quilt covering the double bed. She looked at it with longing and fear and excitement. Deliberately and carefully she removed her clothes one by one as though in some slow-motion film, then she pulled back the bedspread and slid beneath the cold sheets, waiting for him. He had been watching every movement she made, standing motionless with a look in his eyes that she could not decipher. Then suddenly he was galvanised into action, his garments dropped in urgent haste and he was beside her, his arms, hard and relentless, pressing her close as though he wanted to melt into her for ever. Then she gasped as he released her. Surely it wasn't going to happen again, that terrible withdrawal of not only his body but his whole being? He must have seen the agony in her eyes.

'You are so beautiful,' he gasped. 'I must just look for a moment,' and then looking was not enough and his hands were stroking her and his lips caressing. She felt the warmth of him and she held him to her tightly, fearing to let him go, and she heard his heart thundering against hers. The full wonder and joy of their coupling rushed over her like the pounding of the sea on that rocky shore below the house, and they were totally one in a joy and elation that she had never dreamed of before. In the deep, satisfying quietness of the lonely croft they knew the full depth of their love and passion for each other. There were no interruptions and nothing to spoil their delight.

Later they slept, slept on and on in the soft warmth of the deep feather bed, and even the bright May sunshine intruding early through the small windows failed to waken them. At last when Miriam opened her eyes, expecting at first to find the narrowness of the hard bunk and the heat of another day, she discovered only the softness of the billowing feathers and the hard, lean body of her new husband sleeping peacefully beside her. He moaned slightly as she moved closer into his arms, then he too awoke and smiled at her, and they made love again, and then later that morning ran down to the sea together and plunged into its icy waves. They laughed and splashed and kissed, and even the capricious Scottish weather was kind, for the sun shone gently, making their happiness complete.

There was no radio in the croft, no news.

'This is our week,' Chaim said when Miriam commented on it. 'I just want you to know that Israel is my second love. You are my first. That's why I'm here with no radio. It's deliberate.'

It was the most wonderful thing he could ever have said.

CHAPTER TWENTY-FIVE

May–June 1967

'CAN we manage a day or two in Bristol on the way home?' Miriam pleaded towards the end of the most wonderful week of her life.

'I hope so,' Chaim said. 'I've been looking at timetables and I think it'll be possible if we leave here a day early. We promised to be back on the fourteenth.'

'It seems such a long way to come for such a short time!'

Skye was so beautiful, so peaceful, and Miriam surprised herself with a sudden disinclination to go back to Israel so soon. It wasn't that she wanted to stay here for ever, just a little longer, and a week with her parents would have been wonderful.

'You aren't regretting anything, are you?'

She heard the anxiety in Chaim's voice and at once her slight regrets vanished. She ran over to him and threw her arms round his neck.

'Of course not, silly,' she said. 'Wherever you are will always be the most perfect place in the world to me!'

He laughed. 'I won't take that too seriously. There are some pretty awful places.'

'Like where?'

'The desert. A battlefield!'

Miriam shuddered and suddenly the world was cold and frightening. 'There won't be a war,' she said, as if speaking the words made them true. 'There can't be a war now. The weather's too beautiful!'

The foolishness of what she had said made them both laugh, and that was what she wanted. The light-hearted, happy mood of the past days must remain at least for a little longer.

In Bristol Graham and Margaret were watching the television news.

'As long as Syria and Egypt don't join forces against Israel there probably won't be an all-out war,' Graham commented. 'But I'm pretty worried about all these terrorist attacks the Syrians are making in northern Galilee. It's too near Rosh Hazim for comfort.'

Margaret usually had little interest in world events, but recently she listened to almost every bulletin. Israel seemed to be mentioned constantly.

'Why couldn't she have decided to live somewhere nice and peaceful like Switzerland if it had to be abroad?' she moaned as Graham turned off the set.

They arrived in Bristol at the end of the week. Graham met them at the station, and Miriam burst into tears of happiness and emotion as he pulled the car into the drive. It was the first time she had been home since the previous August.

'It's lovely to be here with Chaim at last,' she said, trying to regain her composure, and she took his hand and pulled him through the front door. 'I've been thinking about this moment for so long, and I never thought I'd cry!'

She wiped her eyes quickly, then laughed a little, and she went through to the kitchen and bounded up the stairs to her bedroom. It was just as she had left it, and a few tears threatened again.

'I've put you in the guest bedroom,' Margaret called up to her. 'I thought you'd prefer it.'

Miriam blushed. To be sleeping in your parents' house on your honeymoon was slightly embarrassing. She hoped that Charles wouldn't make any bawdy remarks! For a moment she was glad that it was only for one night.

The short time passed quickly and the following day Graham drove them right to Heathrow. Again there was the sadness of parting, and Miriam was glad when their flight was called. She turned quickly away from her father and walked bravely with Chaim to the plane. Her real life was about to begin now. She was going to be an Israeli wife, a mother too one day, perhaps, and all her thoughts must be for her husband and her new country.

She sat in the seat next to the window and stared out at the green countryside of England as the plane forged its way further and further up into the blue of the sky. There were few clouds and after a while she could see the small winding lanes of the countryside, and here and there a wide new road slashing its way forcefully through the green. Then there was the sea and England was behind her, left for who knew how long. She turned to Chaim at last and smiled at him.

'I'm glad you've come back to me,' he said. 'I began to think you wanted wings to jump out and fly back home!'

'Home is Israel now. That's our future. I can't wait to get back.'

'And Scotland? Would you like to live there?'

She looked at him in surprise at the question. 'No,' she said. 'Your knees are too knobbly to wear a kilt. I prefer you in jeans!'

'Shorts are out, then, are they?'

They laughed and he kissed her. The future would be

good, Miriam thought. If they could always laugh together then it would be good.

They were welcomed back with much joking and good humour, and Chaim proudly produced the shirt he had purchased in Macleod tartan. Miriam had a silk scarf to match.

'We're not putting these in the communal box,' he said. 'No one here has a right to wear them. They're only for Macleods!'

'You might have brought a kilt,' his friend teased. 'We could find out what Scotsmen wear beneath them then.'

'Too hot for Israel,' Chaim said, 'and too expensive. Now what's the news?'

'Great celebrations tomorrow for Independence Day. That's the good news.'

'What's the bad, then?'

'The newspapers say we're planning a major move against Syria and there are rumours that Egypt is massing troops in Sinai. The reserves haven't been called up yet, though, so make the most of the next few days. It shouldn't be long!'

Miriam shivered as she listened, but she was reassured by the bright and confident attitude of all the young people around her.

Chaim shrugged off the seriousness of the situation. 'There are always rumours—I've grown up with them. And if we do have to fight we'll win.' He turned to Miriam. 'Come on, then, let's get to our stately home. I've got to carry you over the doorstep once again!'

There were plenty of willing hands to carry the luggage and more laughs as they opened the door to witness the handiwork of Charles and James. A shower of confetti fell on Chaim as he struggled through with

Miriam in his arms. There were more shocks in the tiny bedroom and even the shower had not gone un-doctored.

'Just wait until it's their turn,' Miriam said. 'Why didn't we see it was locked?'

When at last all was cleared up and they were alone for a few minutes before their evening meal she turned to him.

'I'm so glad we had that week on Skye on our own,' she told him.

For a moment she thought, with nostalgia, of the sturdy little croft nestling in its lonely hillside with the sound of the sea and the wind and the crying of the gulls. Here she could only hear next door's radio.

'Want to go back?' asked Chaim.

'No, oh, no. I told you—here is home. Why do you keep asking me if I want to go back?'

'I have to be sure, that's all. I love you so much. I suppose I'm afraid of losing you!'

'You don't need to worry about that. I love you, and I love it here too. So you can stop all your doubts. Let's eat—I'm starving!'

The Independence celebrations on the kibbutz the next day were wonderful. Miriam had never experienced anything like it before, and when it was all over and she was lying with Chaim's arms comfortably round her in their large new bed in the early hours of the morning she sighed happily.

'Fantastic! Israelis really know how to enjoy themselves, don't they?'

'Well, we have something to celebrate, haven't we?' Chaim said. 'Israel is nineteen years old today!'

'The same age as me,' Miriam replied thoughtfully. 'I was born in 1948 too! It seems a long time to have been alive, and I haven't managed to accomplish very much during those years. Not like Israel!'

'Just being you. That's enough for me!'

She kissed him sleepily. 'I hope it'll always be enough,' she whispered.

For reply he made love to her again, and they fell asleep knowing that tomorrow would be an easy day. There were concessions and only the vital work would be done. Everybody would need to recover!

'The reserves are being mobilised!'

The news spread rapidly through the kibbutz and struck chill deep into Miriam's soul, and by the end of May her worst fears had been realised. She heard Rabin's voice on the little radio they kept in their apartment. War was imminent, he said, and the army must be fully on its guard. Egypt had closed the Straits of Tiran, was putting all its troops and tanks into Sinai and had made a joint defence arrangement with Jordan and Syria. Help had been promised against Israel by Iraq, Kuwait, Saudi Arabia and Algeria.

'It's terrible. Too frightening to think about,' she said when Chaim came in later. She spread out the map on the table. 'Look at the size of Israel compared with all these Arab states ranged against us. We're so small!'

'Don't worry, it's quality that counts,' he said carelessly. 'We've got quality!'

'Apparently that's all we've got. We're on our own.'

'Like Britain in 1940, and look what happened then. Its greatest hour and all that!'

'I just wish you wouldn't be so cheerful,' Miriam moaned. 'You're going to have to fight!' She emphasised the last word, and he came over to her and tilted her chin up to face him.

'You're a brave Israeli wife, remember?' he said.

'And with me in the Army we can't possibly be beaten.'

She had to laugh at his words, and then she kissed him. 'I truly believe you want to go.'

'Perhaps I do. I don't want to leave you, though!'

'What if you get killed?'

'I'm not going to get killed. But if I do, remember to write and tell Aunt Fiona!'

'You're quite impossible!'

Chaim was called up a few days later. Miriam looked at him in the familiar green uniform and there was a small measure of pride as well as intense misery. Then he was gone, and she was alone, alone among all the other wives. It was later, during the evening of that day, when she began to wonder if she was pregnant. For the first time since her return here, she wept for her mother and father and for her home in the green, peaceful countryside of England.

It was the morning of the beginning of the Six-Day War when she became sure. That day would remain in her memory for the rest of her life. She felt sick and stayed in her bed listening to the news bulletins. Wave after wave of Israeli planes swept over nine Egyptian airfields and nearly three hundred enemy bombers and fighters were destroyed on the ground. It was supposed to be wonderful news and she should be rejoicing, but she turned her face to the wall and wept again, crying for Chaim and for her baby who would be born into this troubled land.

Dinah came to visit that afternoon.

'Try to be happy, dear,' she said. 'Just think that all those enemy planes would have been unleashed upon us. The news is terrific!'

Miriam sat up in bed and wiped her eyes. She looked at Dinah and felt deeply ashamed of her tears.

'Why does the world hate us so?' she said at last. 'What have we Jews done to be so hated?'

'That's a big question for a hot afternoon, and I couldn't answer if I wanted to. Let me make you a cup of tea instead!'

'Thanks. That would be lovely.'

Dinah went to the little kitchen area and put the kettle to boil.

'Don't you hate the world, then, after Auschwitz and all that?' Miriam called to her. 'The Germans, I mean. Surely you hate them?'

Dinah came back carrying a small tray with two mugs of tea and she set them down and sat on the bed.

'I hate the Nazis, but that's not like hating the Germans, the ordinary people, and especially the ones we have here. They are just a nice bunch of youngsters like you who come for a few weeks wanting to help us, and often they tell me that they come with a lot of guilt for what their country did.'

'After I visited Yad Vashem I felt I couldn't speak to a German again in my whole life.'

Dinah smiled and stirred two large spoonfuls of sugar into her tea. 'It always seems worse for you young ones who haven't been through it,' she said. 'But we have so many other enemies now that Germany isn't a problem any more. But even the Arabs, it's not all of them who want war, mostly their leaders and a few terrorists.'

'That's what Chaim keeps telling me.' Thoughts of Chaim brought anxiety once more into the forefront of her mind. 'Is there any more news of the war? I haven't been listening for a while. I felt too ill!'

'Yes. It's good. Our tanks have been advancing across Sinai and we've taken Sharm el Sheik and opened the Straits of Tiran again.'

'What about Jerusalem?'

'Not so good! The Jordanians have bunkers in the Old City, I believe, and the last thing I heard was that they're expecting the battle there to be pretty fierce. It'll be awful if they have to fight in those little alleys.'

Miriam felt icy cold and she shivered in spite of the heat of the June day. She guessed that Chaim would be fighting somewhere in the Judaean hills. She wasn't sure exactly why she felt the weight of this knowledge upon her. It was strange and frightening. He had always said that he wanted to liberate Jerusalem.

Miriam was still lying in her bed, still feeling sick, the next day. She turned on the radio and listened. It was Rabin speaking again, and at first the import of his words failed to make sense. He was talking to his men and his message was being broadcast too for the whole nation to hear. He was saying that he saluted them for the decisive victory they had won at such great cost. She heard the voice through a haze of headache and sickness.

'The fighting was savage and hard, and many have fallen in action. . .generations of Jews killed for the sake of Jerusalem. . .their sacrifices——'

'Chaim,' she shouted. 'Chaim, come home to me, to our child!'

It was Dinah who came instead.

'He will be coming home,' she said soothingly. 'They've taken Jerusalem. They've reached the Western Wall. It's all open to us again!'

Miriam burst into tears. 'He won't be coming, Dinah. I know it!'

The others came home eventually when the war was over, a short war, six days in all, and such triumphant days that the map of Israel had to be drawn all over again.

'For the first time in two thousand years Jerusalem is our capital city,' they said, and there was much rejoicing, but in front of Miriam they grew quiet, not knowing what to say, how to comfort such sadness in the midst of such excitement.

Miriam sat in her little apartment, her mind blank and unresponsive to every effort made for her. To one person only she listened. He had been with Chaim right through the fighting, at his side when he died.

'He achieved the thing he wanted more than anything,' he told her. 'He fought his way right through to the Western Wall and he stood there completely happy in that moment of his triumph. He was killed by a solitary sniper, but he made it, he touched the Wall.'

'Did he say anything? Can you tell me what he said?'

'I saw tears in his eyes. Most of us had tears that day, and then I heard him quote from the Bible, "I rejoiced when they said unto me, Let us go unto the house of the Lord. Our feet are standing within your gates, O Jerusalem!"'

'But he wasn't religious. Are you sure he said that?'

'Quite sure. No, he wasn't religious, but I think we all were at that moment, whatever our normal beliefs.'

Graham and Margaret arrived the following day.

'We couldn't get a flight any earlier,' Margaret said. 'We've come to take you home.'

Miriam stared at her mother through tear-reddened eyes. 'Home? This is home, and I'm staying. I'm pregnant, and do you think I could bring up Chaim's baby in any other place but his Israel?' She was shouting, and she cared nothing that plenty of others must be able to hear the angry words. 'My baby will be a Sabra, a true Israeli-born Jew, but he'll only be that if I stay here. You can persuade me all you like, but I'm staying!'

Graham was more calm, more understanding than Margaret, although just as deeply upset.

'You must do what you believe to be right, my dear,' he said quietly. 'How about a long visit to England, though? You need a rest, and we could look after you.'

Miriam looked at him with deep affection. She knew that what he said made sense. The thought of her lovely cool bedroom at home was tempting. They would truly look after her. She knew she would want for nothing, but she knew too that if she left she would never return. To come back here alone would be unthinkable. If there were no baby then perhaps. . .

'No.' Her voice was immensely sad, but with a core of steel. 'No, I can't. Please, please don't ask it of me. I'll come later on after the baby is born. Could you stay with me a little bit, though? I should love you to stay for a few days.'

'Yes, of course we'll stay.' It was Margaret speaking now. 'And I'll come over again when the baby is due, if you want me.'

'Thanks, Mum, that would be wonderful.'

Miriam put out her arms to her mother and they hugged each other and mingled their tears.

'I'm so glad I'm pregnant,' Miriam said to them later when they were having supper. 'I just know it'll be a little boy who will look exactly like his father. It seems such a long time to wait, though.'

Margaret was silent. She recalled clearly her own similar thoughts twenty years ago. She too had wished for a little boy just like his father. She looked at her daughter with the old remembered guilt and with deep compassion for her sadness and plight. She had vowed at her birth that she would do everything in her power to bring this child happiness and security. Never in her life had she felt so helpless to fulfil her vow as she did at this moment. It was Miriam's hour of greatest need, and there was nothing she could do except to look on and suffer with her.

PART THREE

HANNAH

CHAPTER TWENTY-SIX

1978

'PLEASE, Mummy! I should really love to go.'

Hannah, Miriam's ten-year-old daughter, held a letter in her hand, a letter from Margaret. Her blue eyes were anxious, and there was a worried and slightly frightened look in her fair, delicate features.

Miriam felt the customary wave of annoyance as she stared at the little girl.

'Grandad says he'll pay for us,' Hannah pleaded, 'and Moshe says he thinks it would be a good idea. He said he hopes you'll agree.'

'You mean you asked him first without my permission?'

Hannah was silent for a moment. Most of the kibbutz parents were relaxed with their children, but her mother wasn't like that at all. In fact Hannah was a little frightened of her. Miriam had always been strict, and hugs and kisses had been few. Granny was different. Hannah thought of Margaret with a thrill of pleasure. She really loved her grandmother.

'I thought it might make you say yes if Moshe agreed.'

'You needn't have asked him. He doesn't rule our lives!'

There was an edge to Miriam's voice that Hannah didn't fully understand. She knew that the secretary of the kibbutz had some influence, and the more people she could get ranged on her side the better.

'Well, I'll think about it. Now run away and play. I'll

come over and see you this afternoon.'

Miriam watched her daughter turn and walk sadly away from the little apartment. She dragged her feet, scuffing the gravel path, every line of her young body showing despair. A great wave of guilt encompassed Miriam as she stood there. Why could she not love this child who had been born in such sadness ten years ago? She remembered the moment she'd first seen her new-born baby. Her mother had been with her, and she would never forget the look on Margaret's face as she handed the little scrap to her. There was sheer adoration in her eyes, and Miriam was jealous, desperately jealous. In all the years of her growing up she had never been able to bring such a look of devotion to her mother's face. Oh, yes, it had been there for her brothers. How her brothers had been loved! But for her there had always been a carefully hidden coldness, and when there was affection she felt that it had been forced. It was true that Margaret had shown love to her during the later years, on her visits to Israel, and she had thought that the bond between them would become closer when Chaim was killed. But all that had changed when Hannah was born. Margaret loved the child from the first, and Miriam felt left out again, an outsider watching a love blossom between granddaughter and grandmother in which she could have no part.

She recalled the first glimpse of the fair hair and blue eyes of her new little daughter.

'Where on earth does she get that blonde fuzz from?' she had asked in her disappointment. This child, this girl was never going to look like Chaim, never going to recompense her at all for his loss.

'She isn't like any of us, is she, Mum?' she remembered saying. 'So fair, and look at those blue eyes!'

There had been a sudden faraway look on her

mother's face, and then tears—tears that were hastily brushed away. But from that moment Hannah had belonged to Margaret more than to her. In spite of the distance between them, the miles that made visits difficult, there was a deep bond and a love that Miriam couldn't understand. Margaret came frequently to Israel to stay, sometimes accompanied by Graham, and those visits were always more welcome to Miriam. She didn't feel quite so alone when Graham was there.

As soon as Hannah could read and write the letters started, and although at first she was included in the correspondence Miriam soon realised that they were always personal, full of secrets shared and little jokes that she often didn't understand. Soon she stopped bothering to read them. Let Hannah and Margaret have their friendship, their love. She would try to understand and be glad, but the hurt went on and would not be healed.

Now Margaret and Graham were inviting Hannah to go and stay for the whole of the summer. They were going to Scotland, they said, as well as Cornwall, and it would be a wonderful chance for the child to see her father's birthplace, the little croft which was her inheritance, and to meet her Aunt Fiona.

Miriam shuddered. She had never been back. Nothing would persuade her to visit again the place of her happiest days, the sacred, precious little house on the mountainside where she and Chaim had spent the most wonderful week of their life together. She was not keen to let Hannah go there either. The child mustn't think of Scotland as part of her heritage. It was important that Israel must be first in her thoughts and her affection. This was the place she must grow up to love and to serve. Chaim would have wanted that. She was a Sabra, Israeli-born, and nothing must be allowed to interfere with her true destiny. There were the cello lessons too. Hannah had a great gift and her teacher had ambitious plans for her. 'The Israeli Philharmonic, perhaps, when you grow up, and if you work very hard,' he often told her.

Throughout the day Miriam thought about it. It was her turn to work with the small children and she looked after them automatically, seeing to the needs of each one with her customary diligence, but feeling remote and detached.

She liked this job usually, but today it was irksome. Hannah wouldn't let the matter rest, she knew that. The child was persistent when there was something that she really wanted to do. She was like her father in that, Miriam thought ruefully. She might not have inherited any of his physical characteristics, but her nature was very much Chaim's. There was frequently a sunny cheerfulness about her, but with sad undertones, and the remote, faraway look in her eyes sometimes reminded Miriam of the way he had stared at the hills of his native Skye. It seemed to her occasionally as if the Highland blood in his veins was striving for recognition, denied in him and now surfacing in this strange child whom she so often failed to understand.

'But, Mummy, Gran wants you to go to England too. She says she hopes you'll go. Please, let's both go. It would be wonderful to get away from here for two whole months!'

The day's work was done at last, the evening meal finished, and Hannah had come to her mother's apartment as the children always did for an hour or two before bedtime. She slept in the chldren's house with all the others of her age, and Miriam guessed that frequently she would have preferred to stay there after supper. This daily visit was a task that the child forced herself to perform.

'What do you mean, get away from here?' She was aware of the anger in her voice and she tried desperately to moderate her words.

Hannah paled. 'Well, I like staying with Granny and Grandad, and our visits before have always been so short.'

'What about your music?'

'Granny says she has a friend who has a cello and she'll lend it to me if I'm very careful with it. She doesn't play it any more.'

They seemed to have it all worked out between them. Miriam felt defeated. She knew in the depths of her heart that Hannah, who had known almost nothing but this way of life since her birth, wasn't really happy. She thought frequently of her own sheltered upbringing in the lovely home in Bristol, of her father's love for her, and of the presents showered upon her, of the family holidays spent camping in France, or in Switzerland or Spain, and she wondered if she was being quite fair to her daughter. Since Chaim's death she had become more fanatical in her love for this land of her adoption. She knew and recognised it, and she was powerless to change herself even if her child was to be another sacrifice!

'Would you like to go on your own, without me?'

There was a moment's hesitation after she spoke, and Miriam held her breath. She wanted this child's love desperately, even though she had so little of herself to give in return. She hated the thought of rejection, but she felt powerless to bridge the gap between them, and so often she couldn't help herself saying or doing the very thing that would deepen the lack of understanding between them.

At last Hannah spoke, slowly and carefully as though she too had a glimpse of the sadness in her mother's heart.

'Well, I think Granny would be very sad if you don't go, and I know Grandad hopes very much that you will. I should be awfully lonely on the journey too. Please!'

Suddenly Hannah ran across the small room and threw her arms round her mother in an unaccustomed display of affection, and Miriam returned the embrace gladly and in surprise. This small act changed her mind. It was a gesture probably meant to persuade, she thought, but it was so unexpected and so sweet that the words were spoken before she could reconsider.

'Right! We'll go. I'll telephone Grandad straight away!'

Everything was just as she remembered it, and Miriam felt a small thrill of pleasure as she stepped from the car into the coolness of an English midsummer evening.

Margaret was standing at the door to greet them, and they all laughed at Hannah's first words to her grandmother.

'*Shalom*, Granny,' she said as she rushed into her arms. '*Shalom, shalom.* It's wonderful to be home!'

Miriam winced a little as she heard the last word, but she was determined to let nothing spoil her daughter's pleasure and indeed her own too. Yes, it was good to be 'home'.

They had a room each now that her brothers had left, and she was grateful for the quiet privacy. She unpacked her things quickly. There wasn't much. Smart clothes weren't often necessary on the kibbutz, and she stared at the two dresses and assortment of jeans and blouses with slight dismay. They had seemed good enough when she put them in her case, but here they looked shabby and unfashionable. She must go into town and get one or two things, she thought, and something for Hannah too.

The first week passed quickly and easily with shopping expeditions, walks in the country and a visit from Charles with his wife and two small children. He had resolutely refused to follow his father's footsteps into accountancy and was now teaching maths at a local school.

It was James who had given all of them the greatest surprise.

'I was really scared that I was going to lose him too when he went off to Israel just as you did during that long summer holiday,' Margaret confided one evening. 'Do you remember how keen he was?'

Miriam laughed. 'Yes, I thought at one time that he intended to apply to the kibbutz for membership, and I suppose I was selfishly a little pleased. I was feeling particularly lonely just then, and it would have been nice to have a brother around. He was a real dark horse, though, wasn't he? He kept his Christianity jolly quiet.'

'Didn't he give you any clues as to what he intended?'

'None. Except that he went off to Tiberias quite a bit, and when his six weeks with us were up he stayed for a week at a Christian hospice in Jerusalem. I must say I thought that a bit odd.'

'He's been two whole years now as a curate, and I think he hopes for a church of his own soon.'

'I just can't imagine James as a priest, although I suppose he always had a deeper side to his nature.'

'He's very popular with the young people in the church, I believe, takes them on camping holidays, climbing and walking and things.'

There was immense pride in Margaret's voice, and Miriam sighed a little. She knew that her life had been a sort of failure in her mother's eyes, an example of wasted opportunity. Well, maybe Hannah would make up for it, perhaps with her music. The little girl bounced into the kitchen at that moment, full of excitement.

'Jane has been showing me her pony. She says I may have a ride on him tomorrow if the weather's all right.'

'Only if her mother agrees and stays with you,' Margaret said. 'You've never ridden before, and he's quite lively.'

'She said something about a leading-rein, so I'll be quite safe, Granny,' Hannah said. 'She's going to teach me to ride properly.'

Graham, overhearing, came to the door. 'You can have proper riding lessons if your mother agrees,' he said. 'There's a good riding school on the Downs. I'll take you.'

Hannah turned to Miriam, her eyes glowing with pleasure. 'Oh, please, Mummy! Can I?'

'I suppose so. If there's time before you all leave for Scotland.'

Miriam had resolutely refused to go with them. She would stay here, she said, and look after the house. The quietness and the peace would do her good, and there was the dog to think of too. She had always loved dogs and had been sad when she heard of Ricky's death. There was another dog now, a fat and fussed golden retriever called Lana.

'You can't take her all that way,' she'd said, glad of the excuse. 'She must be getting on a bit now and she'd hate that long journey in the back of the car. She and I will be good company.' She'd stroked the dog's silky head and was licked enthusiastically in return. 'Besides, you said that James might be coming, didn't you, Mum? I couldn't miss James.'

They left a few days later.

'Are you sure you'll be all right?' Graham wanted to know. There was anxiety in his voice and he kissed her and looked straight into her eyes, and she knew that he understood more than her mother about the reasons why she could not go.

'I'll be fine, Dad,' she said, smiling cheerfully at him. 'Stop worrying about me. I'm a grown woman!'

It was a joke between them, and they laughed together. Miriam wondered again, as she had done so many times during her life, why this adoptive father of hers was so much closer to her than her real mother. She watched him affectionately as he tucked a blanket round Hannah's knees in the back seat of the car.

'Must keep you warm, young lady,' he said. 'After all that heat you're used to!'

Miriam stood at the door and waved and blew kisses to all of them as he reversed down the drive, and she saw her daughter's small face staring up at her through the window. Just before the car was out of sight Hannah pressed her hand to her lips and returned her mother's kiss, and then they were gone. Miriam turned slowly and went indoors. She made herself coffee, turned on the television and sank into the luxury of the large settee. How strange her life had been, she thought as she looked around her at the well-loved and familiar room. In this place she had grown up. This was her home, and here was everything she had loved as a child and teenager. Her roots were here, and she suddenly shivered. For one moment it was almost as if the last eleven years had never been. If it were not for the fair-haired little changeling girl to whom she had given birth she could almost put the clock right back and start all over again. She sat and watched the programme on the set before her and saw nothing.

Was she the same person who had left here for the excitement of a holiday job on a kibbutz? Was she the same girl who had thrown away the chance of a place at Oxford for an ideal, for a young man with a wonderful smile and a way with words? In spite of her fanatical love for Israel she sometimes wondered in the secret places of her heart whether it was Chaim's dream that was keeping her anchored so firmly there or whether it was her own vision. It was a question she couldn't truthfully answer. She constantly affirmed to herself that it was the latter.

James asked her a few days later when he came for the weekend. They had finished their meal and were sitting either side of the fireplace staring at Margaret's elaborate flower arrangement in the grate.

'What keeps you there, Mirry?' he asked. 'I mean, I know it's very beautiful and a challenge and all that, but it's hard, isn't it? Life could be so much easier here. You could leave Hannah with Mum and do your degree, get a career for yourself. You're not old yet!'

'I've thought about it—don't think I haven't. I suppose I feel I would have failed Chaim dismally if I brought his daughter up here. She'd go to a good school, Dad would see to that, and learn to ride and do all the things a nice middle-class English girl does, and she would forget all about the land of her birth and her father's sacrifice. I'd have a permanent sense of guilt. I'd see Chaim's face accusing me constantly.'

'That's totally stupid!' James's voice was almost angry. 'I didn't know Chaim very well, but from the little I did know I'm sure he wasn't like that. He was far more easy-going. He'd want you both to be happy.'

'You may be correct, but I have to be true to myself, James, and do what I believe is right for us both, for Hannah and me, even though it might not be the easiest thing. And I love Israel too. It has me in its thrall as much now as when I first went there.'

'Fair enough. What about marriage, then? Chaim has been dead for ten years now. Anyone else?'

'Is it because you're a mini-vicar that you think you can question me like this?'

James roared with laughter. 'Mini-vicar? That's a new name for a curate. No, Mirry, it isn't that. I want you to be happy, that's all, and I've a feeling that you aren't. I suppose it might come from my constant dealings with people. You get a sort of second sense.'

'Well, no more talking about me. I get enough of that when Mum and Dad are here. Mum wants to have Hannah here permanently, and Dad would like me around, so they both have goes at me from time to time. If I ever get back to Israel it'll be through sheer determination on my part! Now, what about you? Girlfriends? Good thing you're not a Catholic—I should hate to have a celibate brother!'

'Well, yes, there is one, but no names or anything yet, and no mention of her to the parents, please, not for a bit. She's a vicar's daughter, so she's well used to the privations of marrying a clergyman.'

'Have you asked her to marry you, then?'

'Don't ask questions. I'll invite you to the wedding, and I hope you'll come. We shall want Hannah for the bridesmaid!'

'That might be difficult. You'd better hurry up! Can't you have it while we're here? You're nearly thirty now, after all!'

'What has that got to do with it?'

'Well, it's quite old, isn't it, really?'

They laughed and changed the subject, but that night Miriam recalled his words and wondered when the wedding would be and how on earth she could manage to get away again. She knew it wouldn't be possible. It was another cause to feel guilty about Hannah. She would absolutely love to be a bridesmaid in the ancient little parish church on the hill!

Meanwhile in Scotland Hannah was having a wonderful time. Not wanting to stay in the little croft which Margaret knew had such poignant memories for Miriam, they booked into a hotel in Portree on Skye and went to see Chaim's Aunt Fiona.

'So this is Ian's daughter,' she said, wrapping the little girl in her arms. 'I've been that excited since I had your letter! Oh, yes, we call him Ian here,' she explained. 'It was his first name, actually, and that funny "Chaim" was his second. I could never get used to that.'

She turned to shake hands with Graham and Margaret, and then led the way into her house.

'We'll have a bit to eat and then go over to the croft. There are some folks on holiday in it at the moment, but I've told them we're coming and they don't mind us going in.'

She took them to the sitting-room and then went to put the kettle to boil.

'We have to let it, you see, to pay for the upkeep,' she went on when she came back. 'I'm hoping it'll be properly lived in one day.'

They left for the croft later that afternoon, and Hannah could hardly keep still in her excitement.

'It's like fairyland!' she exclaimed when she first saw the Cuillins.

'There's a song about those mountains,' Graham told

her. 'Come on, Granny, sing it for us.'

Margaret obliged, and they laughed as she tried to remember the lines, but Fiona looked grave as they rounded the bend in the hill and saw the little building tucked beneath its sheltering hillside.

'I was hoping that Ian would come here to live and farm perhaps, and then after he was killed I thought that Miriam might come with the child, but I don't suppose it was a practical idea. Too lonely and too many memories.' She looked at Hannah, who was staring speechless at the small house. 'Well, you're here now anyway, dearie,' she said to her. 'It's been waiting for you all these years. It belongs to you now, you know, kept for you under your grandfather's will. Maybe you'll be the one to come and love it when you grow up.'

Hannah said nothing at first. She followed the older woman inside. It was warm and welcoming with toys on the floor and flowers at the window.

'Don't touch any of their things,' Fiona said to her, 'but you can wander over the house and look into all the rooms.'

Graham and Margaret watched her fondly as she walked from room to room staring from each small window and then, back in the living-room, she paused and looked up at the framed photograph that stood on the mantelpiece.

'That's Mummy and Daddy, isn't it?' she said. 'When they were here. Look, they're standing outside the front door.'

'I came over one day and took it while they were on their honeymoon,' Fiona said, and Margaret noticed the tears in her eyes.

'I want to live here,' Hannah said quietly. 'It's the most wonderful place in the whole world!'

None of them took her seriously. Graham persuaded her outside and took photographs, and they went down to the beach and paddled in the cold sea, and then they left.

'I like it because it's lonely,' Hannah told them in the car later. 'There are too many people in Rosh Hazim, and it's too noisy.'

When it was time to say goodbye to Fiona she shook her hand solemnly. '*Shalom*, Aunt Fiona,' she said. 'I'll be back one day. I absolutely promise!'

CHAPTER TWENTY-SEVEN

1978

IT WAS to be a long time before Hannah could keep her promise and return to Scotland.

'No, Hannah,' Miriam said firmly. 'We are not going to stay here in Bristol with Granny and Grandad, and we are certainly not going to live in that lonely croft. We're going back to Israel, and that's final, so don't let me hear any more about it.'

Margaret looked sadly at her daughter and granddaughter. They were staring at each other with a complete lack of understanding between them, and it reminded her, with an unwelcome pang of guilt, of her own early relationship with Miriam.

There were just two days more before the dreaded return, and she wondered how she would fill her time when they were gone. The bond between herself and Hannah was sweet, and her heart wept at the thought of the child's unhappiness.

'How about going to the zoo this afternoon?' she said in an effort to keep cheerful. 'We could have tea there and a walk over the Downs too. It's a lovely day.'

'Not me, thanks, Mum,' said Miriam. 'I hate seeing those animals in cages, but you take Hannah and I'll start packing. We seem to have bought so much since we arrived that I don't know how I'm going to cope with getting it all home.'

Hannah brightened visibly. 'Will you take me, Granny? I'd love to go.'

'We'll leave straight after lunch, then. Now go and

pick me a lettuce and I can make a quick salad.'

Hannah ran happily out to the kitchen garden behind the house, and Margaret turned to Miriam.

'So you really have made up your mind not to let her go to school here? We'd pay for her to fly out to you every holiday—you know that.'

'Yes, I know, Mum, but it wouldn't do. I couldn't go back to the kibbutz without her. It just isn't done. An expensive English education wouldn't fit her for the life she'll lead in Israel. It would make her an outsider, and I want her to belong, really belong. It's her country, her father's country, and mine too now.'

Margaret sighed. 'All right. I won't spoil your last two days with any more persuasion. I suppose it's selfish of me really anyway. I know I shouldn't live through my family as I do.'

'You should get out and make some friends and take up something, some hobby,' Miriam said. 'Then you won't miss us so much.'

Margaret knew that she was speaking the truth. She had always tried to be the perfect mother, sacrificing herself for her children, and now that they all had lives of their own she knew that she had perhaps been wrong. She had a life too, and she must take it with both hands and make something of these remaining years and not try to live them through Hannah. In two days' time she would make a new effort; now there was lunch to see to and the visit to the zoo.

She washed the lettuce efficiently, whipped up a dressing, cut ham from the joint she had cooked the day before, and mixed tomatoes, beans, and nuts.

'Lovely,' Hannah commented. 'The lettuce always seems kind of floppy at home.'

'That's because it's hot and dry most of the time. Lettuces like nice rainy weather.'

'So do I,' Hannah said. She wrinkled her nose appreciatively. 'It smells nice here when it rains.'

They all laughed.

'Well, it's not raining now, so come on and we'll pay those animals a visit.'

They walked hand in hand round the monkey cages, laughed at the antics of the young gorillas in their large, airy enclosure and stared in awe at the lions. Suddenly Hannah turned to Margaret.

'Didn't Mummy look pretty last night?' she said. 'I've never seen her sort of sparkle like that before.'

Margaret smiled. Charles had hopefully brought one of his friends home during the holidays, and Tom had called frequently after that first introduction.

'An eligible bachelor, rich, successful and nice,' Charles had whispered to his mother. 'Perhaps he'll do the trick where the rest of us have failed.'

Tom had charmed them all, not least Miriam, and when they had driven off together in his gleaming white Opal the previous evening with Miriam looking lovely in a dress bought especially for the occasion, Margaret's heart had lifted in hope.

'She smelt lovely when she kissed me goodnight, and she was so bright and bubbly,' Hannah went on. 'She isn't like that very often at home.'

Margaret smiled a little sadly. It was strange for a child to be so perceptive. 'She just needs to be happy, that's all,' she said, 'and Uncle Tom seems to be making her laugh a lot.'

'I like him too. I wish he'd marry Mummy and be my daddy and we could stay here.'

The words came out in a rush, and then she released Margaret's hand and ran over to look at the kangaroos.

'Look—oh, look at that baby one with his head just sticking out of his mother's pouch! He's really cute!'

* * *

The weather was still beautiful when Margaret stood with Graham at Heathrow two days later watching the plane become smaller and smaller until it was lost in the distant shimmering sky, and she felt that with Hannah's leaving half of her heart had gone. She was sad for Miriam too, of course, she reminded herself with guilt. She remembered the deepening pleasure she had felt all those years ago when her relationship with her daughter had improved so much. But Chaim's death had brought a hardening to Miriam, and as Margaret stood staring into the empty sky she felt tears stinging her eyes. Tears for both of them, but especially for the lovely, sensitive and lonely Hannah, the child who was unwittingly repeating the pattern of a difficult relationship between mother and daughter. Her startling likeness to Karl, to her unknown grandfather, was perhaps the source of all their problems.

Back at home a few hours later Margaret went into the child's bedroom and saw the cello in the corner of the room where it had been carefully placed ready to be taken back to the friend who had loaned it. Then suddenly as she touched the beautiful polished wood her memory flipped back to the distant past and she recalled some long-forgotten words of Karl's.

'That's Corelli,' he had said, surprising her with his knowledge when they switched on the big wooden wireless in the farmhouse kitchen one day. 'I play the violin, and that's my favourite piece.'

As the memories came flooding back she could see him staring at his work-roughened hands.

'I'll need a lot of practice before I'm any good again,' he had said.

Hannah played well. It was one of the main delights of her young life, and she was being taught competently too. Her talent was recognised, Miriam had told them, and she was taken regularly to one of Israel's best teachers as well as having excellent weekly lessons.

'She'll be given every chance,' she had said proudly. 'She may go to a music high school or perhaps join one of the youth orchestras later on.' Then there had been a questioning look at Margaret. 'No one in our family has any musical ability. I wonder where she gets it from?'

Hannah was silent for a long time as the plane flew evenly through the bright, cloudless sky. She stared down at the passing fields, the green fields of England, and then at the sea far below. It had been a wonderful holiday and there was so much to remember. The tiny croft nestling into its lonely hillside had impressed her perhaps the most. She wondered about her father and why he had left such a lovely place.

'Why did Daddy go to Israel?' she asked at last.

'He had no choice,' Miriam said, wondering at her own choice of words. 'He was only four years old. His mother was Jewish, of course, and she had never really liked Scotland.'

'Didn't he want to go back there to live when he grew up?'

'No. By then he'd grown to love Israel, and all his friends were in the kibbutz.'

There was another long silence.

'Tell me some more things about Daddy,' Hannah said at last.

Miriam often talked to Hannah about her father. She had dredged her memory for every tiny fact and Chaim often seemed to come to life as she spoke, but now she was tired and there was a strange unwillingness to go through it all again. Out of the total span of her life so little of it had been spent with Chaim, and yet he had made such an impact, changed it completely.

'I think I'd like to close my eyes and have a little sleep first.' She pointed to the television screen above them. 'Look, there's a film just starting. If you put on your headphones you'll be able to hear it.'

Hannah obediently picked up the instrument and fiddled to get the sound that matched the picture, and then she settled back to watch and Miriam leaned thankfully back in her seat. She thought about the long holiday and all its experiences. Most of all she remembered Tom and his immaculate good looks, his expensive clothes, his charm and the way he made her laugh. She had never met anyone so different from Chaim and yet with power to attract her. Yet she had deliberately turned away from him, refused his invitation to a weekend in Paris, and here she was flying back to a life of work and heat and old clothes, and Israel! Israel was there waiting for her and for Hannah. Her heart gave a little thud of happiness, but mixed with it was a tiny measure of doubt, doubt that had never been there before. She hoped she had made the right decision.

She had forgotten the heat! Weeks spent beneath a gentler sky had dulled her memory. The encompassing blanket of heat met them as they stepped from the plane, dogged them as they dragged themselves through Customs and seemed even worse outside the airport where the blinding intensity of the sun and the weight of their suitcases increased their discomfort to almost unbearable proportions. Miriam put her burdens down on the pavement for a moment and groped for a handkerchief. She mopped her wet forehead and looked at the rapidly wilting child at her side.

She opened the zipped holdall that was stuffed with everything they were likely to need on the journey, and congratulated herself that she had put Hannah's white floppy sun-hat on the top.

'Put this on,' she directed, handing it to her. 'You mustn't get sunstroke.'

Ever since Hannah's birth she had needed to be careful with the fair, delicate skin that was so unlike her own. It must always be protected.

'How about you, Mummy?' asked Hannah.

'Don't worry about me—I can stand the sun,' Miriam replied, her spirits rising suddenly. 'Look, I'll get us some orange juice from that stall over there. You stay with the luggage.'

They both felt refreshed after drinking the welcome, familiar juice.

'The bus won't be long, and then we'll soon be back and we can have a swim tonight. Doesn't that sound wonderful!'

Hannah smiled. 'I've missed the pool,' she said. 'That's the only thing I don't like about Granny's house, no pool!'

Miriam laughed out loud at that, but there was a slight tinge of bitterness in her next words.

'I'm so pleased there's something here that you like!'

The slight sarcasm seemed to be lost on Hannah, and Miriam, feeling guilty, hoped it was.

'Oh, yes, there's lots I like. It's just that I don't seem to belong, somehow.'

Miriam was surprised at the adult sentiment in the words. Was it her appearance? she questioned as she stared at her daughter. Surely it couldn't be? There were plenty of fair-skinned Israelis almost as blonde as Hannah, but the child's remark held some truth. There was some quality about her that seemed to make her different. Perhaps it was just in her nature, nothing to do with her looks. But Miriam decided that she must put an end to these unwelcome ideas ruthlessly. What you constantly affirm becomes fact. It was one of her strongest beliefs, a belief learnt from Margaret and never forgotten.

'Yes, you do belong. More than I do, in fact,' she said. 'You were born here, and that makes you special, something to be proud of. You're a Sabra, Israeli-born. Don't forget that!'

The bus rattled to a shuddering stop in front of them and cut short their conversation. Their luggage was stowed away in the back and they sank thankfully into two empty seats at last. This was the last stage of the long journey, and Miriam couldn't wait to get back to Rosh Hazim and start her life again.

Hannah's thoughts were different. She looked out of the window and pondered her mother's words.

'A Sabra!' She said the word silently to herself and sighed, wondering why it was so special, more special than being born a Scot or English or anything else. She had asked her teacher what the word really meant.

'Well, actually it's a cactus plant that's prickly on the outside but nice and sweet inside. I suppose that's what we Israelis are supposed to be like. Don't ask me why!'

Hannah had wondered about it often after that. I'm not prickly, she thought. Mummy often is, and she isn't a Sabra. Perhaps it's because she wants to be one. Perhaps she's jealous!

CHAPTER TWENTY-EIGHT

1986

'WHY have you come here to Israel?'

Hannah pushed her long, straight golden hair from her face and stared at the handsome young German. She went on without waiting for an answer. 'I'm sorry my mother was so abrupt with you, but she's always had a feeling of hostility towards Germans. Her best friend was in Auschwitz. She still has the numbers tattooed on her arm.'

'Yes, I've seen them on several people here. Don't worry about your mother. I expected some antagonism—it's understandable. I don't really know why I've come. It was something I had to do, I suppose, to atone in some way. My grandfather fought in the war.'

'That doesn't make him bad. A lot of good Germans must have fought.'

Kurt Posner smiled, and Hannah, watching him, felt for the first time a disturbing flutter of kinship, of oneness. Yet how could she feel anything for this stranger? She hadn't known him for more than two weeks. There were plenty of young men on the kibbutz who were constantly pestering her with their unwanted attentions. This one was different.

They were working together in the stifling heat of the enormous building where the dairy cows were kept. Kurt changed the subject.

'Cows are usually outside in the fields in Germany during the summer. Much better for them, I should think.'

'My grandmother says the same about England. She worked on a farm during the war and she remembers having to bring them in twice a day to be milked.'

'Three times here. It doesn't seem right to me.'

'We have to get as much as we can from the land, and that includes the animals, and it would be too hot for them outside anyway!'

She went over to switch on the sprinklers that rained water down from pipes in the roof on to the patient beasts below. It had to be done frequently during the hottest months, and the cows obviously enjoyed its welcome and refreshing coolness.

'Do you like living in Israel? You seem to talk a lot about your grandparents and England,' Kurt said.

Hannah looked at her watch before answering. 'Time for a break and a cold drink. Come on.' She led the way outside, into the burning, blinding heat. They fetched some cold orange juice, and then found shade and sat down on the grass together.

'You asked if I liked living in Israel,' Hannah said. 'That's a big question.'

She paused and stared thoughtfully at the eucalyptus trees and the bright flower borders. It was a question she was always asking herself, and she had to admit that she had come to no satisfactory conclusion about it. For all of her eighteen years, apart from holidays, she had lived in this one place, and she still wasn't sure whether it was where she wanted to be.

'I like England,' she said, 'and I still remember the longest time I spent there. It was when I was ten, and I cried for endless nights after we got back. It made Mum very sad, and ever since then I've tried my best to please her and to like it here, and now I think I've succeeded. I'm half Scottish too, though. There's a little croft in Skye that belongs to my family. My father was born there. That accounts for the Macleod bit of my name—very un-Jewish, of course.

Kurt laughed, not understanding all her words. 'Born in the sky. What do you mean, sky, and what is a croft?'

'Skye is an island off the west coast of Scotland, very beautiful, and a croft is a little cottage. It has thick stone walls painted white, and it's all alone by a beach and some mountains. I've a photograph of it in my room with me standing by the door. The croft and a few fields around it belong to my family—to me, actually, ever since my father was killed.'

'You mean you have a house of your own and you stay here?'

'How could I go and live there, and what would I do? There's my music, and Mum too, of course. I couldn't leave her alone here.'

Kurt got up and fetched them both another drink. 'Who looks after it?'

'There's a great-aunt who lives in a little town nearby. She lets it to people for holidays, but I don't know what'll happen when she dies. She must be pretty old now. I can just remember her, but it was a long time ago. I've only been there once. It can't be sold, you see. My grandfather, the Scottish one, left it in trust or something so that it must stay in the family.'

'I wish you wouldn't see so much of that German,' Miriam said, and there was annoyance in her voice—more than annoyance, perhaps. She was angry that of all the young men Hannah knew, she seemed most dangerously attached to this one. She had grown slim and beautiful during the past two years, and there were many young and highly suitable *kibbutzniks* who were obviously attracted by her fair golden beauty. Her personality, too, brought her many friends of both sexes. She was sunny and bright—like her hair! Miriam often thought.

'In no way can you ever marry a non-Jew,' she said firmly.

'Oh, Mum, for goodness' sake, whoever said anything about marrying anyone?'

'Well, these things happen. One things leads to another. I married your father when I wasn't much older than you.'

'That was different. You hadn't a career. Have you forgotten I've got a place at the academy in Jerusalem for the autumn?'

Miriam remembered her own place in Oxford thrown away willingly for this land and for Chaim. She still had not fully decided whether it was the land or the man for whom she had made the sacrifice.

'That's what I'm worried about,' she said, remembering.

They strolled together round the path just inside the perimeter fence. Above the comfortable sound of the cicadas they could hear the clicking and gentle splashing of the sprinklers which brought precious water to orange groves, gardens, fields and lawns. Miriam often remembered Chaim when she heard them. He had frequently remarked that it was the best way of watering. 'One day we'll have them,' he had told her proudly, 'for the bananas and all the other crops.' They were installed now, and he had never seen them, never known the pleasure of the coolness and the increased yield that they gave. She had recovered outwardly from her grief at his sudden and unnecessary death, but there was an inner core of sadness that sometimes surfaced, and sometimes she could almost feel him again at her side, his young strength supporting her and his enthusiasm for this country still keeping her here.

Hannah put her arm through her mother's and they walked in silence for a while, each deep in her own thoughts.

'Why, Mum? Why couldn't I marry a non-Jew? Others have done it—in fact, Granny did. You're only half Jewish.'

Miriam's heart leapt uncomfortably at the words. She had never told Hannah that Graham wasn't her true grandfather, that she had no idea at all about her roots on her father's side. Perhaps he was Jewish? Margaret was the only one who could answer her questions, and this she resolutely refused to do. That he was a good man and that her mother had loved him was the only comfort she could get even now.

She cast around in her mind for an answer to Hannah's question. To keep our race pure? For the sake of Chaim who died that you might have a country, that the Holocaust should never happen again anywhere in the world? So that you will stay here in Israel and give yourself and your family for this land? Nothing sounded right.

'The law will not allow it,' she said lamely, hoping that it was true.

'What law? What law says I may not marry a Christian?'

'If there isn't a written law then it's an unwritten one. There's a Christian church and a synagogue. You can't get married in both, or in either one. No rabbi would ever conduct a ceremony with a Christian bridegroom.'

'Then I wouldn't have a religious ceremony. A civic one would do. We're not very religious, are we, anyway? It wouldn't matter!'

Miriam felt her anger mounting. 'It would matter. It

would matter a lot. Hannah, you cannot marry a non-Jew!'

Hannah pulled her arm from her mother's and then laughed. 'I really don't know what we're arguing about. I told you, I'm not planning to marry Kurt or anyone else for a very long time. I still have too much to do!'

Miriam, relieved, laughed a little too, but warning bells rang in her heart in spite of the girl's confident words.

In her lonely, narrow bed that night she lay and pondered the conversation with her daughter, and she thought too of her own dreams that had only recently been taking shape. She had come lately to hate the drab clothes that she wore each day. Her mother frequently sent magazines, and there was a pile of them now on the coffee-table. Every time she looked at them the clothes that stared at her from the glossy pages sent shivers of excitement through her. I want to study design, she had told herself with surprise more than once. I know I could do it. Perhaps I could go away and learn and then come back here and start a small industry on the kibbutz designing and making simple smart clothes for sale. I'm not too old to start a new career, am I?

The thoughts, mentioned to no one, had grown in proportion over the last few weeks and she wondered how to forward her idea. She was sure that it wouldn't receive a very enthusiastic welcome and she doubted whether they would consider releasing her from the teaching duties that took most of her time. She was valuable for teaching English, and there was no other suitable candidate now that Dinah had given up. During the last few years, though, there had been news of changes on some of the kibbutzim. It wasn't all agriculture now. She remembered reading of one that was producing a device for cleaning swimming-pools and it had been successful in exporting abroad, another was making dolls, and only the day before during supper her neighbour had remarked that he was interested in the irrigation control systems being made in a kibbutz down in the south. So why not designer clothes? She fell asleep at last with happy images to dream about and her mind filled with a new purpose. At last perhaps she could contribute something of her very own to this country that needed more now than just soldiers and oranges.

Hannah shared a small apartment with two other girls, and she too lay in bed that night thinking about her mother and her life and wondering what would become of them. She had to admit that Kurt had become important to her, but he would soon be back in Germany, she would be in England with her grandparents for a short visit, and she hoped that she would forget all about him. But suddenly life seemed bleak, and the bleakness was the coming absence of Kurt. It was a long time before she slept.

'I'm going to spend a week touring around a bit before I go back to Germany,' Kurt said. 'Would you come with me? You know Israel. You could show me the sights?'

'Just the two of us? My mother would never allow it.'

'Hannah, you're eighteen. What's the matter with you, for goodness' sake? This is 1986. You don't have to do what your mother tells you any more!'

'I know that. I don't like upsetting her, though. She's on her own.'

'That must be her fault. She's very attractive. Haven't there been any other men?'

'A couple, yes, but she didn't care for either of them. There's one in England that I think she liked, but that was ages ago. I was quite small, but I remember him from all those years ago. He writes occasionally.'

'Jewish?'

'I'm not sure. He might have been.'

'Anyway, are you coming?'

Hannah looked at Kurt and her heart leapt. She suddenly decided that she would go. For the first time in her life she would defy her mother and do just what she wanted. It would be a tremendous effort, but she would do it.

'Yes, I'll come. How are we going to travel? On buses?'

Miriam was furious, upset, and finally resigned.

'If you let her go without too much opposition,' said Dinah, 'she'll probably come back and forget all about him. If you oppose her it'll make her all the more determined to stick to him. Believe me, I know what obstinate youngsters are like!'

'You're probably right, but it takes some doing, smiling when your heart is breaking.'

'He's a nice young man, though. I talked to him the other day when he came over with Hannah.'

'I don't know how you can!'

'Because he's German?'

'Well, yes. Even hearing the language must make you remember, surely?'

'I suppose it does give me shivers occasionally. But he wasn't speaking German. He speaks passably good English.'

Miriam looked at her friend and marvelled. 'You're a wonderful woman, Dinah,' she said. 'I just wish I could be so good and noble.'

'Fiddlesticks! Come and have some coffee and cheer up.'

The coffee was hot and sweet, the work of the day done and the evening warm. Miriam felt better. Nothing had changed, but her mood had lightened. She hoped that Dinah was right. She wouldn't oppose Hannah any more and probably the affair would end as quickly as it had begun. She couldn't possibly marry Kurt. She knew that.

'We'll stay in youth hostels,' Hannah said. 'I'll only come if you agree to that. No tent!'

'I agree,' said Kurt. 'In fact I was going to suggest it. I don't much care for backpacking in this heat.'

They spent two days in Jerusalem.

'So this is the Western Wall,' Kurt said. 'It's just an ancient wall. Why is it so special?'

Hannah stared at him in horror. 'You mean you don't know about it? My father died here, right here, fighting for this place! It's. . .'

She couldn't go on. Tears threatened to overwhelm her as she looked. Chaim was just a name to her, his photograph all she had of him, but suddenly he became real and she understood a little of her mother's feelings.

Kurt, standing beside her, was concerned. He groped in his pocket for a paper tissue and pressed it into her hand.

'I'm sorry I was so stupid,' he said.

He took her hand in his when she had dried her tears and held it tightly. She looked so young and so vulnerable.

'I love you very much, Hannah,' he whispered. 'I wouldn't say or do anything to hurt you.'

It was a precious moment, and she turned to him with damp but glowing eyes.

'I love you too, Kurt.'

They walked back through the maze of narrow little streets of old Jerusalem. Arab traders seeing them together, fair and beautiful, called to them to look at their wares, buy jewellery or antiquities.

'No money,' Kurt kept on saying, and Hannah laughed at him.

'They think we're tourists.'

'Well, we are, aren't we?'

'You might be, but this is my land. I can't forget that in a hurry. Mum reminds me of it every day of every week!'

'It belongs to the Arabs too, though, doesn't it?'

Hannah turned to look at him. 'Now don't go saying things like that to Mum, will you?'

'Why not? It's true.'

She sighed suddenly. 'Oh, Kurt, I sometimes long to live somewhere where life is simple. Here there's always conflict of some sort. I'm not the fighting kind, but I have to go in the Army soon. Girls go as well as boys, you know.'

'I'll marry you and carry you off, then you won't have to be a soldier!'

The words were spoken in jest, but he looked at her as he spoke and the laughter suddenly died on his lips.

'Would you let me, Hannah?'

She was silent for a long time and when she spoke there was uncertainty in her voice and sadness too.

'But I'm Jewish, Kurt. You're German. It's not a good mix, you know.'

'Love overcomes all those kinds of difficulties. I shall keep on asking anyway. Do you mind?'

'Keep on asking,' she repeated, then she laughed and pulled him towards a stall with cheap trinkets. 'I shall buy you a little Star of David on a chain. You can tell your friends that a Jewish girl gave it to you to remember her by.'

'And what can I get for you?'

'A little ivory cross. I shall wear it underneath my blouse next to my heart. It will be a sign to me that I love a goy. My mother will have a fit if she sees it! So will all the others. Jews don't wear crosses—that's why I want it. So that I'll have a secret that no one knows about except you and me.'

'Is that really what you call me, a goy?'

'Of course. A non-Jew, a goy!'

'You're laughing at me!'

'Why not? We're on holiday and we're in love, what could be better? It's a good reason to laugh.'

Hannah arrived back at Rosh Hazim alone. She had waved Kurt goodbye at the airport, and she felt desolate. It was the first time in her life that she had been dependent on another person for her happiness. He's the other half of me, she told herself sadly, and I won't see him for months. How can I function with half of me missing?

Her mother was relieved to have her back alone. Now that Kurt was safely away she would be sure to forget him, and there was the short holiday in England before she started her new term in Jerusalem at the music academy. Life would be exciting. Kurt wouldn't be part of it.

Margaret and Graham whisked them straight down to the cottage in Cornwall when they arrived.

'The weather isn't too good, but it's still nice there,' said Margaret, forgetting that the last thing they were coming for was weather.

Hannah loved it as she always did. She breathed the

fresh, sparkling air with delight and took full advantage of the rough seas, frightening them all as she strode out into the breakers with the old wooden surfboard held above her head to prevent it being wrenched from her hands by the force of the waves. She walked miles each day on the cliff paths with the dog in the wind and the rain, and felt healthier and more full of energy than she ever did under a hotter sky.

Miriam was surprised to see Tom again during the week. He came down and stayed a night in a hotel nearby and told her that he absolutely had to come and see her once more after all these years.

'Not married, then?' she asked.

'Almost, but not quite.' He laughed. 'She walked out on me two weeks before the great day. That was three years ago, and I've been a bit wary since then. How about you?'

'No. One or two proposals, of course, but no one who suited!'

'Are you going to stay out there ruining your beauty with all that sunshine?'

'Of course. It's my country now. And the climate suits me. I love the heat!'

'Your daughter doesn't!'

'How do you know that?'

'It's obvious. She's so fair, so beautiful too. Watch her, won't you?'

Miriam felt slightly irritated by the conversation, but she had to admit that he was nice to be with. Perhaps it was his uncanny knack of getting right to the truth and presenting it to her that piqued. She missed him when he went, and she was not very happy with Dottie's and John's visit on the last day of the holiday. She had never liked John very much. He seldom spoke to her, and he stared at Hannah, stared so much that she wondered why she wasn't more embarrassed.

For Margaret the holiday had been a joy. She loved having her family round her, and when Tom came, still a bachelor after all these years, her heart had risen in hope. She had to admit that she had told him that Miriam would be with them. Graham had laughed affectionately at her matchmaking efforts.

'I don't think you'll ever stop trying to get her back, will you?' he said. 'It's been nearly twenty years, and you're still at it!'

On the last evening Margaret and Miriam walked along the cliff path near the cottage, leaving Hannah engrossed in a game of chess with Graham. After a day of rain the weather had suddenly cleared and the sun, shining at last, was just about to sink out of sight again below the line of the sea as it always did on this north Cornish coast. It left the sky a blaze of fiery red with a flaming pathway dancing from the horizon to the beach and seeming to set each grain of sand alight. A few gulls were soaring and calling beneath the red-gold clouds, their wings touched with fire.

Margaret looked at them and her heart lifted as it always did when she heard their haunting cries. She turned to Miriam, desperately wanting her daughter to be as happy and fulfilled as she was.

'Will you be able to do anything about this fashion designing?' she asked as they walked down towards the beach.

'I don't know. I haven't mentioned it yet. It'll have to be discussed at our monthly meeting—it's a bit revolutionary for a kibbutz.'

'How about studying here, in London? Graham would see about it. You could go back afterwards.'

'You never give up, do you?' Miriam said. The words, which could have been hard, were spoken in a kindly tone, and Margaret laughed, thinking of what Graham had said to her earlier.

'No, and I don't suppose I ever will, and you'll never give in, not for me at least. Hannah seems a little strange and remote this holiday. Is she in love, do you suppose? I thought I could detect some of the signs?'

Miriam shuddered slightly. 'I'm desperately hoping not. She spent a lot of time with one of the volunteers that we get burdened with during the summer—German, of all things!'

It was Margaret's turn to go pale, but Miriam couldn't see the shock on her mother's face in the darkening sky.

There had been a letter for Hannah from Germany, from Hamburg, and Margaret had wondered about it, but she hadn't given it much thought until this moment.

'What's his name?'

'Kurt something-or-other. Posner, I think. Yes, Kurt Posner, and he's a Christian, of course, certainly not Jewish. Can you imagine anything more of an affront to her father's memory than to marry a German?'

Margaret was silent for a time. The anger in her daughter's voice shocked and frightened her. She didn't want to argue; it never did any good with Miriam. She spoke at last, quietly and with sadness.

'But he was killed fighting Arabs, wasn't he?'

'Of course, but that hasn't got anything to do with it.'

There seemed little logic in Miriam's statements, and Margaret wondered how to comment. Suddenly she remembered something she had read recently.

'I read in the newspaper a few days ago about a Jewish girl who was marrying a Palestinian Arab. Now that would be even worse, wouldn't it?'

There was a slight element of amusement in her voice. It was deliberate, meant to lighten the conversation. Miriam recognised it and laughed. It was difficult to remain cross with her mother for long.

'I suppose it would. Yes, much worse, but thankfully that's not my problem.'

'It's becoming more and more of a problem, though, isn't it? The unrest in the occupied territories, I mean?'

'Yes. I don't know what's going to happen. More fighting, probably, but just now I don't want to think about it. Let's go back—I'm getting cold.'

They went into the cottage and its cosy warmth welcomed them. The chess was finished and Hannah was sitting at the small desk writing a letter. There seemed to be a great thickness of pages already.

'Cup of Ovaltine?' Graham asked them all.

'I'll get it, Grandad,' Hannah said. 'Just let me finish this last page to Kurt. I want to get it in the post early tomorrow.'

'He must be rather special,' said Graham, winking at her. 'You seem to write him a lot of letters.'

Her delicate skin flushed scarlet and she smiled at him. 'He is rather,' she said quietly. Her mother had gone upstairs to take off her coat and she hoped that she hadn't heard.

CHAPTER TWENTY-NINE

1986–1987

MIRIAM was not looking forward to the next general meeting. It was for all the adult members of the kibbutz and was held in the dining hall regularly to discuss anything that affected their lives. It was very democratic and everyone had a vote, but she dreaded setting out her ideas.

'I can't stay here in that school teaching all those unruly children for another twenty years, though,' she confided to Dinah one afternoon as they sat on the porch drinking tea together. 'I'm thirty-nine, and it's now or never. I've got to do it. I've got to put it to them anyway, however mad they think I am.'

'Not mad. I don't think you're mad at all. It's a great idea and you'll have my vote. It'll be difficult to persuade the die-hards, though.'

Miriam stretched her legs into the sunshine that was edging on to the porch. 'Why do I feel so frustrated, Dinah? I wish I could be settled and contented like I used to be.'

'You should have married again,' the older woman said. 'A woman alone here is bound to feel out of things—it's a family place. How's Hannah getting on, by the way? Have you heard?'

'Fine. She likes it at the academy. She thinks Jerusalem is great too.'

'She's a super girl, a daughter to be proud of. I'm sure she'll do well with that cello of hers. Perhaps she'll be famous one day.'

Miriam laughed. 'I just want her to be happy, that's all. She's never been too thrilled with kibbutz life. I've tried to blind myself to the fact, but I honestly think that she'll leave eventually. I just hope that she meets a nice man at college, someone with the same interests. Perhaps she'll settle down in Tel Aviv or Jerusalem one day.'

'Will you stay?'

Miriam stared at Dinah. All her life, all the past twenty years, had been centred here. But her friend's words focused her deepest and frequently rejected doubts.

'Of course,' she said, affirming what she didn't feel. 'If my clothes-designing ideas really do get some support I shall have the purpose I need. You know all about my dreams. There are vast possibilities. We could have fashion shows in the dining-hall, invite buyers. There are plenty of women who would love to help me.'

There was a doubtful expression in Dinah's eyes. 'Do you really think you've got the courage to do all that in the face of opposition?'

'Opposition? You just said that it was a great idea.'

'Of course it is, but there's bound to be disapproval from most of the old-stagers who came here to work the land and produce essential things. They'll think that your idea is frivolous and that nice clothes are just fripperies.'

Miriam laughed. 'I like that word, fripperies. It could be the name of my company!'

'You're hopeless!' Dinah said. 'But I wish you luck anyway. When are you putting it to them?'

'Tomorrow, and I shall need an awful lot of luck!'

The meeting was a disaster. As Dinah had predicted,

Miriam's idea was indeed laughed at and dismissed.

'You know that a kibbutz isn't a prison,' Dinah comforted later. 'Why don't you do what your mother suggested? Leave, get your training in England and then perhaps come back. They might think more of the idea then—especially if you'd made some success. Or you could go to Haifa or Tel Aviv and set up there in a small way, a little shop or something!'

'I couldn't do that. I need money and support, and I can only find that here or at home, home in England. And I don't want to go back. It would be a sort of failure!'

'Think about it, though,' Dinah instructed. 'There must be a way. Don't give up too easily—you'll just be frustrated and bitter. A kibbutz is only for those of us who really want to be here, those who are enthusiastic about the way of life. It's not like a Chinese commune. No one is forced to come or to stay.'

The words sounded severe, but Miriam knew what her friend meant. She had been enthusiastic, boundlessly enthusiastic, but was she still as whole-hearted? She couldn't answer, she didn't know. There were conflicting wishes and desires in her life now struggling for recognition where before she had been single-minded.

She was completely diverted from her plans and problems when she read the letter that arrived the next morning from Hannah. She opened it eagerly, anxious for news. Jerusalem was a wonderful place to live and study, and she was thrilled for her daughter, thrilled that the kibbutz had recognised her talent and sent her to one of the best of Israel's music schools. It was only the increasing unrest in the West Bank and Gaza that troubled her. There were small pockets of terrorism in East Jerusalem too, and she worried.

But it was not a Palestinian uprising that caused her dismay as she read. Hannah wanted to go to Germany for Christmas, to stay with Kurt's family! He had written to say that his parents were willing to pay her air-fare and could she have her mother's blessing, please?

The consternation that coursed through her body was like a physical pain. She felt unable to make any conscious decision, unable to eat or think. She knew now with a sickening, deadening certainty that Hannah would leave eventually, leave not only the kibbutz but Israel too. Perhaps these past twenty years had been a sacrifice after all, a sacrifice of her own life for the sake of Chaim's memory, for an ideal that she was incapable of fulfilling. It was a terrible thought.

'Aren't you over-dramatising it all?' queried Dinah. 'After all, plenty of people have affairs and then change partners lots of times before marrying. She may not stick to this Kurt, and she's so young.'

'I'd like to think you're right, but you don't know Hannah as well as I do. There's been something about her ever since she met him and I have a feeling, a premonition if you like, that this is how it will be.'

'And there's no way that you can call your life a sacrifice either,' Dinah scolded. 'You've been happy here, and you've contributed a lot to all of us. I don't know what I'd have done without you next door for all these years.'

'Thanks, Dinah—me neither,' she said ungrammatically. 'Ever since Mum had this little apartment when she came over to try to win me back to England all those years ago we've been friends, haven't we?'

'Yes, it's been great.'

'Why do you speak in the past tense?'

'Well, you'll go, won't you? I get premonitions too,

you know, and I have a feeling that you'll be away soon. Well, come back one day and design me a wonderful dress to make me look glamorous. That'll be the hardest job you'll ever have!'

They both laughed, and Miriam felt a little better, but she hadn't made any decisions. She suddenly wished desperately for Chaim.

Hannah went to Germany and came back radiant but apprehensive.

'I'm so sorry, Mummy,' she said when she came to visit on her next day's holiday. 'I'm so sorry that I couldn't fall in love with someone who you would approve of, someone Jewish.'

'I told you before—you can't marry him, Hannah. He's totally unacceptable to me and to everyone here. You have such promise and such talent. This is your country and your father's country. You must give him up!'

'I can't believe what I'm hearing,' Hannah said. 'I just can't believe that you're saying these things to me. This is 1987! I'm eighteen and a free person, not some bargainable property like a medieval princess!'

'You don't understand. Of course you're free, but not totally free. No one is.'

'What do you mean by that? That I have to submit to an arranged marriage like the Arab girls?'

'Of course not!' Miriam's voice was raised in anger. 'Of course not—don't exaggerate. But you can't marry this German of yours and bring him here and expect me to accept him as a son-in-law. I never could. Go to Yad Vashem and spend a day there, and then you might change your mind.'

'I've been to Yad Vashem, and yes, it was terrible, but it's over, Mother. It's over. It was a long time ago, and Germany is our ally now, or hadn't you heard? It's the Arabs who hate us, not the Germans.'

Miriam flinched. She had heard those same words so many times, but still the vision of the Holocaust haunted her, the piles of bodies, the magnitude of the slaughter. She knew she was probably being fanatical. Most people here had come to terms with the past, had put it aside.

'Why do I feel so strongly about it?' she asked Dinah the next day after Hannah had returned to Jerusalem in a rebellious silence.

'I don't know really. I suppose it's partly because of the way Chaim died, and because you haven't any more children. All your hopes are centred on the one, and if she fails to carry on his ideals, then you feel that you've failed too.'

'I remember some of the things Chaim said when he was called up in '67. He said that the State of Israel was special because it was a place at last where Jews could be in charge of their own destiny, not persecuted and murdered as they have been for two thousand years. I suppose that if Hannah marries a non-Jew, and a German at that, then I will feel a deep sense of betrayal.'

Dinah sighed and her fingers subconsciously worried at the tattoo marks on her arm, the marks of Auschwitz that she would carry to her grave.

'If I can forgive, can't you?' she said.

The month of May had come to England with storms and rain that summer, and on the day of Margaret's birthday the wind was howling unseasonably round the house. There was no reason to suppose that this day was going to be different from any other. Graham had left that morning before the post arrived. There were ten birthday cards from friends and family, and she opened them happily.

'I can't believe that this time next year I'll be an OAP,' she said to herself. 'Fifty-nine today!'

She saw the letter from Hannah as it fell from the large bright card and she took it up eagerly. Letters from her granddaughter were precious. She read it carefully, and then she sat down and poured more coffee and read again. After the third reading she laid it carefully aside in her bureau and started to plan, both her day and what she would do about Miriam.

There were gulls in the sky outside the house, driven inland by storms at sea. Their haunting cries seemed to echo Hannah's sadness and took Margaret's thoughts back to that other day exactly forty years ago. To her nineteenth birthday. The events of that day could never be erased or forgotten, and neither could they be hidden any longer. Miriam must know about her father!

She filled the day with ordinary things and prepared the birthday meal for herself and Graham. She took the flowers he brought her and there were tears in her eyes as she found a vase.

She kept up her careful façade of calm while they ate, and then she handed the letter to him.

'I shall have to go to Israel,' she said when he had finished reading. 'I shall have to tell Miriam. She must know about Karl at last. I can see that I should have told her long ago. This fanaticism of hers might not have developed if she had known. I can't let her ruin Hannah's life because of my silence.'

'Would you like me to tell her?'

Graham's words were careful, measured. She knew that his offer had cost him a lot. It was the last thing he would want to do.

Margaret got up slowly and looked at herself in the long mirror. She pushed back her greying hair and stared at the lines in her face. She suddenly felt old, very old. The mistakes of years ago had a habit of reappearing when you were more vulnerable, less able to cope with them.

'No, I must do it.'

She suddenly turned to Graham and felt his sorrow. He had adopted Miriam and loved her as much as his own sons, and Hannah too was precious to him. Miriam knew that he was her adoptive father, but she had never told Hannah. Margaret didn't understand her reasons, but had abided by her wish. The truth would hurt them all in different ways, but for Hannah's sake it must be told at last.

'I'll go into the travel agent's and book you a flight,' he said. 'Is your passport in order?'

She threw herself into his arms and hugged him tightly. 'I'm so sorry,' she whispered. 'Can you forgive me?'

'There's nothing to forgive, absolutely nothing, and it's not so terrible a secret after all. Don't be too dramatic about it. And remember I love you very much.'

They had breakfast the next morning together as they always did, with Graham reading *The Times* and Margaret watching television. She stared at the news pictures. Israel, of course, and more terrorism, more unrest.

Graham peered over his paper. 'I wish you hadn't got to go. Make sure you don't go anywhere near the West Bank!'

Margaret looked at him affectionately. 'Don't worry, darling,' she said. 'I'll be all right. They call it Judaea and Samaria now, by the way.'

* * *

Three days later she arrived in Tel Aviv, and Hannah was there to meet her.

'You needn't have come all this way, Gran,' she said. 'Although it's wonderful to see you. I feel guilty, though—about my letter, I mean. Pouring it all out to you like that.'

'Stop feeling guilty. There's nothing in the world for you to feel guilty about.'

She remembered hearing Graham saying the same thing to her, and she wondered. Was there any guilt, and whose was it anyway?

'I know that I want to marry him, Granny. I'm quite quite sure, and Mum's almost having hysterics about it.'

'Leave it to me,' Margaret said with more confidence than she felt. 'Just leave it to me. Come and find me a taxi—I want to get to Rosh Hazim as quickly as I can and see if I can talk some sense into your mother. You're coming as well, are you?'

'Yes. Just for one night.'

'I want you to leave us alone for a bit, Hannah. There are things I must talk to her about without you around.'

'Of course. I shall want to be with my friends. I don't see them often now that I'm studying in Jerusalem.'

'How's the work going?'

'Fine. I shall be in the youth orchestra if my audition next month goes well.'

'How will that fit in with this love of your life?'

Hannah smiled. 'We shall get engaged first and it'll be a longish time before we actually get married. I have to finish my studies here and reach an acceptable standard so that I can go on with my music anywhere we might choose to live.'

She sounded so sure of her decisions. It had never

been like that back in the 'forties and 'fifties, Margaret thought. Today's young were so much more confident, more poised. If they had doubts then they kept them beneath the surface, or at least they seemed not to worry about them.

A taxi pulled up at the kerb and they settled themselves comfortably. Margaret remembered the first time she had come here and had been so scared. But she was quite used to the big *sherut* taxis now. She had even learned a little Hebrew, and she addressed the driver with some carefully chosen words.

Hannah laughed loudly when she heard them. 'He's a Christian Arab, Granny,' she said. 'He speaks Arabic, and English too, probably as well as we do. I shouldn't bother with Hebrew! Keep that to impress the *kibbutzniks.*'

The journey was long and hot as always, and Margaret was silent for much of the time. Hannah didn't seem to mind, perhaps sensing that there was some trauma ahead that she didn't understand.

Miriam was still working when they arrived, and they walked through the entrance gates towards her apartment.

'It's hotter than usual today,' Hannah said. 'A four-shower day!'

'What do you mean by that?'

'I judge the temperature by how many times I want a cold shower. Today I need about four!'

They laughed, and Margaret put aside her travelling clothes and settled for thin cut-off trousers and a simple white blouse.

'Super trousers,' Hannah said, eyeing them with some envy. 'I wish Mum could get her design thing going. We might be a bit more fashionable then.'

Miriam soon joined them, and after they had drunk

endless cups of coffee and exchanged news, Hannah went to find her friends. Then there was a silence between the two women and for a moment each was caught in a web of her own thoughts, a tangled web that must be unravelled so that the past could no longer disastrously affect the present.

Miriam spoke first.

'Why have you come so suddenly, Mum? It's lovely to have you, but so unexpected. I hope you're all right?'

There was anxiety in her voice, and Margaret, looking at her, was saddened by the worry lines in her face and the slump of her slim body.

There was no reason to stall. If the truth must be told then now was the time. She came straight to the point and her heart nearly failed her for fear. She was full of conflicting emotions too. The memory of Karl was bright and vivid in that moment of time and their past love for each other still precious. She was frightened of her daughter's unknown reaction. There was bound to be anger, perhaps scorn. Contempt would be the most difficult to bear.

'I must tell you about your father!'

Miriam sat up straight and stared at Margaret with fierce brown eyes. 'Then you haven't come to scold me about Hannah and Kurt?'

'No, no, of course not. And if I had, you're a grown woman. Oh, Miriam, why have we so often tortured each other so with our words?' There were tears in her eyes that made the telling even harder. 'You've always wanted to know who your father was. Now is the time to tell you. I can't withhold the knowledge any longer.'

'Is it so awful, then?' Miriam's face was white beneath the tan.

'He was a good man—you already know that. He was clever and talented, a violinist.'

Miriam clenched her hands tightly. 'Hannah! Her cello. I must tell her. But why——?'

'His name was Karl Schormann, a prisoner of war. From Dresden.'

There was another silence, a terrible silence that Margaret thought she would never forget, then Miriam spoke at last and her voice was flat, drained of all emotion. There wasn't even any anger.

'I must go to Dresden,' she said. 'I must go to Dresden and find my father.'

CHAPTER THIRTY

1987

'How do I get there?' Miriam demanded. 'How on earth do I get to Dresden? I don't even know where it is!'

They had eaten and said nothing yet to Hannah. The conversation had been stilted and forced in the dining-hall, but secrets could never be discussed there anyway. There were no small tables, no privacy.

There had still been no accusation from Miriam. She was simply polite and correct. There wasn't even a trace of anger, and Margaret feared that this strange, almost emotionless reaction would have disastrous results later. They were all three to sleep in the small apartment, and she rather dreaded the coming night.

'I've put clean sheets in my bed for you, Mum,' Miriam said suddenly. 'Hannah and I are having camp-beds in the living-room.'

Margaret stared at her daughter. How could she talk about mundane things, about sheets, at a time like this? 'Do you really think you should go and find Karl? He has no idea that he has a daughter.'

Miriam turned on her then with anger in her voice. It was the first emotion of any kind to surface from the calm, cold void of her mind.

'How could you? How could you not tell him? And after I was born—didn't you feel guilty every time you looked at me, knowing that my father, my real father, had no knowledge of my existence?'

Margaret didn't want to make excuses. 'You don't

understand how it was then. You can have no knowledge of it at all. You grew up loved and cosseted, and Graham was everything any father could ever be to you, and more. By the time you were old enough to understand about sex and life we were into the swinging sixties and you couldn't know about the trauma and disgrace of having a baby with no husband in 1948.'

Her words seemed to have no effect on Miriam. There was still the cold anger in her voice when she replied.

'I suppose the fact that he was German made it just too difficult for you too! Of course you knew what they were doing to girls who slept with German soldiers in France? They shaved their hair off and called them traitors. I was reading something about it the other day. I never dreamed my mother was one of those!'

Here was the contempt that Margaret was so frightened of. It degraded the magic and the beauty that she had carefully built around her memories of Karl. She got up and walked out to the porch and leaned on the wooden balcony, breathing deeply of the scented air and listening to the sounds of the night, sounds that always reminded her of Israel.

'Come and sit out here, Miriam,' she said. 'Come and listen and I'll tell you all about it. Please.'

She talked for what seemed like an hour at least, and Miriam listened quietly. Then she got up and went to make coffee. Margaret could hear her clattering about inside. She came out at last carrying two mugs and there were traces of tears on her face.

'Thank you, Mum,' she whispered. The anger seemed to have gone from her voice now. Only a blankness remained. 'Thank you for telling me so much. I'm trying to get used to the idea that my father was a German. It's been a shock. You know how I feel about Germany since I came to live here, don't you? A German! It's too horrible.' She shivered in spite of the heat. 'How can I stay here now? How can I ever face Dinah and the others who were in Belsen, Sobibor and Treblinka? All those camps have survivors here.'

'But he wasn't a Nazi, Miriam. Hundreds of Germans were murdered too for standing out against Hitler. Please try to see and understand. He was a good man—I've always told you that. Would I have loved someone who was not?'

'I shall go and find him. Then I shall know. If it's possible I shall go!'

'John and Dottie hear from him now and then. He's married and has a son.'

It was another blow, and Miriam turned on her in amazement.

'So John and Dottie know about it too? They're in the conspiracy of silence. No wonder John looks at me so strangely on the few occasions when we meet, and never wants to talk to me much. Of course, he would have known Karl. The pieces are beginning to fit together!'

'We decided that Karl must still not know. It was far too late to tell him then. I made Dottie promise not to tell when she wrote.'

'Dresden was bombed, wasn't it?'

'Terribly. It was one of the most beautiful cities in Europe before the war, so they say. In fact Graham's father went there when he was a student and he almost wept, apparently, when he saw the pictures of the devastation.'

At that moment Hannah came swinging across the square of grass with a friend. She was laughing and looked serenely happy. For a moment Margaret envied her youth and dreaded bringing any sorrow to her young life.

'Are you going to tell her?' she asked.

'No, you can do it. I couldn't bring myself to speak the words—the irony is just too much. I'll leave you alone. I could do with an after-dark swim. The pool is best in the late evening.'

Miriam grabbed her bikini and towel and rushed out, passing a surprised Hannah on the way.

'Back soon,' she called. 'I'm hot!'

So the story had to be told all over again, but it was not so difficult the second time. Hannah listened, incredulous, and when it was finished her reaction was not quite what Margaret had expected. She laughed! She laughed almost hysterically until tears were streaming down her face.

'Oh, dear,' she said at last. 'Poor Mum—a German father! I can't think of anything she would like less.' Then suddenly the full implication hit her. 'But she can't possibly object to Kurt now, can she?'

'I don't know. That's the reason I came, Hannah. Because of you and Kurt. Don't you see?'

Hannah threw her arms round her grandmother.

'Oh, Granny, thank you so much. I'm so grateful. I don't know what to say.'

'I just hope it all works out all right. Your mother wants to go to Dresden and find Karl. I'm not sure that it's the right thing to do, but she seems determined.'

'Is it possible? I mean, it's behind the Iron Curtain, isn't it, in East Germany? It isn't the sort of place people go, especially with an Israeli passport.'

'I don't know. We'll have to see. Perhaps she'll change her mind. It's in the German Democratic Republic, by the way. I don't think they like it to be called East Germany any more.'

It was a long time before Miriam returned. When she did she was quiet and calm.

'I've been to see Amnon and told him that I'm leaving. He's the new secretary of the kibbutz,' she explained to Margaret. 'I'm going back to England with you. I can't stay here now.'

'That's a bit extreme, isn't it, Mummy?' Hannah said. 'There's no need, you know. I'm quite sure that there's no need to make a decision in such a hurry. And what about me?'

'Well, what about you? You have your place in Jerusalem, and you still belong here as well. You don't need me. You can make up your own mind now about your life. You can write and tell Kurt as soon as you like.'

Suddenly Hannah too was dismayed by her mother's quiet resolve and calm, hard words. She regretted her laughter. For herself the news had really been good, at least the result was going to be satisfactory, but she knew that for her mother it was a disaster, and she grieved for her, wondering how she could help. But there seemed no way, no comfort that she could possibly give.

The weather had improved when they reached Heathrow.

'Why do we always think about the weather in England?' Margaret said as they stowed their cases behind their seats on the train. 'In Israel it isn't a matter for conversation!'

She had been trying to find things to talk about all the way home, but Miriam answered in monosyllables. It wasn't until she saw Graham waiting for them on the station that she began to take any interest in anything around her.

'Hello, Daddy,' she said, reverting to the loved, familiar title. 'It's great to be home.'

He wrapped her in his arms and hugged her, looking at Margaret over her head, a question in his eyes.

She smiled at him but said nothing.

'I've been doing a bit of research,' Graham told them later. 'It's possible to get to Dresden—not only possible but quite easy. There's a travel agent who specialises in short holidays there. You can have a package tour, two days in Berlin, one in Leipzig and two in Dresden. If you're really determined to go then that's the way to do it, I think.'

'I'm quite determined,' Miriam said.

'You can't go alone.'

'Why not? I'm quite capable!'

'I know that, but I think you should both go.'

Margaret stared at him, incredulous. Surely he really wasn't serious, wasn't going to throw her back into Karl's arms after all these years?

'I've loved you for forty years,' he said later when they were lying in the spacious luxury of their large, comfortable bed. 'During all that time you've been a wonderful wife and there's never been anything to make me feel a grain of jealousy. Nevertheless there's always been a sort of ghost in the cupboard, the memory of Karl sometimes coming between us. I want you to go and see him and then come back to me and I shall know that you're really mine.'

'But he's got a wife and a son. I can't do that!'

'Yes, you can. You can easily do it. It was all a long time ago—and there's something you don't know.'

'What's that, then?'

'His wife died last year. Dottie and John told me when they heard, but we all decided not to say anything to you. Dottie said that it might unsettle you. But now you had to know. I don't suppose you could have gone if she was still alive.'

Margaret gasped in amazement. 'And you still don't mind my going?'

'No. I want you to go. I know that the man you still have in your mind is one who doesn't exist any more. Go and see the real Karl and put your dreams to rest.'

They stood together in the foyer of the great Semper Opera House in Dresden. Margaret's letter to Karl had been brief, merely telling him of her visit and that she was bringing her daughter who wished to see that part of Germany. There had been an enthusiastic but equally short reply, and the travel agency had booked three seats for them for a performance of *La Traviata.*

'It'll be a good idea for us to meet him somewhere like that,' she had said to Graham. 'It's an organised trip, and with an opera to watch we won't need to talk much.'

'Don't say anything about me being his daughter at first, will you, Mum?' Miriam had said anxiously. 'Just leave it. The right moment will come.'

'But I thought that's why we were going?'

'No, it's for me to see him! Please don't force anything.'

'Go all that way and actually see him, touch him, and not tell? You must be joking!'

But Miriam had been adamant. 'Maybe it would be better if he doesn't know who I am. I'm just asking you to wait and see!'

Margaret looked at her as they waited in the entrance

of the magnificent building. They had both dressed with great care, and Miriam was lovely. The worry lines had lessened since they had left Israel, and her natural flair with clothes had led her to just the right dress. Margaret caught sight of herself too in one of many mirrors.

'I don't look almost sixty, do I?' she said aloud, and Miriam laughed nervously.

'No, Mum. You look wonderful.'

'Margaret?'

She turned, and the years suddenly melted away as though they had never been.

'Karl!'

He kissed her hand, and people around turned to stare at them, the tall, handsome German and the English tourist. The meeting between them had been officially arranged, the wartime friendship explained and the guide in charge of their party smiled affably, but they were aware of no other person but each other.

They stood for a moment, her hands held in both of his, and the moment seemed to be frozen in time as if it would never end. She forgot about Miriam standing quietly beside her. Then, eventually, she pulled away from him and turned, bringing Miriam into the circle of their love.

She wanted to say, 'Our daughter,' but she forbore, hoping for the right time.

'This is Miriam,' she said simply.

They sat in the deep, comfortable seats, letting the music flow over them. Margaret was glad that their first meeting should be in such awe-inspiring surroundings. She couldn't cope with his nearness and with making conversation too. Just the feel of him beside her was enough. Tomorrow it would be easier, the first traumatic shock of seeing him again would be eased a little. They had arranged a day of sightseeing together.

'I shall pick you up at your hotel after breakfast,' he said, smiling at them after the performance, and then he clicked his heels in the way she had forgotten, kissed her hand and Miriam's and disappeared into the night. Their Reiseburo guide fussed around them, shepherding all her party into the waiting coach, and there was no time to talk. Margaret felt there was nothing she could say to Miriam either. The evening had exhausted all her emotions.

They each lay in their narrow, identical beds some time later beneath great feather duvets in their hotel room, and each was waiting for the other to speak. At last it was Miriam who broke the silence.

'It's Hannah who should be here,' she said, 'not me. He's so like Hannah! Now I know where she got that fair hair and those striking blue eyes. Sometimes I think that there's nothing of Chaim in her at all.'

'Did you like him?' Margaret was anxious, desperately anxious to know.

Miriam turned on to her side in the bed and looked at her mother in the dim glow of the light. 'Yes. I liked him!'

It was all she would say that night. She closed her eyes and Margaret could hear her steady breathing, although whether she was feigning sleep or had really fallen so soon into blissful unconsciousness she couldn't tell. She herself crept out of bed and groped in her toilet-bag for a sleeping tablet. It was a luxury she seldom allowed herself, but she knew that tonight, if she was to sleep at all, it would have to be induced. She swallowed and soon slept too, and her dreams were of a windswept shore and a gull calling.

In the cruel morning light Margaret stared at Karl and wondered if she too looked so old. He was handsome still and his smile turned her heart as it had done all those years ago beneath a Cornish sky, but the once thick blond hair was almost white and there was a slight stoop to his tall, muscular body. There were sadness lines too in his face, and his blue eyes held depths that had not been there before.

'I have the car ready,' he said. 'Have you any preferences, or will you leave the choice of places to me?'

'To you, of course,' she said. 'I think Miriam would like to see Meissen, if that's possible, though.'

'It's a very interesting little town, and some of it is like Dresden before the bombing. Where is your daughter? She's very beautiful, and she reminds me a lot of you.'

Margaret smiled at him, longing to tell her secret, but she knew that this wasn't the right time. There would be the perfect moment today, later. She would know when it came.

'She's just getting some traveller's cheques cashed. I think she wants to buy some presents today.'

'She has a daughter too, you said. Hannah, was it?'

'Yes, Hannah. She lives in Israel and she plays the cello.'

'My son plays too—the violin, though, like me. Do you remember that I told you once that I played?'

'Yes, I remember. Your hands—they were spoilt with hard work on the farm.'

'It took a long time before I could start again, and

now I only play for my own pleasure. My son is very good. He's in the Leipzig Gewandhaus, a symphony orchestra.' There was immense pride in his voice and he looked down at her and smiled. 'He's married and has two small daughters. They live in Leipzig, of course, so I don't see much of them. They are always busy.'

There was no closeness between them at the moment, and Margaret felt that she should mention Gisela, the wife with the pretty name, the unknown wife whom she had often thought of with a tinge of jealousy.

'I was sorry to hear that your wife had died,' she said, groping for the right words.

'Yes. She was ill for a long time. I'm just beginning to recover from her loss. We were very happy.'

Miriam ran down the steps of the hotel at that moment.

'There were a lot of people at the desk,' she explained. 'I hope I haven't kept you waiting too long.'

Karl smiled at her and took her hand, kissing it as he had Margaret's.

'There's no hurry,' he told her. 'We have all day, and I'm really looking forward to showing you my country.'

Your country, Margaret thought. And it could have been mine too!

Meissen was lovely, and they chose small pieces of porcelain to take home. They visited the cathedral and the old castle, explored the narrow cobbled streets and then drove back to Dresden.

'Now I shall show you my own town,' Karl said. 'My beautiful Dresden.'

It was during that afternoon that Miriam could feel herself being challenged, all her ideas, all her prejudices being overturned. They visited the museum, saw pictures of the town as it had been before the terrible nights of February 1945, and they stared at records of the bombing.

'I shall take you to the Frauenkirche,' Karl said. 'It is preserved as a memorial.'

Margaret stared at the sad fire-stained ruin and the bomb-marked stonework of its once beautiful pillars.

'It's a little like Coventry,' she said sadly. 'We do such terrible things to each other, don't we?'

'It all happened so quickly,' Karl said. 'A great firestorm over the city and hundreds of years of beauty destroyed in a few hours. Thousands were killed, mostly burnt to death. Almost the whole city was burnt and flattened. Coming home and seeing it was the most terrible experience of my life. There was almost nothing left, just acres of ruin and desolation.'

'Why? Why did they do it?'

'We did it,' Margaret said. 'It was our Lancasters that did it. I want you to grasp that fact, Miriam.'

They were cruel words, but she had to say them. One of the most important reasons for coming here was to help her daughter to come to terms with her birth and so to become more tolerant with Hannah, more tolerant altogether, perhaps.

They walked down the Pragerstrasse.

'It's very modern,' Karl said. 'I'm not sure whether I like it, but we couldn't have reconstructed the town in the old style. Most people are very proud of all our up-to-date buildings. A new city has risen from the ruins.'

Miriam looked around her and at her parents, for she suddenly realised that these two who she had never seen together before were her parents. It gave her a strange feeling, a sort of numb sense of shock and a sudden fear for Graham, the man she had loved as father all her life. She suddenly wanted to be alone for a while. Today had been one of the most traumatic of her life. She had to rethink many of her deepest beliefs, come to terms with things she had never considered before.

'Would you like a trip on the river?' Karl suggested. 'We could take a paddle-steamer and you could see the town from the water.'

'That would be wonderful. Would you like that, Miriam?' Margaret asked.

'I think that I should prefer just to stay here on my own for a bit,' she replied. 'I can walk and explore, and I expect you two have a lot to talk about.'

She sat for a long time on the seat where they left her, staring into the dark, swirling river water. 'The Elbe, I believe,' she said to herself. 'I never expected to be here in Germany, did I? Germany!'

She thought of Israel, left in such a hurry, of her friends in that so different country, of Dinah and the camp marks on her arm, of Yad Vashem in Jerusalem, and then of Chaim who had died fighting so that there would never be another Holocaust, so that Jews would have a place of their own and never be hounded to death again. She wondered if he would have fallen in love with her had he known that her father was German. She looked up at the passers-by, ordinary Germans of all ages and types. There were women who smiled enquiringly at her, knowing she was foreign.

'But I'm not!' she wanted to shout. 'I'm one of you. My father is one of you!'

She sat silently and watched them and wondered who had survived that terrible night, who had heard the Lancasters in the sky, who had lived through the terror they brought.

An old man walked past and then sat on the next seat and took out a newspaper. Hannah stared at him. Perhaps he had been in the war, a camp guard? She shuddered, and then almost laughed at the stupidity of her thoughts, of the futility of racial hatred.

'I'm half German, half Jew,' she said to herself. 'A battlefield!'

Margaret stood beside Karl on the boat and wondered if the time had come to tell. Miriam had decided after all to leave it to her to do the telling. She shivered a little, and then surprised herself by thinking suddenly of Graham. The thought of him began to grow in her heart like a small grain of warmth and peace. He had always brought her peace.

'I hope your daughter won't be lonely. Tourists are still fairly rare here and she might get a few interested stares,' Karl said.

'She'll be fine. She's very capable. She likes to be on her own.'

He looked down at her and took her hand in his. She remembered the roughness of his farmer's hands years ago, and the strength in those long, artistic fingers. They were smooth now. There was no sign that he had ever done any manual work. He lifted her hand and cupped it in both of his.

'And you, Margaret? Are you fine too? How have you been all these years? Is your marriage a happy one?'

The directness of the last question took her by surprise.

'Yes, Karl. I've been happy. Graham has been good to me.'

The little inner glow in her heart began to flourish again as she remembered Graham. She stared down at the dark brown water swirling round the side of the boat, and she brought her thoughts back to the man at her side.

'I wanted to come to England for you,' he was saying. 'You know that, don't you? I wanted to marry you. But it was impossible. Impossible to get the necessary papers, and impossible too to imagine you in this place, this town which was almost completely a heap of rubble!'

She turned from him and looked across to the new buildings shimmering in the summer heat. 'It's beautiful again, though—Dresden, I mean.'

'The best we could do,' he said.

'You know, I think I would have followed you anywhere if it hadn't been for Miriam. For her sake and for yours I had to stay in Bristol.'

'Miriam? What did Miriam have to do with it?'

'She's your daughter, Karl. Miriam is your child.'

He dropped her hand and stared at her, and she saw the colour drain from his face.

'Oh, Margaret, Margaret,' he said at last. 'Why didn't you tell me? Why did you run away and cope with it all on your own?'

She paused before replying.

'There were so many reasons. So many reasons, and often they all seemed totally stupid to me. But I suppose I knew that it would never have worked—you and me, Jew and German! Not then, not in 1947. For a long time I wondered if I had done the right thing, and then Graham rescued me, adopted Miriam and we were happy—we are happy. When she went to Israel and took Israeli citizenship I wondered again, though. And now she has a daughter, Hannah, who wants to marry a German.'

'I'm beginning to understand why you came,' Karl said.

For the rest of the journey on the river they did little more than sit beside each other, talking occasionally, seeing nothing of their surroundings.

'Does she know?' he asked eventually.

'Yes, she knows.'

When the little boat docked Miriam was waiting for them. There was a hesitancy and then Margaret watched with tears in her eyes as Karl took both of Miriam's hands in his and slowly pulled her into his arms.

'My father,' Margaret heard her say. And she turned away, not wanting to see the tears on his face. She was crying too, and the sorrow of all those early days in Bristol was purged. Life had come full circle. Hannah would marry her Kurt, and she would have Miriam's blessing now. Margaret was sure of that. The stigma of race and war would be forgotten in their love.

Miriam turned and stepped over to her and taking her hand pulled her towards Karl.

'We're complete now,' she said. 'Don't you see? We are a family, just for this precious little time.'

Then she smiled at both of them and walked away, and Margaret was alone with Karl. They each looked into the other's eyes and knew that it was for the last time. Margaret understood suddenly and with great clarity that although Karl held her heart in a dream world of the past, yet happiness lay not in dreams but in the substance of today's living. She longed strangely in that precious moment for the strength and comfort of Graham's arms, Graham's embrace.

'How will you remember me, Karl?' she asked. 'As I am now, or. . .?'

'You will always be beautiful for me,' he said. 'But I shall see only a girl on a clifftop with the wind in her hair as I have done through all the years.'

'And a gull crying,' she added. 'Always a gull!'

CHAPTER THIRTY-ONE

1987

GRAHAM was waiting for them at the station. There was trepidation and hope together in his heart as he stood bareheaded on the cold platform. The train was late, and he paced up and down, his thoughts a confusion of memories. He saw Miriam lying in that second-hand pram in the small yard of the terraced house in St Pauls and he heard again Margaret's voice. 'But I don't love her,' she had said. He remembered the agony in her words and the affection for both of them that had surged through him then and had remained and grown into deep love through the years. All the traumas and joys of their life together seemed to flash before him in a jumbled kaleidoscope. He had willingly agreed to their visit to meet Karl, but the short time that they were away had been full of anxiety and he knew that if his fears were realised, if he lost either of them now, it would destroy him utterly.

He waited impatiently on the cold, impersonal platform, constantly looking at his watch and then up at the flashing announcement-board hanging above his head.

At last he heard the rumbling of the train and his heart thudded uncomfortably. His eyes searched the coaches as they rolled slowly past him and all he could see was a mass of faces, all alien, all concerned with their own affairs, and he felt alone and lost in his own city. Then suddenly they were there, further down the platform, waving to him and smiling. Thank God, they were smiling!

'I love you, Graham!' Those wonderful words were the first ones he heard as his arms went round Margaret. 'I love you,' she said again, and in that moment his world was good, mended totally, his fears banished. He looked into her eyes and knew that at last she was his with no other between. He released her and took Miriam's hands in his.

'How was it?'

She smiled and kissed him. 'A fantastic experience, Dad,' she said. 'Thank you for not minding.'

He picked up their bags and they walked together to the car, mostly in silence.

'We'll tell you all about it over tea,' Margaret said, but the look on her face confirmed his happiness, and when she turned to him in the luxurious warmth of their huge bed later that night he knew that he would never again suffer from the spectre of jealousy that had all too often secretly haunted his lovemaking and even his waking hours.

'Tom has asked me to marry him!' Miriam announced a week later, and the glow in her eyes and the new confidence in her whole bearing spoke worlds to Margaret.

'And will you?'

'Probably. Well, yes, I think I will, actually.'

Margaret laughed. 'You sound very calm and composed about it.'

'I've told him about the dress-designing course I'm enrolling for and he thinks it's a great idea.'

'Is that your reason for marrying, then?'

'No, of course not. Love comes into it as well, as a matter of fact!'

'And what about Israel?'

'I feel awful about deserting it while there's so much

unrest and strife, and I shall always love it and feel partly Israeli, but it's had half of my life and I'm going to put Tom and myself first now.'

'I'm so very, very glad, my dear,' Margaret said, and it was the biggest understatement of her life. 'But you're sure?' she added anxiously, feeling that the news was just too good to last.

'Honestly, Mummy. You spend about twenty years trying to get me to stay in England and now that I'm going to do just that you start worrying!'

They both laughed together, and Margaret knew suddenly that the bond between them was strengthened and renewed. They could talk easily now, there were no secrets.

1988

The mist was thick on the hills when Hannah at last kept her childhood promise to Fiona and returned to the home of her ancestors, her fairly new husband at her side. Rain slanted out of the sky, and they shivered as they parked the car outside the little croft.

They pushed open the creaking door and Kurt lifted her into his arms, carrying her over the old doorstep. He set her down before the fireplace, and she took the old faded photograph from the mantelpiece and stared into her mother's face and at the young man who stood with his arm round her shoulders, the father she had never known. She held it out to Kurt.

'Ian Chaim Macleod,' she said. 'My father, who loved Israel more than this and who gave his life for it.'

'Which do you love?' Kurt asked. 'Which is really your place?'

'Wherever you are,' she said, and they laughed together and kissed, and there was only the sound of the sea worrying at the shingle on the lonely beach and the calling of the gulls to break the quietness that surrounded them.

'Don't you see? There's a sort of pattern about it all,' Hannah continued. 'It started with Granny and Karl all those years ago, then Israel and the purging of the wounds of war, then Mum coming to terms with her birth and with our marriage.'

'And Scotland?' Kurt asked.

'I don't know yet. I know that I love it. That I feel Scots as much as Israeli, although I haven't lived here. It's in my blood, I suppose. We couldn't make our home here now, could we, but one day perhaps we might? Or one of our children!'

'I know,' said Kurt, teasing. 'We'll have three. One can be German, one Israeli, and one Scottish!'

'And we must go to Dresden, mustn't we? I must meet my real grandfather. It's from him that I get my musical ability, Mum says. His son is in the Leipzig Gewandhaus, apparently. I'd love to go to a concert there.'

'A bit of a shock, suddenly finding out that you've got another whole family!'

'Him or me, do you mean?'

'Well, both, I suppose.'

Hannah was silent for a moment. She loved Graham and it was strange to know that he wasn't her real grandfather after all, but she quickly shook off her slight misgivings.

'I think I'll like him—Karl, I mean. I shall call him Karl. There could never be another Grandad. Granny told me all about him. It's all very romantic—sad too, in a way.'

'We'll go next summer,' said Kurt, 'if at all possible.'

'You must help me with my German. I want to be fluent.'

Kurt laughed. 'And you had better teach me Hebrew. Then there's Gaelic, of course. All the bits of us are important!'

Miriam's wedding to Tom was a grand occasion.

'The kind of wedding you couldn't have with Chaim,' Margaret said, and although there was some sadness in Miriam's heart at the memory of that faraway day under a hot Israeli sky, it was all so distant now, precious still but of the past, and the future was Tom's and hers to take with both hands and to enjoy. She determined to let no high ideals mar her present happiness.

Graham walked beside his daughter down the aisle of the old church, as proud as any father as he held her arm affectionately.

It was only Margaret who surprised herself by seeing vividly in her mind and through her tears another figure, one who no longer existed except in the deep places of her heart. He was young and strong with a handsome, smiling face, short-cropped fair hair and blue eyes, and he bore no resemblance at all to the elderly man she had met in Dresden. She brushed away the tears as she heard, in her imagination and over and above the strains of the organ, the calling of gulls, and she saw, for a fleeting moment, not the flower-filled church but a lonely beach and a restless, white-flecked sea.

Then she looked at Graham and the picture dimmed in her mind and she squeezed the hand of Hannah standing beside her. They smiled at each other, and in the happiness of the day all the old memories seemed suddenly to have their fulfilment and were laid to rest. And she knew, as her daughter standing there proud and beautiful at the altar knew, that true joy lay in taking today and holding it carefully, treasuring it, savouring it, and never letting it be lost in a hankering after yesterday or even tomorrow. Tomorrow belonged to the baby in Hannah's womb, today was here and now. It was hers and Graham's to have and to hold as long. . .He came and stood beside her in the old oak pew, and she saw the pride and the love in his eyes and she was totally content.